PROSPECTS
of a
WOMAN

PROSPECTS
of a
WOMAN

A Novel

WENDY VOORSANGER

SHE WRITES PRESS

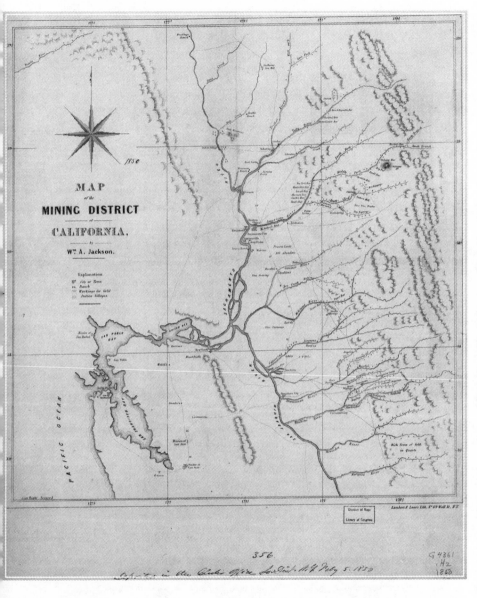

Jackson, Wm. A, and Lambert & Lane'S Lith. *Map of the mining district of California.* [S.l, 1850] Map. Image courtesy of Library of Congress Archives.

Published 2020
Printed in the United States of America
Print ISBN: 978-1-63152-781-4
E-ISBN: 978-1-63152-782-1
Library of Congress Control Number: 2020908451

For information, address:
She Writes Press
1569 Solano Ave #546
Berkeley, CA 94707

She Writes Press is a division of SparkPoint Studio, LLC.

Interior design by Tabitha Lahr

For my sister Karen, an extraordinary California woman, and for all the generations of California women who came before, and now

Author's Historical Note

In early America, a woman was legally dependent on her father, then on her husband. Upon marriage, a woman lost any right to control property that was hers prior, and she had no rights to acquire any property during marriage. She could not make contracts, keep or control her own wages or rents, transfer property, sell property, or bring any lawsuit. She had little right to divorce, and had no rights to her children if she left her husband.

Drawing on the traditions of Spanish civil law, the California Constitution adopted in 1849, and subsequent sections added upon statehood in 1850 and thereafter, granted California women the first set of broad equal rights in America. Both single and married women in California were allowed to own property, manage business affairs, divorce, and share custody of their children. These rights gave California women unprecedented social and economic power to work as ranchers, lawyers, writers, architects, doctors, publishers, hoteliers, nurses, politicians, artists, teachers, clothiers, mothers, and wives. Generations of powerful California women helped build the thirty-first state of America into the fifth largest economy in the world. *Prospects of a Woman* strives to tell of those beginnings.

"We will remind them that this dear California is a gorgeous edition de luxe of Palestine of old . . . that every spot in it has its hills and dales. Our Holy Land, our Promised Land is this golden spot, and we want the sages of Babylon to pay us a visit."

—RABBI JACOB VOORSANGER
EMANU-EL, 1896

PROLOGUE

North Fork of the American River,

Summer, 1850

The river ran angry that day, with water raging loud at the sun for burning it off the peaceful granite slopes of the High Sierra. Falling into a spring melt, it tumbled down, flowing as something altogether different through the pine canyon. Flowing cold and fierce. Even with the river talking to her, telling, Elisabeth never could have predicted. In all her circular thinkings and imaginings, her mind never conceived of such a day. She didn't yet know a man could turn like that.

She threaded her fingers through her husband's, grabbing at his strength as her own. Together, they stood staring at the little log cabin across the river. It didn't look like the leaning shanties and mud-strewn tents they'd seen in San Francisco. The cabin tucked up tidy against the steep ravine, looking sturdy and permanent with logs laid atop one another level and dried mud caked in between the chinks and wood shingles neat on the roof with a bit of moss growing. It looked like the beginnings of a homestead back in Concord, not a gold claim at the edge of civilization.

They waited a long while, watching the faint puff of smoke slipping out the slight river rock chimney. Watching for him to come out. When the sun set low behind the ridge and dying light cloaked mysterious around them, Nate squeezed her hand and let go.

"Look like something your father built?" Nate asked.

"No idea."

"Time to find out," he said.

Nate crossed the river first, leaping from boulder to boulder, elegant, balancing on logs placed across as makeshift bridges. When he jumped to the far side, he waved for her to follow. She picked her way across careful, trying not to look down, trying not to think what might happen if she slipped. Trying not to imagine being sucked into the rapids, pulled along, gasping. Smashing against the rocks. Drowning. When she finally made it to the other side, she let loose a trembling of fear.

Nate put his arm around her as they walked up to the cabin. He knocked on the door.

"Hello? Mr. Goodwin. Henry Goodwin? It's Nathaniel Parker."

No response.

Nate spoke again.

"Mr. Goodwin. I'm here with Elisabeth. Your daughter."

Still nothing.

She should've walked away then. Walked away, not knowing. Not seeing. But Nate tested the door, pushing it in slow, and she peeked inside. A dozen candles lit the place up like the fire of Hades. Lighting up the man, and his bare backside, hairy and pale, with pants flopping around his ankles, going at it hard on a woman, bent over a table.

"Jesus," she said.

She covered her mouth but didn't look away. The man didn't bother to stop his business with the woman and instead looked defiant over his shoulder at them, his long graying beard bouncing as he kept on humping that woman up and down, faster and faster, holding on to her long braid and hooting like he was riding an animal, showing off. That woman seemed to enjoy all that roughness, moaning with a pleasure that cut Elisabeth sharp. When the man flared his deep-set green eyes, Elisabeth stumbled backward. Nate caught her from falling down as the door closed with a slap.

"A shame. A shame for you to see," said Nate.

A wave of nausea hit her hard. She steeled herself from getting sick, flexing her middle, trying to keep down that measly bit of jerky she'd eaten earlier in the day. But their last bit of foodstuff came up without her permission as she leaned over retching. Nate placed a hand on her shoulder for comfort as she wobbled weak. He took her elbow, guiding her over to a cottonwood beside the river. They sat down and leaned against the trunk as clouds gathered overhead, squashing the lingering twilight dark. Nate told her to sip water from the canteen. Wrung ragged, she obeyed, leaning back heavy on Nate's chest. He kissed her temple and covered her with their blanket. As her insides settled, she wished for a sliver of sun to come back out. Just a small spot of setting sun to show her a sign of a merciful universe. Or a slice of moon, gleaming glorious. She needed to see something. Her faith was dripping out slow like the sweet sap of a maple going dry. At this rate she'd have no more faith by the time she reached twenty-one.

"Let's wait, to be sure," said Nate.

She looked at the black night closing in with no moon and no familiar tastes blowing on the western wind, and listened to the river rage over the rocks. She started biting at her fingernails, pulling off bits of skin with her teeth until her fingers bled, wondering 'round and 'round. Wondering why she'd thought coming all this way to find her father was a good idea. Wondering what she'd tell her mother. Wondering how she'd face Nate in the morning light with such shame shining nasty over the Goodwin family. Wondering how they'd get something to eat in the morning with all their money spent through. Wondering why the woman splayed backward across the table seemed to like it that way.

At dawn, two mourning doves called melancholy from the branches above, coo-cooing in lament. She sat up, rubbing her eyes, as white puffs of cottonwood fluff floated atop the river on the early morning breeze without a worry. A shadow covered her face, and she looked up at Nate.

"He's got something to say."

"What?"

"He better tell it himself."

Over at the cabin, Henry Goodwin stooped, looking much older than she remembered, grizzled too thin with his wiry hair grown out long and wild. He stood hardened, with sacks at his feet and a girl sidled up too close. Not a woman after all, but a girl. An Indian girl. A slight thing, maybe younger than Elisabeth. She wore a deerskin shift slipping indecent off one shoulder and stared straight at Elisabeth with a round face and wide-set eyes looking sassy. Like she owned that spot beside her father. Elisabeth glared back, folding her arms across her chest, waiting on him to explain.

"You shouldn't a come," said Henry.

"But you wrote us about the claim," she said.

She pulled the letter from her pocket and shoved it at him. Henry looked at the paper but didn't take hold of it.

"You made a mistake in coming," said Henry.

Elisabeth crumpled the letter and threw it at him.

"We're giving up the claim. You and your man can have it," said Henry.

"We?"

Henry scratched his nose and sniffed, looking shrunken and sick since she'd last seen him nearly three years ago, yet standing taller, too, which confused her beyond measure.

"There are times when a situation looks simple, 'Lizbeth. When, in fact, you see . . . there comes a turn far more complicated, requiring more of man than he's capable," said Henry, stumbling over the words.

"That's quite a luxury. Getting out of what's required," she said.

With a slow sweep, the Indian girl flung her braid over her shoulder haughty, and Henry started stroking her head like she was his pet. Elisabeth could hardly believe his manner. That damn Indian girl had him under some sinful spell, taking away his love. Hiding it. Locking it away.

"You'll come to understand when you're older," he said.

"You said you were coming back home!" she yelled.

She couldn't contain herself any longer and started flapping her arms and barking out words like a rabid dog.

"We waited for you! Me and Mama and Lucy and Samuel. You left us with nothing but those goddamn rotten apples!"

"There's nothing for me back in Concord," he said.

"What about Mama? What about me?"

"You don't need me no more."

"Please don't leave me, Papa," she said, thinking softness might get him to stay.

"You got yourself a husband now. And you got Samuel and Lucy. I'm sure they're getting on the same . . ."

She wanted to tell her father. Make him sad, make him hurt. She wanted to tell how her sister, Lucy, had gotten her hair tangled up in that wicked warp at the mill, her scalp yanking clean off with her long brown curls still sticking to it. Lying mute in the hospital, with half a head and a horrible infection for months and months. She wanted to tell how she'd nearly gone mad herself, still working the loom all day and worrying at Lucy's bedside all night, watching her head swell nearly twice its size, and how Lucy had died crying out something terrible. She wanted to tell how Samuel had gotten furious with her for not keeping little Lucy safe, and how they hadn't told their mother for fear she'd try to kill herself again. She wanted to tell about marrying Nate, a man she hardly knew. The first man who'd paid her attention. How she'd left her job at the mills. Left Samuel on his own at Amherst. Left her mother sinking into madness at the Worcester Asylum. Left everything on hope of finding him. Certain it was the right thing. Certain he'd give her back the happiness she'd lost. Instead, she lashed out, hysterical.

"You don't get to know about Samuel or Lucy or nothing!"

"Fair enough," he said.

"Samuel knew you were a louse. He said you weren't coming home," she said.

"Listen here. We can't all live down here on the river together. That ain't gonna work. I gotta move on," he said.

Unleashing her pent-up empty insides in a spring of hate, she pushed her father with all the force she could muster, hoping he'd fall backward and get the sense knocked back into his head. But his wiry self didn't budge, and he stood staring at her like a statue. His indifference fueled her, and she lost herself completely, pounding on his chest over and over, and he took it stone-faced, like she was giving a punishment to someone other than himself.

"I thought you loved me!" Elisabeth screamed, spit flying from her lips.

When he stumbled ever so slight she kicked his shins until he fell, then she turned and slapped his Indian girl on the face hard with an open palm. She slapped her for taking her father away and making him forget and making him wild and making him happy and making him nothing. The Indian girl didn't put her hands up in defense or slap back. She took the slap, holding her chin high with a slight smile sitting on her lips as if daring Elizabeth to do it again.

"Listen to the wind," the girl said. "It's saying our souls are connected."

Enraged, Elisabeth made a fist to strike the girl harder. But Nate stepped in, holding her wrist, saving her from herself. Saving her a bit of dignity.

"What a load of nonsense," she said, shaking Nate off and smoothing the front of her skirt.

The girl went to Henry lying on the ground and helped him up.

"That old Henry Goodwin you know is gone," he said, facing Elisabeth. "Good as dead. Can't find him in me no more. He up and left my soul the first year I came out here. Can't say I'm sorry for it, either. I've made a new man of myself. And this here good woman," he said, pointing to that Indian girl. "We'll, I'd be dead if wasn't for her."

He talked a selfish gibberish that she had no point of reference to understand.

"There's still gold in the river, I'm sure of it," said Henry, picking up his sacks to go.

"I don't want your dirty gold," she said.

Nate finally spoke.

"Hardly an honorable way to end it, sir."

"Nothing to be done about it," said Henry, nodding to the girl.

Henry didn't shake Nate's hand. He didn't touch Elisabeth, either. Didn't hug her like when he'd left their orchard for work with the Hudson Company three years ago. He simply walked away, crossing over the river with his Indian lover following behind. Elisabeth planted her feet solid into the California dirt, determined not to run after him like some dog begging for scraps. She watched him walk along the far bank and up the trail and into the forest and wilderness beyond, like a stranger she never knew. She watched long after he'd gone and the tall pines fuzzed together into a hazy mass of dark dusky green.

"That's no way to treat family," said Nate.

Something inside her broke at hearing Nate say it aloud. Shattered. Cracked into pebbles. She screamed at the searing loss stabbing through her soul. She gasped and choked and sobbed heavy, raging like a mad woman. She raged for her father leaving. She raged for her little Lucy dying without her hair, and for her mother gone mad, and for Samuel at Amherst, and for herself, stuck out west with a husband she hardly knew. She ran behind the cabin to a pine grove shaded from the strong sun, and Nate followed.

Falling to her hands and knees, she crawled around in circles on the forest floor, shaking and crying until her nose ran with snot and her eyes swelled red and she filled full with shame and guilt. Nate didn't tell her to shush but simply sat down beside her as she curled up in a bed of pine needles. Sylvan softness diffused the grove and a soft breeze fluttered the branches overhead, oblivious to her ravings. She refused to listen to the wind like the girl said, and instead listened to a squirrel skittering down a trunk and a Steller's jay flying back and forth through the afternoon light streaming through the trees. She thought she might turn to dust, then remembered Emerson's words—*"the whole of nature is a metaphor of the human mind."* She came together slow then, steadying her breath as it matched the rhythm of the river flowing in the distance, long and deep and constant, knowing she'd never beg for a man again. Never beg like her mother. Never again fold up with madness. However cracked and fragile and lost, she was bound now only to Nate, alone.

Part 1

Upon hearing a circus had come to town, an excited farmer set out in his wagon. Along the way he met up with the circus parade, led by an elephant, which so terrified his horses that they bolted and pitched the wagon over on its side, scattering his vegetables and eggs across the roadway.

"I don't give a hang," exulted the jubilant farmer as he picked himself up. "I have seen the elephant."

—NINETEENTH-CENTURY AMERICAN FOLKTALE

1

E lisabeth counted the stitches holding together their dingy canvas tent. Twice. She got 946 both times. Cooped up in the midday heat, she seethed at Nate for leaving her alone. They'd lost too much time already. Refusing to wait another goddamn minute on his frittering and scheming, she untied the tent flaps and crawled out, stretching her arms long overhead. A soft air of relief touched her cheeks. Aching with hunger, she stumbled downriver, in the direction of Culoma Town. She hadn't eaten since a bite of beans for breakfast the day before.

Nate had left early that morning, again. Gone digging for gold in the river, refusing to let her join. Telling her to stay put. Warning about unsavory men roaming around, men with a mind to take what they will. Elisabeth was done waiting on him to bring her something decent to eat. She grabbed her satchel and headed for the river trail, thinking on how she'd get food in her belly with no money left.

She wasn't thinking about the roaming men but about the blisters on her feet still burning something awful from that long journey getting to the river. Elisabeth walked all afternoon alongside the American River roiling loud, cutting through the valley, tempting her. Tempting Nate. Her eyes burned with the honest light shining lush and vibrant through the narrow valley. The grass glowed golden along the river trail, and the rich green pines marched up the steep sides of the canyon, swaying alive and standing taller and fuller than the scraggly pitch pines at home in Concord. Warm air whooshed through the branches, spreading a sweet smell around.

Arriving in Culoma Town, Elisabeth picked her way through a mess of empty tents strewn haphazard. Plopping down on a log in the center of town, she unlaced her boots to let her stockinged feet breathe and witnessed new beginnings. Industrious fellas buzzed around, hammering up buildings with fresh-hewn boards and siding and plank floors and shingle roofs. Jabbering and rushing. Heaving pails and shovels and pans and timber. Haggling for food and supplies. No women milled about, and she wondered if they were all hiding away too.

Some of the fellas in town noticed her sitting alone on the log. One man dropped his hammer and walked over, stammering and stuttering as if he hadn't seen a woman in years. She smiled polite, introducing herself as Mrs. Nathaniel Parker. More men came. And more. Until over a dozen stood around gawking at the only woman in Culoma Town. She pulled at her dress collar. Shifted her bottom on the log. Cleared her throat. When a few of the men sat down in the crisped-up grass like they had all the time to waste, she wondered why but didn't dare ask. A fella with a long curly beard dripping down his chin offered her a cup of cool river water. She took it, gulping. Wiping her cheek with the back of her hand, she reddened with shame. When one man tossed two bits into her empty cup she looked at him coolly, thinking him daft. When another coin clinked into the cup, then another, she didn't give them back. Didn't look at the coins either. She simply stared up at the clear sky, fanning herself with her shabby straw hat, acting like she couldn't care less if those foolish men wanted to waste good money just to sit near a woman looking not exactly pretty.

"I'm not out here to beg," she said.

"Of course not," said the long-beard fella.

She shuffled her unlaced boots, tamping down the dry grass.

"I'm simply out getting some air," she said.

"We all see that," he said.

An older man, wrinkled up like a prune, scooted up to her left knee. She caught him looking her up and down, leering, and she wanted to slap him for the lack of manners but held back. Letting men stare for money was unseemly, no matter the circumstances, but she knew each clink of a coin meant she and Nate would eat tonight. Oh, he'd be furious, of course. He'd probably even accuse her of flirting. Maybe she was. Flirting. Encouraging. She didn't care. She needed a proper supper and a hot bath. Besides, the men seemed harmless.

She considered how many coins those fools had given her, but was too afraid to count for fear they'd wise up to this absurd payment-for-gawking scheme and demand all those coins back. The men stared at her wide-eyed while a pecker pounded on a nearby trunk, knocking and knocking for grubs, matching the thud in her head.

"Any of you know a Henry Goodwin?" Elisabeth asked.

"That your husband?"

"My father. He settled a claim up the North Fork," she said.

It'd been nearly a month since he'd run off with that Indian girl, and she still stung sore and angry at his leaving. She convinced herself he'd change his mind. Convinced he'd return to the claim eventually.

"Sing us a song?" A prune-face fella asked.

"Not hardly," she said.

"Can't? Or won't?"

Not exactly delicate, Elisabeth lacked the finer qualities admired in most ladies. Her singing sounded more feeble frog than melodious finch, and she had no patience for sitting still for parlor conversations, finding the feminine topics of curtain colors and canning peaches dreadfully dull. Nate said she walked too heavy, but she knew he'd appreciated her strong back when they'd taken turns pushing their cart loaded down with his case of books through the foothills and into the river basin.

"Can't," she said.

Conscious of her mousy plaits splayed loose and messy, she smoothed stray strands behind her ears and slipped a hand into her skirt pocket, touching the little booklet she carried always, Ralph Waldo Emerson's essay, "Self-Reliance." It was a parting gift from her dear friend Louisa May Alcott, inscribed by the author himself: *"In the highest civilization, the book is still the highest delight. He who has once known its satisfactions is provided with a resource against calamity."*

She'd read the book over and over again, until she could nearly recite whole sections by heart, stuffing herself up with more learning than she'd ever known. Her mind stumbled through the chapters searching for an understanding, making her feel halfway educated, however far below the intellect of Louisa May, whose parents actually believed in educating a woman toward betterment.

She fingered the worn spine of the book, listening as the men gathered around peppered her with questions teetering on the edge of aggressive.

"You got something else for us, then?"

"Something sweet?"

"What you got, lady?"

"Sing for us."

"One song, lady. Won't you?"

Their voices mixed together into an animal chorus, like pups yipping with eager expectation, falling all over themselves looking for mischief but baring sharp teeth nonetheless. She wasn't about to encourage them in the wrong direction. A trickle of sweat dripped down her brow as she squeezed her eyes shut, more than a little afraid of what she might've gotten herself into.

"My husband is returning any moment," she said.

"Why'd he leave you alone?" the prune-face fella asked.

The question lingered in her ears as she wondered why, indeed. Wiping her forehead with her dress sleeve, she stuffed her fear and studied the faces of the men circled around. They looked as if they'd spent months ripping their hands raw digging for gold in the river with nothing to show but a head full of dim-witted dreams. Way too skinny, the lot of them. All sun worn and covered with a thin layer of dirt and dust, and stinking with a western rank she couldn't place. Covered in sweat mixed with burnt grass and warm sunshine and hope, they looked in sore need of comfort, all the while grinning like they knew a secret she hadn't yet learned. She wondered what brought them west, if they'd been desperate like her, or sought adventure. Either way, who was she to say no if they wanted to rest in the grass flipping coins into her cup for nothing?

"Perhaps I'll read aloud," she said, hoping to redirect their attention.

She cleared her throat like Louisa May's mother did before saying something important.

"In 'Self-Reliance,' Emerson says our minds are subject to an unhappy conformism. He lives in the town where I grew up. Concord, Massachusetts. "

Opening the book in the middle, Elisabeth began, reading Emerson's words slow and deliberate.

"The power which resides in him is new in nature, and none but he knows what that is which he can do, nor does he know until he has tried."

After two pages, the prune-face fella sidling up close put a hand on her boot, but she didn't flinch. When he slid his hand up to her ankle, she kept on reading, wondering how far he'd go. The other men didn't say a thing about prune-face fella's wandering hand. Perhaps they didn't notice, too caught up in Emerson's words coming out of her mouth. When the prune-face fella ran his rough fingers up her stockings, she still didn't stop him, finding herself aching pathetic for the attention. When his hand went up her skirt, nearly reaching her knee, she stopped reading and looked down into his face. He smiled with a mouth full of white teeth, not looking old after all, just wrinkled up red without a hat under the California sun. With sudden contempt for both the man and herself, she kicked prune-face fella's shoulder harder then she'd meant, and he fell backward onto his bottom with a crunch in the grass.

"Keep your hands off!" she said.

Prune-face fella laughed wild and loud.

She closed "Self-Reliance" with a slam, and another man spoke up.

"Don't scare the lady, Joe," said the long-beard fella.

"You leave her be, Joe. Her reading's fine," said another.

"Awww. She don't scare so easy," said prune-face Joe.

As she laced up her boots, the men asked her to stay. Pleaded. Begged her to read more. She shook her head no. When the long-bearded fella handed Elisabeth a slice of bread, still warm and soaked with butter, she hesitated, knowing nothing came for free.

"Go on, ma'am. It's a gift. For reading," he said, sounding earnest and kind.

She was too hungry to refuse and grabbed the bread, gobbling it down in three bites, spilling crumbs down the front of her dress. She looked down at her palms, crusted over with calluses from pushing the cart loaded down with supplies. Her nails stuck out ugly, ripped ragged from her nervous biting. Those lovely gray gloves Nate had given her as a wedding gift had torn to shreds weeks ago. Traveling west had stolen her womanliness. With a pride all but gone, she figured it was time to get up and walk away with that slice of bread in her belly and all those coins jangling in her cup. They wouldn't dare stop her. As she finished lacing her boots, two more fellas walked up, talking loud and boisterous. One man took of his hat off and whistled.

"Looky here, Chana. A real live woman! Well, aren't you a sight. The pink of perfection."

"Pardon his rudeness, mademoiselle. My friend hasn't seen a woman for so long, he's forgotten himself," said Mr. Chana, tipping his hat.

She straightened up, nodding polite.

"Jim Colton's the name, ma'am. I come from West Virginia. Figured diggin' gold from a river out here beats digging for coal down a mine out there. This one here's my digging partner, Claude Chana. He's from France," said Mr. Colton.

"France!" she said, amazed he'd come from all the way across the world.

"I must say, ma'am, you're a beam of beauty. Those green eyes! A solitary sight bringing a man to tears. Offering a bit of joy in the hardness of life. Piercing our blindness with a rainbow of color," said Mr. Colton.

His words sounded silly, like a joke at her expense. She knew she looked a mess with stinky stockings and unwashed hair gone all catawampus. Even so, she liked the man's humor.

"Oui. Belle," said Mr. Chana, his voice heavy with a French tongue.

"Like our mothers and sisters and wives all rolled into one," said Mr. Colton.

She placed a hand over her lips to prevent a nervous laugh from escaping out her mouth, and stood up.

"I was just leaving. Good day, gentlemen," she said.

"You know mending?" Mr. Colton asked.

"Of course," she said, turning around.

"I done torn my shirt. See here?"

Mr. Colton peeled off his shirt before asking her price. She'd never seen a naked man. She'd only been married eight months and had been traveling most of that time. The few times she and Nate had been intimate, he'd kept his shirt on, leaving her to imagine his naked body by running her hands along the muscles in his back.

She couldn't look away from Mr. Colton's bare chest. His big belly flopped generous over the top of his dusty brown trousers. He filled out paunchy in the gut with thick patches of hair sticking out all over his shoulders down his chest like a mangy dog, but his arms looked better suited for a younger man, sinewy and firm. Elisabeth was surprised she didn't feel a lick nervous seeing a man standing in front of her half naked. On the contrary, she felt calm and in control. She took his shirt, turning it over, wondering on a fair wage for fixing a two-inch tear. If she asked too much, Mr. Colton might balk. Too little, and he might not take her serious. Remembering the price gouging at Brannan's Dry Goods in San Francisco, she bet on the value of scarcity.

"A rip along the seam like this will split your whole shirt in no time," she said.

"I figured," said Mr. Colton, slapping Mr. Chana on the back.

"Two dollars."

"Deal."

"Merde, Jim! You really need that chemise fixed? The Chinamen will fix it up for half."

"Mind your damn business, Chana. I aim to cheer the lady."

"I've only white thread. It won't match the gray."

"Matching don't matter t'all. Take your time. But not too much, otherwise that afternoon sun'll burn me up like a spit pig," Mr. Colton said, laughing hearty.

She dug around in her satchel for a thread and needle. Relieved at negotiating an honorable trade, she now sat tall on the log, threading through Jim Colton's shirt, while he and Claude Chana sat down with the other men in the grass watching her work. She pulled tiny, tight stitches through the shirt slower than necessary to make Colton think he was getting his money's worth.

"Smaller stitches hold up better with rough digging," she said.

"Mmm," said Colton, looking on with the rest of the men.

Prune-face Joe was sitting a ways behind Mr. Colton, and she relaxed her shoulders, again trying to interest the group away from her womanly self.

"Finding any gold?"

The men split open up like a sack of beans then, spilling out tales of digging and finding just enough flecks to keep them fed. A few grumbled about luck being stingy, but Claude Chana bragged, saying he'd pulled a fortune from the river. Everyone listened as the Frenchman boasted on and on while she mended Mr. Colton's shirt.

As the sun hung low over the far ridge, she cut the thread with her teeth and tied the ends, then folded up Mr. Colton's mended shirt, pressing the wrinkles flat against her chest. When she held out her hand for payment, Mr. Colton dropped two dollar coins in her palm, and she plopped the money into the cup with the rest of her earnings. She handed the shirt to Mr. Colton, who shook it out, admiring nothing at all.

She'd never made so much money for so little effort. It had taken barely fifteen minutes, although she could've sewn it up in two. She was giddy at how easy she'd earned it, just sitting on a log sewing. Making as much sewing up Jim Colton's shirt as she would've standing on her feet fourteen hours for six whole days back at the Lowell Mill, weaving her shuttle fast enough through the fabric to keep up, lest she lose a finger to the loom. Or worse, losing half her head like little Lucy.

Sewing Colton's shirt was the first time she'd earned money for herself. Not for her brother Samuel's schooling at Amherst or for Nate and his books. She'd earned it for her own supper and a hot bath. She figured the whole setup too good to be true. A fluke. A single shot of luck. A woman earning money couldn't be that easy. She half expected some law man to come out from behind a manzanita bush saying a woman making money like that was against the law. She couldn't wait to count up all the coins back at their tent.

Elisabeth looked down at the grass and saw a swarm of tiny black ants scurrying up her boots. She hated ants. Jumping up with a start, she kicked and stomped. The men on the grass jumped up, too, hooting along like they were all dancing together. Then she noticed a big group of diggers coming up the riverbank toward the commotion, lugging pans and picks, looking worn and tired, but still joking and jostling each other. Among the motley crew of Orientals and Americans and Californios in various states of dishevelment walked Nate, unshaven and bedraggled, his suit vest buttoned up uneven, his white shirt gone drab. His blond hair had grown out too long in the past months but still looked endearing, flopping bright in the late afternoon light, although she couldn't get used to his beard, scraggly and unclean. In Lowell, he'd shaved meticulous and always wore natty clothes.

Nate smiled easy, with his arm draped around the shoulder of another gold digger like they were old friends. She hadn't seen him so lively since leaving Massachusetts so many months before. She pricked with envy. Catching his eye, she saw his brightness dim into a scowl, and his joyful smile leaked away like water from a cracked pail. As he diverged from the diggers and plodded in her direction, she dropped the coins from the cup into her skirt pocket and slipped a few down her boot, quick.

2

*"The great man is he who in the midst
of the crowd keeps with perfect sweetness
the independence of solitude."*

"What the hell were you thinking, leaving the tent? Coming into town! What sort of addled-headed woman are you?"

Nate wasn't a man to curse, no matter how frustrated. His sharp tone gave her a fright.

"You needn't insult me."

"I told you not to mix with those men. It's dangerous," he said.

They argued in the dark outside Shannon and Cady's Store, a newly painted white clapboard building with real windows gleaming bright from lanterns inside. Nate gripped Elisabeth's elbow, preventing her from going in.

"You're the one left me alone, getting sidetracked digging in the mud. I took care of things myself. Earned us a proper sit-down supper," she said.

"I was digging for gold!"

"And?"

"It isn't as easy as all that . . . pulling up gold from the river in a hat. That's a myth. It's hard going and takes a strong man. I dug all day without stopping while teaching English to a man named Cho digging beside me. He gave me some rice in exchange," he said.

"I want more than a bowl of rice," she said.

"Jesus, 'Lizbeth. Have you no pride?"

"Plenty enough."

"How much did they give you?"

"I earned it."

"Earned it, did you?"

Standing outside the store, her insides growled angry and her bones screamed for a soft, plush chair after so many months of traveling and sleeping on the ground. She wanted to stop bickering so they could sit and eat. Instead she flickered hot like a flame, burning back at him.

"I'm not a girl to turn down work," said Elisabeth, her voice dripping heavy with sarcasm.

"Sewing for *all* those men?"

She looked toward the lit window and started biting her thumbnail. She knew a good wife should be honest, and she truly wanted to be a good wife. A terrible guilt ate at her that she'd dragged Nate all this way with promises of joining her father resting fat and happy on a prosperous gold claim. She'd never expected he'd abandon them. Leave them with nothing.

"And a bit of reading," she said, still not looking at him.

"You took money for reading?"

"I earned it, Nate."

"Damn it, Elisabeth! Don't be naive. For your own good, you gotta stay away from those men. They'll take advantage," said Nate, seething through clenched teeth.

She knew she shouldn't argue with her husband but was having a hard time staying quiet. Fourteen years older, Nate had taken on the role as her protector soon after they'd married, insisting his greater years made him more knowing. In the beginning, she relished having someone else care enough to help make her decisions. But during their long journey west she'd come to understand that Nate didn't always know best, like that day they'd arrived in San Francisco on the roiling tide of thousands of other intrepid souls.

When the Humboldt sailed through the Golden Gate, they'd huddled together on the bow holding hands, weary and dizzy with hunger. Hundreds of ships filled the harbor full, lined up side by side, left abandoned by whole crews jumping off to join the gold frenzy. Elisabeth and Nate had climbed like rats from ship to ship with the rest of the passengers, hauling trunks over bows and sterns to reach the sandy shore. As fingers of fog streamed overhead, she'd wanted food and a bath. Instead, Nate had wasted nearly sixty dollars on gold-digging supplies: a pick, a shovel, a pan, and a handcart. She'd pleaded with him to return at least the pick and shovel, explaining her father surely had sufficient supplies at his claim. Instead he'd boiled up a single shrunken sprouted potato for dinner. For her bath, he'd found an old tin bucket half-buried in the sand and went to find fresh water while she pitched their tent on a barren dune behind a bush, scrubby and small. When he returned with a bucket full of tepid water and a cleaned rag, she'd seethed, trying to wash her grimy mosquito-bitten self as the San Francisco wind swirled sand through the tent flaps and stuck to her wet skin, while he stood outside, holding the canvas ties closed against the gusts, yelling that they'd recoup their investment in no time.

So far, she'd seen no recouping of all the money he'd spent unwisely. They'd been grubbing around for scraps of food for weeks, ever since her father left. She was starving.

"How much you get?" he asked.

"What?"

"How much did you get off 'em?"

She hesitated. She could barely reconcile her understanding of fair value back home being completely at odds with the astonishing condition of financial matters in the West. She'd been shocked counting out the coins when Nate relieved himself behind a tree. Eighteen dollars! Those men had given her eighteen whole dollars just to sit near her, plus the two dollars she'd stuffed down her boot for sewing Mr. Colton's shirt. She knew Nate would surely have trouble making sense of this new economic reality, too, and would struggle at seeing her new value out here.

"How much did they give you?" he asked again, giving her arm a little shake.

"Eighteen," she said, wiggling out of his grip.

In the dim light cast from the windows, Nate's mouth went slack.

"Come again?"

"I earned eighteen dollars."

"For reading? And sewing? Well, I'll be damned."

Unable to tell if he was mad or pleased, she shifted nervous on her feet.

"Enough for a square meal for us. And a bath."

"Eighteen dollars, you say?"

"I can make more, too, I know it. I'm not waiting around for you anymore. I aim to work."

"Hand it over," said Nate, holding out his palm.

"What?"

"The money."

"I can manage it," she said, holding her chin up and pursing her lips.

"Now how's that gonna make me look, 'Lizbeth, if we go in there and all those men see my wife lay coins down on the table for my meal?"

In all her rush of hunger and impatience, she hadn't considered his pride as a man who regarded caring for his wife a rather serious affair. After all, it was savings from his book-lending business that had paid their way west. She'd given all her mill money to Samuel for his schooling at Amherst.

They stood outside in the dark, faltering and tentative, an unease creeping in between them like a louse you can't see, but making an itchy sore nonetheless. Nate sighed heavy and rubbed his temples with his fingers like he hurt. Feeling guilty, she emptied the coins from her skirt pocket into his cupped hands.

"For safekeeping," he said, pocketing her money.

"Suit yourself," she said, weary from their go 'round.

"You've a bit of dirt here," he said, touching the tip of her nose, gentle.

She spit on her finger and rubbed the line of dirt off her nose. She knew her face looked freckled something awful from the California sun; Nate had said so a few days back. Still, she pinched her cheeks so they'd glow rosy and opened the door for herself.

Shannon and Cady's served as an all-around everything place in Culoma Town. Dry Goods. Restaurant. Bar. That night the place was stuffed full of diggers from every creek, gulch, and ditch all around the American River Basin, enjoying a plate of food and a stiff drink after a long day prospecting. The tables and chairs set up on one side of the building served as a restaurant. A store took up the other side with bags of coffee beans in a corner, next to big barrels of flour and beans and pickles and dried apples. Shelves overflowed with tea canisters and jerky and sacks of potatoes. Pans. Rope. Tin cups. Boxes and boxes of nails. Hammers and picks and saws hung on the wall. Bolts of fabric and hats and pants filled up boxes on the floor, half-unpacked. The smell of new oak planks and fresh coffee rankled Elisabeth; she hadn't had a decent cup of coffee since leaving Boston. An oak bar ran along the back wall, fashioned fine with a shiny brass footrail underneath.

Scanning the room, she recognized a few of the men at the bar who'd circled around her earlier in the grass, including Mr. Colton and Mr. Chana. To her relief she didn't see the prune-face fella, Joe, who'd taken liberties with her leg. A man behind the bar noticed her and boomed louder than a foghorn.

"A lady in my establishment! 'Bout time they start rolling in!"

All the men turned 'round to look, and she flushed with embarrassment as Mr. Chana waved friendly in her direction. Dirty in her ragged gray working dress with a tear at the bottom, she smelled rank. She now regretted not dressing proper, but she'd been too hungry to walk all the way back to the claim to change into the emerald-green Sunday dress Nate had bought her the day after they'd married when he'd found out she'd borrowed the widow Avery's old wedding dress for the occasion. She'd worn that old gray working dress every single day for the past four months traveling, keeping the fancy dress folded up neat in her trunk for something special. She only had the two dresses. She'd given up her corset altogether while walking across the Isthmus of Panama, making breathing the thick tropical air easier, so she probably looked slouchy now standing in Shannon and Cady's. At least she'd tried to clean up a bit, washing her hands in the river as best she could without a bar of soap. Nate said wearing his woolen shirt and duck overalls was better than sticking out as a dandy putting on airs in a broadcloth suit.

The barman stood tall and imposing with hair running wild and long, even more unkempt than Nate's. But a white beard sat atop his face close cropped. He introduced himself as Captain William Shannon, pumping Nate's hand up and down and slapping him on the shoulder informal, saying how everyone was welcome in Shannon and Cady's. When Nate introduced Elisabeth, Captain Shannon placed a hand on his heart.

"Thank you for bringing in your lovely wife, Mr. Parker. It's pleasure for all of us, entirely."

Nate didn't seem to mind the men staring at her now. A wave of pride settled over his face, and he puffed up taller having her standing by his side like a special prize he'd won at the county fair.

"I assure you, Mr. Parker, I ain't no Sunday man. This here ain't no hog ranch. It's a pillar of respectability in Culoma."

"The only pillar," called out one of the men at the end of the bar, laughing.

"Oh, calm yourselves. It ain't like you never seen a lady before," said Captain Shannon.

A little spittle settled on the captain's bottom lip as he talked to Nate.

"Ignore them pikes. They're a harmless bunch taking in the sights. Your fine woman here being the most fetching sight they've seen all year."

Nate beamed and Elisabeth bristled as Captain Shannon yelled over to the men at the bar again.

"Bend an elbow, boys. A nickel a shot for the next half hour. Or a pinch of your pockets. Whatever you got."

Captain Shannon nodded for his barman to pour up, then showed Nate and Elisabeth to a table. Elisabeth sank down in the chair, her hips relaxing back into the smooth wood, hankering for bite of food. When the captain poured water into real glasses, she knew she'd been right to let the men stare for money. She was going to eat a proper supper. The captain sat with them while supper cooked, sharing rumors of recent strikes in and around the river, listing off digging spots he'd heard were paying out. She followed the conversation, learning the names of gulches, ravines, and streams while the men at the bar stole glances, making her feel far more pretty than she was in that old working dress. She'd take what she could get. It'd been too long since she felt pretty, with Nate always saying he was far too exhausted by all the unfamiliar travel and the digging for married loving.

"Tell me about your travels," said Captain Shannon.

Nate told of how they'd boarded a clipper in Boston nearly five months back, making their way down the Atlantic, then across the Isthmus of Panama, and up the Pacific.

"You must be a brave woman, Mrs. Parker, agreeing to come out west," said Captain Shannon. "All that hard travel getting out here, with only your husband to help you along. It must've been difficult for you."

She didn't tell him how the travel itself hadn't been nearly as difficult as the uncomfortable discord growing between her and Nate since they'd arrived.

"We came out here to find my father. Henry Goodwin. Know him?" Elisabeth asked, not knowing exactly why.

Nate kicked her under the table, like she shouldn't have mentioned Henry. Like the shame of him running off with that Indian girl was something they should keep a secret, or forget altogether. Captain Shannon leaned back in his chair and slipped his stubby fingers through his suspenders.

"There's a Henry comes in here for a whiskey pinch now and again. People call him 'Big Bear,' and that's not on account of his ursine resemblance," he said.

"Goodwin?" she asked.

"Never did know his family name. This Henry dared a grizzly. Come away with a huge gash on his face, and a bear head. Showed up here in Culoma Town with that bloody head slung over his shoulder, boasting. Been called Big Bear Henry ever since."

"A trapper, then," she said.

"All them old mountain men are trappers," he said.

"My father worked for the Hudson Company. Came out here trapping in '47."

"There ain't no Hudson men around here no more. Just diggers. But that Big Bear Henry's a dabster, all right. Traps skins like nobody. Trapped up the whole valley when it was only Sutter and those Mormons. When I opened my store last year with only a broadcloth and a board laid up on barrels, Big Bear come in welcoming me with a passel of cottontail as holdings on a rye account. He offered to skin 'em right then, whip me up a rabbit robe, of all things. I told him I don't open no accounts on rabbit skins. I deal in cotton and silk, for dressing lovely ladies such as yourself, Mrs. Parker. I'm fixing things up in here finefied for when the ladies arrive. My customers don't want no bunny skins."

"We had an apple orchard. It caught the blight," she said.

Elisabeth explained that her father had fought the fire blight, pruning and washing the trees till his hands bled. But the disease wormed its way deep into the roots, cracking the trunks open with black ooze until the branches bent down to the earth. When all the Pippins and Baldwins shriveled into ugly nubs, he took up work with the Hudson Bay Company, saying it was the only way to support his family. She left out the part of him loving on the Indian girl.

"Big Bear Henry might be a lapper, but he's no family man. Lives up on there on the North Fork with his squaw."

Her heart fell at hearing about her father traipsing that Indian girl all around town proud for everyone to see.

"He ever find gold on his claim?"

"Heard he made a decent strike. Never short of money when he came in here."

Captain Shannon's barman placed plates filled with roasted chicken legs, boiled potatoes, and salted beans on the table. She dug into the greasy leg, chewing off nearly half before tasting the beans, salted and seasoned delicious with bits of pork and onion. The supper tasted like heaven.

"Seen him lately?" Elisabeth asked the captain in between bites of beans.

"Seen who, darlin'?"

"Big Bear Henry."

"Not since early spring."

Captain Shannon called over to a man sitting by himself at a table near the window, reading a Bible of all things.

"Don Gabilan, you seen Big Bear around?"

The man looked up from his Bible and tipped back his wide-brimmed hat, slowly shaking his head no.

"I'm surprised you're still around, amigo. I thought you'd a gone back to the Gabilans by now. Stop those Americans from stealing your family ranch."

"Not yet. Soon, maybe. Soon."

Don Gabilan didn't wear a serape like the other Californios she'd seen coming up the trail on horseback. He wore a black woolen vest over a white shirt, pressed neat with a black necktie, pulled taut. Smooth and brown, his face had no whiskers, only long thin sideburns. He was the cleanest thing she'd seen in months.

"Don Gabilan here's a fancy ranch man," said the captain.

She'd heard about those old aristocratic families. Descendants from the first Spanish settlers who'd come out nearly a hundred years ago spreading Catholicism to the Indians by building a trail of missions. Mixed in with the Mexicans and Indians too. She heard they were wealthy. Extravagant. Lovers of art and music and all sorts of other unseemly vices. And they owned all the land in California. Controlled all the ranching and farming. Ran the government. They held onto their power with a sense of refinement, hiding their low opinion of the incoming Yankee foreigners under a heap of courtesy.

The captain walked over to the Californio, gripping his hand, familiar.

"Out slumming, amigo?" asked the captain, laughing hearty.

"Sí, El Capitán. Like you," he said in clear English, with only a slight accent.

The captain pointed to a pen in front of Don Gabilan.

"May I?"

"Of course," said Don Gabilan.

The captain picked up Don Gabilan's magnificent metal nib pen, turning it over in his fingers, appreciating the tiny bear carved into one side of the bone handle. When Captain Shannon showed the pen to Nate, that Californio set his dark eyes on Elisabeth. He didn't gawk like the men at the end of the bar but smiled with his eyes mischievous like he was about to start something. Her face flushed hot, and he kept looking and looking deep into her eyes until he nearly burned a hole right through 'em, and she couldn't stand the honesty of it a second longer and finally looked away. She straightened up in the chair and put down her chicken leg, wiping the grease off her chin with her fingers. She sipped water from her glass delicate, acting like she was the lady she wasn't. When she caught a glimpse of her own rough hands with dirt caked underneath her ragged nails, she placed the glass down harder than she'd meant to, nearly breaking it. Disgusted with herself, she hid her hands below the table wishing she could buy new gloves.

"Care to part with it?" Captain Shannon asked Don Gabilan.

"I'm here for supper. Not business," he said.

"Can't blame me for trying, with the all that finery you always got on you. I'm a business man, amigo."

She took little bites of her beans now, spooning them slowly into her mouth, careful not to appear too ravenous in front of Don Gabilan. Nate inhaled his meal, then sucked the chicken bones clean. After, Captain Shannon cajoled him to enjoy a drink at the bar.

"Let your woman finish her supper in peace!"

"Maybe one rye," said Nate, standing up.

She flashed Nate a nasty look, hoping he wouldn't drink up her earnings. When Captain Shannon turned to her, she reached out to shake his hand like she would've meeting a new mill boss back in Lowell. He hesitated, leaving her hand hanging in the air so long a wave of foolishness crashed over her. When he finally reached out, taking only the tips of her fingers, she let her hand float like a dead fish supposing it more ladylike.

"Pleased you're here, Mrs. Parker," he said, patting the back of her hand.

Nate joined the men at the bar, making merry. Slapping backs. He seemed to forget completely that most of those men had flocked lascivious around her earlier in the day. Annoyed, she tapped her foot, hoping that Californio might pay her some attention. But when she looked over, Don Gabilan had already gone. Disappointment spread through her like a hot rash as she pulled "Self-Reliance" out of her pocket to read, alone.

3

"I will do strongly before the sun and moon whatever inly rejoices me and the heart appoints."

E lisabeth touched herself through her petticoat, rubbing and rubbing, desperate. The devil had settled inside her blood, stoking a fire, burning her up. Sitting by the rushing river as the inky California night pooled around, she pulled off her boots, careful not to spill out the coins she'd hidden from Nate. She rolled out of her stockings and slipped her toes into the water. It felt cool yet silky, too, and soaked the bottom of her dress, but she didn't care. She hiked up her skirt, and a delicious draft glided over her bare skin, tingling. The air floated gentle and dry, nothing like the sticky air in the East, hanging heavy and thick.

Falling back in the sand beside a boulder, she ran a hand between her legs, remembering Nate kissing her in the alleyway behind the mill in Lowell. He'd pushed her up against the bricks with a kiss that smothered away her sadness at losing Lucy. His lips had tasted soft as butter on her neck as he whispered she was his everything. Smarter than all the other mill girls in all the boardinghouses he'd visited with his book-lending business, he'd said. After, he'd brought flowers and books, and read her poetry. He'd sucked her in with his fancy words and liquid blue eyes. Now he hardly ever kissed her. A peck on the cheek here and there. Nothing so moving.

After supper at Shannon and Cady's, she'd tried to tempt him once again, saying she'd clean up better. They'd found a bathhouse straddling the creek but got a shock at the posted price of two dollars a soak. Three for hot water. Nate said a bath wasn't a wise buy, after forking over the ridiculous sum of nine dollars for the chicken supper. They'd need to save the rest of their money for food. Instead of making the long walk back to the claim in the dark, Nate suggested they sleep outside the tent, down by the river in the night air.

"We'll buy some food stores in the morning before heading out," he said.

They curled beside a boulder, and Nate put his arms around her, warming her. They breathed together, yet mismatched and out of time, until Nate started fidgeting as usual, tossing about in the sand.

"I can't get comfortable," Nate said, sitting up.

"Let me help," she said, placing a hand on his lap.

"Aw, 'Lizbeth. It's no good. My nerves are kicked up again tonight."

"I feel the same. All nervous and wiggly. It's probably the supper making us so. We haven't had full stomachs since I can't remember," she said.

"It's no good," Nate responded.

"We just have to practice, is all. Get used to each other," she said.

"No. The digging. The digging's no good. I think I'm doing it wrong," he said. "That's why I haven't found any gold yet. There must be a special technique. A secret I gotta know."

"Digging?"

"I'm going back to ask Captain Shannon."

When Nate got up, she sighed, irritated.

"Please don't spend our money on drink."

"Not a chance, darling," he said, kissing the top of her head.

Lying alone by the American River, she waited impatient for his return. She loosened the collar on her blouse and wiped off the tired stink under her armpits, wishing she had a bit of lavender soap to wash proper. Then she slipped both hands in her drawers. She didn't mean to start the pleasuring, but thinking of all those men stirred her up. Before she knew it, wetness dripped between her thighs. Touching herself was a poor substitute for a man. She couldn't help herself. She wanted more. Working both hands back and forth, she wiggled her bottom into the warm sand like a woman deprived of a special love you get when agreeing to marry. Perhaps the wildness of California itself was infecting her, burrowing deep into her bones. Or maybe she simply wanted too much. Either way, she yearned for a husband's touch. Not the fumbling affairs she and Nate shared under the quilt after they'd married, over so quick she hardly got going. She wanted something else altogether. She wanted Nate to set about her with passion. But he always clammed up on her, hiding his pearl of love away tight.

Now all that pent-up want was turning into a naughty thirst quenched only by her own fingers. Biting her lip, she rubbed that little knobby bit faster, aching and throbbing and swelling and surging as the water danced over the river rocks and a sharp sliver of western moon rose up behind the black silhouette of trees on the ridge beyond. She slid a finger inside and a squeal escaped her mouth as her familiar New England sensibility of shame slipped off like an onion skin, revealing the bittersweet rawness of lust. Peeling away. Growing. Turning over. Transforming into an insanity of want. She forgot about Nate as her whole body vibrated with nature. She imagined those men from earlier in the day. Gathered around. Reaching out. Touching her, naked. With strong hands, large and soft and rough. All over her. Offering up warmth and passion and love. And that Californio with the dark eyes. Taking her for his own. Touching her. She imagined her fingers as his fingers. As his body, moving in and out with frenzy. Rising and rising, reaching for more and still more, sending her into a stream of sultry shuddering as an explosion of stars shot down from above.

A thin strip of moonlight shimmered across the river and a coyote moaned in melancholy from somewhere up on the ridge. Elisabeth felt as lonesome as ever and wondered what lies she'd write to Louisa May in the morning.

4

September 1850

My Dearest Friend Louisa May,

I trust this letter finds you well and settled into your new family lodgings in Boston. You will be relieved to know we finally arrived at my father's claim and he welcomed us joyful, expressing deep gratitude we'd come so far to find him. As I suspected, he accepted Nate as the ideal son-in-law. We spend our nights together around the hearth fondly recalling the Goodwin Farm with Mother and Samuel and Lucy. Oh, the joy of family, Louisa! Our reunion gives me a sense of wholeness, fulfilling my every longing for security and happiness.

Father's claim is expansive, covering a wide swath of the river basin. He holds a second claim a few miles upriver, where he spends a good deal of time, giving me and Nate the privacy much desired in a young marriage. He visits every Sunday for supper, when we discuss our weekly yield of gold from the river. Our physical comfort is much more than I expected in such a wild place as yet unsettled. The sun shines in a sky of brilliant blue with an autumn air blowing strangely warm. There is no hint of the coming winter signaled by a morning chill and only a few river birch burst familiar in a show of orange and yellow leaves. The beauty overwhelms and confuses me with a breathtaking constancy of the vibrant green pine trees. It's true what you've read in the papers. Many men are swept up in gold folly, succumbing to the surge like Odysseus's sailors in the land of the Lotus-eaters, driven by blind greed. Fortunately, my dearest Nate has not fallen in with that lot. He stands by my side giving me a singular companionship I could've only hoped for in a husband. So, you must now forget your worry that I married in haste as a purely economic resolution to my prior unfortunate circumstances. Traveling for so many months has not at all proved hard on my marriage nor strained our collective sensibilities, as you suggested might happen. On the contrary, settling down on Father's claim was the right decision worth the arduous travel. This splendid place shifts us closer with affections and expectations beyond our imaginings, by the day. Nate gives me more than a wife should want and cares for me better than I'd thought a man capable, dressing me in finery of silk and insisting I have three pairs of gloves and a new church hat with an ostrich feather, if you can imagine! He even procured me a horse in San Francisco to carry me comfortably up into the foothills, saying no wife of his should rip her stockings walking the river trails on foot. I grow embarrassed by the riches he bestows upon me, as you know I am a simple woman not requiring luxury.

I do not blame you for doubting our union, as I understand a woman without a husband cannot know yet of such delicate conjugal matters. One day soon, God willing, you, too, will be blessed with the love of a man such as Nate. Until then, rest assured I am not on a journey of doubt but have found a home in my marriage, sheltering me in the truest of loves.

But how I wish you were here beside me to share in this glorious untamed nature, as I know how you dread *the crowds and muck of the dreary Boston city! You must long for Hillside House in Concord, as I, too, long for the Goodwin Orchard next door in its finer days. Considering the urgent social work of your mother, you've not acquiesced but adapted to a difficult situation for the sake of family, as all women must. I've no doubt you will manage in the cramped quarters of the city apartment with grace. As you say, dear Louisa, our pride and taste and comfort suffer for love. We rarely bend a new condition to our will but bend ourselves into the new condition. I may remind, your present predicament provides far less than the discomfort you endured living through your father's bungled experiment at Fruitlands, however noble. Thus adapt you will, as the seasons change.*

Meanwhile, please express my most heartfelt love to your mother and your sweet sisters. Tell them I miss our evenings whiling away in lively curiosity at Hillside House, and our innocent days running through the fields toward Mr. Emerson's library for our lessons with Miss Foord. Most especially, convey to your father and Mr. Emerson that "Self-Reliance" has been my greatest source of strength since leaving Concord. At your earliest convenience, please post word to Culoma Town, California, sharing your current situation and success in writing. You simply must.

Your loving friend in the West,
Elisabeth Parker

5

"Fiction reveals truth that reality obscures."

After posting the letter, Elisabeth asked around Culoma town after her father. She knew it was stupid, still stewing over where he'd gone and if he'd come back. Even so, she couldn't help herself. Near the livery, a tall black woman squinted at Elisabeth from behind a rough pine table, then pointed to a board carved with the word *Bakery* hung over the door of a shack. When the woman lifted up a rag, Elisabeth smelled the fresh-baked bread and her mouth watered.

"You wanna buy a slice?" asked the woman.

"You know a man named Henry Goodwin?"

"Who's you?"

"Elisabeth Parker."

"Nandy Gootch," said the woman, nodding matter-of-fact.

Nandy grabbed a serrated knife with big hands, knobby like a man. Her skin didn't look black but only a shade darker than Elisabeth's, browned up from the California sun. But Nandy was smoother like a caramel apple, not at all uneven and splotchy with freckles like Elisabeth. Nandy wiped the plank table with a wet rag, whistling and rubbing the pine clean, polishing nothing to polish.

Behind the table an open fire burned low with a Dutch oven tended by a lanky-looking black man wearing a vest over a flax shirt open at the neck. He crouched, poking at the embers with a wooden stick. Seeing Elisabeth, he pulled his leather vest straight and sniggered.

"A dollar a slice. Two for butter," said Nandy.

Elisabeth stuck out her chin, shocked at the prices for the least little thing. Still, chatting with this woman felt right, seeing as she was the only other woman around. But buying a slice with the coins stuffed in her boot seemed wrong. She planned on saving them, just in case.

"I'm not buying."

Nandy flopped down the rag with a thump and put her hands on her hips. Squinting, her thin eyes nearly disappeared inside the full folds of her face. She wore a blue kerchief covering her head with soft puffs of hair popping out. She was much older than Elisabeth's twenty years, and with a filled-out waist she looked better fed.

"You drooling over my bread. That's what you doing."

"I'm not drooling."

She was, in fact, drooling. She wanted to grab the whole loaf, biting off hunks without even slicing it. And she was jealous too. Jealous that this woman looked so healthy while her dress hung loose.

"All the folks drool over my bread."

"Not me."

"You's plain lying."

"Nope. Simply conversating."

"You got money?"

"Not two bits for bread."

"You a beggar girl."

"Nope."

"Who's you then?"

"Henry's daughter."

Nandy smiled with the most beautiful white teeth, big and square and completely straight.

"I knew you was coming," said Nandy.

Elisabeth ran her tongue along the inside her mouth, feeling the uneven, small, and rather misshapen teeth, wondering if Nate found them ugly.

"How's that?"

"You married?"

"Yes."

"Where's your man?"

"Over at Shannon and Cady's stocking up."

"You said you got no money."

"I said no such thing."

"Little 'uns?"

Elisabeth clasped her hands in front her, thinking she'd never have children if Nate didn't give her any loving.

"You're awful nosy."

"Come 'round here," said Nandy, flicking a finger at Elisabeth for her to follow behind the cabin.

"Why?"

"That's fine, you don't wanna hear my story. I gots work to do anyhow," she said.

Nandy grabbed a lump of dough from under a red-and-white checkered towel and flopped it on the table, pounding and pounding the dough with her fist, then lifted another towel, revealing a steaming loaf of bread. The smell made Elisabeth's stomach ache, and she twisted her plain gold wedding band on her finger and swallowed. An emptiness stuck dry in her throat.

"Did you hear me earlier, asking after Henry Goodwin?" Elisabeth asked.

"I ain't no idiot."

"Never claimed you were."

"What do you think I'm doing out here? Traveled to the West like a fancy lady?"

"I suppose not."

"Now, I done told you, I got a story."

"What story?"

"You like stories?"

"That depends."

"On what?"

"If it's true."

"You only like 'em true?" Nandy asked.

"I don't mind lies, as long as I know they're lies," said Elisabeth.

"Well, I got a good one."

"A lie? Or a truth?"

"How 'bout you tell me which, once I tell it to you," Nandy said.

"I'm listening."

They walked behind the cabin to a crude cut bench under an oak. Elisabeth sat next to Nandy in the afternoon heat, examining the dirt for any sign of ants. She had a terrible fear of those buggers, crawling creepy all over her and getting up into places she'd rather keep to herself.

"I got quince," whispered Nandy, pointing to a canvas sack leaning on the tree trunk.

Elisabeth grew irritated at the woman's bragging.

"What's the story?"

"I is 'bout to tell it. You got to be patient."

Nandy folded her arms across her chest, sighing loud. Then she closed her eyes like she struggled to remember. Elisabeth waited. When Nandy started breathing deep and slow, Elisabeth thought the woman might've fallen asleep. Minutes passed. The oak overhead cast large leafy shadows on the yellow grass, floating and flitting on wafts of wind like dancing ladies. Elisabeth pushed her boots back and forth, crunching the grass flat to make a proper dance floor for the leafy ladies. The day grew long and languid as she waited. When a jay squawked in the distance, she leaned in close toward Nandy's face, taking in a smell of warmth and sugar. She poked Nandy in the shoulder gentle and her flesh gave way to ropy strength underneath. Nandy jerked with a start and began meandering toward a tale.

"Me and Billy," she said, pointing to the man tending the fire. "We was brung from Missouri five months ago. Brung out by Master Sappington."

Elisabeth sat back down on the bench, listening.

"Master Sappington comes back from the diggings every afternoon wanting his bakery money, but he don't know nothing 'bout no quince," she said, winking. "Found these over the ridge. Sweetest quince I ever ate."

Nandy handed one to Elisabeth.

"Go 'head. Smell it."

She turned the fruit in her hand. Green and hard and shaped a bit squat, it smelled familiar, like an underripe pippin.

"I can't pay," said Elisabeth, handing it back.

"And I ain't asking you to. They's mine. Picked free as God's bounty. Eat," said Nandy.

Elisabeth bit into the quince, puckering and savoring the crunch. It tasted tart, and harder than an apple, but delicious.

"That the way they is. Got a tang a lemon," said Nandy, biting into one.

The two women ate, sizing each other up with the branches overhead protecting them from the growing heat. A Steller's jay landed on the quince sack, screeching. It pounced around, pulling on the cotton fabric, bold and stubborn, while Nandy looked on.

A few black ants crawled onto Elisabeth's boot, and she flicked them away.

"They ain't gonna hurt you," said Nandy.

"I hate ants," she said.

"Them ants is so dumb they walk in a line one after the other, not thinking where they's going. One of 'em gets off track, the others follow till they all lost. Now them Stellers is smart as all. Always remembering where my store's at. Them little bird brains hold more than you'd 'spect," she said, tapping her temple with a finger. "But they's greedy buggers, too, stealing. Taking more than a fair share."

Nandy shooed a flat hand at the bird. The jay didn't fly off but held its ground, cocking his head with a dark blue Mohawk flopping and beady eyes peering. Suddenly, Nandy lurched forward, waving both arms big and powerful, squawking like a mama bird. The jay fled up to a twisty branch but kept screeching down.

"That Steller's my teller. Plenty of jays come 'round, keep a running conversation. But that one there tells me what's gonna happen. In the future," she said, pointing up. "That's how I knew you was coming."

"That so?"

Elisabeth wondered if Nandy was dim-witted.

"Times I don't know what he's saying till after the happening. Early yesterday morning he was fussing when I seen a fawn come into camp. Slight thing, small like you. I was watching and thinking 'bout my own little Andrew in Missouri when that fawn ran to a buck down that hill. I ain't ever seen that. A fawn running with her daddy. No mama in sight."

Elisabeth considered what sort of mind conjures a notion like that from seeing a couple of deer, but she kept quiet and listened.

"First time my jay talked to me, Big Bear came," said Nandy.

"Big Bear Henry?"

"Now let me tell it," said Nandy, hotly. "I don't like rushin'. I tell it how I like to tell it."

"Are you always this rude to customers?"

"I don't see no customers," said Nandy.

Billy let out a huge belly laugh by the fire pit.

"Fair enough," said Elisabeth.

Elisabeth nibbled the last of the quince and chucked the spent core in the grass.

"One Sunday my jay was clamoring and noising about more than usual, flying crazy from branch to branch. I was sweeping the brush away from the cabin, and Billy was out collecting firewood. Master Sappington sat in front of the cabin on his rocker, tapping his pipe and reading his Bible, sore as usual with my jay's disturbings. He looked up every now and then, hollering, but my jay paid him no mind and kept on fussing. Then my jay left the oak in a hurry, leaving bad feels around the cabin. Sappington declared he was glad to be done with the racket, but I knew my jay flew away for a reason. A hot second later the devil's spawn itself swooped down and landed atop the bakery table, giving Sappington such a fright he toppled off his rocker onto his bottom. A beast of a creature stared him down, standing nearly three feet tall with black spiky feathers all around its neck. A nasty thing, with a wrinkly raw head, pink and yellow, and black eyes. Hissing and grunting, that beast let loose a river rat from its beak atop the table, squeezing that poor critter in its talons, making it flop and squirm and squeal something awful. It started the work of shredding it up then and there, gulping bits of gray fur and flesh and itty-bitty pink paws still wiggling for mercy down its gullet. When old Sappington got up from the dirt and took a step toward the table, that beast spread its wings wide as a house, flinging blood onto Master's white Sunday shirt. What a sight! Sappington scrambled into the cabin, coming out with his gun. But the beast beat off in a whoosh like you never did see, circling overhead, taunting and taunting, till Sappington done used half sack of powder shooting at the sky. When he sat down in his rocker, sweat pouring from under his hat, that's when Big Bear come."

"Big Bear Henry?"

"No interrupting," said Nandy.

"Big Bear come clad in animal fur saying California is free, earned her freedom through war with the Mexicans. Saying all folks out here is equal. Saying men and women dig equal for they own selves. Big Bear claimed this land a free state. Said we is free. That sound like your daddy?"

"No."

"Well, he didn't say nothing but curse words for Sappington. Pointed his rifle at him. Tried to run him off. Of course, he don't like that. Stayed put. Called Big Bear's bluff, saying he'd be swinging from a tree by sundown if he killed a wealthy Missouri man like his self. And I know 'bout that. Mmm hmm."

"What happened next?"

"Big Bear stormed off, spewing words for the devil. That's when I knew my jay was talking to me. Telling me the future."

"Did he have an Indian girl with him?"

"Nope. But came again, when Sappington gone out digging, telling me and Billy we is gonna be free soon. He come four more times after, too, saying the same. We is gonna be free. Well, we isn't free yet. I's still waiting. I know Big Bear is telling the truth."

"Did you ever get to his claim on the North Fork?"

"I never left this spot in three months. I ain't free yet, girl."

"I got a need to know about him. How he lived. What happened," Elisabeth said.

"We don't always know the why. He gone now, sugar, that's all we need to know."

"How do you know?"

"On account of that daddy buck I saw. He done ran away when his fawn wasn't looking. That sorry thing walked around in circles for hours confused till it figured it could move on by itself. It didn't need a daddy no more."

"That's a queer view of it," Elisabeth said.

"Where's your mama?" Nandy asked.

She'd tied a knot on that thread, preventing a loose memory of melancholy from unraveling inside her mind.

"Massachusetts."

Nandy flipped a loaf, browned to perfection, onto the table from the Dutch oven. Elisabeth stared at the warming lump, still suffering with morning hunger, even after eating the quince.

"You got any food?" Nandy asked.

Elisabeth shrugged, staring at the warm lumps of bread, downright crazed with hunger, probably whipped up more by eating the quince.

"You far away from Massachusetts now, girl. You at the far ends of the earth. Far away in here too," Nandy said, pointing to her temple.

"I get your point," Elisabeth said.

"The world is different out here. And not a slight different. A big different. People get all mixed up sideways. I seen it. But it ain't all bad, I tell you. This place is special. It presses into you, no matter what you got to say about it. Like a stranger offering a gift you didn't know you needed. Once you take it, you ain't never gonna be the same."

An idea slipped into her head. If a slice of buttered bread cost two dollars in town, one quince might sell for three, or three and a half in the diggings. Maybe four or five further up river. She posed the idea to Nandy.

"Listen, I appreciate the story and the advice and all, but I'd be better off if you'd lend me that sack of quince. How about I sell them down in the diggings and give you twenty percent," Elisabeth said.

"Twenty percent? For my very own quince?"

Nandy giggled and giggled, with her whole chest heaving.

"I thought . . . since you can't leave here, and all. On account of Sappington," she said.

"I may be a slave, but I ain't stupid. My quince is more to me than all the gold I could hold in my hand. Seeing as I ain't got no rights to spend it. Yet."

Embarrassed at trying to get an advantage over Nandy, Elisabeth turned to go. But Nandy called out.

"I saw you sewing for those men yesterday."

Elisabeth turned around to defend herself.

"That's my business!"

"I ain't judging. Just sayin'. You got more thread?"

"Yes."

"Then you be fine," Nandy said, handing her a single slice of buttered bread. "You Big Bear's girl."

6

"Adopt the pace of Nature.
Her secret is patience."

With a whole quince and a slice of buttered bread filling up her belly, she bounced along the trail with Nate, feeling buoyant and strong. More than strong. Making money on her own terms had forged a strong nugget inside her, changing the balance in her marriage. There was no going back now. She'd pushed Henry's leaving down into the deep holes of her mind so she could forget and move onto something better.

She'd already made twenty-eight dollars mending an overcoat, three shirts, and two pairs of pants for diggers while Nate swirled his pan in the river nearby waiting on her to finish. He wasn't sore anymore, now realizing they could keep fed with her sewing while he panned for gold. She asked for more money downriver, sewing slow and smiling pretty, knowing those diggers were pleased to hand over the coins if she delivered the sewing with a bit of flirting. Not too much so she'd seem too loose. Just a little giggle. A toss of her chin over her shoulder. A slight batting of her eyelashes. Nate scrunched his nose at her sly acting and the men staring, but she didn't sew faster, and he couldn't say a thing about it. She was the earner now.

She refused to sulk over Nate drinking at Shannon and Cady's the night before, either. She'd relished the time alone, touching herself, imagining. Besides, Nate had returned before dawn, lying next to her in the sand, draping his arms around her middle, and only smelling faint of drink. When the sun rose, he'd rubbed her shoulders until she stirred awake, mumbling "my darling" in her ear. When she opened her eyes, he'd smiled sweet, telling her how the men at Shannon and Cady's explained how to use a rocker box to get at the gold. Walking back upriver toward the Goodwin cabin, they planned to find Chana's claim for a demonstration firsthand.

Elisabeth soaked up the deep, rich, never-ending blueness soaring overhead, unfettered by any cloud. Spread clear and expansive, the western sky unlocked endless possibilities, unlike the grayness in the east sagging like a wet blanket, dulling the senses. Even in summer. When the sun moved directly overhead, they stopped to eat near the river. Nate peeled an orange, picking off the white inside skin meticulously, bit by bit. He put eight slices on a small flat rock for her and took only two for himself. Sucking on a slice, she watched Nate peel an egg and sprinkle it with a pinch of salt from a tiny pouch. He handed it to her, smiling like he was just fine with his wife doing the earning, and the sour crack between them filled in with a sweet sauce of tenderness. The egg-orange lunch seemed a feast to Elisabeth, and her spirit sang with the meal and mending and the clear sky and the surging water, and her smiling husband.

"The river," she said, speaking over the loud cadence.

"Huh?" Nate asked, pulling out his notebook.

"I like being with you, beside the river," she said.

Nate tapped his finger light on her nose. She hated it when he did that. Dismissed her, like a bothersome child. He put on his round reading spectacles, sliding them down his nose, and started writing. She leaned over, peeking at the pages, and Nate pressed the notebook to his chest.

"Do you mind?" Nate asked, snippy.

"Wondering what you're writing is all," she said.

"Nothing of consequence. Simple observations about the West, and such. Not worthy of your attention."

She skipped flat rocks, waiting for him to finish his daily writing. She marveled at the American River, flowing powerful and with intent, completely different from the Concord River she knew back home. Slow and meandering, the Concord lay languid and lazy, contented and steady, bloated with convention. And the muddy Merrimack in Lowell, slogged sick and strangled with production. The American ran fresh and fervid with no manners or tradition, shooting and exploding in every direction, alive with adventure and no regard for any known canon. The water rushed past, full of rapids in the middle, pulling sticks and leaves and anything else caught up, infusing her with the confidence it carried, whispering. Encouraging. Prodding. Insisting she share in the adventure.

After writing two pages, Nate blew the ink dry and tucked the notebook into his knapsack. They continued on the trail, rounding an oxbow, toward two dozen men digging on a shallow gravel bar. Chana's claim. She stood in shock seeing all those men tearing at the mud and rocks, digging deep trenches alongside the river and in the flats, and diverting the water into a long, wooden sluice. Mr. Chana called out orders, telling the men to cull the upended riverbed for gold. With hunger and hope on their faces, they destroyed the natural course of nature, cracking rock with pickaxes and shovels and even bare hands, and dumping buckets of mud into boxes atop the sluice, rocking and swishing for gold. Absolutely nothing remained untouched but the air itself.

"Would you look at all that!" Nate said.

Mr. Colton greeted them and took Nate down to the water to show him the particulars of the sluice mechanism. Elisabeth noticed a few Indian women crouched on the far side of the gravel bar, swirling reed baskets through the water. Elisabeth wondered if they worked for Claude Chana too. They wore double-fringe deerskin aprons barely covering their bottoms, and their naked breasts flopped and shook with every swirl of their baskets. Magnificent red markings swooped around their shoulders, and white bones pierced through their earlobes. A ripple of envy skidded through Elisabeth at seeing those women working half naked among those men with such ease. They looked so intent and useful yet carefree, too, sifting the gravel over and over in smooth, rhythmic motions. They carried themselves strong and proud, with no hint of shame to cover up, and none of the discomfort or fear she carried around like a sack of weakness. Elisabeth felt an unreasonable urge to rip off all of her clothes and join those women splashing around in the river. She imagined slipping naked through the silky water with them, giggling along as the warm pine air flowed through the canyon and prickled up goose bumps on her bare nipples. A familiar voice startled her back to reason.

"Bienvenue! Bienvenue!"

Claude Chana waved and came up close.

"A pleasure, madame," said Mr. Chana, kissing her cheek, then the other.

"Oh!" said Elisabeth, uncomfortable with such public affection.

"A Frenchman greets a woman with kisses," he said, pulling back with a grin.

She tipped up her straw hat to get a better look at Chana, taking in his thin mustache and tidy blue silk vest. She liked the sound of his French accent and the strength of his pointy chin. Wiry and slighter than Nate, he carried his short self tall and vibrant under the California sun, with an air of optimism and no hint of worry. And his face looked golden tan, not a ruddy red like Nate's face.

"You must be exhausted, after such a long walk from town," Chana said, offering his wooden chair.

She declined and remained standing, feeling nervous, the sort of nervous that made her feel excited.

"You have any mending?" Elisabeth asked.

Mr. Chana smirked.

"Do I look like I need mending?"

"What about your men?"

"Look here," he said, pulling a nugget out of his pocket.

He held it between his fingers, and she whistled, marveling at the bit, odd shaped and sparkling golden, with a smooth round side and spiky bits poking 'round the other side.

"So that's what all the fuss is about," she said.

"Lovely, isn't it?"

"Yes."

As she reached to touch it, Chana slid the gold nugget into her palm. It was cold and hard yet soft, too. When Chana rubbed the gold up her sleeve, and to her shoulder, she froze. When he touched it to her cheek and brushed it across her lips, she gasped but didn't back away.

"If you were my wife, I'd not make you roam the river for supper. Dirtying yourself for a man," he said, his French accent enticing.

"Mr. Parker doesn't make me work."

"Looks to me like he does."

He pointed out her muddy working dress, and her face flushed hot with embarrassment. He wiped a spot of mud from her blouse, touching her breast, slow and lingering. Her nipples hardened like her body had a mind of its own, yet she didn't flinch.

"I want to work."

"Mr. Parker has no prospects," Chana whispered in close.

"Meaning?"

"What I mean to say, madame. Mr. Parker offers you very little. I, on the other hand . . . I can offer you more," he said, pocketing the nugget.

She found his directness refreshing and imagined what it might be like married to a man like him. A strong man in control of his fortune. His future. A man with charm and passion. When he lifted her chin, she let him, standing still under his touch. Nate was only twenty yards away by the river with Mr. Colton.

"Your eyes are stunning. Green, like the Pyrenees in spring."

"Mr. Chana. You're too much," she said, flirting back.

"I'm lost in your eyes."

"Don't be ridiculous," she said, egging him on.

"I assure you, madame, my offer is not in vain. Consider the opportunity. Divorce is possible out here. I know men, accolade governors who will help."

"Divorce?"

She blinked wide-eyed at the nastiness of it. Cutting loose from a commitment. Breaking a promise made before God, for a bit of gold and a few exciting kisses. Just like her father.

"You will consider it. A woman like you, too beautiful for a measly man like him," he said, tilting his head toward Nate down by the river.

When he slid his arm around her waist, she realized she'd taken the flirtation too far. She tried to wiggle away, but Mr. Chana held on tight.

"Let off," she said.

"You want me."

"No, I don't," she said, more forcefully now.

Nate turned around just as she pushed Mr. Chana away. Nate tossed the rocker into the sluice and marched up the riverbank, slow and deliberate. Elisabeth went to his side, shaking with shame.

"What's this all about?" Nate asked.

Chana straightened his vest.

"I'm simply offering her a choice. There is no crime in that, surely."

Nate balled his hands into fists.

"You've quite a nerve. I demand an apology."

"I'll not apologize for offering the lady a choice. Me, or a man who makes his wife work."

"She has no choice. She's married to me."

"Leave it be, Nate. Let's go," she said.

"I'd not make my lady work for her supper," Chana said.

In an instant, Nate's decorum dissolved. With ferocious speed, he jumped atop the Frenchman, pushing him into the mud, pinning his chest down with his knees and hitting him in the face over and over again, smashing his nose. Blood splattered on Nate's shirt, but he didn't stop, punching and pummeling the Frenchman harder, grunting like a bear. Chana didn't seem to have an ounce of muscle to fight back, lying limp in the mud. She stood transfixed at the squishing sounds of fist on flesh, watching with a mix of awe and disgust while Nate beat the Frenchman into a pulp of oozing blood and snot and sweat and disgrace.

When Mr. Chana coughed uncontrollable, Nate took a pause, and two of Chana's men grabbed him and held him back. Mr. Chana rolled away, breathing hard and holding his face. A deep line of red leaked from his nostril into his mustache and chin and all over the front of his fancy blue vest. He crawled away through the heavy sludge and spit a bloody tooth into the mud.

"I submit. *Je suis désolé*," he said, mumbling through his swelling lips.

Still held down by Mr. Chana's men, Nate thrashed and flailed, landing a few more kicks at Chana's right leg. When a shot cracked above the commotion, everyone turned to see Mr. Colton pointing a rifle to the sky, its barrel smoking. He dropped the rifle and held up an Indian basket. One of the Indian women tried to grab for it.

"Stop your fighting, Claude. You'll get all the ladies you want later. Looky here in this basket! We're rich! Stinking rich!" said Mr. Colton.

The men let go of Nate to help up their boss. Mr. Chana pulled a white handkerchief from his front breast pocket to stanch his bloody face and staggered over to inspect the find, clutching his nose. Nate scrambled up from the mud and ran to his wife, holding her close, smoothing her hair and whispering calmness over and over as if to soothe himself.

"I've got you. You're all right. You're all right now."

Nate draped his arm around her shoulders like she was a delicate bird and guided her toward the trail. She didn't spoil the sweet moment with the truth: She'd encouraged Chana's advances. She'd led him on. And she wasn't scared by Chana or the fight, either, but stirred up by the violence of watching men fight in the mud. She looked over her shoulder at Claude Chana holding up a chunk of golden rock nearly the size of a man's fist, as if to show her what she was missing. The Indian women waded into the water with their apron hides billowing out around them as they clutched their reed baskets and floated away downstream into a kinder uncertainty.

7

"We but half express ourselves . . ."

Back at Henry's claim, Elisabeth and Nate didn't bother sleeping inside their tent, as the night filled with a gentle heat, sweet and dry. Under the bright stars, they curled up together as the sounds of the river canyon lulled them. A screech owl echoed *who-who-who-who* off in the trees, and the crickets chirped hypnotic and in sync. As the warm wind drifted through the pine tops and the water tumbled rocks along the river bottom in a smooth crunching chorus, the strange place cracked Elisabeth wide open with expectation.

Wrapped in Nate's arms, all her knots loosened and wilted with want. He smelled of books and beans and kindness and family. She nestled in closer, wiggling her bottom up against his trousers, hoping to get him excited. His breath quickened heavy and he kissed her neck, his scruffy beard scratching her skin. He turned her around to face him in the dark and worked his lips around on hers, sloppy and urgent, causing a tingle between her legs. Light and floating, she wanted more. She let out a moan, perhaps a little forced. As Nate unbuttoned his pants, she scrunched down her drawers and lay on her back waiting for him. The moonlight streamed down on Nate's privates, lying limp like a rag. Undaunted, she kissed him with fast, little kisses on his cheeks and neck, searching for his lips. Instead of kissing her, Nate turned his face away. Instead of touching her, he started touching himself. When she put her hand on his to help things along, he pushed it away.

"Let me do it," he said.

Nate fell upon himself with vigor, pulling and pulling as if he were alone. She propped herself on her elbow, watching with curiosity as Nate worked on himself, moving his hand back and forth in long pulls, faster and faster. Seeing him yank on his privates struck her as odd. She didn't understand why he found more pleasure from his own hand than with her body lying ready. Perhaps he simply lacked the quickness of a younger man, needing extra effort loving himself before loving on her. It seemed exhausting work, requiring a strong arm. She used to think a man needed a wife for this sort of pleasure. Since marrying Nate, nothing had quite gone as she'd expected.

They'd left the mills after the wedding. The first leg sailing from Massachusetts to Panama was crowded and uncomfortable. She'd remained patient, huddling in steerage below with Nate and a hundred other passengers during the baleful storms. Nate had complained about the atrocious food: first bland bits of boiled chicken, then measly rations of too salty pork. Crossing the Isthmus of Panama proved easier. Elisabeth had relished walking on solid ground, and Nate had acted more joyful, picking her bananas and singing silly sea shanties he'd learned from the sailors up on deck. But the exorbitant price of travel and supplies bled their meager savings. When the donkey drivers and bungo boys charged far more than expected to get them upriver to Panama City, Nate had turned rude, griping loud when the rain soaked them through and sniping at the bungo boys for the least thing, telling them how to pole the river bottom and where to tie up for the night, as if he were the river expert. Instead of sleeping in the bungo beside her, he'd raged on the muddy riverbank like a madman, swatting at the mosquitoes with his hat, cursing foul at the demon creatures, as if he were the only one getting bit. She'd responded with an unhealthy dose of silence, wrapping herself up in her shawl against the bites at the bottom of the hollowed-out bungo boat to sleep, thinking a few little biting bugs shouldn't turn a man whiny and weak. She wondered then if she might've made a mistake in marrying him, like Louisa May had warned.

That last stretch onboard the coal ship up the Pacific had passed in dreadful misery. The Humboldt Captain had taken on more folks than the ship could hold and promised more food than he'd stocked. The tea ran out during the first week. She conserved her share, taking bits of leaves from the bottom of her cup and drying them flat in the pages of her Emerson book. For the next month, they had only tepid water from a rusty barrel, insipid stew and hardtack. Traveling left them exhausted, with hardly the energy to make conversation. Nate spent most nights up on deck pacing with worry at not getting enough to eat, while she lay awake on the hard boards below, lethargic and empty and itching something awful with the angry welts left on her once-smooth skin by the Panamanian mosquitos. She believed in the puritanical notion of a devoted woman, holding in her anger when Nate stumbled down at sunrise smelling of rum. Most mornings he'd only manage to mumble a few words before drifting into a deep sleep, his chest rising and falling with the motion of the rolling sea. During those long days sailing up to California, she'd watched him dream while she seeped through with salty disappointment like the rusty cleats on the railings above. She believed the difficult travel made Nate distant. Uncertain. She'd tried to look past her disappointment and focus on the possibility of growing closer once they made a home out west.

As Nate worked at himself by the river, she fixated on his blond tuft. Seeing him yank into a frenzy made her hot and tingly, which seemed lurid and lovely and wrong, but she didn't care. When he pointed straight up in the moonlight, the tingle between her legs swelled to a throb. Not wanting to lose the moment, she slipped off her dress, tossing it aside in the sand. She felt wild, lying naked in the open, waiting. Nate moved over her, keeping hold of himself, still tugging. When he started poking the tip on her thigh she reached out, but his stiffness recoiled like a shy creature with a mind of its own. She let it go, fearing her forwardness turned him off.

"I told you. I gotta get it going by myself," he said.

When he started slapping himself against the inside of her thigh, awkward and rough, she closed her eyes, trying to find the pleasure in it but worrying she should help in some way. And worrying, too, that her own throbbing might weaken.

"Put it in," she said.

He didn't hear her, just kept jerking furious.

"Quick! Do it now," she said, louder. "Put it in."

When he moaned lusty, she thought he'd begin the loving on her. But he remained oblivious to her lying in wait, and grunted and grunted, coming on louder and faster with the speed of his own hand shaking and shaking, until his whole self surged and trembled, and he spurt out on her leg. The heat inside her faded away into emptiness. With a sour sorrow oozing off her, she looked up at the moon waxing angry and cursed silent at his selfishness. She rolled to the edge of the blanket, ashamed at them both and disgusted at the crevasse splitting wider between them.

"I didn't mean for it to go like that, 'Lizbeth."

He covered her nakedness with the quilt and stifled a snivel with a cough. Raging silent with sadness, she listened to the American grumble by while trying to convince herself his faint capacity for loving might be for the best. She couldn't see mothering a child way out here in the wilderness anyhow.

8

"A man must consider what a blindman's bluff is this game of conformity."

With no alternative prospects presenting themselves, Elisabeth and Nate attempted to make a go of the Goodwin Claim, panning side by side on the riverbank in front of Henry's cabin, swirling and swooshing in the mud, trying to find something, trying to build something out of nothing. She understood now Henry had been the single source binding them together, like a mast on a clipper ship rigging the top and bottom sails. With Henry gone, they'd lost all wind, flapping loose and limp yet side by side. Instead of ripping apart, she settled on floating alongside Nate, trying to fix her tenuous marriage. Trying to figure out how to make him happy.

During those early fall days they eked out a meager living, realizing that nothing divided a woman's work and a man's work on the American River. With so much to be done, the work itself emerged as the great equalizer. They found a few flecks of gold in the river, which was better than nothing, storing them up in a leather poke Nate wore around his waist. In between digging, she kept up mending. She carved a sign on a board with a penknife and staked it at the juncture on the river trail. *Mending—50 Yards Upriver.* It was closer to 150 yards, but she knew once a fella got to walking in a direction it wasn't easy for him to turn back. At least a dozen or more hopeful miners passed by the Goodwin Claim everyday, hiking along the river looking for good spots to dig, and she asked every single one if he had mending or washing that needed doing. Quite a few did, or said they did, anyhow, presenting her with torn-up pants and shirts and overcoats for her to fix. She turned a decent profit, given she conserved thread, and soon started making soap using ashes from their fire ring and a spot of pork fat, adding crushed-up pine needles she'd collected to the soap for a sweet scent. For an extra dollar she'd wash miner's clothes, or sell them a sliver of pine soap if they wanted to wash their stinky selves clean.

Nate kept mostly to himself, picking and panning and doing other useful chores that needed doing around the claim. That first month he was ambitious, splitting logs and stacking cords of wood to keep them warm through the coming winter. And he built a proper outhouse a ways downriver, digging a deep pit, for which she was grateful. Working around the claim seemed to sap Nate's strength. At night, he avoided getting close, sharing the warmth of the fire ring at a respectful distance, quietly eating a measly grub of beans with bits of pork off tin plates. After supper, Nate wrote in his notebook by the firelight, never sharing his musings, while she read and reread Emerson for answers, wondering if the man had considered the fairer sex when writing "Self-Reliance," and what he'd thought of the womanly expectations of marriage, reasonable or otherwise. They still slept in their tent since Elisabeth insisted loudly she'd never set foot inside Henry's cabin.

"I'll not sleep in the same place where he was loving on that girl," she said.

"Then let's pray for a mild winter," he said, rolling his eyes.

When Nate smirked, he somehow managed to look both irritating and charming. She saw flashes of the man she'd fallen for back in Lowell and believed that however distant he acted toward her now, that man was still inside him. Somewhere. He might still crack open and offer her loving.

After writing, Nate went directly to sleep. They slept under the marriage quilt she'd made for their wedding back in Lowell, but

Nate closed himself off, keeping a space between them, never touching her. A few times, she placed a hand on Nate's shoulder, but he didn't respond, sighing heavy as if he was irritated she'd disturbed his dreams. She couldn't help but feel an invisible barrier dividing them, spoiling her efforts, preventing them from growing closer. She blamed herself for his cool distance, worried her previous advances made him feel inadequate. Nevertheless she remained hopeful, each night washing with her soap and putting on her clean pantaloons and undershirt before crawling under the blanket beside him. Just in case.

Maybe seeing her dig like a man in the river repelled him. She could hardly blame him, knowing she no longer looked beautiful. She'd become something of a sight with the man pants she'd made herself, which she now wore under the gray working dress she'd cut short and mended up below the knees. It proved a practical outfit on the river, but not at all attractive for a woman. Her full hips had thinned and hardened with the rough, physical efforts of panning and her boots had busted clean through, so she dug in the river wearing an old pair of boots she'd found stashed under Henry's cabin stoop. Wearing his boots somehow kept a drop of hope alive that he might return someday, no matter how foolish. She still stored her green dress folded up in the trunk inside their tent, seeing no occasion to ruin it digging in the mud.

When her straw hat cracked in the middle, she bought a tattered felt hat off a fella passing by for a dollar. It was a crime, taking the man's hat for so little, but he was despondent, saying he had a mind to sell every stitch of his clothing from here to San Francisco even if it meant getting to his family back in Georgia naked. Wild-eyed and haggard hollow, the man said he was done, sapped of all spirit, his strength drained from the hard going of digging in the river with nothing to show for it. Elisabeth felt pity for the man and gave him a slice of jerky for his journey. They couldn't spare it, but her heart saved a soft spot for a man willing to risk so much for his family.

Her motley-man costume looked peculiar, and diggers passing by often mistook her for a man, until she tromped through the shallows, waving and calling out, asking if they need sewing done. Then they'd stare and stare, trying to make sense of her man pants, too-big boots, floppy hat, and long braid frayed frizzy down her back.

She'd smile and let them look, knowing a warm manner meant more money for mending.

With her sewing and their gold finds, they managed to keep fed in beans and dried apples and the occasional slice of salted pork or jerky—not quite enough to stave off the perpetual state of hunger. Nate bought their food from a new town sprung up on the ridge called Coyoteville, saying it was closer than walking the way back downriver to Culoma Town. He hiked up the ridge once a week to buy what little food they might afford, going alone, insisting she stay around the cabin in case someone got a notion to jump their empty-looking claim. In truth, she relished the time alone. When it got dark, she climbed into her tent and rubbed herself, letting her mind wander back to that Californio she'd seen weeks before at Shannon and Cady's store. She thought back to those dark eyes. Those long fingers handling his fancy pen. She pinched her nipples and touched herself inside, trembling and moaning under her own hands, biting the quilt, shaking and shuddering. Loving on herself left her only temporarily satisfied, and after she felt even worse.

When the first rains came, the days stayed warm but the nights fell into coldness. One frosty morning, Nate said he was ready to move out of their old tent and into Henry's cabin for the coming winter. Elisabeth stomped her feet, but Nate held up a hand in front of her face.

"I'll not let my books ruin in the next rain. The moisture isn't good for them. Besides, it's about time you stopped feeling sorry for yourself about Henry. He's not coming back. This is *our* home now, so you better start acting like it."

"I could give a fig about Henry," she said as Nate walked toward the cabin.

Nate propped the cabin door with a river rock and went inside. Elisabeth followed him as a smell of musty sage slunk up her nose. The cabin wasn't as sturdy as it looked from the outside, with light poking in from chinks gaping in between the logs. Bundles of dried herbs and flowers hung from the rafters of the pitched roof, but the dirt floor didn't have proper planks, only a massive brown bearskin rug with no head. There was a crude hearth and a wooden bedstead with a dingy white ticking. There were no pots, pans, plates, cups, axes. No windows. Nothing useful but an old bedstead, a rickety rocking chair, and a rough side table with a pair of three-legged stools. A broken coffee grinder lay on its side, with a dozen beans spilled across the table.

Flopping in the rocker near the hearth, she pressed off the dirt floor with the tips of her toes, testing its sway. The chair felt too big for her liking. She rocked on anyway, stewing about how to turn Henry's shack into a decent home, when she noticed a woodblock carved with a landscape hung over the bedstead. She pulled the block off the wall, examining the carving of a barn and a long fence reaching into the distance, toward a lovely farmhouse placed peaceful amidst an orchard. An orchard! Elisabeth recognized the trees. All those miniature apple trees, heavy with summer bounty. The picture was carved in reverse, but it was the Goodwin Orchard, to be sure.

"This is my home back in Concord," she said out loud, realizing that was no longer true.

Nate examined the wood carving as she looked around the room for clues. Answers to what sort of man her father had become and why he'd run off with an Indian girl half his age. A gallon tin jug sat by the door. Popping the cork stopper, she got a whiff of stale drink. She put the jug to her lips, but it was empty. She dragged a small trunk out from under the table, opening it. Inside sat two cans of ink, a stack of paper, several blocks of wood, a sandbag, and a leather fold. She unfolded the leather, running her hands along the wood carving implements tucked neatly inside, then rifled through the sheets of paper at the bottom of the trunk. Each paper was printed with a Goodwin Orchard picture from the woodblock, each with varying degrees of ink. Underneath was a book: *The Art of Wood Engraving*. A wave of sadness splashed over her; she didn't know her father was an engraver. Behind the trunk was a small Indian basket with nuts inside that she didn't recognize. Green and pointy at the bottom with a brown "hat" at the top.

"What the hell are these?"

She picked up the nut, took off its "hat," and bit into it. It was bitter and rubbery. She spit it out onto the floor, then threw the basket down, kicking it around harder and harder until the river reeds snapped and the basket splintered to bits and the nuts smashed under her boots into the dirt floor of Henry's cabin.

"He's gone, 'Lizbeth. Now move on. Make the cabin homey-like. Add a woman's touch," Nate said.

He began dragging their two small trunks inside, as well as his case of books. Then he broke a branch off a pine tree and handed it to her. She grabbed the bough in a huff and started sweeping out cobwebs from the creepy dark corners of the dirty cabin while Nate opened his case and took out each book, rubbing it with a cloth and placing it on the table.

"They need to breathe," he said.

His precious case, filled with six rows of ornate leather-bound books, each the same size for a total of thirty six, was the only evidence left of the life in Lowell he'd given up to come out west with her. His life as a prosperous book lender. He'd chosen the collection with care, considering the entire range of knowledge and entertainment they'd need out west. He'd included a whole row of books just for her. She remembered being touched by the gesture before they set out. She hardly cared now. In truth, she didn't even enjoy the titles he'd chosen for her, preferring instead the rows of Shakespeare and Homer to the sappy romances taking up her row, like *Waverley* and *The Bride of Lammermoor* by Sir Walter Scott.

"Take the ticking and rug outside. Air 'em out," he said.

Figuring Henry probably wasn't coming back, she toiled tirelessly over the next weeks making the cabin a comfortable home for them. First, she repaired the cabin chinks by stuffing mud and bits of wood into the holes between the logs. Then she organized the kitchen area and the mining tools inside the cabin, and scrubbed the bed, tables, and chairs clean. She simmered up crushed pine needles and hacked up a cedar branch into shavings, stuffing them into a new bed ticking which rid the cabin of ranky air. She made a simple tablecloth with a bit of gingham she'd brought from the Lowell Mill and put the most strangely beautiful bushy blue-lavender flowers she'd picked off a fragrant bush growing up the autumn slopes in a tin cup atop the table. She hoped Nate liked her feminine touch.

Elisabeth settled in for her lot cast on the American, knowing she was more fortunate than most women, with the cabin and the claim and a good man, however distant. Nate treated her kindly and wasn't entirely unpleasant. But as the days got shorter Nate began staying overnight in Coyoteville on his weekly Sunday run for their food stores, and they grew even farther apart, with vast distances spreading out wide between them.

"It's not all that easy, hiking back in the dark with the boulders and a creek to forge," he said.

"Whatever suits," she said.

She wanted to act the agreeable wife and not push him further away with her demands, even as she ached with loneliness.

"I'll be back early in the morning," he said, grabbing his poke of gold flecks they'd collected that week.

"Buy a candle this time?" she asked, turning the wax stub over in her hand.

"We've only enough for a bit of coffee and jerky this week."

She didn't push, wanting to avoid the discovery of an uncomfortable truth scratching under the surface. Maybe he didn't love her. Maybe he, too, thought marrying was a mistake. Instead of picking at a thread barely holding them together, she forced a meek smile. When he left, she sat on the stoop outside reading about Odysseus and his faithful wife, Penelope. As the cricket song grew louder and the pages grew dim in the afternoon shade, a big yellow dog loped up from out of nowhere, dropping a stick at her feet. He whined and whined and cocked his head.

"What do you want?"

The dog grabbed his stick and tried to push past her into the cabin, like it was his very own. She shouted at the dog, but that didn't deter the thing. He dropped the stick and grabbed at the folds of her skirt pulling playfully, his big ears flopping back and forth.

"Get off!"

The dog let go of her skirt.

"Go away," she said, flailing her arms to scare him away.

The dog didn't take her meaning and started barking and barking, like he was trying to tell her something. Then the dog jumped up on her, putting his paws on her shoulders and licking her face wet and slobbery. Scared, she kneed him off, and the dog yelped and scooted under the stoop, whimpering.

Feeling guilty, she got on her hands and knees and peered under the stoop. The dog looked back with droopy eyes.

"Come on out from under there. I'm sorry."

He whimpered and whined and backed up, scooting deeper under the cabin frightened.

"Suit yourself," she said, standing up.

Angry at being rejected yet again, and by a dog no less, she clomped up the step and went inside, slamming the cabin door in a huff.

9

"God offers to every mind its choice between truth and repose. Take which you please; you can never have both."

Hiking out of the steep gorge was goddamn difficult, going barefoot over all those sharp rocks and prickly pine needles. She couldn't very well wear Henry's man boots with her only fancy dress on her first visit to Coyoteville, so she wore nothing on her feet. Done feeling sorry for herself, she was fixing to find some fun of her own. That Yellow Dog loped up too close underfoot, and she tripped on a rock sticking up on the trail, falling hard on her knees and tearing her emerald-green silk dress nearly to the waist, showing her dingy drawers underneath. Yellow Dog lay down on the trail beside her while she cursed and cursed, holding her toe, ripped open and bleeding. When he whined and licked her bloody toe, she pushed his muzzle away irritated, and stood up. She pressed on, stepping slower and careful now, walking and walking up the hill, reaching the top just as dark fell.

She limped over to a huge open-air tent lit with lanterns and lurked just outside, mesmerized. Wild with abandon, men culled from every race and nation mixed up crazy, dancing a twisted waltz with each other to a comic tune played out of time on a banjo, a fiddle, and two harmonicas. A bare-chested Nisenan accompanied the band with rattles tied 'round his ankles, strutting and gyrating and puffing like a grouse. Half the men wore pants patched front and back across their man parts with flour sacking that read *Self-Rising Haxhall.* Others wore sacks bearing the name of a Mexican hot chile. Having no women didn't hinder the men, with some overcoming the difficulty by taking on the feminine role. Transfixed, Elisabeth studied the men and figured the ones wearing the patches were acting as women, prancing coy and light, following the lead of their men. Those not dancing cradled the arms of their partners, cheering and clapping ladylike, while the real men hooted and stomped furious to the bawdy music.

It seemed the ordinary order of things had gone askew, like some dirty dream brought on by fever. She watched the men, hips swaying, lips pursed, arms wrapped around each other. They groped and sucked on bottles, passing the drink in sacred, merry fraternity. The tune changed, and the fiddler led the couples in the Lady's Chain square dance, blurting out steps in between plucking and bowing, the drunken men joining in verse. She knew she was witnessing something women shouldn't see, something sick and sinful. But it seemed somehow sweet, too, as if the dancing cured the men of a vast loneliness that'd spread across their hearts since coming out west to find the women hadn't yet arrived. She couldn't turn away, fascinated. She spied the men from the dark fringes, when someone came up behind her.

"Have you come for the Fandango?"

In the sinister light cast from the lanterns stood a man, imposing and peculiar. He wore a black velvet vest so short it barely reached the top of his loose-bottomed pants. Rows of shiny brass buttons ran down the sides of his pants, and he had a fine leather holster strapped around his waist. Without a hat, she recognized those moody eyes and shoulder-length curls. It was that Californio from Captain Shannon's store. Out here the man seemed less lovely than she'd remembered. His hair splayed too long down around his face, and he swayed like he was a little drunk. She ignored his question, looking back at the dancers as her stomach screamed with hunger.

"Señora Elisabeth Parker," he said with a wobbly bow. "Buenas noches. Soy Don Nemacio Gabilan."

She looked him up and down, wondering if he intended to join the degenerate ball in the male role or strap on a sack.

"Good evening," she said, cool.

"I don't think that particular Fandango is for us," he said, nodding toward the tent and pulling on his own green glass bottle.

"You're drunk too."

"Ahh . . . señora. A matter of perspective. Perhaps not nearly as drunk as them," he said, leaning his hand on the tent pole behind for support.

"Is that so?"

Yellow Dog bared his teeth at Nemacio.

"Settle!" she said, snapping her fingers.

Yellow Dog listened, lying down next to the tent pole, watching Nemacio.

"Dance with me," he said.

"I won't join in that," she said, pointing at the tent.

Seeing the lewd lot under the tent put her in no mood for dancing. Besides, she'd learned from Mr. Chana that flirting with a man other than your husband is dangerous. Still, she'd worn her silk emerald dress for the first time since coming west and felt like a woman, even with her drawers showing through the rip down the side. Sure, she was barefoot with a toe stubbed bloody. But she'd combed the tangles from her hair and arranged it up high on her head with a green ribbon she'd been using as a bookmark in her Emerson book, and she'd scrubbed her skin raw with pine soap and hot water. She dressed decent, and knew she smelled clean.

"Let's dance outside the tent," said Nemacio, putting down his bottle.

Before she could object, Nemacio slipped his hand around her waist and turned her in circles, moving elegant and masterful, like he was used to handling a woman. Against her better judgment, she didn't resist, allowing herself to be led around in the dark, forgetting all about her sore feet and the raunchy squawking fiddle.

Nate had never danced with her. They'd married in a sensible affair at the Christ's Church of Lowell with no drink or dancing, only the pastor and a few mill girls from her boarding house as guests, and a slice of cherry pie to celebrate. Samuel couldn't get away from his studies at Amherst to join the celebration, and Little Lucy wasn't there as witness, dead and buried in the dirt of the churchyard. Nate's brother Joseph came from his job as an accountant at the Baldwin Locomotive Works in Philadelphia, but he'd remained sullen through the ceremony. Nate said Joseph hadn't been the same since their parents died five years before in a terrible accident involving a reckless coach. It wasn't the wedding she'd hoped. Her marriage wasn't what she'd hoped either.

"We have a ranch, with many fiestas."

Nemacio trailed off into a Spanish she didn't understand, but she didn't care. She pushed out thoughts of Nate and let Nemacio's voice melt around her like warm butter, and she gave in, soaking up the lovely moment with this Californio man pulling her in close, warming her from the cool wind picking up. Stirring her up. She imagined herself a Spanish lady in a red silk dress at a lavish party instead of who she truly was: a neglected wife stuck out west with no dancing shoes and in want of new drawers. She was just imagining. She wasn't flirting. It was only dancing, innocent. Polite.

"A grand ranch," he said.

Twirling her around in circles, Nemacio made her feel beautiful. Swept up in his attentions, all her worries and wants dripped away. Swirling and reckless, she stepped closer into his arms. He stared down at her face, his breath slow and heavy and full against her cheek. He smelled of the earth and the river, all at once familiar and frightening, mixed with a faint of drink.

"Your eyes are . . ." he started.

Too nervous to look at his face, she instead concentrated on the intricate letter R adorning the top brass button on his vest and forgot about being thirsty and hungry and cold with a bloody toe.

"Your husband," said Nemacio, nudging her.

"Yes, I'm married," she said, leaning back to put a more respectable space between their bodies.

"No. Your husband. There. Dancing," he said, nodding toward the tent.

She stopped hard to see Nate pull a man onto the dance floor. Nate took the lead, bumbling around in the center of the crowd with a man wearing a flour sack patch and frolicking around like a giddy girl. Clearly in control, Nate led his partner around the tent with joyous revelry. Her husband smiled bright like she'd never seen. When the song ended, Nate traded in the first man for another with fine-boned cheeks and a black braid dangling down his back. A new ditty began and the pair danced, the lady-man wrapped up silly in her husband's arms, his patched pants signaling his preference. Nate rubbed up close against the man's front patch, and Elisabeth gaped, confused. When Nate led the man into the shadows, she crept up, looking. From behind a rock, she saw the man drop to his knees and fumble with her husband's trousers. She stumbled backward, and Nemacio caught her before she fell into the dirt.

"I don't understand. What is he doing?"

He held her hand tight, pulling her away.

She wiggled away and snatched Nemacio's bottle near the tent pole, stealing a long drink, the nasty liquid burning all the way down.

"It's mezcal. Not for women," he said.

"Ha! And you know what women want?"

"It's no problem. Mr. Parker is simply enjoying the company of men," he said, enunciating each syllable slow.

Nemacio tried to grab the bottle away, but she took off with it. Yellow Dog followed as she ran away from Nemacio, away from the tent, away from the fading fiddle and her husband with the lady-man. She stopped to swig again, her veins flowing warm. The drink tasted more medicinal than repulsive now, blunting the sharp edges of her jagged thoughts. Nemacio caught up, out of breath.

"No deberías tomar el mezcal."

"Speak English, you!" she said, turning and poking his chest.

"You should not drink that."

"You think I can't handle it?" she asked, holding the mezcal behind her back.

"It will make you sick," he said, gentle.

Drinking again, she turned away from him, looking down into the vast darkness below where the river must lie. The elixir drifted up toward her head, letting her loose, floating. The night hung heavy, with no moon, but the mezcal made everything clear, as her stormy marital mist drifted away to reveal the truth. She stared up at the night sky, seeing for the first time, the stars burning true.

"He will come back to you in the morning," he said.

"Do you go with men too?"

"No, señora."

She plopped down in the dry grass, tucking her silk skirt in between her legs. Yellow Dog sidled up, putting his head on her lap. She had no plan for getting back down to the claim. When she took another drink, he didn't try to take the bottle but sat down with his arms around his knees, watching her.

"Where are your shoes?"

"Are you a Mexican? Or a damn Spaniard?"

Silence.

"Well . . . where are you from?"

"From here. I am a Californio."

They sat quiet. Crickets thrummed. An owl hooted melancholy as she slipped into an unfamiliar spirit, coated clear yet dulled and dimmed delicious with disregard, like a careless captain sleeping down in the bowels of his ship instead of up at the helm navigating around a treacherous rocky shoal.

After a while, Nemacio spoke.

"Is it enough?"

His voice sounded distant and muffled as she grew heavy and weightless and oddly warm given the cooling night. She no longer minded her hurt foot, enjoying the blankness, feeling like a book whose words magically disappeared, leaving room for something new. She stared up at the sky again, focusing on one particular star, thinking it might guide her. Tell her what to do next. She took one final sip, the mezcal dripping down her chin sloppy, then handed the bottle back to him.

"Where do you sleep?" he asked.

She let her body fall back, stretching open into the earth.

"Waaaay back there," she said, pointing down into the river ravine.

She hoped she wasn't lying near an anthill. She hated those damn ants. Tears slid down her cheeks. She covered her face with the crook of her arm, hiding. She didn't want him to see her cry like a ninny who couldn't handle her drink or her husband. The wind whispered through the ponderosa pines below the ridge, sounding wistful and strange, like water running low in the distance, flowing free and wild, broken off a distant glacial main, thawing, finding a rhythm, running toward a mysterious unknown. She listened, and passed into a sedate bliss. Nemacio picked her up and carried her back to his tent, with Yellow Dog following close behind.

10

"Space is ample, east and west,
but two cannot go abreast."

Elisabeth arrived back at the cabin with Yellow Dog the next day to a shambles. Nate stumbled toward her, throwing his arms around her and hugging too tight, stammering. His voice shaking.

"Oh, dear God! My prayers are answered. You're safe."

She stayed rigid in his arms.

"I thought something awful happened to you. I'd a been shattered. Shattered with guilt. I should've never left. I'll never leave you alone again."

"You can leave. I suspect I wouldn't mind," she said.

Nate didn't hear. Or didn't want to hear. He turned, fussing frantic over his books.

"A bear broke in. Thank the Lord you weren't here, or who knows what might've happened. Look! All my books. Rifled through," he said, holding up frayed pages.

Nate scuttled from book to book, picking them up and dusting them. He looked pathetic and weak; the accomplished book lender from Lowell had long disappeared. Seeing him dancing with that lady-man drowned out all the affection she'd felt for him. All her hopes of a happy marriage now lay dead at the bottom of his dirty well of deception.

"The beast rummaged through the food cabinet. It's all gone. The pork, dried apples, the beans. The damn thing even ate the salt. I'll have to go back to town for more. We need a gun. Thankfully, it didn't get your Emerson book," he said.

She snatched "Self-Reliance" out of his hand as words and accusations sat dormant and unformed on her tongue, the vocabulary for his actions nonexistent. She couldn't look at him and turned toward her satchel, dumped open with various spools of thread strewn about. The two remaining bolts of fabric she'd brought from Lowell lay unfurled and torn. She collected her spools, putting them back in the satchel, then sat on the dirt floor of the cabin rolling up the fabric.

"Where were you last night?" Nate asked.

"Where were *you*?"

Nate fell to his knees, taking hold of her shoulders.

"Oh, 'Lizbeth. I'm sorry I left you alone."

She pushed him away.

"What's got into you?" Nate asked.

"All kinds of something, apparently," she said, feeling an unfamiliar rage bubbling up.

"What?"

"I saw you, last night," she said.

Elisabeth saw his eyes flash with fear, but he kept quiet. An ant crawled on her skirt, and she flicked it away as her mind slipped back to the night before. Her husband kneading himself up against that lady-man. Fragments had trickled to her all morning, banging in her head like a bag of jagged rocks as she hiked down from Coyoteville. Her head thudded and clunked with each step, her skin smelling strange and her mouth filling with acid.

She remembered Nemacio. The drink. Nasty and delicious, drifting warm and swirling her sloppy into an eddy of oblivion. She remembered Nemacio placing her on a feather quilt, the softness sensual, luxurious. She savored that remembrance, and bubbled up more. Perhaps she wouldn't let go of his neck. Maybe she tried to kiss him and he peeled her hands off and tucked her under a soft blanket. Maybe she tried to take off her dress. Pull him close to her. Had she gotten sick? Maybe he cleaned her lips, gave her water, tucked the blanket under her chin. She captured a slight memory of him washing her feet. Had he rubbed her heels, or did she imagine it? In her fuzzy memory, he'd left her to sleep alone. She'd awoken inside his tent that morning to a hardboiled egg and a single red Indian paintbrush flower placed in a tiny basket. And Yellow Dog licking her blood-crusted toe clean. She wondered now where Nemacio had slept last night, not seeing him anywhere that morning in Coyoteville; she'd wandered around the single street strewn with lean-tos for a solid hour before giving up.

"What did you see?" Nate asked.

"I saw you . . . dancing with that lady-man."

Nate sucked in air, sharp like he'd been stung by a bee, as she trolled his face for some recognition of the man she knew back in Lowell. Her gentle husband. Sophisticated. Dignified. Managing his own business. The man who read aloud to her and brought her flowers and books and told her she was his everything. She couldn't see that man in his face now, all squished up with deceit. He leaned in too close, his breath fouled with betrayal. She turned her head and started biting her nails again, spitting bits of skin onto the dirt floor. She bit and picked until her pinky burned raw, blood pooling bright, until she had to suck her wounded finger to stanch the bleeding.

He began, slow and deliberate.

"I don't know what you think you saw, 'Lizbeth."

"I saw you with a man!"

"Darling," he said, kneeling close. "The West has unmoored us. Set us adrift. Confused our sensibilities. Without the steadiness of my book business, I'm at a loss. And with your father gone, you've been quite difficult to care for."

She hated when he made excuses. Blamed her.

"What's taking care of me got to do with you loving on a man?"

"Oh, darling, you misunderstand. All men have a common desire toward gentlemanly fraternity. It's perfectly natural, especially for me, contributing so pitiful to our livelihood. You've weakened me. Made me dependent upon you in ways I don't find comfortable."

"You're saying me making money sewing and washing, me keeping us fed . . . that's what caused you to go dance with men?"

"Don't be ridiculous. I was simply enjoying my companions. A man has a right, even if his wife buys the bread."

"Gentlemanly fraternity? Is that what you call it?"

"I'm more comfortable with the diggers than with you, 'Lizbeth. I enjoy cards. Drinking. Reminiscing about home. You've become a hard, rough woman."

His words split her like rock smashed under a pick, all consideration and affection crumbling out, slow and sour. Another ant crawled along the length of her dress, scurrying frantic by the upending. She flicked it, too, sending it flying, disoriented and damaged, its lower half ripped clean off. She wished those damn ants hadn't found their way into the cabin.

"I don't believe you," she said.

"Which part?"

"You don't even know how to love a woman!"

Hearing her spite, he got up and left, slamming the door behind him. She stayed inside all afternoon tidying the cabin, struggling for some sort of understanding. Forgiveness. She thought back to the Pacific crossing aboard the Humboldt, when Nate had left her below many nights, saying he needed air, a walk on the deck for his constitution. She hadn't followed him to see what sort of fraternity he'd sought in the dark. She wondered if his peculiar gentleman wanderings had begun then, with the dark sea as cover for his sins.

Nate returned later that afternoon as if nothing happened, offering her a tin cup.

"I got coffee from the boys upriver," he said.

A whiskey whiff on Nate suffocated her. Hoping coffee might stop her thudding head, she took the cup, leering at Nate, wondering what he was drinking in his cup.

"From your lady-man?"

Nate ignored her snide question, holding out his palm.

"I picked some blackberries for you."

She reached for a berry, savoring the ripe sweetness.

"I tore my skin getting those for you," Nate said, pulling up his sleeves to show the little dots of dried blood on his forearms.

"I'm not sorry for it," she said.

"Come here," he slurred.

"No."

Nate reached out with a surprising force and grabbed her wrist. He placed his mouth on hers and slid his tongue along her teeth, trying to pry her mouth open.

"I don't want to," she said, turning her head from side to side.

"Sure, you do," he said, running a hand up her leg, sloppy.

She rolled her eyes like she was bored.

"You can't even do it proper."

"Yes, I can," he said, squinting as if he was bringing her into focus.

She watched him remove his shirt and drop his pants, struggling clumsy to free each leg. In the candlelight, he cut a handsome figure, tall and ropy from months digging in the dirt. When she saw him lying limp between his legs, she pointed and laughed.

"I told you so!"

He threw her down on the bed, kissing her cheeks, and she laughed and laughed unhinged, taunting, "you can't do it."

"I can," he said.

She stopped laughing. She pulled up her skirt and opened her legs to him.

"Then do it. Give me some love."

When he hesitated, she sighed in exasperated disgust and started to crawl off the bed. He pushed her backward, rough, flipping her onto her stomach with surprising force. He pulled down her drawers and tried sticking his tip in and out of her, but he lay limp.

"Soft as a flower," she said, her sass turning nasty.

"You want it?"

"Not anymore."

"You like it?" he said, pressing his hips down onto her bottom.

"I can hardly feel it."

"I'm gonna give you what you want," he said, an unfamiliar fire in his voice.

He stank of sour mud and madness.

"Get off me!"

She flailed out from under him and stood up.

"I thought you wanted to," said Nate, reaching out toward her, gentle.

"You don't know how to love a woman."

She hoped to shame him into feeling something for her.

"I do. I love . . ." he said.

"Men! You love men! You don't love me."

She was crying now, but she wiped away her tears, not wanting to look weak. Nate turned away in shame, pulling on his pants. He fled out into the night, and Elisabeth curled up in a heap on the bed, staring at the shadowy log walls. She was disgusted and angry but guilty, too, that she'd shamed him so. And she'd said it out loud. Said the thing maybe she'd already known. He couldn't love her; he loved men. She listened to the crickets outside, the noisy rhythm shutting out the vision of him dancing up against those men the night before. Loving with that man in the shadows. She started picking again, biting her fingernails to the quick, as her ears rang harsh. Grasping for an understanding, she felt the ground shift beneath her, with relations emerging far more complicated than she'd previously known, with a gradation of morality and no fixed points to grab hold.

Elisabeth felt used. Her mother would've understood, having gone crazy from being used up by Henry, worn down to a nub of nothing, making her feel there was nothing fine left. Nothing special to hope on. Nothing but soreness and hurt, and a heavy load to carry up a steep, endless mountain, like a donkey being dragged along by a rope. A torrent of guilt and regret swamped her. She should've shown her mother greater patience and kindness and love. She should've told her she was worth more than how Henry treated her, with his leaving them with nothing. Maybe then her mother might not have crumbled and crushed and split open by a sickness as bad as those cursed apples.

Lightheaded, she lost focus. She closed her eyes as darkness spun round and round inside her head, and she faded, falling into a void of regret she couldn't escape. She wished she'd never married and come west with Nate looking for her father. A vicious rage flowed through her blood, solidifying her heart like molten lava cooling into a heavy rock. She knew she'd never rid herself of that weight; she'd carry the burden forever.

11

October 1850

My Dearest Friend Louisa May,

I haven't yet heard from you and am sorely missing your company, especially your particular frank perspective, full of sharp wit and humor, so deeply refreshing and never veiled. I find myself lacking the necessity of your particular female companionship, even as I discover the true meaning of loving in my marriage. There is so much to tell, I hardly know where to begin.

We revel in Father's riverside home, which is vast with many rooms and comforts I never knew back East. I was surprised to find, even without my mother's touch, Father managed to fix up this western Goodwin homestead quite nicely, with lace curtains on all the windows and an impressive set of china on which we enjoy our supper. He's filled the walls with extravagant prints in every color made from his woodcuts, brightening up my mood with every glance. We even have a red mohair divan where I take my respite every afternoon in front of a cozy fire and an oil lamp to light my way though the pages of "Self-Reliance." Our large front porch is simply the perfect place, filling with sunshine as I take morning tea with the scones made from the wild berries I find growing in abundance along the river canyon.

My days are not so difficult. I dig leisurely in the river with Nate, as I cannot wile away all my hours and days reading. Women grow bored by doing nothing of significance. I need something to occupy my spirit, as do you. I never struggle alongside Nate, practically scooping gold up in my bonnet. We've nary the hours to tally up our finds! The work is far easier than what I knew at the orchard or the mill, with the benefit of a glorious air giving me vigorous good health in mind and body, and no angry machines threatening to rip off my scalp. The nature here is singularly spectacular, far more than I could put into words. The river ravine is steep and wild with a large variety of majestic pines and other trees, too, and a blinding sunlight so clear that it's quite painful to the eye. I take daily walks through the canyon, losing myself in the pristine beauty. The air is soft and gentle and safe, and the river itself offers me a great source of comfort, filling me with a sense of calm and hope, never murky or rippling with discontent. The fears I once shared with you about Nate becoming silent with bitter disappointment on false promises of family hold absolutely no merit. We grow richer in love by the day, as he shares his mind with constancy. He dances with me under the moonlight, whispering what a fortunate lot he's drawn in marrying me. I'm relieved I make him so happy, as a good wife should, although, I must admit, with only men for company, loneliness creeps upon me now and again, and I miss you dearly. Fortunately, a big yellow dog has taken up my favor, following me around like a shadow everywhere I go, sitting by my side at the riverbank as I dig. At first, his blind loyalty struck me as rather stupid, as I never feed him and push him off when he puts his slobbery face in my lap for a cuddle. But his incessant love has grown endearing, and when he greets me on the porch in the mornings, I'm filled with such a *rush of warmth that I take hold of his chin in my hands and whisper praise and love into his floppy ears, not at all minding his stinky slobber. How silly I am!*

I think of you often, squished together with your whole family in that little Boston apartment, wondering how you manage. As you adjust, I do hope you find space between lessons in your current position as teacher and governess to post word to me in Coyoteville. Tell me about the stories you're writing under your mysterious nom de plume, Flora Fairfield. Is your latest a thriller or a children's yarn? I implore you, LM. Do not stop writing, no matter what stumbles you up or blocks your path. You must find a way. A woman must truly have something of her own before embarking on a partnership with a man. Please write when you're able.

Your gold digger friend in the West,
EP

12

"It is one of the beautiful compensations of life that no man can sincerely try to help another without helping himself."

Nate stumbled back to the cabin in the middle of the night, acting a baby, saying he'd been bitten by a snake. Trying to make her open the door, he pleaded in a trembling voice outside the cabin. She'd barred the door with the table so he couldn't get inside.

"It's coming on something terrible. My whole leg's swollen up, 'Lizbeth."

What a great pretender, just like that hognose snake that bit her back on the orchard in Concord. She'd been climbing trees in the back row of the orchard. When she jumped down, she'd landed right on top of an old hognose. It put on such an impressive display, puffing up and hissing fierce. When it lunged and bit, her father had come running with a stick. He didn't even have to beat that snake. As soon as it saw the stick, the hognose had started writhing around, vomiting, then let its tongue loll out like it was dead. The bite in her leg was shallow and clean; it hadn't even required a bandage. She remembered her father saying she had a better chance being killed by lightning than a snake, but he'd picked her up in his arms anyway, carrying her back to the house gently. When she looked over her father's shoulder, the snake had righted itself and slithered away.

Nate rapped weakly on the door, whining.

"I come all the way from Coyoteville. Getting us a gun. Open up, 'Lizbeth. Please. Please. I'm hurting real bad."

What a fool. They didn't have the money to buy a gun. She ignored his begging, letting him go on and on about the pain like that sneaky hognose, pretending. She wasn't about to let Nate trick her into taking him back inside. He could sleep in their old tent, suffering all night, for all she cared. She stuffed her fingers in her ears to drown out his cries and fell asleep on the bed.

When she woke the next morning, she slid the table away and opened the door to see Nate crumpled up on the stoop with a new gun and Yellow Dog licking and licking his knee. His pant leg was torn nearly off with a bandage wrapped tight around his right calf. As she removed the wrapping to inspect the wound, he stirred.

"'Lizbeth? That you? My sight's blurring," he said, blinking and squinting.

"Hold still," she said.

His leg looked fat, nearly twice its normal size, with two red blood spots near the ankle where the snake must've grabbed hold. She ran to the river, filling a bucket of water. She heaved the heavy bucket back to the cabin, scooting Yellow Dog aside. The dog whimpered as she put down the bucket, kicked open the door, and dragged Nate inside. She grabbed a bolt of fabric she'd been saving from Lowell and tore off strips. Dipping the rags into the bucket, she tried to clean the wound, but the whole lower half of his leg had swelled grotesque. She dumped all the water onto his leg, muddying up the dirt floor inside the cabin, then ran to the river for more. She made six or seven trips, filling the bucket up and dumping water onto his bitten leg. She held his head and put a cup of water to his lips. Most of the water dribbled out the side of his mouth. Nearly delirious now, Nate mumbled.

"You're the smartest girl at the mill. The smartest . . . I do love you. I love . . ."

She was determined not to let him worm his way back into her heart.

"'Lizbeth?"

"I'm here," she said.

"I'm such a rat," he said in a whispered mumble.

When his head fell slack to the side, she shook him.

"Damn you, Nate. What the hell do I do now?"

When he didn't answer, she unbuttoned his shirt and wet his chest with a cool rag. Against his skin, the rag turned hot as if she'd set it on a firebox, nearly burning her hand. She replaced it with another cool rag until that one heated up too. Trying to cool him down all day, she ran back and forth to the river until dark, filling up the bucket and pouring cold river water onto his calf, then cooling his skin with rags, hoping someone would come along their claim to help. Of all the days, no miners passed.

By nighttime his fever cooled slightly, but the wound turned an awful sight of blackened, rotted flesh, smelling putrid and sticking to the rag. No amount of soaking would leach out that damn snake poison. She wondered if this was how it would end between them. Nate would die and she would become a widow, free of her lady-man loving husband. Free to start over. She felt sick at her wicked thinking.

He lay still on the muddied floor of the Goodwin cabin, his breathing shallow and labored. Yellow Dog nudged into the partially opened door, looking up with big dopey eyes. She had no heart left to shoo him away, so he stayed inside while she cradled Nate's head and dripped more water into his mouth. She remembered cradling her mother the same way when she'd cut her wrists through, Samuel wrapping the bandages down tight to stop the blood. A weird breathing had come out of her mother's mouth then, strange and eerie, yet somehow peaceful too. Now she'd endure another loss. A fourth loss. First her mother into madness. Then little Lucy. Then her father. Now Nate. Perhaps this was the grand price God demanded of her. She'd affronted Him, surely. Now she'd pay. Leaving her in the West alone to fend for herself like a feral cat.

She dropped the cup and prayed with her hands clasped silently, asking for mercy. She asked for herself and for Nate. She pleaded, saying he wasn't a bad man. He was her family, and she didn't want him to die. When she ran out of prayer, she listened to him breathe. When his breathing slowed too quiet, she nudged him.

"Nate? Can you hear me?"

His face winced, but his eyes stayed closed.

"Nate. Nate!"

When he didn't answer back, she realized she couldn't live with herself if he died. She flew out the door, planning to run all the way to Coyoteville in the dark for a doctor. Under a full moon casting creepy shadows from the sugar pines, she ran twenty steps before bumping into a man walking down the trail. He stood short and stout, with a guitar strapped around his shoulder and a wide straw sombrero on his head. Frantic, she spit out the story of Nate and the snakebite.

The man said his name was Álvaro and he'd come all the way from Culoma Town.

"You've got to help me," she said, shaking the stranger's shoulders.

Álvaro followed her back to the cabin to see Nate, lying lame on the floor.

"Mmmm. Looks bad, señora," he said, taking off his guitar and leaning it up against the cabin wall.

"What should we do?"

"Some say if you bite the snake after it bites you, the wound will heal," he said.

"What?"

"And tobacco," he said, pulling a string of rosary beads out of his pocket and fingering them. "I once saw an Indian put tobacco leaves on her boy's leg after a snake got him. Next day he was running around after the cows."

"Is that true?"

"Sí, señora. When my uncle stepped in a rattlesnake nest, mi madre used guaco leaves. The baby rattlers are the worst. Horrible."

"Stop," she said, replacing the compress on Nate's leg. "Stop with the stories! Help me."

"Do you have any tobacco?" Álvaro asked.

"No."

"Did you suck out the poison?"

"No."

"Then he will lose it."

"What?"

"The leg. It must come off."

Oblivious to the decision before her, Nate lay still with closed eyes. She blinked back at Álvaro and pleaded for him to get a doctor, promising him money without a clue how she'd keep the promise.

"A big reward if you bring whiskey too. I'll pay."

"Sí, señora. I leave my guitar here."

With Álvaro gone, she sat on the floor, leaning her back against the wall next to the guitar, waiting. Still holding a cool rag on Nate's leg, she lost all sense of time, drifting, falling, dreaming. She dreamed of her father back on the orchard, climbing a tree, plucking apples from the tallest branches, saying, "I can see heaven." He lifted her little eight-year-old self to the highest branches, holding her legs tight as she peeked out from the treetop to see the white house, the holes in the leaky barn roof, the rotting fence falling away, the Concord church steeple poking up to heaven, and her mother thinning carrots in the garden, looking placid, with no hint of her coming madness.

"Señora. Wake up, señora. El médico está aquí."

She squeezed her eyes tight and poked her temples, trying to recapture the images of her once happy family back on their orchard in Concord. Trying to uncover the deep holes of her mind to find them. Her parents. Her family. But someone shook her, dissolving the remembrance.

"Señora. El doctor está aquí."

She woke up confused, then remembered telling a man to run to town for a doctor and whiskey. Elisabeth grabbed the jug and dripped whiskey in Nate's mouth, hoping it might help him endure the pain. Drops of rain began pattering the roof overhead, slow and deliberate, as the doctor explained how he'd cut the leg. Álvaro held Nate's shoulders down, and the doctor sawed back and forth like he was cutting a branch from a tree. The whiskey didn't quite numb Nate senseless, and he writhed and squirmed with force at the cutting, but he didn't holler out. She admired him staying brave, getting through the cutting by kicking his good leg out and digging his boot heel into the muddy floor to brace himself.

"Hold him still, woman!" the doctor said.

She obeyed, holding Nate's working leg down, pressing with all her might until her arms shook and sweat dripped from her forehead. The rain began pounding down harder on the cabin shingles, but it didn't drown out the sickening sound of metal on bone. Blood pooled on the dirt floor of the cabin as the doctor finished sawing. When the doctor severed bone with a crack, Nate fainted limp under the pain of losing a piece of himself. She let go of Nate's good leg, cringing at the sound of the doctor scraping bony shards smooth with a file.

"So no pointy parts break through the skin," he said.

Nate twitched, and Álvaro poured more whiskey into his mouth. When Nate's eyes rolled back and settled calm, the doctor pulled the extra flaps of skin taut over severed leg bone and sewed it up with strong horsehair, like a woman at a quilting bee.

"I'll leave an opening here so it'll drain," the doctor said, pointing to his work. "Keep it clean with hot water so it doesn't turn putrid."

She looked down at the snake-bit leg lying alone on the dirt floor, bloated black with poison. A spate of guilt filled her lungs at thinking how she waited too long before going for help. What sort of woman had she become, stalling, musing that a dead husband might've made her free? Feeling sick, she gulped for air over and over like a duckling drowning without a mother or a father, and grabbed the bloody shank and ran out of the cabin.

"It's all my fault. It's all my fault!"

She ran through the rain and into the pine grove behind the cabin, falling to her knees and clawing and scraping the dirt, opening up a muddy hole. Yellow Dog helped her dig, and she shoved Nate's limb, wet and gooey, down into the shallow hole and covered it up until even his toes disappeared beneath the earth, burying away any reminder of her heartless self.

PART 2

"There is no estimating the wit and wisdom concealed and latent in our lower fellow mortals until made manifest by profound experiences; for it is through suffering that dogs as well as saints are developed and made perfect."

—JOHN MUIR

13

*"We return to reason and faith. There I feel
that nothing can befall me in life,—no disgrace,
no calamity, which nature cannot repair."*

Separating Nate from the rotten leg saved his life, but didn't quite bring him back to the living. Over the next weeks he fought a god-awful fever, tossing about in bed between fits of sleep laced in hazy understanding that his leg ended without a knee. Elisabeth fixed on helping him, cleaning the stump, changing his bandage, and emptying his piss pot. With no appetite, Nate didn't want food. She spooned sips of pork broth into his mouth anyway, knowing he'd need nourishment to live. Through a fevered daze, Nate apologized, babbling on about being sorry, saying he amounted to a nothing. A failure. A sorry excuse for a man. A sinning bugger. She didn't disagree, letting him ramble on until sleep took him again.

With Nate's leg gone, she was stuck with a broken husband, but she took her duty as a wife serious. She wasn't the sort of woman to leave a husband out for the wolves with a sick fever and only one leg, no matter how bitter her thoughts. Whatever love she'd once felt for Nate had washed away at seeing him loving on that man in the dark.

Even so, she wasn't like Henry, who'd abandoned his family so easily. She'd stay, knowing he'd die if she left him alone. She felt the whole thing was her fault anyhow. If she hadn't married him and convinced him to come looking for Henry, he might not have gone up to that Fandango. She might not have seen. She might not have taunted him. Then he wouldn't have run off like that, getting himself bit by a snake.

She thought church might be the only thing to save her from drowning in despair over caring for a feeble husband all by herself in such an untamed place. But Coyoteville didn't have a church, and it was nearly a days' walk back to Culoma Town from the North Fork of the American. Besides, Culoma Town didn't have a proper church yet, only a little log cabin she's heard about being built by the Catholics, and no self-respecting Protestant would sit in that church just because of broken-up insides, even if it was the only one around for miles. She figured God had forsaken her, like her father. She turned to Emerson instead, flipping back and forth through the pages of "Self-Reliance" over and over again, looking for clues on what to do when a husband couldn't love her.

She came to understand Emerson believed a man should follow his own instinct and ideals, but drifting along dwelling on the sad state of one's soul seemed a luxury she couldn't afford. She had to consider the more pressing practicalities of filling her belly. Winter was creeping up, and they didn't have the food stores to sustain them through, and she still owed the doctor forty-five dollars for the cutting, a painful sum. Fortunately, Álvaro asked nothing in particular for running to get the doctor, saying he'd see her later.

Determined to make something of a dreary situation, she turned toward the river, finding a private place to bathe upstream in a pool settled calm by a clump of huge boulders separating the main flow. She scrubbed her short-cut skirt, pantaloons, and bodice thin, hanging them over a cottonwood branch to dry, and waded into the edges of the water wearing only her drawers and camisole. The coldness gripped her breath as she sunk down, her toes feeling the soft gravel bottom. Dunking under, her hair flowed long and free, and the water cleaned her clear, washing away layers of dirt and grief and hurt and helplessness. She opened her eyes and saw the small river rocks lying peaceful on the bottom, oblivious to the current above. Coming up from below, she looked down at her bare feet standing on the rocks through the translucent water like a magic window revealing a twin more pure than her diluted self. The river pulled her. Even in the calm of the pool, it gently tugged her toward the faster, deeper, dangerous current. She flapped her arms and captured the eddy, gripping the gravel near the bank. Climbing out wet, she shivered, not with cold but with revival, as if the river had jerked her out of some murky underworld, remaking her anew. Not like a baptism, but more like the American was the River Styx giving her miraculous powers, making her invulnerable, like Achilles.

She scrambled atop a granite boulder, solid and large and flat on top with a six-inch wide gap split down the whole length. Sprawling out on the larger half nearer the river, she watched the water surge and gurgle. She looked up to see the ponderosa pines rising tall out of the river basin. The rich dark green of the branches appeared almost black, with light green, too, and all the greens in between, mixing together into a dazzling fullness. Sugar pine smell hung heady in the air as she stretched out flat on her stomach, drying by the heat radiating up from the split rock into her body, baking her new. She rested her chin on her hands; a soft fall breeze brushed goose bumps along her arms, and she heard it talking. The wind. She listened careful to hear if it might say something to her, when she got distracted by an elegant osprey soaring overhead, with white underwings blinding bright against the blue sky. When the bird pointed down straight for the river, she sat up to watch it dive in with a determined plunk. Lifting up, the osprey faltered. Graceful gliding turned into ridiculous flopping as the bird weighed down heavy with a big fish gripped in its talons underneath the water. The osprey refused to let go of the fish dangling below and instead spread its wings and settled in the water like a floating duck, thinking on a strategy. Determined, it turned itself around in circles atop the water using its wings as oars, mustering up strength. When the osprey sprung up in a whoosh, Elisabeth saw it had a fish nearly as big as itself gripped in its talons. The fish wiggled and wiggled, making things difficult on the osprey, who bumbled along bumping the fish along the surface of the water. She figured the osprey might have to let loose the fish or sink itself, but it refused to give up, stretching wide with wings a little longer and a little stronger than before, lifting up and soaring magnificent, gripping its prize tight, with no hint of the prior lacking grace.

Back at the cabin, she shoveled dirt onto the bloody spot on the floor where the doctor made a mess sawing off Nate's leg. Patting it down flat with her bare hands, she wished for a wood floor but knew they hadn't the money for planks. After, she worked the claim, crouching along the riverbank, panning with the rocker box Nate had fashioned when he still had both legs. Yellow Dog crowded up too close, slobbering. When she shooed him off, he slunk low, his big brown eyes pleading patient, waiting on food or love or something else. But he never left her side.

In between bouts of panning, she encouraged Nate to sip soup and drink water. Her anger at him fell away, replaced by a wave of pity as she cleaned his stump with boiled water as the doctor instructed. She rolled him over and wiped his bottom when he messed himself, and scrubbed his dirty trousers and ranky blanket in the river. After three weeks, his fever broke, and she made him sit up in bed to eat a meager pork broth she'd cooked up from a small shank she'd been picking off over the past weeks. The broth brought the color back to Nate's cheeks, and he rubbed his stump, looking forlorn with a crumpled-up face.

"Nothing to be done about it. At least you're among the living," she said.

"That I am," he said.

"You can't stay in bed forever."

She handed him a cup of water, knowing he'd have to get up into the chair soon. He sipped, then let his head drop back on the bed.

"We've got to work the claim. Or we'll lose it," he whispered.

"I know."

"The mining laws say if we don't work it, someone else can claim it," he said, closing his eyes, drifting.

"I understand. I've been working it while you've been healing," she said, sharper than she'd meant.

Yellow Dog whined outside the cabin door, softening her. The cabin reeled rank from Nate's swollen-up stump, so dog stank wouldn't make it much worse. She opened the door and let Yellow Dog inside. He crawled atop Henry's bearskin rug in front of the fire, and she got on her hands and knees and hugged him. Yellow Dog put his chin on her shoulder and nuzzled back, then together, they curled and fell asleep.

In the morning she opened the cabin door, and Yellow Dog darted out. A moment later he came back with a tiny pika in its jaws, dropping the furry thing at her feet. Before Yellow Dog could tear at the fur to crunch and gulp it down whole like she'd seen him do before, she grabbed the pika, cutting off his head and throwing it to Yellow Dog as a gift. She gutted the pika and stuck it through, cooking it over the morning fire until the smell of singed fur filled the cabin. She ate the tiny meal, pulling off the meat and skin with her teeth, picking the bones clean, without offering even a bite to Nate sleeping in the bed.

As winter crept up, fewer miners traveled by their cabin, instead hunkering down from the cold in one of the dozens of mining towns sprung up around the placers. That meant less mending and less money for food. They had no choice but to hang on at the river claim, eating the last of their beans mixed with miner's lettuce found growing wild in the forest, hoping on gold. By month's end, she helped Nate out of bed, setting him up in a chair by the fire.

"You're gonna need to buck up. Help out."

"Will do," he said.

She cut a tall pine branch for him to balance his weight on and encouraged him to walk. If Nate suffered in pain, he never complained, just hobbled around with his stump flopping and wiggling every which way something ugly, stuffed in a trouser leg she sewed up short. Praising his efforts, she said he'd soon grow strong as ever. She was careful not to go overboard, knowing false praise would hurt his pride. She pretended getting around on one leg was no different from getting around on two, even though she knew it wasn't true. When he'd gained a bit of strength, she encouraged him to get outside for some air, helping him to a stool she set down by the river. She wrapped him in blanket and thrust a pan in his lap.

"Good to get out," he said, managing a slight smile.

Nate started helping by swirling through the sand she dug up, but the cold proved slow going for them both. Most days, they collected only a few small gold flecks, which alone didn't even amount to enough to trade for food, but together added up to a nibble of glitter that keep them going on a foolish hope. She suspected the larger more substantial gold remained elusive, hiding in rocks below the river's rush, so she kept digging and encouraging him to keep looking in the pan. Out of desperation, she piled up small round river rocks beside her so whenever she saw a pika or a chipmunk dart around the banks, she'd pick up one and throw it. She managed to land about one out of every five throws, so some nights they had a tiny creature to share for supper. Nate insisted on giving up the bed to her, saying it only seemed right his wife should sleep proper. She snorted at his comment, understanding they weren't a proper husband and wife.

"I'll take a spot on the rug so I don't wake you with my rolling. I always wanted to sleep on a bear," he said, smiling at his attempted humor.

She protested on account of his condition, but not too hard, knowing a man needed to control something. That night he took the floor on Henry's bearskin rug in front of the fire where she'd been sleeping during his past two months' recovery. Secretly pleased, she made a new bed ticking for herself, sewing up pine needles into her leftover fabric from Lowell. Sleeping separate became permanent, and they closed themselves off from each other for good.

Even on her new bed she slept in a fit, never getting used to her belly aching something awful for food. Nearly every night she'd wake from a nightmare with flashes of nasty images floating through her dreams in a torrent. A slice of apple pie, warm and steaming. A boot squishing the treat to juicy bits, right before she could take a bite. She woke sweating and shaking and sick with terror at having so little to eat, as she listened to Nate's snoring on the floor thinking back to that Fandango and Nemacio and his mezcal. If she got her hands on some drink, she might sleep solid through the night without any nightmares. She stewed on how to get some.

The sound of gentle pattering of rain soaking up the dry grass around the river basin came as a welcome relief. With only one light rain since arriving out west, she'd thought the American flowed by magic. She listened to the haunting gusts of wind whistle through pine tops and rain stutter and spatter on the rickety shingle roof. By morning the sky cleared to a radiant blue again, crisp and cold, but the muddled banks of the river were up nearly two feet from the day before. The rushing roar goaded her nerves and stoked her fear. She knew she'd need to learn to hunt or they'd starve. No more picking off chipmunks with river rocks. They needed a real meal. She took the gun Nate had brought back the night of the snakebite out from underneath the bed, turning it over in her hands. Yellow Dog jumped up and down, waking Nate, who looked up at her from the rug.

"Show me how to use it," she said.

From a stool in the pine grove, Nate explained how to stuff powder into the Hawken and ram a wad of grass down the barrel with a rod, like he'd been shooting his whole life, when she knew he'd spent his childhood in a Cambridge townhouse. His knowledge of rifles ended with stuffing the barrel, so she rolled up her sleeves, setting up targets of pine cones and sticks, imitating the shooting position she'd seen her father use when hunting deer back on the orchard in Concord. She'd grown strong in the West, and handling the shotgun proved easy, even with the kickback. She practiced shooting at the targets and reloading the barrel until her face smeared with gunpowder.

"We need some help," said Nate, running a hand through his blond hair growing out long.

"I know," she said, resetting the targets.

"Digging. The two of us won't do."

"I know!" she said, irritated at him for explaining like she was dim-witted. "That's why I'm working on getting us something to eat."

She threw the small sack of gunpowder over her shoulder and set off into the woods in search of food with Yellow Dog loping behind.

"Be careful, 'Lizbeth!" he called out.

Getting away from the claim buoyed her spirits. The forest in California didn't frighten her like the dank, dark forests back home. In Concord, she'd been afraid of the woods with the thick, brambly underbrush crawling around scary and mean. Playing with Louisa May as a little girl, she always stayed in the wide open fields running back and froth between the Alcott's Hillside house and the Goodwin Orchard House, never venturing close to the forbidding edges of the forest. In California, the forest grew open and airy with pine trees spaced the perfect distance, letting in slivers of light dappling down friendly on the soft ground, making her feel brave and at ease, like nature itself was seeping into her soul, giving her strength. Still, she was glad for Yellow Dog as company.

She didn't walk too far before flushing out a covey of quail stirring under a manzanita bush. They scattered at a run up the steep hill. She shot and missed, aiming too high. After, she spent the whole day walking through the forest shooting at quail and grouse and turkey and even passenger pigeons, missing them all. When a rabbit hopped in front of her, she took aim. The rabbit stopped, looking back at her like it wondered what a woman was doing wandering alone out in the woods. Big and fluffy, the rabbit would make quite a supper. Her mouth watered as she pulled the trigger, but the shot flew wide and the rabbit hopped away much too slow to even deem her a threat. Yellow Dog took chase, but the rabbit zigged and zagged every which way, taking cover in a burrow. She reloaded and shot again and again, hitting nothing, like a fumbling disaster, until she threw the Hawken in the dirt and kicked at a pine trunk with her man boot in a tantrum until her whole leg cramped up and she sank to her knees knowing she'd endure another night with nothing in her stomach but wild onions and a few beans. Leaning her forehead against the rough bark, she shivered with a creepy feeling that Henry's Indian girl was lurking around. Turning around fast, she saw nothing but quiet and Yellow Dog panting patient by her feet. She leaned down to pet him, thinking he deserved a better name better than Yellow Dog.

14

"In the midst of wild Nature, the self becomes one with being and God; differentiation, alienation, and struggle cease."

It took Elisabeth five more days of walking through the forest shooting all manner of creatures and missing until she landed a shot at a white rabbit nibbling sweet fennel. She crept up quiet, aiming at its fluffy bottom. She checked and rechecked her aim, holding the rifle steady. The bunny paid her no mind, and when she pulled the trigger it fell over with a quiet thud. She jumped up and down and yelled out loud with a silly glee for no one to hear but herself. Yellow Dog knew what to do, bringing the bunny back in his mouth gentle and plopping it down at her feet. She put the bunny in a sack, carrying it warm and limp over her shoulder back to the cabin. Nate hobbled up, hugging her with a joy that filled her near happy. Even so, she brushed him off.

"Nothing to it. No need to get all worked up," she said.

Nate trimmed the bunny up for dinner, tearing off the fur and throwing the guts to Yellow Dog as a reward. The next day after panning, the Hawken proved too much for quail, its blue-gray feathers and white chest exploding to bits. She shot a turkey next, more plump than she'd imagined, clipping the head clean off. Back at the cabin Nate cut off the wings and feet, plucked the feathers and roasted the turkey over the fire while simmering up the innards in a pot with wild onions for a soup. The meat tasted juicy, and she was proud at keeping them fed.

She enjoyed the ritual at the end of a long day of digging, putting down her shovel and picking up her rifle to hunt in the forest. Finding something to put in their bellies proved far more pleasing than lazing around reading with Nate in the cabin, no matter how tired she felt. And it kept her from feeling so lonely. One time, she shot a yellow-bellied marmot resting on a rock ledge, enjoying the wide view of the river valley down below. Seeing that creature torn up by her shot with its little childlike face twisted up in a grimace of pain made her ache. They ate it anyway. Nate staked it through and roasted it for hours over a fire outside, but it tasted both tough and too fatty, not at all a meal worth putting up with on account of the haunting little face.

When the air grew colder, the turkey hid. She saw quite a few deer, but they always ran off before she could aim on account of her unfortunate clomping in the man boots. So she kept to shooting at the bunnies bouncing all around the river gorge, both cottontail and jackrabbit. They seemed deaf to her heavy footfall, and she had a knack for anticipating which way they'd run. With all that practice she could shoot a rabbit darting around crazy. At close range, she aimed for the head. If she hit the rabbit anywhere else, the ball tore it up terrible, making a measly meal. Nate complimented her clean shot, even when it wasn't, skinning the rabbits from his spot on the rocking chair near the hearth. She saved the skins, stitching the rabbit pelts into a scarf to keep her warm while she hunted. She was working her way toward making a rabbit-fur blanket for herself, now done shivering under that lame old wedding quilt she'd made when Nate asked her to marry, now gone shabby and dirty with the stitches pulled apart like their marriage itself. She'd make a rabbit-fur blanket for Nate too; she couldn't very well let him freeze on the bearskin while she slept cozy under a bunny blanket on the bed.

By early December she ran low on gunpowder but didn't yet have enough gold flecks to buy more.

"I'm going up to Coyoteville for more powder," she said.

"With what?" Nate asked, setting out cups of warm water steeped with bay leaves.

She threw another log on the hearth to keep him warm and grabbed the last two dollars she'd made sewing from her savings tin. Then she opened his trunk of books.

"One of those Scott novels should fetch something," she said, grabbing *The Bride of Lammermoor.*

"That's your favorite."

"I never liked that one," she said, gulping down the tea.

"Oh?"

"Too sappy."

"It's quite a walk to make it up and back in a day. Ask after a woman named Luenza. She takes in boarders."

Elisabeth grabbed the Hawken, nodded to Nate, and whistled for Yellow Dog. She was more sure-footed switchbacking up the slope in her man boots than the last time hiking up barefoot to that Fandango. Still, it was hard going. She stopped to catch her breath often, but the challenge of the climb spurred her on and she managed to shoot two bunnies along the way, which she stuffed in a sack slung over her shoulder. She arrived at the top of the ridge midday and continued toward town along a flat trail, when she came upon a man leaning up against a buckeye tree. His eyes were wide, but his mouth hung open stiff like a man singing a long holy note from a hymnal.

"You all right, mister?" Elisabeth asked from a good distance.

When he didn't answer, she walked closer. She poked him in the shoulder with a stick, and he fell over, dead. She knelt down, examining his face. He looked young and thin, but not sickly, with red hair and skin white as a crystal. She wasn't scared at seeing him dead. She'd seen little Lucy dead, and this man had no gaping wounds oozing through bandages. Nothing stinking him up or rotting his flesh. He looked as if he'd simply sat down and given up. She wondered where he'd come from and who he belonged to. Someone, somewhere, must be wondering about him. Wondering where he'd gone and when he was coming back. His mother. His father. Maybe a sister or daughter. Either way, he wouldn't be needing his coat. As she worked his stiff arms out of the scratchy gray wool, the dead man slid sideways, falling over into a pile of pine needles. She shook out the coat and smelled it, grateful it wasn't too rank. She knew she wasn't sinning. It wasn't stealing if the man was dead. Besides, he didn't need it. Why should a perfectly good coat go to waste freezing overnight on a dead man? She slipped herself into it confidently, buttoning up the front, feeling warm and toasty. She pulled at the shoulders to test the fit, knowing it would be good as new with a soft bunny-fur lining sewn inside.

She walked into Coyoteville by midday, surprised it'd grown into a real town from that makeshift camp on a hill where she'd danced with Nemacio only a few months before. Hundreds of people packed into a proper Main Street now, with eight wooden buildings and tents lined up and down a dry creek housing a laundry, a blacksmith, and a tool shop. She tried to remember the location of Nemacio's tent but got turned around all topsy-turvy by the crowd and streets and gave up looking, figuring he'd moved on to another camp or town or claim, like so many other men moving around from strike to strike. She had more pressing business anyhow.

First, she went to the Stamps Store. Inside, she tugged off her wedding band and placed it on the counter.

"How much for this?"

Mr. Stamps picked up the gold band, examining it through a loop.

"It isn't pure, like what's coming out of the river. This is rose gold. See the tinge of red?"

He handed her the loop to look.

"It's got a bit of copper mixed in."

"A fake?"

"I'd not say that. It's decent, hard and solid," he said, biting the ridge to demonstrate his point. "But it's not real. Real gold is much softer, and going for over twenty dollars an ounce. I'll give you ten for this."

"That's thieving!"

"I don't need to buy it at all, Mrs.," said Mr. Stamps, looking her up and down.

She shuffled self-conscious wearing the dead man's coat but straightened up anyway, smoothing the collar down flat.

"How about you give me sixteen?"

Mr. Stamps shook his head no.

She spun the ring on the wooden counter, stalling. It was just her luck, getting a fake ring for a fake marriage. That damn ring had strangled her finger as a bitter symbol of all the lies told and lived since her wedding day. She wanted to get rid of it.

"What about this book?"

Elisabeth placed the Scott book on the counter.

A woman came from out behind the backroom shelves, introducing herself as Mrs. Millie Stamps, and Elisabeth smiled happy at seeing another woman in town, the first woman since Nandy Gootch back in Culoma. The woman looked fancy with a clean cotton dress and no dirt under her nails and pretty blond hair pilled up tight. Mrs. Stamps leaned on the counter with her elbows up and her chin in her hands, blinking with wide eyes, listening as Elisabeth explained the story of *The Bride of Lammermoor*. Hungry for money, she sold the story hard, needing to buy the powder and food, and to pay off the doctor for cutting off Nate's leg.

"It's an adventure beyond imagining. A tragic love affair, offering many nights of entertainment, I assure you. And after you read it, you can resell it."

"Oh, yes! Yes! Yes!" Millie said, clapping her hands together.

"I'll give you five dollars for the book. Ten for the ring," said Mr. Stamps, eager to please his wife.

Elisabeth laughed.

"This book is worth more than its weight in gold. I'll take no less than twelve for the book alone. Twenty for both," she said, placing the ring on top of the book.

Mr. Stamps placed his hands on his hips, scowling. She didn't budge.

Millie Stamps pulled her husband into the back storeroom, and Elisabeth heard her insisting, saying she wanted the book. She needed the book. When Millie pounded her heels on the wood floor in a fit, a baby cried awake, and Mr. Stamps relented. Millie came out from the back room with a baby on her hip, handing Elisabeth twenty dollars in coins. She turned right around and used the money for a sack of gunpowder and dried apple rings and a slab of jerky. She also bought a tiny tin of MarJax salve for Nate's aching stump, even though she craved coffee. Turning to leave, she caught sight of a broadsheet tacked to the wall.

"What's that?"

"The Great Seal of California," said Millie, opening the book with one hand while balancing the baby on her hip with the other.

Elisabeth leaned over to examine the intricate seal. The goddess Athena sat in the foreground with a bear feeding on a grapevine, and a miner with a pick and pan at his side. In the background spread a grand bay with four sailing ships, and in the distance were snowy peaks with a great river flowing out of them. Around the top of the seal were thirty-one stars. Below read the motto: Eureka.

"What does it mean?"

"'I found it'. . . from the Greek, I think," said Millie, placing the book down. "I think they put a woman on the seal because of California coming into the union as a free state, and of all the rights we've got now."

"What rights?"

"Equal rights, as women."

"You can't be serious," said Elisabeth.

"I overheard man come in from Placerville tell about it. Said he read the front page of the *Mountain Democrat* about women's equal rights being set down in the California Constitution," said Millie.

Elisabeth was shocked and wanted to know specifically what equal rights might improve her lot.

"So what rights do we get?"

"Can't speak to the specifics. I haven't yet read the paper myself. I'm trying to get my hands on a copy. Either way, the woman is beginning to awake to her true position . . . and surely in California she can see there is work for her hands to do."

Elisabeth wondered if the new state of California meant Nandy and Billy were now free, out from under Sappington. She wanted to write a letter to Nandy about hoping she was freed, but she worried a letter might cause Nandy trouble. Instead she decided to wait until she learned more. She planned to come back next week to ask Millie. In the meantime, Elisabeth wrote one letter to Louisa May in Boston, one to Samuel at Amherst, and one to her mother at the Worcester Asylum.

She chose her words to Louisa May careful, ever mindful of not writing beneath the intellect she thought her friend required. The lies were temporary. Innocent musings set down until she could think of something more pleasant to write about than her current predicament. She needed Louisa May's friendship. Even with the great distance spread between them, Elisabeth longed for Louisa May and still wanted her to think she was as clever and worthy of her friendship as when they were young.

She wrote to Samuel saying they'd arrived safely to Henry's claim but he'd gone, which wasn't exactly a lie. She couldn't find the words to tell the truth about the Indian girl, knowing he'd respond with an *I told you so about Henry.*

To her mother, she wrote reassurances of love. She didn't mention any particulars, knowing she'd not likely understand much. When she last visited her mother in Worcester to explain she'd married Nate and was going west to find Henry, she'd stared back blank with the gashes on her wrists healed to thick flopping scars as evidence of what she'd done to try to end her pain.

After posting the letters, Elisabeth had only three dollar coins left. She walked over to the doctor's place, finding him inside pulling a man's tooth. She interrupted, telling him forty-five dollars to cut off a man's leg was criminal.

"I'll settle up what I owe with these," she said, flopping the sack of rabbits on his desk.

The doctor took off his spectacles and peered into the bag at two hefty jackrabbits.

"Shot through at the neck," she said, so he'd know he was getting more meat.

When the doctor hesitated, she cocked her head cute, trying to act a little silly and stupid so he'd feel sorry for her.

"Awww, come on, Doc. It's all I got, besides a bum husband. And you already did the cutting, so you ain't losing nothin'," she said, slow.

He pulled the sack behind the counter and lifted his chin, motioning her off. Giddy, she slipped out the door quick, feeling only a little sheepish at acting so lumpish to get what she needed.

She walked up the road past the livery to find a woman throwing piss water into the nearly dry ravine beside her tent. She wore a red calico dress with a once-white apron and her hair split into two messy buns on either side of her head. The skin on her face sagged with pockets hollowed around her mouth and under her eyes. Three grubby little boys ran around, teasing each other. A rough flat board sign painted above the tent read: *Boarding, $10 a night.* A dozen tents circled around a giant sugar pine. Elisabeth peeked inside one at four wide benches, each with a tattered blanket at the end, folded up neat.

"Can I help you?" the woman asked, from behind.

"Are you Mrs. Luenza Wilson?"

"Who's asking?"

"Is this a hotel?"

The woman looked her up and down with a sneer.

"Not that sort! I run an honest business. Those other ladies work further down. Git on," she said curtly, shooing at her like she was a fly.

Elisabeth furrowed her brow, looking down at her man boots and cut-short skirt poking out from below the dead man's coat.

"Oh! No. No. I must I look a mess."

"Most folks look a mess when they come rolling in here. You're no exception."

Admiring the woman's frankness, Elisabeth put down the sack of powder and gun.

"I hold claim down on the river with my husband, Nate Parker. He told me to ask after Luenza. I assumed that was you," she said, pointing at the sign.

"Nate Parker has a wife? Well, good for him!"

She extended her hand, introducing herself as Luenza Wilson. After seeing the woman handling chamber pots, Elisabeth hesitated slightly, then grabbed her hand.

"Luenza," she said, pumping her arm up and down strong. "A misunderstanding, Mrs. Parker. I'm just trying to establish a respectable place. I don't get many lady customers, is all. You won't likely wanna be sleeping with the men. You can bunk with me and my boys for five dollars."

"Five?" she said.

Elisabeth stepped back incredulous, shaking her head. At that price, she'd manage the walk back to down the canyon in the dark. After buying the powder and food, she wasn't about to waste her last dollars sleeping in a tent with bratty boys.

"I've already turned away a dozen men. I take in forty boarders each night, and they behave or I kick 'em out in the cold. As it is, I'm giving you a discount. I charge those men ten a night, knowing they'd pay almost anything for a solid meal and a warm bed."

Doing the math in her head, she figured Luenza a rich woman collecting nearly four hundred a night!

"Oh," she said, disbelieving.

"My husband Stanley's always out digging. Looking to get rich quick. I keep saying, nothing comes quick. You gotta work every day. Be patient. Put in your due. He never listens."

Luenza explained how she started out in one day, buying two boards off a man, and with her own hands laid them up on some barrels for a table. She bought a few chickens over at the Stamps Store on credit, and when Stanley came back that night he'd found a dozen miners eating supper with his wife. As Luenza bragged on, Elisabeth's mind flipped around on the particulars of a woman getting up and going all by herself.

"From that first day, diggers came to eat. So I got some tents, and there you go. I clear a fair bit of profit after my costs. Joseph Stamps charges me a fortune to get the chickens up here from Sacramento, but I plan to raise my prices even more once the snow starts falling. Grab an even bigger share. I'm saving up to build a real hotel."

"Impressive," Elisabeth said.

"Out here's the only place I know a woman can get a fair dollar for her work. Of course, I took my husband into partnership anyway, just to keep him from griping on me."

What a curious arrangement, a wife taking her husband into a business partnership. She peppered Luenza with questions about costs, supplies, and profits. Luenza offered her a chair and told of her success. She listened in as Yellow Dog sat nearby turning with mild interest at the youngest Wilson boy pulling his tail. The two other boys kept hitting each other with sticks and playing gunfight, making an awful racket. They acted like wild animals, smelly and grubby, but adorable, too, with not a care in the world. She envied them something awful. When Luenza turned to talk to a customer, she leaned down to the little Wilson boy.

"My dog's gonna bite you bad, you keep that up," she said, stern. "He's meaner than he looks."

The boy ran away toward the creek quick, and Luenza started up talking again.

"Stanley works around here only when it's too cold to dig in the river. He's framing up a house around back, when he gets a mind to it. I hired a cook yesterday, an old man from Georgia, with knees too achy for kneeling in the river."

A woman getting a solid business going in California from nothing so quick seemed a marvel. If Massachusetts had that sort of opportunity for women, Elisabeth might not have been so hasty in marrying and coming west. She wanted to move up to town, get something going for herself. But she didn't want to give up the claim, as she'd surely regret hearing about someone digging up a fortune after she'd left.

"How about I help out in exchange for you giving me a bed?"

"I don't need help. I told you I just hired myself a cook."

"How about I watch your boys?"

"Do they look like they need watching?"

She looked over at the boys running wild down at the creek. One threw a rock and hit a miner in the shoulder, who stood up and hollered. She realized that she didn't at all take to children, especially unruly boys like the Wilsons. But she needed food and a warm place to sleep that didn't cost five dollars.

"Damn it, Luenza! Control your hellion!" the miner yelled.

"I'll tell them a story," Elisabeth said.

"You get my boys washed clean and get some learning into their head tonight, and you pay only a dollar for a meal and a warm bedroll," said Luenza.

"Deal," she said.

Corralling the Wilson boys proved torturous. She pleaded and cajoled for them to wash in a bucket of water as they ran around and wrestled with Yellow Dog, hollering in a painful pitch that exhausted her. When the oldest Wilson boy jeered at her man boots and kicked at her toe, she grabbed his earlobe until he turned red and nearly cried, while his two brothers watched, stone-faced.

"Get clean with that bucket, then sit for a story, or you'll get worse than pinched. I'll paddle the lot of you . . . just you test me!"

After her show of force, they sat quiet, listening. She hooked the boys with a story of Odysseus battling the one-eyed monster, describing in great bloody detail how the Cyclops ate the men one by one until Odysseus blinded it with a wooden stake. The boys looked affright at the tale, but she kept on going, aiming to scare them into submission. After a while, they fell asleep, and she ate a whole chicken supper before climbing in a warm bedroll beside the boys, feeling thankful Nate hadn't gotten her with a baby. She lacked the patient temperament for rising up a brood. She heard Luenza cleaning up the dishes and pots but didn't offer to help, thinking she'd paid her dues watching that woman's hellions. Elisabeth slept sound for the first time in months.

The next morning, she said goodbye to Luenza and walked back down the ridge into the river canyon below. Arriving back to the claim as it began to drizzle, she saw Nate on a rock near the river looking sweaty and pale. He clutched a rope set down into a deep pool near Split Rock while two muddy men loomed over him.

"They're showing me how to fish with a basket. Damn if I didn't think of that!" Nate said, giddy.

Tired and wet, she went into the cabin to dry. When Nate crowded in with the men, they all took off their wet boots, setting them by the hearth to dry. She stoked up the fire, noticing one of the men held a string of fish, cleaned and ready to fry. The other man wore a serape and waited near the door. Nate limped over to the rocking chair, removing his hat and slapping the water off against his stump.

"Isn't this the luck, eating fish with our new partners," said Nate.

"Partners?"

In the dim firelight, one of the men took off his hat and nodded. "Good to see you, señora."

She recognized Álvaro then, with a guitar strapped over his back. "Álvaro!"

"We meet again," he said, standing short and round and smiling, with his arms out wide.

"I expected you earlier. So I could pay you proper for your help," she said.

She explained to Nate how Álvaro had run for the doctor the night of the snakebite. In a rush of gratitude, Nate jumped up from his chair and threw his arms around Álvaro.

"I would've died! It's fate! Fate, I tell you! Fate you were kicked off your claim for being foreigners."

Álvaro's companion spoke up from the dim corner of the cabin. "I'm no foreigner. I was born here."

Recognizing his voice, Elisabeth dropped the fire poker on the dirt floor. Taking off his hat, Nemacio looked worn, with long whiskers grown out full like Nate. He wasn't clean-shaven like she remembered, but she couldn't mistake that curly black hair, even in the firelight. Or that thick voice, no matter how soft he spoke. He introduced himself, placing a hand on his chest and making a small bow. Then he looked directly into her eyes, as if boring a hole of desire right through her.

January 1851

My Dearest Friend Louisa May,

Your letter comes to me as Sunlight Incarnate, with your poem of the same name gracing my dark winter days, "piercing the depths of the forest dense." I read your letter, savoring each word, and gaining strength from you, however far, as I must.

Our days took a terrible turn since summertime. A tragic accident befell Father and Nate, the details of which are too terrible to tell. Father is gone now, and Nate is left in a state from which he must now recover. He remains fortunate to have lived at all. I know he'll regain strength soon and be a strong man once again. I blame myself for his current condition and suffer a terrible guilt, although he does not condemn or accuse with grievance. He holds up brave and without complaint, joyful at a second chance at living. I do admire his temperament, for I am not sure I'd manage as such under the same circumstances. At times the burden caring for such a man in this wild place leaves me unable to breathe. But I am not afraid. I simply follow his example and try not to think on it. I've come to understand the undue difficulties facing a prideful man such as Nate, who has always had me depending upon him for security. We now move forward with grace into a brighter future, including all the tender loving a wife desires. Holding up physical love as a manifestation of soulful love may seem silly. I understand you cannot miss what you've never had, Louisa May. But I do, oh, how I do! Never you mind. One day you will, God willing, know loving from a man. From my experience, I've found the secret to getting love lies in the not wanting. As you've said, wanting too much leads to disappointment. You should know, dear LM.

The good news is, I've become a hunter, shooting rabbits for dinner. Can you imagine? My growing contribution is quite satisfying. We've taken on two partners at the claim, and just in time, if you must know the truth, as Father's claim holdings are too large for the two of us to work as winter comes upon us. I'm deeply grateful for the Californios, Nemacio and Álvaro, considering Nate's contribution is somewhat limited, given his current condition, however temporary. The Californios know the land and show us new techniques for finding the gold, giving us a spectacular chance for greater success in our enterprise, and in other more delicate matters which I dare not expound upon presently.

It gives me great joy to know you are writing again, with your ambition mirroring mine out here at the far end of civilization. It pains me, however, to read of your complaints. I cannot believe you truly think your family pathetic. Perhaps you're simply sodden down with the great weight of poverty, which clouds your current perceptions. I understand how your father tests your patience, pushing his radical ideas into an unaccepting world while sacrificing the comforts of his own wife and daughters. A touch grandiose perhaps, but pathetic he is not, as he shows a paternal constancy, be it in a form you still might disapprove. Am I wrong to think family is like a boat keeping you afloat, however rusted and filled with holes the hull might be? Your family comes with a safe keel for which I forever longed. Perhaps I over romanticize the value of kinfolk, with my understanding somewhat clouded in the unfamiliar fog of the West.

In the meantime, I anticipate great fortunes by the coming spring, with sunlight as my comfort, as you say, "in the light of an eternal home." For now, I have more than adequate. More than I deserve. I've enclosed a sprig from a giant sugar pine growing tall and proud upriver from our claim, and hope the glorious smell sweetens up your city room while I await your next letter. I beg you humbly for more poems and stories, as well as your contemplations on my notions set down here on paper, however contrary or agreeable.

Your rabbit-hunting friend on the American River in California,

EP

15

*"If you are true, but not in the same
truth with me, cleave to your companions;
I will seek my own."*

Maybe Nemacio came looking for her. Or perhaps it was a coincidence. Either way, her tide turned when the Californios arrived down at the river claim that winter. Nemacio and Álvaro pitched their tent in the pine grove and joined in the tedious labor, hunching over dirt-filled pans in the river, digging and swirling. Working outside froze up their hands and sent shivers running through them cold as a knife blade, but they all endured with a collective hope a generous vein of gold might reward them. Nemacio and Álvaro used their own pans and fished at the same time, with clever reed baskets dropped into the deeper sections of the river. Nemacio showed Nate how to fry up the salmon with sage and garlic he kept in a tin. She savored the pink fish, picking every last bit of flesh off the bones and feeling full for the first time in months. During the day, Álvaro smoked the extra salmon so they'd have a stash for the winter, hanging thin strips over a low smoldering fire near the river on a structure he'd fashioned with pine sticks. He stored the smoked strips in one of Henry's Indian baskets, hanging high over a tree branch.

"To keep bears away," said Álvaro.

The Californios suppered in the cabin, warming themselves while waiting for their soaked socks and shirts to dry out on a rope strung above the hearth. Elisabeth averted her eyes when they undressed, not wanting them to catch her staring at their bare chests, but it proved difficult in a single-room not to steal a few glimpses now and again. In the candlelight she spied Álvaro with his big brown belly, round and rolling like dough when he laughed. Nemacio was lighter and taller and more brawny, smooth like a piece of twisted madrone. She struggled to look away from his beautiful broad chest, forcing herself to stare instead at his face, that hard-angled jaw and heavy chin with a deep dimple, right in the middle. He kept his face shaved clean after that first day arriving at the Goodwin Claim, and every morning there after, kneeling by the river with a straight razor and a little round gilt mirror he kept in his knapsack. Even in the rain.

Whenever her insides got churning at seeing him without a shirt, she pretended to read in bed by candlelight. Thankfully, Nate always stayed up while their clothes dried, rubbing the MarJax salve on his stump, giving the whole no-shirt situation an air of innocence. When their clothes dried, Nemacio and Álvaro always dressed and returned to their tent outside to sleep.

At first, Nemacio acted so polite and formal, Elisabeth thought maybe he didn't remember dancing with her outside the Fandango tent. But one night when the firelight dimmed in the cabin, and Álvaro shut his eyes with exhaustion and Nate snored in the rocker, a log tumbled and crackled in the hearth. She looked up from her book to see him with his back against the door, his knees up and his arms gathered around himself, his eyes fixed on her, black like river stones. No one had ever looked at her like that before, long, with bare honesty and a hint of expectation and desire that made her unfurl inside, like a blanket being shaken out fresh on a warm summer day. She looked back at him, holding his stare, and she knew. He remembered. Their dance. Lovely and romantic and fraught. After a long while, she couldn't stand him staring anymore, couldn't stand the honesty of it. She wanted to turn away but found she couldn't. She sat transfixed, locked in his gaze, trapped. When another log dropped heavy on the hearth with a pop, Álvaro startled awake, and Nemacio stood up, putting on his shirt. Opening the door to go, he turned back, nodding with a wink, and her heart dropped down nearly to her toes, her whole body rearranging its particular parts without permission.

That winter turned into one long battle of resistance. She resisted his long, lingering looks, his charms and kindness. Or tried, anyhow. It wasn't easy on the days when the cold bore down in the gorge, making panning and hunting difficult, and they all huddled in the little cabin together. Having him so near was torture. She could smell him from across the room, a musky mystery floating up her nose that made her skin fidget uncomfortable, yet it was delicious too.

Compared to Nemacio, Nate remained flat, without any taste and texture, like a piece of dry toast with no butter or jam as flavor. Both Nemacio and Álvaro were infectious, always spreading good cheer, patching up a hole that Elisabeth carried around for so long. Álvaro filled the cabin with music, his fingers flying along the frets and strings of his guitar, strumming and picking and pulling out luscious, percussive melodies with force, then quieting into dulcet longing. He tapped his guitar above the strings with the palm of his hand, drumming, like he worked two instruments. She'd never heard flamenco before, and it flowed through her, intoxicating and romantic and strange, growing into a resonate lump inside her throat. Whenever Álvaro played, she sat near him with Yellow Dog's head in her lap and closed her eyes, listening. Nate relished the music, too, rocking peacefully to the melody with his one good leg tapping out a tempo and a slight smile settled on his lips.

When Álvaro wasn't playing, Nate read aloud to the Californios. Nemacio encouraged him, leaning over his shoulder, asking about certain words he didn't know or characters he wanted more information about. When Nate grew tired of reading, Nemacio took over, stumbling over unfamiliar English words, his low voice deliciously thick and sticky as sap. When Nemacio read, she didn't so much hear the words but felt the lushness of his voice running through her, lulling, reminding her of that moment dancing on the ridge. She savored the moment in her mind, turning it over again and again greedy, like a secret cache of gold.

When the salmon run quit for the season, Álvaro and Nemacio caught trout for a few weeks. But the steelhead and rainbow were smaller than the salmon, so Elisabeth went back to hunting so they could eat rabbit now and save the salmon Álvaro had smoked for the difficult winter days ahead. When she came back from the forest with rabbits, the Californios always stopped panning, throwing down their pans, clapping and hooting in a big show of appreciation, filling the camp with a joy that thrilled her. Nemacio's charm even started rubbing off onto Nate some, making him less uptight and more light-hearted, like he'd been back in Lowell.

In charge of the kitchen now, Nate learned to prepare rabbit with herbs that Nemacio had collected to add more flavor.

"I don't want to interfere in your preparations," said Nemacio.

"Please, by all means, interfere," said Nate, handing Nemacio a knife.

"I don't imply your cooking is bad."

"I understand."

"Only if you want."

"Yes. Please. Show me how to cook like a Californio. I want to learn," said Nate.

Nemacio clapped and rubbed his hands together.

"Then let's do it. I'm rabid with hunger," said Nemacio, laughing at his own funny pun.

She noticed Nate standing far too close to Nemacio as he smeared the bunny with a garlic and rosemary paste, frying it up with wild onions in a pan of pork fat. Nate studied Nemacio as he worked, learning the fine art of Californio cooking with the plants growing natural throughout the canyon. Soon Nate was experimenting on his own with inventive ways to stretch a single rabbit into a meal for four by adding flavors from herbs and plants Nemacio brought back to the cabin. Sage and bay and miner's lettuce and wild onions and fennel. Nemacio showed him how to make a rabbit stew, rich with flavor from balsam and shooting star roots and buried tubers. Cooking suited Nate, and he seemed to relish the role, announcing new concoctions with a flourish and pride at suppertime.

"I present a supper of Bunny Shepherd Mash. Boiled buckeyes mixed with roasted shepherd's purse seeds under roasted bunny bits," he said, trying to impress Nemacio.

Elisabeth hated seeing Nate getting so friendly with Nemacio. Hated seeing him flirting, flipping his blond hair to the side, acting halting and nervous when he read aloud, just like he had back in Lowell when he was courting her. She caught him sizing up Nemacio in the candlelight, looking at his strong back longer than a man should look at a man. It made her sick seeing Nate lusting after Nemacio like that. It wasn't right, she and her husband wanting the same man.

Nemacio never let on he knew about Nate's peculiar tendencies with men. How he'd seen Nate at the Fandango doing something sinful behind a rock with that lady-man. Nemacio didn't seem to hold that night against Nate the way she did. He didn't judge but treated Nate with a respect Elisabeth thought undeserved.

One particular blistering cold afternoon, Nemacio found Henry's old woodcutting tools and started sharpening them. He didn't ask who the tools belonged to, simply took each knife out one by one, pulling them along a flat river rock back and forth until sharp, then fashioned a single crutch for Nate out of a pine branch, with an arm pad from a bit of rabbit skin. She watched him whittle, mesmerized by his long elegant fingers peeling the wood straight and smooth, and as he carved a picture of a snake into the length of the stick, twisting down and back up to the top where the stupid thing was eating its own rattle, devouring itself. He turned the stick round and round, creating an intricate diamond detail along the snake's back, and burning it beautiful with the hot fire poker.

"Now you have the rattlesnake's power," he told Nate.

"What a gift," Nate said, testing the fit under his arm.

He lost his balance, throwing his arms around Nemacio to stop from falling. He hung onto Nemacio's neck awkward, pressing his chest up too close. Nemacio held Nate's shoulders at an arm's length, putting some distance between them as if helping him stand. Jealousy ran through her like boiled water.

"Walk around," said Nemacio, motioning his finger in circles.

Nate hobbled around on the dirt floor, attempting a smooth gait using the snake stick.

"It's perfect. Perfect," he said.

Nemacio had a way of directing his full attentions toward a person, listening with rapt intensity. She'd never seen a man so generous with his spirit before, pulling out a person's better self and reflecting it back to them in ways they didn't know themselves before. He flattered everyone, with an earnestness she found beguiling.

He told Elisabeth she was strong and steady like an unmoving river rock in a powerful spring thaw. No man had ever said anything like that to her before, and he'd said it right in front of Nate and Álvaro. She laughed out loud at his ridiculousness, knowing he must be joking but hoping he wasn't. Nemacio stared back, serious. She worried Nate might suspect something between them. Not that it mattered; she and Nate lived like brother and sister now, not husband and wife.

Nemacio showed a tenderness she'd never seen in a man, like when he tickled the pads of Yellow Dog's paws, giggling to himself. Or when his eyes watered at hearing Nate read a lovely poem aloud, and his heavy brow furrowed as he stared into the fire as if he worried on something troublesome. He had an elegant strength about him but also wore vulnerability around proud like a buffalo robe, which only made him seem more powerful. When she asked why he came to dig in the river, he said it was for family.

"They are the air I breathe. I cannot live without them. So, I dig."

He explained how the Americans were after his family's ranch, and how they were taking over all the Californio ranches up and down the state.

"Four generations of Gabilan held our land, but the Americans now say our boundary maps aren't solid proof. They want deeds and money."

"How much?" Nate asked, impertinent.

"More than the Gabilans have, and we have a lot. So here I am. A desperate digger."

"Taking your land is illegal. You should challenge the claim," Nate said.

"How?" Nemacio asked.

Nate acted like he knew all about California law, explaining the particulars of how to get a letter to a senator. Irritated, Elisabeth interrupted, rolling up her right sleeve to show Nemacio the angry red blisters bubbling up on the inside of her right forearm.

"My arm is itching something terrible."

"Poison oak," said Nemacio.

"Leaves of three, let it be," said Nate.

"I know that!" she said.

"Poison oak has no leaves in the winter. You can hardly see the sticks," said Nemacio.

He boiled up yerba buena and manzanita, making a poultice. When he pressed the medicine gentle on her skin, she flinched with desire.

"It can't hurt that much," he said.

"No."

"I'll hunt with you tomorrow. Show you the sticks," he said, still holding the compress to her skin, soft.

"If you want," she said.

Maybe the poison caused a heat to rise to her skin, but she burned under his touch. It had been so long. Her only source of affection came from Yellow Dog nuzzling up dirty against her thigh. She'd not realized how withered up for affection she'd become, like a rotted sack of potatoes gone soggy out in the rain, spotted and ruined.

Nemacio wrapped her arm in cloth, tucking the ends in neat. When he let go she wanted to grab his hands and place them all over her body, but instead she looked away, hiding her face pinking up like a raspberry.

Over the next few weeks, the rash grew into an oozing mess that itched like Satan himself had settled in her arm, but she grew glad for it, because it meant he'd touch her. Tend to her. Each night he sat close beside her on the cabin floor, healing her pain, while Nate rocked by the fire absorbed in a book, blind to the growing affections between them. The sound of Álvaro's dulcet guitar was a secret blanket hiding her quickening breath as Nemacio pressed the poultice down onto her rashy arm, wrapping the cloth slow, taking his time. Nemacio leaned in close, whispering.

"Does he touch you?"

"No."

"A shameful disregard."

"I don't mind it."

"A woman needs loving," he said, his dark eyes set serious.

"I don't need loving," she lied.

"All women need loving."

"Can you catch it from me?"

"Catch what?"

"The poison," she said.

"That depends," he said.

"On what?"

"On what sort of poison you're talking about," he said.

She wanted more but didn't know how to ask.

16

"Nature is made to conspire with
spirit to emancipate us."

E ven on cold winter afternoons, Elisabeth hunted. She wore
the dead man's coat, tromping through the wilderness among
snowflakes fluttering down light and airy, settling on the pine boughs
above and into her hair and onto the forest floor in a thin white
blanket. Marveling at the quietness of the winter forest, she relished
getting away from the stale cabin and out in the crisp mountain air.
The soft sounds of the forest rejuvenated her, the trees swaying in
solace. She usually got a rabbit within an hour, stuffing it into the sack
she carried over her shoulder. One afternoon, she rested by a little
pool below Indian Creek waterfall. Cupping her hands through the
water for a drink, she looked up to see Nemacio crossing the stream.

"You following me?"

"Maybe," said Nemacio.

He opened his satchel for her to see.

"Pine cones."

He tapped a pine cone on a rock, shaking out nuts, then peeled
several and gave a handful to Elisabeth to eat.

"Mmmm," she mumbled.

"You shouldn't be alone," he said.

"I'm not alone," she said, patting Yellow Dog on the head.

"Your choice or his?"

She knew he wasn't talking about Yellow Dog. Intent, he'd had a way of poking and prodding her open. His directness unnerved her.

"I do what I want," she said.

"You should leave Yellow Dog back at the cabin if you want a deer."

"Bunny is fine with me," she said, holding up her sack of bunnies.

"I want more than bunny," he said.

"Then go hunt for yourself," she said, picking up her rifle to leave.

He pointed to a bare branch sticking out of the ground.

"That's poison oak."

"Oh," she said, feeling dumb.

As she leaned down to examine the stick, he grabbed her hand, presumptuously.

"Let's get a deer," he said.

She wasn't a weak woman, nor was she was led easy anymore. Even so, she let him pull her through the trees.

"I already know how to hunt," she said, her hand still in his.

When he turned and pressed his finger to her lips, her insides buzzed crazy like a swarm of yellow jackets.

"I don't need your help. I'm perfectly fine out here, alone."

She followed anyway as he showed her how to walk through the forest without tramping, taking soft, quiet steps. She stared at his strong back, his broad shoulders, his dark curly hair falling out from underneath his hat. When he stopped and listened, she stopped and listened, seeing all manner of creatures scuttling about: a family of ground squirrels, a tiny pika poking a twitching nose out from a rock, a sleek pine marten crossing the path without fear. As she scrambled over a downed log, Nemacio let go of her hand. When she jumped down, he picked up her hand again, and they entwined their fingers. Tiptoeing through the forest, they didn't see a single deer, but she couldn't have cared less. She listened as Nemacio pointed out the names of trees and bushes and animals in Spanish and English, and watched him cut dried thistle, adding them to his sack of pine cones, careful to not prick himself.

"It makes a good tea for a sore stomach," he said.

"How do you get around the prickers?"

"You boil the seeds. But you shouldn't drink too much."

"Why?"

"It prevents baby making."

"I never heard of such a thing."

"All women need to know about thistle blossom tea," he said as he placed a hand on her shoulder, serious.

He filled her with mixed up feelings, both thrilling and confusing. She couldn't quite parse his meaning. But she didn't ask him to make himself clear either, enjoying the mystery of his intentions. She didn't want the walk to end, wanted to stay out in the winter forest with him forever. He talked easy with her, sharing about his family, saying his father had been a great general who died in the Mexican War of Independence from Spain.

"As the eldest son, I have great responsibility. I can't lose our ranch."

She listened with envy as he told of a thousand acres of heavenly earth that sounded unreal, with a grand hacienda and hundreds of head of cattle, and a huge family all living together.

"If that were my home, I'd a never left," she said.

She told him of the apples on the Goodwin Orchard back in Concord going all a blight and Henry leaving and her working at the Lowell mill and losing little Lucy to the spinning machine and Samuel studying at school in Amherst and meeting Nate and coming over on the boat to find Henry. But she didn't tell of her mother and her madness. Nemacio listened, his eyes soft with understanding at all she'd been through.

"Thank you," she said.

"For what?"

"Nothing. Never mind," she said.

How ridiculous! Thanking a man for paying her a spot of attention. A married woman pining after another man turns a woman wretched. Nothing good could come of it. Truth be told, she didn't really care if Nate caught her pining after Nemacio. She actually hoped he'd notice. Hoped he'd see Nemacio was drawn to her too—a woman—and not to him.

They arrived back at the cabin to find Nate hopping around outside on his one foot, swinging an axe at a log, while Álvaro gathered wood across the river. From the edge of the trees in the gloaming, they saw him struggling on his one leg, flopping and flailing, losing his balance. He fell in the mud and picked himself up slow, lurching, and reached again for the axe. He swiped at the log and fell again, hitting the ground with his fists and cursing frustrations, his hollers echoing up the river canyon. She started to go to him. To help. Nemacio shook his head, holding her back. With guilt and pity squeezing her soul, she couldn't watch any longer, and she slipped off into the cabin, alone. She cooked up the rabbit, as a sour slab of envy ruined her appetite. She wasn't sure if she was more envious of Nemacio for comforting Nate better than she could, or envious of Nate for getting the comfort from Nemacio she wanted for herself. Throwing the pan on the dirt floor, she swelled in a thicket of disgust at her mangled thoughts.

Music woke her in the middle of the night. A captivating rhythm, passionate and raw. She tiptoed outside and saw all three men around a bonfire, blazing hot. A dusting of snow sat still on the ground, but the men seemed impervious to the cold, passing a bottle between them, sloppy. Álvaro strummed his guitar while Nemacio sang along, matching the melody with his deep, rich voice booming above the river. *Me estoy muriendo de pena. Por tu sole tu querer.* Even though she couldn't understand the Spanish, the haunting words drew her close. She opened the cabin door to see light from a blazing fire, and Nate fixed a lusty look over Nemacio, who seemed oblivious to Nate's looking. Nemacio just kept singing and sucking on his bottle with an arm strapped around Álvaro. This looked like the sort of fraternity Nate had told her all men wanted. In that moment, she realized she was competing with her husband over the same man. She laughed out loud at the absurdity of it all and went back into the cabin, slamming the door behind her. That night, she picked up Henry's tools, and Yellow Dog snuggled in close watching her work.

Carving woodcuts with her father's tools offered her something to do while cooped up in the cabin with three men during those long dark days of winter, and kept her thoughts off both her spectacular failure as a wife and her pitiful desire for Nemacio. Her first woodcuts looked crude, like rough scratches on wood with a penknife. But she read through *The Art of Engraving on Wood* buried at the bottom of Henry's tool chest, then started over again with drawing. She experimented.

With no tracing paper, she drew simple shapes directly onto wood with a tip of charcoal from the fire, and tested the various engraving tools, digging out triangles and squares. When she got the hang of basic geometry, she moved on to engraving pictures of the forest, plowing through the wood slow and careful with different-sized bruins to create rough tree trunks, then chiseling out the finer details of individual branches. The pinewood left her sticky with sap, so she searched for cedar wood while out hunting in the afternoons. She hacked large branches into flat blocks and scraped the small knots flat with the back of an ax. With the harder cedar wood she mastered more refined detail, giving her the confidence to try more intricate pictures. She carved an image of Álvaro's guitar, but it looked odd, the strings curved cock-eyed and the neck foreshortened, weird. She threw it into the fire. It was slow work but satisfying, too, putting her passion into something other than a man. Working with her father's tools made her think he might've been proud of her, if he'd stuck around. Yet, she figured in the end, he'd probably not care a whit.

Álvaro became a great source of joy for Elisabeth, with his bubbling generosity and goodwill. Impervious to the cold and the hard climb out of the river canyon, he went up to Coyoteville weekly, no matter the weather, to play monte at the El Dorado Hotel—Luenza's El Dorado—always bringing back a sack of potatoes, beans, coffee, or even dried fruit bought with his winnings. Elisabeth asked him to find that paper explaining the women's equal rights in the California Constitution, but he'd had no luck. One time he surprised them with a sack of fresh oranges, a lamp, and a jug of whale oil. He turned on the lamp, lighting up the cabin with his spirit.

"Now you won't cut yourself carving in the dark," he said to Elisabeth.

She jumped up, throwing her arms around him.

"You're the best. How'd you manage?" she asked.

"What can I say? I'm good at monte," he said, giggling to himself.

Much shorter than Nemacio and roughly ten years older, Álvaro wore a round pudgy face, like a boy who hadn't yet grown up, even with a full beard. She wondered what his mother fed him as a child. He kept a flask in his pocket, but no one said a thing about it. She loved hearing him go on, dramatic about his home.

"I am not a Mexican. I am from España. I came to Alta California as a boy, but I am Spanish of the heart," he said.

They all four grew closer that winter, digging side by side. By January the weather turned moody, with sleeting rain streaming down heavy between bouts of snow dustings and blue sky, like Mother Nature couldn't make up her mind. When the winter cold made it difficult for the Californios to keep warm overnight in their tent, Nate made space for them inside the cabin. Álvaro slept under the table next to Nate on the bearskin rug, and Nemacio slept in front of the stone hearth with his own blanket roll. They never asked why Nate didn't sleep up on the bed with his wife, either out of respect or an understanding of the particulars of their marital situation. It was obvious Nate had no romantic interest in Elisabeth.

What came before their time together on the river that winter made no difference. An urgency hovered over them, shifting the equilibrium of convention, requiring them to transcend their past expectations of a natural order. They were in the midst of an altogether different society emerging in California, where old rules didn't apply. It demanded they move beyond stagnant roles, toss aside judgment, and open themselves up to inventing something altogether new. Done with convention, Elisabeth was ready.

When the wet came down unforgiving, they hunkered inside for days in a stretch. Elisabeth carved and Álvaro played while Nate read to Nemacio. When a storm cracked Henry's flimsy roof, streaming water into big puddles on the dirt floor, Nemacio patched the holes in the shingles and plugged the side chinks with mud to keep the water out. They survived the worst of that winter on food stores the Californios provisioned: salmon jerky, nuts, dried elderberries, and various roots and herbs. Whenever the sky stoppered itself, they ventured outside to dig pell-mell in the river, collecting some gold dust and a few nuggets, holding out hope for a big strike. Meanwhile, they stored all the gold bits in a tin.

She found it difficult to keep her womanly privacy cooped up with the men, having to make many trips back and forth through the cold to the privy. It wasn't too smelly since the Californios put a bucket in there filled with cedar chips and pine needles to throw down the hole to keep things fresh. One day, she found a tiny wooden box tied with a red ribbon hiding behind the bucket. Inside was a stack of buckskin pieces, soft and rectangle. Seeing they'd be too thick for ordinary wiping, she realized they must be for her monthlies. Shocked by such a thoughtful gesture, she knew it wasn't Nate, and wondered if Nemacio or Álvaro had made them. Of course, she couldn't ask; she was too embarrassed to even thank them.

She learned to carve well that winter, balancing a sandbag with the woodblock on her lap, turning and turning while holding gravers and chisels to outline different animals she saw around the river basin—a bunny and fox and deer and that sad marmot with its grimace. She experimented with different-sized tools, little by little teaching herself how to cut out all the surrounding parts. When her hand slipped stabbing the bruin into her finger, a painful gash opened. She had to lay off engraving for two whole weeks waiting for the cut to heal, going antsy with boredom and angry at the cold for keeping her cooped up in the cabin. When she started engraving again, she didn't stop, putting in long hours practicing different ways of holding the tools to create the perfect line. She wanted to create an engraving worth printing on paper, but her creatures still turned out clumsy and all alike, the fox with the deer face, the bunny with the marmot body. Frustrated, Elisabeth threw block after block of botched carvings into the fire.

"There goes another one," Nate said, looking up for a moment to watch the block catch fire.

When he returned to writing in his notebook, she didn't let his comment go.

"No need to get so snarky with my effort to make something better," she said.

"None intended, darling," he said, dripping with sugary meanness.

Nemacio stopped their quibbling before it got going.

"What are you going after?" Nemacio asked.

"Something I can print," she said.

"Why not start simple?"

"I want to make something beautiful."

"Simple is beautiful."

She bit the inside of her lip thinking on that principle. She didn't want to make another odd, lopsided picture. The nature in the canyon seemed so complex yet with perfect symmetry and balance, like the ospreys with their different-sized feathers laying into a flat line of even wings. Or the green pine tips splayed up against a blue California sky. Or the pine cone swirling around into itself getting smaller and smaller, each scale hiding a little seed. She'd taken a pine cone apart, pulling off all the scales from the bottom one by one, examining the pieces until the top alone looked like a wooden rose. She could never capture that natural beauty.

"I'm not sure how."

"You'll figure it out," he said, confident.

For some reason she believed him. Infused with his confidence, she carved, slower and more deliberate, with fewer lines. An image seemed to bubble up from some mysterious wellspring buried deep inside her. Split Rock—that special place where she loved to sit by the river. Only six lines for the rock, split down the middle. And a few more lines gouged in varying sizes for the water, flowing into a swirling eddy with one tiny twig caught up in the calm. It looked almost too simple, and maybe not worth printing on paper. To her it was beautiful, and far more meaningful than sewing a straight seam on a pair of pants.

Engraving kept her mind off that Californio, a bit. Having Nemacio sleeping in the cabin that winter wound her up something awful. Practically everything he did aroused her imagination, running it wild with lust. Watching his hands chop rosemary at the table. His thick lips moving sensual as he read aloud. Those silky curls dripping wet after a rainstorm. Smelling his coat hanging on the peg nearly brought her to her knees. Even his feet drove her crazy, long and wide and a beautiful brown compared to Nate's ugly single white skinny foot warming up limp on the hearth. At night when the lamp went out she heard Nemacio breathing, thick and soft. Heard him stir awake. Heard when he'd drifted off to sleep on the floor.

Having him so close turned her wicked, and touching herself in the dark became a sore temptation taking all her strength to resist. She ran her palms along her thighs outside the bunny blanket back and forth each night to warm up, then stopped. If she started on herself, she'd likely not be able to quit, moaning with pleasure and waking the whole cabin up with her fit of shame.

17

"He who is in love is wise and becoming wiser, sees newly every time he looks at the object of beloved, drawing from it with his eyes and his mind those virtues which it possesses."

The rain quit in early spring, and the sky opened into an innocent blue with not a cloud of interference. Elisabeth couldn't believe a clear sky had been capable of releasing such a winter drenching only a few days before. The blueness and the sunshine overhead warmed up the river gorge, making her think of honey and hope. When a robin started tittering and the woodpeckers started knocking on tree trunks, she knew spring had arrived.

Nate had been clever taking on Álvaro and Nemacio as partners. They'd helped them get through the worst of the winter without starving and proved themselves expert miners. With the spring melt, Nemacio acquired three foot-wide planks and a sheet of iron from the blacksmith in Culoma. He and Álvaro fashioned an elaborate Long Tom, hammering the wood into a rectangular sluice with a sloped bevel. They pierced holes in the iron sheet and nailed it to the bevel. All the while, Nate tottered around, growing more comfortable with his fancy snake crutch, hollering out directions about this or that. Álvaro and Nemacio had worked a Long Tom before at the Spanish Diggins. Nate knew nothing about toms or sluices, other than what he'd seen back at Chana's claim, but still bossed them around like a know-it-all, saying, "What you really want to do is . . ." She supposed his bossing made him feel important and useful after losing such a substantial part of himself. The Californios didn't complain but listened polite like Nate was offering up valuable information they'd never heard before.

Nemacio and Álvaro carried the Long Tom north of the cabin to a gravel bar with a flat of quartz underneath they hoped led to a deep vein of gold below. They set the sluice beside the river on a square wooden box and angled it downslope with a flange all around. She stood at the head of the Long Tom, christening it formal like a sailing ship with words from Emerson.

"*Man (or woman),*" she added, in earnest, "*is his own star; and the soul that can render an honest and perfect person, commands all light, all influence, and all fate.*"

She poured the first bucket of muddy water into the Long Tom, and everyone cheered. Álvaro hooted, Nate circled his crutch in the air, whistling loud, and Yellow Dog barked and barked like he knew they were embarking on a marvelous feat of fortune. He jumped up and down, sniffing the contraption, looking inside, trying to lick the water out. *That's it!* She'd name him Tom. A perfect name. She patted Tom on the head.

Nemacio said a blessing in Spanish she didn't understand and crossed himself. Álvaro made the sign of the cross after and dumped in more buckets of gravel. She hoped this magical contraption might offer up enough gold to give her freedom. She didn't yet have a clear plan, but that long winter cooped up in the cabin with Nate had made it clear. She wouldn't stay living down on the river with him too much longer. She didn't love him. She had no idea of what she'd do, or how she'd live on her own. Maybe she'd move up to Coyoteville. Learn business from Luenza. She only knew she had to get away. She couldn't stand being around Nate anymore. Couldn't stand the sight of his grubby face and greasy hair and floppy stump. It took all her strength not to act rude griping at him, and she was sick at herself for being such a terrible nag of a woman. She was still young and dreaded thinking about spending the rest of her days wilting away with a husband who couldn't love her proper.

Nemacio and Álvaro did all the heavy work that spring, breaking and crushing up the quartz rock and carrying it in buckets into the Long Tom. Elisabeth added buckets of water and moved the rock and mud around with a shovel, sifting and examining the find, and pushing the smaller rocks and gravel bits through the holes in the metal plate like a big flour sieve. Nate sat on a stool at the end of the Long Tom collecting the smaller bits as they streamed down, swishing the dirt in a pan, looking for something shiny. He slid the larger chunky rocks aside into the pile of sludge to reexamine later. They labored tireless, each suited for their specific job, finding rhythm. Working the Long Tom proved backbreaking, but it let them sift through the rock faster, so they didn't complain, even when spring rain showed up. They knew the rain would only last a few hours then escape behind white puffy clouds plastered against a brilliant blue sky for another day. Through bouts of rain they crushed and sorted and separated as much dirt in a day with the Long Tom as they had in a whole week with the rockers and pans. Day after day they kept up, even as their bones screamed weary.

After a month ripping up the gravel flat, their luck turned. They started finding larger bits of gold. Shiny and yellower than she'd remembered seeing when Chana held it up in front of her face. With the price of gold at twenty dollars an ounce, filling the poke only a third full added up to a square meal for all four of them at Luenza's for a week. Nemacio restaked their claim perimeter fifty yards up- and downriver from the quartz flat with tall sticks, making it clear for other diggers to keep off.

When fellas passed through the claim Elisabeth still smiled sweet but no longer asked if they needed sewing or mending; it wasn't worth her time to stop digging. Their Long Tom system brought out curious neighbors, as well as claim jumpers from downstream. Twice, Nemacio and Nate banded together against jumpers, brandishing the Hawken and saying their claim was off-limits. On one occasion, five interlopers confronted Álvaro, saying he had no right to dig in America.

"You're an illegal. You gotta pay the assayer your foreign miner's tax."
Nate hobbled over to stand ground with Álvaro.

"We're all Americans here," said Nate.

"You can't work no slaves on your claim," said the claim jumper.
"California is a free state."

Álvaro looked as if he'd been struck, then started laughing and
laughing and slapping his knee. Nemacio didn't find the men funny
and threw his pan down with a clatter in the river rocks.

"You're the foreigner, you filthy gringo," said Nemacio. "I was
born here."

The claim jumpers started yelling then, hollering and spitting.

"They're my partners, you idiot! Now get off my claim," said Nate.

A gang of gruff-looking men they'd befriended up Sweetwater
Creek calling themselves the Sweetwater brothers came downriver to
see about the ruckus. They stood in solidarity with Nate and Nemacio and Álvaro, telling the claim jumpers to scram. Two Sweetwater
brothers even pointed rifles at the jumpers, and Elisabeth worried
things might get rough. Fortunately, the shifty men moved on to find
other diggers to bully.

Afterward, digging life on the North Fork of the American took
on a steady rhythm, with pleasant camaraderie flowing through
the canyon among the other miners claiming a dig. Together, Nate
and Nemacio emerged as leaders, introducing themselves to nearby
neighbors staking out new spots in the American, and in the creeks
and gulches flowing in, and the shallow placers, too, up and down
from the Goodwin Claim. Most folks in this stretch of river were
friendly, more interested in working hard rather than getting worked
up over a few Californios. The river required a leveling, with no one
fawning over the rich or flouting the poor. In fact, you couldn't tell
one from the other down on the river. All that mattered was the
digging, and digging demanded a sturdy lot. California swallowed
up weaklings.

Nate made a huge effort getting to know all the men up and down
the river. After a long day of digging, he'd slowly hop along the trail
with his one leg flopping, talking to all the diggers, showing great
interest. He disarmed men with his self-deprecating manner, introducing himself as Gimpy, and laughing big at himself, then he'd ask

where they'd come from, getting familiar fast, calling them buddy and partner and chief, and asking opinions of things he already knew, flattering. He showed great ability to create cooperation among the men, organizing them into the North Fork Committee Mining District. They held meetings to discuss property boundaries and markers, the spring river conditions, the types of rock surrounding their claims, and new mining methods. He persuaded the committee to work together building a single ditch, with each group taking turns on it diverting off water at different hours of day, so as not to muddy up each other's claims downriver with slag. Nate encouraged civilized agreements among the men, enforced by no laws, striving for honest cooperation instead of dishonesty and deceit. The men agreed, believing the tide of teamwork would lift them all.

The Sweetwater brothers turned up social at the Goodwin Claim often, bringing good fellowship and offering up tips on how to add more riffles to the Long Tom to catch more gold. They didn't look at all like brothers, with some having black hair and some dirty blond. Two talked with thick Scottish accents, and three said they came from Missouri, and four from Pennsylvania. Many nights, all or some of the Sweetwater brothers filled around their camp-fire hurly-burly, swapping drink and stories about luck and hapless attempts at getting gold. Álvaro listened in but never added his two bits, instead playing his guitar in the background. The Sweetwater brothers proved a jovial bunch, getting more loud and more raucous the more they drank, but treated Elisabeth kind, calling her Mrs. Parker out of respect for Nate. Hearing that name made her wince, and she always insisted they call her Elisabeth.

The quartz flat on the Goodwin Claim followed a crevice in the bedrock that looked promising. They dug down a foot and cracked it open, seeing it teem with bits of gold. Taking four days to work it out, they got almost twenty-nine ounces, the most they'd dug up yet! Almost six hundred dollars, in total. Their great stroke of luck continued through the spring, helping put a skip in her digging, and helping her forget about being lonely, at least temporarily. All spring, they worked the vein through, stashing more than seven thousand dollars' worth of gold in flour sacks and yeast powder boxes in a hole dug inside the cabin. A year ago, she'd have thought that a pile of money, but divided four ways, it didn't seem much to her now. She'd need even more to break away from Nate. Start something of her own.

A six-mule train arrived one afternoon, led by a grizzled old man named Sherman. He dropped a load of pine boards, and Álvaro went about clearing out the cabin. Elisabeth danced around in circles, pumping her arms up in the air, ecstatic. Nate remained suspect.

"Planks for a floor?" said Nate.

Nemacio shrugged.

"How much?" Nate asked.

"Sutter owed me a favor," he said, grinning.

"What sort of favor?"

"I got to keep some business private," said Nemacio, throwing an arm around Nate's neck and pulling him in rough.

It took only a day for the Californios to level the dirt, create a frame, and lay the planks down. They hammered in real nails, breaking open that sweet smell of pine to fill the whole cabin. They added a secret spot under the floorboards for their gold stash, hiding it over with a rug Álvaro had won at the monte tables the week before. With a proper floor, Elisabeth started feeling more civilized and less like an animal scratching out a meager living off the river.

Álvaro and Nemacio made regular runs to Coyoteville now, bringing back eggs and apricots and slabs of beef. Nemacio brought more paper for her printings, and she experimented with inking at night, applying tint with a small dauber to her Split Rock engraving. Ever so careful she placed a piece of paper a top the block, then covered it with thin board. Using the burnisher, she rubbed the back of the board. When she peeled off the paper, she saw a fair representation. It wasn't a perfect print, the ink a bit blotchy and heavy in parts, but to her it was remarkable. She hung the print of Split Rock on the wall, along with a few other simple pictures of trees and the river, happy her lie to Louisa May about art on the walls wasn't a lie any longer.

With the salmon run on the river not yet going, she started hunting bunny for supper again, enjoying solitude in the forest after a long winter cooped up with three men. Getting out alone helped wash those naughty thoughts of Nemacio clean out of her head, and she walked up and up, falling in love with the slopes of the Sierra

Nevada range swelling as her earthly paradise, making up for that past hardscrabble winter.

Coming back from hunting, she often stopped by the Sweetwaters' mess of tents, giving them a rabbit or two if she'd shot more than supper in exchange for a cup of their special cider. The boys fell all over themselves polite and solicitous, with a profound and sincere deference, offering her a spot by their fire. She always joined in for few sips, never letting on to Nemacio or Nate or Álvaro how she imbibed with the Sweetwater boys. And she never felt afraid being out among men alone, knowing the scarcity of good women elevated her to a state of near goddess, giving her a power she'd never known back East.

One morning, when the spring river ran too high to work the tom, Elisabeth quit early to hunt.

"I'm done," said Elisabeth, dropping her pan for the Hawken.

"You shouldn't hunt with Tom," said Nate.

"I don't need you to tell me how to hunt."

"Nemacio says he scares the deer," said Nate.

"Maybe," said Elisabeth.

"Maybe it's you who scare the deer, the way you clomp around," said Nate.

She stung with the insult and laid into him, nasty.

"I can't help it, on account of Henry's man boots," she said, holding one foot up for emphasis. "But I suspect you might do well with a more grateful tone, since it's me out doing the hunting for our supper, with you not able to give your wife a proper meal or a proper set of woman boots, or any sort of proper loving for that matter."

It was a mean thing to say, and she knew it the moment she'd said it, but she wasn't sorry. Even if she'd said it in front of Álvaro and Nemacio.

Nate sat near the sluice with his mouth hanging slack. Álvaro looked back and forth between Nate and Nemacio sheepish, like he expected them to do something to calm her.

"I'm sick of bunny too," said Nemacio, throwing down his pan to break the tension.

"Then don't eat it," she said, turning to leave.

Nemacio dragged Tom by the scruff over to Álvaro.

"Hold him so he doesn't follow," said Nemacio.

"Oh, let her go," said Nate, waving Elisabeth off with the back of his hand. "She's used to hunting alone. No doubt prefers it."

"I want deer tonight," said Nemacio.

"Don't mind them, Nate," said Álvaro.

Nate glared at Álvaro, as Nemacio ran to catch up to Elisabeth on the trail.

"You don't clomp," he said.

"Thank you for your opinion on my walking, Don Gabilan," she said, more snotty than she'd meant.

"Did your father teach you to shoot?"

"I taught myself."

"Por supuesto."

He had a habit of slipping into Spanish almost on accident when they were alone. It made her feel closer to him, even though she couldn't always figure out the meaning of his words. She felt as if hearing him speak his first language let her peek into his soul. She never asked him to make himself clear, out of fear he'd stop.

She walked ahead, knowing he was looking at her bottom. Her nerves rattled, but she kept her boots moving and her eyes fixed on the narrowing brush ahead. She ran her fingers through her hair like a comb, making a feeble attempt to pull her brown knotty hair smooth, and secured it into a single ponytail with a ribbon. They traveled on in silence for an hour up toward the ridge, until coming upon a clump of madrone bushes where she knew a colony of rabbits lived. She stopped and waited quiet as mice and squirrels darted about. A red milkweed beetle crawled along the pine needles, so slow she thought she could hear its little feet shuffling along the forest floor. The warm afternoon glow streamed through the pine boughs overhead, diffuse and soft, blurring desire and dream together. When a rabbit jiggled under a bush, she leveled her rifle. Nemacio came up beside her and lowered the barrel.

"What are you doing?" she asked.

"Don't you want more than bunny?"

"Yes."

"Then look up," he whispered, lifting her chin up. "Don't look at the ground."

He held onto her chin and looked into her eyes. She didn't look away but stared back at him, long. Seeing clear. She examined his smooth skin up close, with stubble already growing in even though she'd seen him shave that morning by the river. She wanted to press her finger deep into the cleft in his chin.

"Why are you alone?" she asked.

"I'm not alone," he said.

"You got a woman hiding somewhere?"

"I've nothing yet to offer a woman."

"I doubt that," she said, snorting nervous.

"Once I find gold . . ."

"Ahh . . . the gold."

"I'll give a woman the world."

"I don't need the world," she said, surprised at herself.

"You have a husband," he said, brushing a strand of hair away from her cheek.

It was an innocent gesture, pushing hair out of her face, but it flooded something fierce though Elisabeth.

"He's not my husband."

"Sometimes our hearts travel without permission from God to those not entirely suited . . ."

He didn't finish and instead turned toward a madrone bush, pulling off a thick waxy pink flower.

"Smell this," he said.

She wanted to tell Nemacio that God made no difference; he'd forsaken her long ago. Instead, she leaned into the flower, and an intense honey-like fragrance filled her nose.

"Do you like it?" he asked.

She nodded, grabbing the red bark of the madrone to steady herself and rubbing the soft peeling bark with her fingers nervously.

"You can pick the berries in June, to mix with thistle tea."

She'd do whatever he wanted. Pick berries. Drink his tea. They walked further up the ridge into the mountains beyond, coming upon a clump of birch. Nemacio drilled a tiny hole into the white bark with a long pointy knife.

"Come here," he said, grabbing a reed from his pocket and stuffing it into the hole. "Put your mouth around it."

"What?"

"Like this," he said, sucking the sap from the reed.

She leaned over, sucking. It tasted like water, yet silky and sweet.

"It's good for drinking and washing your mouth fresh. But only in early spring."

Being with him opened up endless possibilities in the forest that she hadn't known before. She followed him off the trail now, farther up than she'd ever walked, deep into the upper slopes scattered in large gray slabs of granite with patches of spring snow still nestling in the shadowy crevices. It looked like a fairyland from a book, with the rich afternoon light illuminating the world into lusty focus. With smooth gray-blue granite and white-barked lodgepole pines and the blinding bits of snow and the little yellow budding mule's ears flowers coming up around the melts. She didn't care about hunting anymore and wanted to lie down on a rock, curled up in Nemacio's arms in the warming spring sunshine.

He stopped sudden and grabbed her wrist. He placed a finger on his lips and pointed toward a rocky escarpment. At first she only saw the rock beyond. Then something else came into focus, but she couldn't make sense of it. It took her a moment to see that blending clever into the dark granite hunched a black panther, only thirty yards beyond.

Elisabeth and Nemacio waited shoulder to shoulder, barely breathing, blending into the air, and into each other, fused like the trunk of a single tree. She had never seen such a magnificent creature. It loomed massive, nearly eight feet long with sleek fur and eyes orange as a pumpkin. Its mouth dangled open, showing sharp white teeth and a long tongue, pink and wet. The panther panted, waiting, stalking a lone blacktail deer below the rock who remained oblivious to the danger above.

Elisabeth leveled her gun, taking aim at the panther.

"There are so many deer," he whispered in her ear.

The panther must've heard his whisper, as it leaped off and disappeared beyond the escarpment, and Nemacio stepped behind her, wrapping his arms around her shoulders to redirect her aim at the deer below the path. Hesitating, she rechecked her aim.

"Go for the neck," he said.

She pulled the trigger. When the deer fell, she let out a breath, realizing she'd been holding it in.

"Perfecto."

Nemacio slipped his arms around her waist then, warming her with his soft breath on her cheek. He brushed his lips down the length of her neck, languid and luscious. She shivered even though she wasn't cold as he held her close, giving her the attention she so longed for. She closed her eyes hoping the moment would last and last, but he let her go, without a word and leaped off the trail down to the deer, heaving it over his shoulders.

"Let's get the deer down the mountain before dark."

She went cold without his touch but followed him in silence all the way down the ridge without asking for more. Back at the claim, Álvaro built a huge bonfire outside while Nemacio and Nate gutted and skinned the deer, leaving the bloody entrails for Tom. As the deer cooked over the fire, the Sweetwater boys came over to join in the feast, enjoying the celebration of her kill and eating up the meat. Álvaro pulled out his guitar and Nemacio pulled out a bottle. Drinking and singing and swaying together, the men no longer saw Elisabeth. She'd become invisible, disappearing into the fog of gentlemanly fraternity. When Nate draped his arm around Nemacio's shoulders, she went into the cabin. Oozing with jealousy, she riffled through Nate's things. Shook out his bedroll. Dug through his box of books. Looked through the pots and pans, the tin of coffee. When she searched his coat pockets, she found it: that damn little red journal. She flew out of the cabin to Split Rock to read it.

18

"My life is not an apology, but a life.
It is for itself and not for a spectacle.
I much prefer that it should be of a lower
strain, so it be genuine and equal, than that
it should be glittering and unsteady."

At first she didn't understand. His words seemed confused, like he was trying to work out something eating away at him. As twilight set itself on the river, as she sat on Split Rock alone, flipping through the pages over again, trying to find the meaning in them. She grew angry and hurt but felt sorry for him too. Even at the more disturbing passages.

Entry #17
That Frenchman with his snakelike charm. He offered
'Lizbeth a better choice. I should have been an honorable
man and given her up. Said yes. Go with him. He's the
better husband. The better man. My pride got the better
of me. Or my shame. Perhaps it's my own selfishness. I'll
admit, I don't want to be all alone out here, without a
familiar face giving me comfort, reminding me of who

I am, who I was back home. I've not been honest with
myself, not believing. I've not been honest with her. I've
not yet wanted to believe. I wanted to convince myself I
was never that man.

Entry #29
Men. I see too many of them out here in the diggings,
and too few women. They scorn tradition, refusing to
settle down with a good woman and start a family. It
confounds me. They don't seem to want a wife, or need
one. They've come out here for something more, roaming
the hills for freedom, fortune, without the constraints of
expectation. Bold and brave. Unencumbered. Oh, how I
envy them, with no worry or care. No responsibility. With
a wife in tow, I've brought the conventional life from New
England with me. Concern weighs on me heavy. I see
the roving eyes of men. I should've come out here alone.
She's in danger.

Entry #41
The warmth inside the tent on such a cool night. The men
letting go of judgment, seeking companionship in a spirit
of freedom and dignity. Finding kindness and comfort and
love. Never in all my years have I known such a warm-
hearted embrace of my true self from another man. With
no hiding. No shame. No fear. And no repercussions for
honoring my own true being.

Entry #64
The diggers look hungry at Elisabeth, a sweet innocence
spread across her face. I am crazed with jealousy. I want
to be unburdened. Must I bear the burden of a life with a
woman abandoned by her own flesh and blood? I can never
leave her. I can never abandon her the way her own father
did. She will be my yoke forever, however much I want to
be digging alone, alongside the men, carefree. I want their
life. I want them.

Entry #82

She hasn't done a thing to deserve my rejection other than be a good woman, a fine companion, offering me nothing but kindness. I'm a wretched soul, mean-spirited and filled with anger at nothing she's done. I regret hurting her pride with my lack of touch but don't believe I've truly hurt her heart. I know her body doesn't fancy mine, just as my body doesn't fancy hers. I suspect a body can't help it. A body does what a body does, comes alive or doesn't. After last night, I understand. I can't make my body sing along to music it doesn't hear. I am no longer afraid to admit I hear only the music of men.

A family of wolves howled through the canyon, but Tom stayed silent by her side up on the Split Rock, not calling back in brotherhood. She slammed Nate's journal shut, knowing for sure now that she'd need to plan a future without Nate. After reading his journal she'd not stay with him. She was no man's pity wife. She had to figure out a way to leave.

Pushing his writings out of her head, she heard faint sounds of Álvaro's guitar in the distance, overlapping and mixing in among the wolf calls. The music flew on the wind gentle and slow and languid, then grew louder and faster with his deep strumming fullness, tempting. The contagious melody carried her back to the claim where a dozen people sat around the fire, drinking and laughing warm, including the Sweetwater boys and some folks she didn't know who dressed like Nemacio the night she'd seen him outside that Fandango tent, with short jackets and brass buttons down the sides of their pants. Álvaro played guitar for the strangers as Nemacio sang in a Spanish melody that vibrated through her. Nate sat close beside him, comfortable as if he understood every word. A woman sat among the men, relaxing with her red frilly skirt pulled up high, showing off bare legs and lady boots. Her white blouse, embroidered with bright blue flowers, flounced around loose, slipping bawdy and low off one shoulder. In the firelight, the woman's brown nipples poked out taut under her shirt and her breasts wiggled up and down as she laughed, brash and much too loud. A thin cigar dangled from her lips, just like a man, but her dark hair flowed long and loose and beautiful all around her. She was stunning. The man next to her draped his arm around her shoulders, lewd.

Elisabeth turned away from the woman and walked up to the fire. Nemacio stopped singing and looked up with his soft eyes, patting the dirt for her to sit beside him. She wiggled in between them, nudging Nate out of the way to sit close to Nemacio. He introduced the strangers, saying they were from Andalusia.

"In Spain, they jumped on a ship and here they are, looking to get rich like the rest," he whispered sloppy in her ear.

His warm, drunk breath sent a tingle through her.

The group went on drinking, oblivious to her desires, eating up the last of the deer meat she'd shot earlier that day. Álvaro looked at home among these people, strumming his guitar soft and sensual, teasing and coaxing with his fingers. Pleasing. Then harder and more dramatic. The Andalusians loved his music, encouraging him on with rousing cheers, and so he gave them more. Two of the men began to sing, and Nemacio leaned over to her to translate. Nate leaned across her to hear him.

"The gypsies sing of their mountain landscape, of murderous highwaymen, bandits," he said slow, through his deepening drunkenness. "Heroes who kill for the smallest sums. Or for honor. They glorify the . . ."

Nate looked past Elisabeth at Nemacio, who remained oblivious to both of their attentions and instead watched the beautiful woman stand up and circle around the fire slow, with one hand holding her skirt up and the other over her head. She snapped her fingers and stomped around in her fancy boots to the rhythm of Álvaro's guitar like a horse, shaking her head back and forth, her hair swinging wild to the group's delight, as one of the men started clapping in rhythm. Elisabeth was mesmerized by how the woman flung herself around. How she wasn't ashamed or shy but proud and sensual. How she wanted the men to look at her and admire.

"You like the gypsy woman," he said.

It wasn't a question but an observation. She shrugged back at him, choking down bitterness. She felt a stranger among the group, not able to be a man like Nate, passing a bottle sloppy without care, laughing along with the song and dance as if she was one of them. She wasn't a real wife with a proper husband. Or a lover. And she wasn't a gypsy woman, either, wearing a short frilly skirt showing off bare legs, getting everyone's attention. Oh, how she wanted to dance around like that, feeling free with no embarrassment, wiggling her hips. Instead, an acidy anger filled her throat.

Nemacio stood up to join the gypsy woman, moving slow around the fire with her, stomping up close. The group whistled and hooted as he and the woman acted out a tawdry dance that Elisabeth found disgraceful and enthralling all at once. Nemacio held his hands up high, dancing closer and closer around the woman, who swished her skirt and flung around her hair in rhythm to his stomping. Nemacio started singing to the woman luscious in Spanish, and Nate looked on with lust splashed across his face. A raw rage swirled through Elisabeth, and she turned to Nate, lashing out.

"You want to dance with him like that?"

"What?"

"Like you did at the Fandango."

Nate blinked at her with heavy eyelids, and she leaned in closer, whispering more meanness.

"You want to do some nastiness with him like you did with that lady-man behind the rock?"

"Lizbeth . . . I . . . I . . . didn't," he said, through his dim drunk.

"I saw you loving on that lady-man!"

When then the gypsy woman flung her skirt in front of Nate and the Sweetwater boys hooted and hollered for him to get up and dance, Elisabeth scooted herself back. She faded away into the shadows at the edge of the firelight as the logs crackled and sparked hot. Not able to enjoy the night, she slunk back to the cabin, sullen and ashamed at her own meanness. Curling up in bed, she listened to the distant music and laughter, stewing angry at Nate and the gypsy woman and Álvaro for playing so loud and Nemacio, too, for not paying her attention, until she fell asleep.

Long after the party quieted, and the Sweetwater boys left and the Andalusians bedded down in their tents staked out along the river, Elisabeth awoke to Nate snoring soundly on the floor, his stump flopped out loose from underneath his blanket. Repelled, Elisabeth slipped out into the dark night, wearing only her pantaloons and camisole.

With the moon long set, she waited until her eyes adjusted to the darkness. She heard quiet laughter coming from one of the tents down by the river. It sounded like sweet happiness. Curious, she tiptoed toward the tents like Nemacio had taught her, stepping slow and quiet so as not to wake anyone. She crept closer and closer until she was just outside the tent, listening. The gypsy woman giggled like Elisabeth had as a little girl, giddy and light without the heavy burden of living with a lame husband who couldn't love a woman right. She never laughed like that anymore. The woman let out a delicious moan. Elisabeth leaned in closer to hear more. When the woman started panting fast and delicate, Elisabeth knelt down on all fours beside the tent in the dirt, listening. The sound of two bodies slapping together faster and faster upended her, and she put a hand over her mouth, breathing in sync to the rhythm inside the tent. Sweat dripped from her armpits, and she went wet in between her legs. She crawled up even closer, peering in through the crack in the tent flap, watching the shadowy figures fuse together, the woman arching her back and the man moving faster back and forth. Elisabeth bit her palm and held still to calm her breathing and settle her heart nearly beating out of her chest, listening as the woman sang out long with delirious pleasure. Then all was quiet. She crept backward on all fours, putting a few yards between her and the tent, before standing up and starting back for the cabin.

"I see you," he said, quiet.

Nemacio sat alone by the fire ring. She burned with shame, hoping he couldn't see her face in the dark. He held up a bottle in the firelight, offering her a drink. She took it, sinking down beside him, sipping and sipping again, feeling sloppy and low and dirty compared to that fancy dancing gypsy. He tossed another log on the fire, and for a long while neither spoke. They passed the bottle back and forth, listening to the wood crackle. As she drank, her shame slowly slipped away with the hot orange bits of singeing sparks popping off the fire, floating up, dancing and swirling away to disappear in the black night.

"What did you see?"

"Not much," she said, matter-of-fact.

The drink swelled her blood, emptying her out, making room for something new. Making room for courage and lust and freedom. Elisabeth wanted to be like that gypsy woman. Powerful and beautiful and wanted.

"You like to watch," he said.

"Like you," she snapped. "Watching her dance around, then joining in all lusty-like."

"She's married to Pablo," he said.

"So that's how it is with you, getting up close to your friend's wife?"

"Only dancing."

"Show me," she said, standing up.

Nemacio turned away, looking into the flames.

"He's a good man, Elisabeth," he said.

"He doesn't want me," she said, her honesty let loose by the drink.

"He *needs* you."

"Stand up!" she said, stomping her foot. "Show me how to do it."

He hesitated, then stood up. He pulled her hips around to face him.

"Pretend you're wearing a skirt, holding it out to one side out like this. With your arm straight," he said.

She pretended, holding out an invisible skirt like he instructed, as the drink traveled up to her head, making her dizzy.

"Now put your hand on your hip, like this," he said, guiding his hand over hers.

She tried not to sway.

"What now?"

"Move from side to side, back and forth. Slow. Swooshing your skirt."

She moved and swooshed and swayed her imaginary skirt as he walked around her, looking at her intense, like he'd looked at the gypsy woman.

"Now take your hand from your hip and lift it up," he said, demonstrating.

"Like this?"

She flung her arm high into the air clumsy.

"No, no. Slow," he said. "Act shy at first. Like you have something inside, bottled up tight, wanting to come out. You don't let it out, not all at once. Comprende? You let the passion out slow, little by little."

He took her wrist and gently put it back down.

"First put your thumb and forefingers together like this, and spread your other fingers wide," he said, showing her. "Circle your hands around, like a flying bird."

She turned her wrists around in circles.

He backed up, studying her hands, serious.

"Slower," he said.

She slowed down, circling her hands twice.

"Again."

She circled and circled her hands around and around as he watched.

"Beautiful," he said.

"Now what?"

He stepped into her close. He took her hand, and she felt him shaking.

"Now take your hand and very slowly move it up from you hips, up along to your waist. Keep moving your hand up to here," he said, stopping at her breast.

Unsteady, she leaned her breasts up against his chest, thinking she might crumple. A tear dripped out of the corner of her eye, and then another and another until she was weeping, silent. He ran his hand along her wet cheek and her lips, then sucked his fingers.

"I taste you," he said.

"Oh," she said, sucking her breath in sudden.

She thought she might faint, but he held her, wrapping her hands behind her back, holding her, trapped. She couldn't move under his grip.

"Is this part of the dance?"

"Te deseo, Señora Parker," he said, staring down at her.

She heard his breath quicken like he'd been running. He put his lips to hers then. Breathing her in, tasting her. Opening her with his lips, his tongue, his heart. She closed her eyes as he opened her up, giving her more than she'd ever known, with a single enduring kiss that seem go on melding them together forever. *Our souls are connected.* When he pulled his lips away she waited for more, but he simply wrapped his serape around her shoulders and walked away, slipping out past the pine grove, and beyond. She stood, stunned as the stars seemed to stop shining, knowing she'd been nothing before that kiss, and would be nothing without it, again.

19

"Who looks upon a river in a meditative hour, and is not reminded of the flux of all things? Throw a stone into a stream, and the circles that propagate themselves are the beautiful type of all influence."

E lisabeth dropped Nemacio's sack in the dirt, waking him in a start. She felt a little guilty for it since he'd built the floor, but she couldn't abide Nemacio sleeping only yards away from her any longer. She'd gone completely daffy over him. If she didn't get him out of the cabin, she might likely crawl up in bed beside him pathetic, looking for loving in the dark. She needed to put some respectable distance between them.

"If it's warm enough to sit outside singing and drinking all night, then you can sleep outside from now on," said Elisabeth.

Nemacio stood up by the fire ring, still smoldering from the night before. The air filled sweet and smoky from all the morning campfires up and down the river canyon. Álvaro and Nate were already up, digging and swishing over by the Long Tom.

"You're angry," said Nemacio.

"Set yourself up somewhere else, Señor Gabilan."

"Lo siento."

"Far from away from me," she said, waving him off.

"You don't mean that."

"Yes. I do."

"What about last night?" Nemacio asked, ignoring her irritation.

"I don't remember a thing," she lied.

"You enjoyed my singing."

"You sang?" Elisabeth asked, incredulous that he talked about singing when all she could think about was his kiss.

"'Malagueña.' I sang it for you."

"Looked like you were singing it for my husband."

"You're jealous."

"Don't be ridiculous."

Nemacio looked over his shoulder at Nate standing near a large white quartz rock upriver swinging his pick clumsy, attempting to cleave off a hunk.

"I danced for you. I sang for you," he said.

"Sing it now," she demanded. "In English."

He started slow, looking at Elisabeth with passion pooling across his face. He sang quiet and unsteady, with none of the confidence brought on from drinking the night before.

"*My Malagueña, your eyes shamed the purple sky,*" he sang. "*You were as fair as I dreamed you would be.*"

He paused, taking off his hat and wiping a trickle of sweat dripping down his brow.

"Go on," said Elisabeth, waiting.

He started again, so quiet she almost couldn't hear.

"*I loved and left you, for I never could deny the gypsy strain in me.*"

"Stop!" Elisabeth said, putting her hands to her ears.

Nemacio stopped singing and closed his eyes. He put his hat back on and walked all the way across the claim toward Nate and grabbed the pick away with force. Nemacio swung hard, hitting the rock with a bang. The deer meat seemed to give him a newfound energy, pouring and sifting, washing and swooshing. She admired him from afar, aching.

She saw Nate pinching a tiny bit of gold careful not to drop it before placing it into his poke. She was sick of him grubbing for those little specks. By the time they'd collected enough to move off this godforsaken claim to something better, she'd be an old lady. She wanted something of her own, away from him. Digging in the dirt for nearly a year had turned her sour. She'd become mud and dirt itself, erasing all the womanliness she once carried. Her hair stuck matted and her clothes hung torn up and tattered. Hip bones poked out from her lady pants, unflattering and strange from too little food over the past winter. Rough hands. Man boots. She'd turned ugly. No wonder Nemacio had walked away after kissing her last night.

Eating the deer meat and getting kissed reminded her of everything she didn't have. Everything she wanted for herself. A bath. Boots that fit and a decent hat and a new dress and some pretty little gloves. And she wanted her hands to not hurt all the time. She wanted to move to town. She wanted Lucy back, and her mother. She wanted kisses. And love, and more.

Disgusted as much with herself as with Nate, she walked past the three men upriver to Split Rock. Tom, who'd been licking and chewing the marrow out of the deer leg, hopped up and ran after her. She walked around the bend and climbed up on Split Rock, just beyond their claim marker. Tom leapt up, too, lying down beside her, stretched across the gaping crack down the middle. The river swelled with the spring melt, running as fast and furious as her mood. Watching the river, Elisabeth felt stuck and angry. Stuck without loving and angry at the fix of a false marriage. She'd grown so lonely out here with all these men and no Lucy or Louisa May for womanly friendship. She chucked a stone into the river, sore at the unfairness of life and her own choices and mistakes, wondering how long she could go on. She threw a smaller stone into the eddy below the rock, watching the ripples radiate outward.

She stayed on Split Rock all day, examining every inch of the granite, dragging her hand along the dark gray base layered in blue and cream, with swirling spots of red. She fingered the uneven pits and divots embedded into the whole rock, cracking with crooked lines deep and shallow, horizontal and crossing and hiccupping in no particular order with rough ridges and knobby bits poking up all over both halves in a rocky chaos of no mistake. The half of Split Rock closest to the river was her favorite. Completely flat with a swath of glorious smoothness inviting her in, encouraging her to stretch out long and give herself over to the stone as it grabbed onto the tiny spot of sanity in her mind, holding it precious even when she couldn't.

As the afternoon drew long, Álvaro walked up the trail toward Split Rock, waving in her direction. He climbed up on the rock beside Tom, who started licking Álvaro's hands.

"Quite a spot," said Álvaro.

"I needed a moment."

"A beautiful moment."

"You're too damn cheerful," said Elisabeth.

"I've seen the elephant."

"What?"

"You know the story about the elephant?"

"No."

"A man who set out with a cart full of goods looking for the circus. Along the trail a man came upon the whole merry circus parade, led by a glorious elephant, who scared the horses. They ran off, pitching his wagon over. Ruined all his precious goods. But you know what?"

"What?"

"The man was cheerful and didn't mind his whole world upended."

"Why not?"

"Because he'd seen that glorious elephant."

It was a silly tall tale, but she was grateful for it.

"Have you've seen an elephant, Álvaro?"

"I sure have."

"Where?"

"In here," he said, poking his chest.

Álvaro smiled broad and jumped off Split Rock, whistling.

"Would you look at that," he said, pointing.

He dragged his finger along a wide line of quartz imbedded in Split Rock, leading down the side into the bedrock beside the river. Álvaro got on his hands and knees, pushing the dirt away to uncover an entire quartz floor that extended broad and flat up and down the river. Sly, Álvaro walked back downriver, pulling up the wood marker staking the boundary of their claim and moving it upstream about ten yards up from Split Rock, expanding the claim by almost twenty yards. Next to the marker, he piled up flat river stones into a two-foot-high cairn, for extra measure. He smiled at Elisabeth, pressing a finger to his lips, before walking back to camp.

20

*"A gem concealed . . .
a burning ray revealed."*

C oming out of the secret path into a small clearing on a ridge, Elisabeth gasped. Down below lay a narrow ravine with a river altogether different from the American, drifting deep and calm, surrounded by giant granite slabs and boulders with a vertical wall on the far side. The water meandered so slow and peaceful that it appeared not to move at all, like a piece of clean glass.

"It's called the Uva. After the grapes growing wild," said Nemacio.

They were supposedly out hunting together again. They'd spent the last month digging, with no time for rest, moving their Long Tom production upriver to Split Rock, hacking up the base where the thin quartz vein widened into a white mass of sparkling ground. Elisabeth felt sorry for breaking up Split Rock but needed more than they'd found to get her freedom from Nate. Start over on her own. So she hacked and hacked at the base with the men until her back ached and her hands blistered and bled. Come Sunday, she took off hunting, and Nemacio insisted on coming along again.

"I'd rather go alone."

"I can help get another deer," he said.

"I don't need help!"

"You can carry it down the mountain yourself?" he asked.

"She's in a mood, Nemacio. I'd steer clear of . . ." Nate started.

"Save your back, Elisabeth. Take my cousin," said Álvaro, cutting Nate off.

"Suit yourself," she said.

Before Nate could object again, they were off in the woods. She soon realized he hadn't come along to help her shoot something for supper. He led her across the river and up and over the ridge for nearly an hour.

"No one will see us way over here," he said.

He threaded his fingers through hers as they looked down from the narrow ridge, seeing through the clear water to the gravel on the river bottom. His hand felt warm and strong and safe.

"I thought you wanted to help me get a deer," she said, sassy.

"Later," he said.

He made himself comfortable, sitting down in the grass on the ridge and pulling a bunch of red grapes out of his knapsack. Her mouth watered.

"Have some," he said, holding out the grapes.

Sitting down beside him, she took a bunch, savoring the sweet fruit. She wondered why he'd brought her here and told herself to calm down, breathe steady. Told herself it was innocent. Just two folks by a river, enjoying a picnic of grapes.

"It's the Uva. Let's swim. You'll love it," he said with a familiar playfulness.

He grabbed her hand and led her down the ridge to the edge of the water. On a boulder beside the Uva, she watched him unlace his boots and take off his shirt. When he dropped his pants she didn't turn away but gawked at his naked backside as he dove deep into the water, gliding under, graceful. He came up treading water, smiling in that way of his.

"Come on. It's perfect," he said, tossing his head to fling wet curls away from his face.

"I don't think so."

"I'll turn around."

She hadn't swum in deep water since she was a little girl back in Concord, and she'd always stayed in the shallows close to Split Rock when washing in the American for fear she'd be swept into oblivion.

"Nope," she said, shaking her head.

He swam to the other side and climbed out, sitting naked on a long slab with his back turned, water dripping down his brown shoulders.

"I won't look," he called out from the far bank, his voice echoing off the granite walls.

The calm waters of the Uva tempted her, and she looked up and down the ravine to make sure they were alone. Feeling reckless, she took off her boots and slipped out of her dress. She sunk into the water still wearing her pantaloons and camisole, shocked at her indiscretion but thrilled too. The cold stole her breath. Gulping in short bursts, she swam around clumsy, grabbing at the water. Putting her face down, she opened her eyes, looking around the crystalline pool with the sand and rocks at the bottom, and tiny see-through fish swimming around her bare feet. She came to the surface and floated on her back, looking up in awe at the blue-gray granite surrounding the river. Gliding downstream, she relished the respite of the Uva away from the claim and all that feverish energy clawing and digging, desperate and dirty in the American for gold.

He slid naked into the water beside her, and they floated on their backs together, holding hands. This surely wasn't an innocent picnic any more, she thought, as the current pulled them toward the river's edge, slow, then unmoving.

"We've stopped," she said.

"We caught an eddy."

"What a hoot!" she said, jumping out of the water onto a flat rock like a wet frog. "I want to do it again."

She bounded upriver, hopping from rock to rock barefoot with her thin underclothes clinging wet, while he watched. She jumped back into the water with a splash, feeling her deep loneliness wash away as she floated down with the current, cradled in the arms of the river. She caught the swirling eddy again, gliding tranquil. Flipping over, she swam clumsy to a flat rock sticking halfway out of the water at the center of the pool. She scrambled out onto the smooth granite and folded her knees up to cover her breasts sticking out taut in her wet camisole.

"What an extraordinary place," she said.

Nemacio treaded in the water close and closer, watching.

"I see you," he said.

"You said you wouldn't look," she said, nervous.

"I can't help myself," he said, swimming closer.

"Liar," she said.

As the sun slipped behind the ravine, the gloaming grew around the Uva. Even in the dimness, the granite and grass and trees, even the needles on the pines swelled more vibrant, as if dusk revealed secrets blinded by the California sun. As he reached the slab, his face looked like a truer picture of itself, the outline of his shoulders sticking out of the water more broad. His cleft deeper. His eyes richer. When he touched her feet dangling off the rock into the water, she shivered even though a warm breeze drifted through the secret canyon. When Nemacio traced his hand up the inside of her calf, she sucked in her breath. He climbed out naked and dripping wet, leaning over her.

"You've got hold of my soul," he whispered in her ear.

She didn't resist when he sucked her lips, draining her weak and delicious. When he pulled her knees open and touched the place between her legs through her wet pantaloons, she sank back into the soft rock like she was drunk, lightheaded and dark together, wanting him to touch her more. This was the touch she was missing. This was the loving she'd never gotten from Nate.

She should have stopped him when he unbuttoned her camisole and licked her breasts, but instead she held the back of his neck, coaxing him for more. Curious how far he'd go.

"I'm desperate for you," he said, tugging off her pantaloons.

She dragged her hands up through his wet curls as he found her, sliding his fingers in. Touching her softness inside, higher. Curling and coaxing her along, longer, making her want, until she was writhing her naked bottom against the smooth granite in the middle of the Uva. Dizzy, she closed her eyes.

He stopped.

She panicked, grabbing at his shoulders.

"Please, don't stop," she said.

"Open your eyes," he said.

And she did, finding herself inside his inky eyes, newly born, as he moved over her, pushing himself in, slow. Filling her whole. Deep and deeper inside, back and forth, until they moved together, as if no light, no dark, no empty ever existed. Only blueness and fullness. He pushed her past the point of reason, unspooling and reverberating beyond, into a primal creature, until she stirred and rippled, bursting open, elemental and raw.

21

"Even in the mud and scum of things,
something always, always sings."

The next morning Nemacio thrust a cup at her as she came out of the cabin.

"Thistle tea," he said.

She drank it down, not able to look at him, feeling shamed. She shouldn't have gone swimming with him. Shouldn't have let him love her like that. Shown her what loving she'd been missing. Pull her down, spill his soul into her.

"There's a pot steeping over by my tent. Drink it all day. We've gotta be careful," he said, winking.

He didn't seem ashamed, just concerned she didn't get with a baby. He ran off to join Álvaro and Nate at the morning dig, looking energized as he swung and hacked with glee at the quartz floor. Sheepishly, Elisabeth took her place in the middle of the Long Tom, sifting through the piles in the rocker box, looking for gold. Down by the end of the tom, Nate collected the smaller bits.

Nemacio walked back and forth, dumping bucket after bucket of crushed quartz and water and mud in front of her. She tried ignoring him, but she could smell the sweat and dirt and love on him every time he came over to dump a bucket, and it made her want him something powerful. Turning away, she concentrated on the work of sifting through the rock for what seemed like hours without stopping. Her hands cramped up and her back started aching as she worked through the gloppy pile, sliding the slag down the sluice toward Nate at the end who looked like a little ant, swirling a pan, looking for flakes, hunched-over back and too-thin arms. With his odd-shaped head and pointy chin he could actually be an ant. An ant with one leg, hobbling along to his little anthill. He was turning into a disgusting ant right before her eyes. A hairy ant man, with a straggled blond beard crawling around a stinky pile of leftovers. Oh, God! She was losing it. Losing her senses. Her grounding.

When Nemacio dumped another bucket into the Long Tom, he leaned down and whispered.

"I can still taste you," he said.

His hot breath in her ear sent a rush of heat through her body, like she'd been set on fire.

"Get away," she said, serious.

He leaned in closer as if he was telling her something about the sluice, talking below the river's roar.

"I can't. You've got hold of me, in those gorgeous eyes, and your . . ." he said.

"Stop! He'll hear you," she said, looking over at Nate.

But Nate was looking down into the pan, lost in the swirling dirt like he was examining his future in a crystal ball. Nemacio grabbed her arm, speaking with an anger under his breath that frightened her.

"This isn't a game! I want to throw you down in the mud, right here beside the river. In front of your husband. Make him watch as I love you. Make you scream with pleasure. Beg for more."

Elisabeth blinked, wide-eyed.

"Pero me resisto," he said, dropping her arm. "For the sake of your honor."

When he walked back over to Split Rock, she let out a huge sigh, releasing all her pent-up energy and frustration and want, and smashed the pile of rock in front of her with the back of a shovel, sending mud flying onto her dress, her hair, her face, her eyes, up her nose, even in her ears. She almost had a fit right then, flipping over the entire idiotic Long Tom contraption in frustration, when she saw it. A nugget. No, not a nugget. A hunk. A big yellow hunk shining bright out from under the brown glop. She reached her hand out, digging into the mud, not believing.

It was considerable, heavy and uneven. It was gold, and far more than a nugget. A whole lot more.

22

"When it is dark enough,
you can see the stars."

A rumbling in the manzanita up the trail struck her with terror. She gripped the Hawken and stopped. They were walking up to Coyoteville to weigh their find, Álvaro out front carrying his guitar, Elisabeth in the middle with Tom loping alongside, and Nemacio behind holding the gold stone in a sack slung over his shoulder.

After almost a year digging down in the river, they'd found something extraordinary. Seeing the thing sparkling in the sluice, she had squealed. Nate had stood up and Nemacio came running. It was nearly a foot long, embedded in a mass of crystalized quartz, with a clear-cut corner and sides poking out shiny with great brilliance. They cleaned it and passed it around, testing its weight, examining the uneven contours. Nate guessed it weighed nearly five pounds. Álvaro bet Nate it weighed nine, saying he'd been eyeing Nate's crutch and wanted to lop off the pad to make it a fancy walking stick for lolling around San Francisco, now that he was a rich man. They all laughed, delirious at their luck.

Holding the gold, she thought Álvaro was most likely right at nine pounds, giving them a near fortune in one go, on top of what they'd already dug up. After finding the hunk of gold, they'd kept digging through the Split Rock vein another two weeks, cutting out a channel up toward the ridge fifteen feet wide, draining and washing out the ore. The work was like pulling money out of a bank, giving them two thousand more. When the vein slowed up to flakes, they agreed it was time to head to the assayer up in Coyoteville to weigh the gold and file proper claim papers. Nate told them to go on ahead, come back with a donkey to haul up the other sacks hidden under the cabin floorboards. Álvaro had no opinion, just lounged on a rock strumming his guitar as Nate and Nemacio discussed the logistics of expanding their operation.

With her take of the gold, Elisabeth planned to leave the diggings, move up to Coyoteville. She was done digging in the river like a dog. Done caring for Nate. Done sneaking around like a hussy with Nemacio, hoping on proper loving. She'd figure out a way to make a decent living in town. Maybe start a book business of her own. Selling, not lending. Perhaps offer woodcut prints too.

As they headed out of the canyon at dawn that morning, she looked back at what a sight to see: Nate hobbling around, moving quicker than a man with both legs, doing the job of four, still dumping, sifting, and swishing all by himself, hoping to find more.

"I'll have more luck when you return. God willing," he called out, pumping his snake stick high above his head.

It wasn't luck at all. Or God's work. It was human work, picking through rocks all day, never stopping, no matter how cold or wet or hot or hungry or uncomfortable. Never stopping except to hunt and eat and sleep. That's what got them the gold. Hard work. Not divine providence.

Finished with that life of mud and rocks, she carried the Hawken, along with all her meager belongings in a satchel, including the engraving tools and "Self-Reliance," knowing she wouldn't return back to Nate or the claim. She'd stay up in town. Reward herself with a real bath in a tub of warm water. Buy a proper dress, in fancy yellow silk taffeta with a bow and maybe a new ribbon for her hair, and some fine lady boots with no holes. She'd finished walking around in Henry's man boots.

In a sudden moment the sound grew deafening, and before they could back up, a massive grizzly charged out of the bushes from twenty yards up the trail. It happened in a whirl. The bear stood up tall on its hind legs, growling hideous with massive teeth. As it ran toward them, Elisabeth got off a quick shot with her Hawken, hitting the bear in the shoulder, but that didn't stop it from coming. It leapt on Álvaro, swiping with daggerlike claws, nearly taking his face clean off. The bear clawed and bit as she started reloading, pouring more powder in the barrel with shaking hands, and Tom ran barking frantic and fierce, launching himself onto the grizzly's shoulders, and Nemacio pulled out a pistol she didn't know he kept under his coat. The bear swatted at Tom, flinging him ripped open to the ground with a yelp, then turned back to crunching on Álvaro, who'd rolled up like a pill bug. She put another ball in the barrel and tamped it down as fast as she could while Nemacio plugged the bear in the neck with his pistol in rapid succession six times. The bear flinched with each slug but didn't stop tearing into Álvaro, grabbing his whole head in its jaws. As Nemacio reloaded, she walked right up to the bear, placing the barrel against its head, and pulled the trigger. It let loose poor Álvaro then, staggering back, weaving and roaring with bloody slobber dribbling from its mouth. She backed up as Nemacio shot his pistol again, hitting the bear in the head and face six more times. Heaving, it fell dead. He reloaded and ran to Álvaro.

The forest rang silent. No birds chirped. No squirrels scuttled. The late summer breeze fell flat. The pine trees stilled as angry dead bear stank wafted up evil. Nemacio cradled his friend, rocking him, speaking in Spanish, soothing. Álvaro looked a sight, torn up beyond man, his nose gone, scalp laid open, neck strung out. She fell to her knees. In moments, Álvaro was done, his breath disappeared into a heap of blood and bones and flesh and soul.

Nearby, Tom lay whimpering, his left hip splintered, guts dangling out raw and red pooling around his beautiful yellow coat. His tongue hung loose in the dirt as he panted painful. She reloaded the gun again, pouring and tamping the powder and ball down, slow this time. Tom looked up at her with warm eyes, giving love to her even in his last moments. She placed the barrel to his head and closed her eyes, pulling the trigger with a flinch.

When a low murmur came from the bushes, she turned to see a little bear stumbling out from a hiding place beneath a huckleberry bush, confused. He wobbled over, pouncing on his mama, shaking her shoulders and licking her nose, and crying and crying something awful. When the baby bear curled up beside its dead mama, Elisabeth hunched over and threw up on her pants.

Nemacio and Elisabeth slumped there among the ruin on the trail, the sun reaching high and hot, with the baby bear curled up beside its dead mama, whining. Time folded back upon itself, and she fell into dazed devastation at losing dear Álvaro. When a shadow crossed in front of the sun, she looked up to see two, then four birds circling in the sky, a mass of wings blotting out the light with each pass. One landed on the trail with a thud, standing over four feet tall. Then another landed, and another, with no fear or regard for her or Nemacio or the baby bear. These were no ordinary vultures but grotesque beasts straight from the depths of Hades, with feathers black as a starless sky and bald wrinkled heads, pink and blotchy, and long beaks sharpened to a hook, and bulging necks ringed with a frill of spiky feathers. One stretched its wings, nearly nine feet across, and hopped toward Tom, cocking its head and staring sinister with evil eyes, unblinking. She'd never seen such a bird, so massive, so bold and unafraid. Another hopped closer, kicking up dust with each stamp of its huge clawed feet. She felt trapped crumpled in a heap with all those tall birds towering around. Nemacio still cradled dead Álvaro, staring into a void. When the bird lurched closer, she kicked at it, but it didn't startle. When it pecked at Tom's paw, a screech came out of her in a voice she didn't recognize. Nemacio leapt up, throttling the bird by the neck and flinging it down and pounding its chest while it flopped and flapped until its heart stopped and its eyes rolled back into that bulging head and it went limp. The other birds looked on, unmoved by their brethren's fate. She stared at Nemacio, horrified.

"I have its power now," he said.

Gripping the dead bird in his fist, he stumbled back down next to Álvaro lying lifeless. She shook with silence, stunned and spent by the bloody mess of killing and death raining down upon them. A group of men walking up the trail found them: dead Álvaro, Nemacio kneeling beside, still holding the bird by its wrung neck, Elisabeth keeping guard over Tom, and the baby bear curled up by its dead mama. The men hollered, and the menacing birds flew up in a whoosh of wings to circle overhead. Someone roped the baby bear and dragged it off by its neck, howling. Another man gave Nemacio an old blanket to wrap up dead Álvaro. Nemacio carried him over his shoulder the rest of the way to Coyoteville, while he dragged the bird by the neck, its talons carving grooves into the dirt its talons carving grooves in the dirt. When someone offered to help lighten his load, he kicked and shouted.

"No!"

She had the sense to grab their sack of gold that had rolled under a bush, slinging it and Álvaro's cracked guitar over her shoulder. She picked up her Hawken and satchel, struggling the rest of the way into town under the heavy load. Several men offered to help, and she let them carry her satchel and the guitar, but she held on tight to the sack of gold with that big nugget inside.

As they walked into the streets of Coyoteville Nemacio searched for a priest, cradling dead Álvaro over his shoulder, his head hanging limp down Nemacio's back, blood leaking through the blanket, staining it wet. In a stupor, she followed him into the El Dorado, where he placed dead Álvaro out on a table and yelled out for someone to find el padre. He flung the huge bird on the oak floor with a thud, and all the men hushed. He drank, and Luenza came over and hugged Elisabeth, saying something sad and somber she couldn't hear. Luenza placed food in front of them, but she didn't eat, just suffered empty. She couldn't believe that lump on the table wrapped up tight was Álvaro, dead. She couldn't believe his days of playing guitar and singing and laughing and joking and digging alongside them were done. Done so quickly, and with such savagery.

Nemacio cut his meat deliberate and graceful, even now with his hands still smeared with Álvaro's blood gone dry. He downed shot after shot of whiskey; someone kept filling up his glass. Descending into a stupor, he struggled to maintain decorum, pausing to wipe his lips clean with a napkin, then calling out again impatient and slurring for el padre who wasn't there. She couldn't see what difference it made: el padre or a reverend. No religion would help Álvaro now, his luck run out after finding such a fortune. She pinched her face, hoping it was all a dream, some sick nightmare, with her mind playing tricks. The pinch hurt. It was real.

They were a strange pair, the Californio and Mrs. Parker, sitting in Luenza's El Dorado Hotel now fancied up far beyond that clump of tents she'd started with the previous summer. Elisabeth's smelly clothes were worn to tatters, and out of place in the real wooden building with two stories and windows and crimson velvet drapes and flowered wallpaper, and a long oak bar with a gilded mirror and paintings of nude women hanging on either side. But the diggers didn't give a hoot about her appearance, gathering around, buying more shots for Nemacio to honor dead Álvaro and drinking along in sympathy. The piano man played something sweet as word spread around about the bear mauling. Many of the men had played monte with Álvaro, and now they toasted his considerable skills, his generosity and humor. Nemacio didn't console Elisabeth over what happened but kept drinking and slipping farther away from her, mumbling to himself in both Spanish and English, and yelling out like a lunatic for el padre.

"Dónde está el padre?" he asked, slamming his fist down on the table. "Damn it! Get me the priest!"

Someone came to fill Nemacio's glass again; it was Luenza's youngest, Tyler. Elisabeth stole the drink, gulping it down. When Nemacio didn't notice, she did it again, not minding the taste of whiskey one bit. Little Tyler brought her a glass of her own and kept filling it while he held her hand, and she drank until she became light itself, gazing at the windows sparkling with light streaming inside as the sun sank and the dust fairies started dancing in a radiant stream, glowing all around. Her mother had told her about those dust fairies, the little people, sometimes visible in afternoon light. If you looked real close, she said, they came out to say hello and bring luck. She'd believed the story when she was young, and wanted to still. Perhaps Álvaro danced among the fairies now. She reached out, grabbing at the light stream. Eluding her grasp, the fairies disappeared through her fingertips as Tyler poured again and she drank, wanting to soar with the fairies light and carefree into another world. As darkness loomed, the fairies disappeared, leaving her alone and bereft.

When el padre finally came, Nemacio slung dead Álvaro over his shoulder and stumbled toward the door.

"Vámanos, Elisabeth. El cóndor," he said, pointing.

She stood, swaying slightly, looking into the unseen spaces of the room. She picked up the dead bird and Álvaro's mangled guitar, and concentrated on walking straight toward the door. Outside, the cool air filled her nose, reviving her a bit, but she was drunk, and the wrung bird felt much heavier than she'd expected, maybe thirty pounds or more. She followed him to the graveyard on a little hill behind the town, dragging the bird behind her while the motley group of men from the El Dorado followed as a drunken death procession, with torches gleaming through the night.

A shallow hole waited for dead Álvaro. Nemacio leaned down and placed his friend in the dirt, tucking the bloody blanket around him tighter, as if that'd keep him extra warm underground for eternity. El padre wasn't a Californio, rather Father John Shannon of the new Catholic church being built on the hill. Elisabeth couldn't understand his Irish brogue, but it made little difference. All manner of God's grace had escaped her, like river sand slipping through her rough fingers. She'd as likely look to the California sun for comfort, which had made her far happier in recent days than God. Or the river, where she'd known real love for the first time.

Nemacio knelt alongside the hole, pushing the dirt over dead Álvaro with his bare hands for long while. When the men tried to help with shovels, he swatted them away. Elisabeth looked up at the little white stars above, flowing and blurring together in the darkness, making her dizzy, as Nemacio patted around the mound. He took the bird from Elisabeth, who hadn't realized she still held it. When Father Shannon started to pray over dead Álvaro, Nemacio staggered away, like he'd forgotten about his urgent desire for a proper burial. She didn't understand why he left and ran to catch up, wanting to share their sorrow. She followed him toward a fire ring tended by miners down at Coyote Creek, where he skinned the bird whole without plucking it, and threw its bloody carcass crackling onto the fire and stuffed the skin and the feathers and that nasty beak into the sack with the gold. She followed him to the livery after, where he bought a donkey and gave a man directions down to the Goodwin Claim.

"Bring Nate Parker up to town, and I'll pay the rest. I'm at the El Dorado."

He seemed slightly sober now compared to her wobbling.

"I don't want him up here. He's not my husband," she mumbled.

Nemacio didn't regard her comment, just plodded back to the El Dorado, and up the stairs. She followed him toward a door at the end of a long hall. He opened it.

"We'll settle up the shares later," he said.

She threw her arms around his neck, but he didn't move. She pressed up against him, but he didn't hug her back, leaving his arms by his side.

"Come inside," she whispered heavy, not letting go. "I want more loving. I need it."

"One night is not enough," he said, standing still.

"Then stay. You can have me, for always."

He peeled her hands off his neck like she was a child and took a step back, away from her.

"You're eating my soul . . . making promises you can't keep."

"I won't beg," she said, slurring slightly.

"I can't do this to Nate."

"He'll try to get with you now."

"God is punishing me."

She wanted to say God didn't kill Álvaro. It was the bear, but she couldn't form the words.

"I'll have Luenza bring you hot water for a bath and clean clothes. And a comb."

Nemacio closed the door, leaving her reeling in the center of that fancy room. She didn't touch a thing, only looked around at the cast-iron tub and the fluffy bed with a white lace spread and the glass vase with little bluebell flowers set on a table, smelling like perfume powder and happiness, and she drowned deeper in drunken sorrow. It was too luxurious for her alone, and far more than she needed. She missed Tom sidling up, nudging with his wet nose, even though he would've stunk up the fancy air something awful. She missed Álvaro. She wanted to rewind the days, give the gold back to the earth, and listen to her dear friend playing his Spanish guitar by the river, singing and laughing true. She balanced the smashed-up guitar in the corner and sank to the floor in a slump, thinking she should've told him how much she loved his music.

23

"Nothing can bring you peace but yourself."

" I don't care if his mama is the Mother Mary herself, I don't register no foreigners or no women to any claim in this county. And by the looks of it, I'd say you owe me twenty dollars in foreigner tax for every month you were digging down there," said the assayer in Coyoteville.

Elisabeth laughed out loud right in the assayer's office, inappropriate and brash. Nate glared at her, but she didn't care.

"I'm no foreigner," said Nemacio.

"You look like one. And that name—Nemacio Gabilan," the assayer spit. "That's a Mexican name."

"You are the foreigner, sir. I am Californio, with American citizenship. The Treaty of Guadalupe Hidalgo promises me full rights," Nemacio said.

"I didn't promise you nothing," said the assayer.

"Sounds to me like you don't understand the law in California," said Elisabeth. "All citizens can register names on a claim. Even me."

"Only your husband can sign, Mrs.," said the assayer. "That's the way it's always been. You got no legal rights apart from your husband."

Elisabeth had done her research. Millie over at the Stamps Store had finally gotten her hands on last year's issue of the *Mountain*

Democrat with all the details of the California Constitution and shared it with Elisabeth. She'd read through twice, studied the particulars before making up her mind.

"There's where you're wrong," she said, wagging a finger in his face. "Out here in California I got all sorts of rights. I can own property, take custody of my children, if I had any. Hell, I can even sue if you do me wrong."

"No need getting your dander up, lady."

Nemacio stepped up to her defense, patting his hand on the claim certificate.

"A woman needs no permission to file a claim or own land in California. My mother holds fifty thousand acres in her name alone."

"That was before. We're in California now," said the assayer.

The assayer turned away from Nemacio and spoke to Nate like he was the one in charge.

"You giving your lady permission to sign?"

Before Nate could answer the assayer, Elisabeth yelled, all worked up at the man's ignorance.

"I don't need permission from him!"

"Calm down, darlin'. All I'm saying is, why bother putting your name on a claim, when you got a husband here to take care of all that trouble for you?"

"I've taken care of most of the trouble so far. I'm an equal partner, and don't need anyone to sign for me. I can even divorce, and you'd still have to let me sign."

Nate stared over at her, horrified. But Elisabeth turned toward Nemacio, looking for his reaction. He gave way to none, just kept staring down the assayer.

"I'll let you, if it's all right with your husband. But I still ain't registering no foreigner on this claim," said the assayer, pointing to Nemacio.

Nemacio grabbed the assayer around the collar. The assayer's assistant reached for a pistol out from under the counter, pointing it at Nemacio's head. The click of the pistol cocking echoed off the bare wood walls. Nemacio put his hands up. Nate stepped in between the gun and Nemacio.

"Settle down," said Nate. "We don't mean trouble. Just want to set the claim title correct."

Nate placed a reassuring arm around Nemacio's neck.

"Why don't you go wait outside while I get this all straightened out," said Nate.

Nemacio slammed his fist on the counter and stormed out. The assayer slid the claim registration form to Nate as his assistant holstered his pistol. Nate signed the form, and Elisabeth grabbed the paper away before the ink was even dry and added her name. Their gold chunk weighed 6.9 pounds, worth $2,040, and the sack of seven thousand they'd dug up all spring. Álvaro would've won the bet after all, leaving Nate crutchless.

"You lost the bet!" Elisabeth said to Nate, laughing.

If Álvaro had been alive he would've laughed too. He would've roared and roared and elbowed Nemacio and Nate, and bowed to Elisabeth, cheeky. So she laughed like his ghost was in the room. After all, if he hadn't moved the claim stake that afternoon at Split Rock when he'd told her the tale of seeing the elephant, they would've never dug up all that gold.

Álvaro had always given more of himself than expected, relishing in the simple moments with good friends and sweet music. Not even a week had passed since the mauling and she missed him terrible, with a hollowed-out ache draining her empty. She missed him more than her mother and father, and even little Lucy and Louisa. It didn't make sense why she missed him so much, but she thought it might've something to do with how he'd truly understood her. God knows, he was plenty tolerant of her moods. He saw her honest and put up with her patient, even with her ugly finger picking and her dirty hair and her sore temper flaring up when she got tired. He'd been constant.

After the assayer exchanged their gold for bills and coins, they sat down to a private, corner table at the El Dorado. Nate divided up their earnings of nine thousand in coins and bills, putting them in three separate hemp sacks. Elisabeth grabbed her sack of three thousand and stuffed it in her valise, gripping it tight in her lap, knowing even that much money wouldn't go far out here. Over steak supper, she listened quiet as Nate talked to Nemacio about adding him to claim as an equal partner.

"The definition of citizen is apparently now up for debate. As soon as we prove you're an American, this whole mess will be settled. Do you have documentation?"

"Criminal! These gringo laws," said Nemacio.

Nate suggested Nemacio write his uncle, asking him for the proper paperwork from the Accolades in Monterey. He assured Nemacio they were equal partners even without proof of his citizenship, drawing up a note guaranteeing his one-third ownership right then at the table from a page torn out of his journal. It wasn't an official-looking document, but Nate said he'd honor it forever.

With new money, the three partners looked altogether different from the week before, and entirely at ease in the fancy El Dorado with its polished oak bar and gilt mirrors and piano man playing a tinny tune. The men were clean-shaven, but Nate fashioned his blond mustache long and waxed straight out to the sides. He dressed in a new suit, with a white collar pressed rigid and a light blue silk tie. One leg of his pants fit short to his stump, hemmed up by the town tailor, not by Elisabeth. He wore a silk top hat that sat much too high on his head, making him look haughty. Not the best choice for digging. Nemacio wore new clothes, too, dark brown pants and a white shirt with a leather vest buttoned up to a brown necktie. He'd hung his new brown felt hat on a rack behind. Nate hadn't bothered to take off his hat at the table.

Elisabeth had taken a long, hot bath, washing off the dirt from the hard winter, scrubbing some of the woman back into herself. She thought it best not to waste her money on that fancy yellow taffeta she'd dreamed of, but instead dressed in a simple flax calico dress buttoned up to a white lace collar. The dress wasn't sunshine yellow either, but more of a light mustard. It reminded her of Tom. A size too big, the dress hung loose, but taking it in would be foolish. She planned to eat at least twice a day now that she was staying in town, filling it out with hearty flesh on her hips within weeks. She didn't buy a new corset, and didn't bother with a bustle either, cutting the bottom of the dress off just below her knees like she was used to wearing, and fashioning it with a neat ruffle. Underneath, she wore a pair of lady pants she'd made from a pretty lace petticoat, more practical for the muddy streets of Coyoteville. Her new woman boots fit perfect with no heel, buttoning up the side. She even bought a new lacy sleeping shift from Millie over at the Stamps Store, keeping it folded up at the foot of her bed upstairs in her room over the restaurant, in case Nemacio came back to her. She hadn't bought a new hat. Eventually, she'd buy a simple straw one, sturdy and practical. For now, she planned to save her money. White gloves had seemed frivolous, but now looking down at her rough hands, she wished she'd bought a pair. A year digging and hunting and engraving had leeched her hands of all feminine delicateness. They looked like man hands now, with thick calluses and short jagged nails. She hid them in her lap underneath the table as Nate and Nemacio discussed plans for expanding the claim. She waited for a long while listening to them talk particulars. When Nate suggested they pool all their profits together and create a mining corporation, she finally spoke up, saying she was keeping her share.

"I've an idea for something here in town," she said, steadying her shaking hands below the table so they couldn't see.

"That doesn't make sense. The claim's finally paying out," said Nate. "We've gotta go bigger."

"Work it without me. I'm staying in Coyoteville," she said.

Nate's mouth still hung slack.

"You're gonna stay up here?"

"I aim to build a business."

"By yourself?"

"Not like you want me down there anyhow. Either of you," she said, glaring at Nemacio now. "You two can work the claim without me. Hire another man on."

"Oh, no! No. No," Nate said, shaking his head vigorous. "You've got to come back to the claim."

She figured he wasn't interested in her and only wanted her share of the money, and her hunting his food and washing his drawers.

"My mind is all set," she said, her face set firm.

Nate's face fell soft and his voice quieted, talking to her as if coaxing a wild horse to calm down.

"I'll build onto the cabin, 'Lizbeth. You can have your own room."

"And how will you do that, in your condition?"

She looked under the table at his half leg.

"You're not being fair."

"I've been fair enough, given the circumstances."

"You know I pull my weight down there on the river, digging and cooking. Come on back and I'll fix things up nice for you. We'll hire more men. You won't have to dig anymore. Right, Nemacio?"

Nemacio didn't try to smooth things over between husband and wife as he usually did; he just looked back and forth between them expressionless, which irritated her to no end.

"Thank you all the same. I intend to stay here. Open my own business," she said.

"What about your share of the claim?" Nate asked.

"The way I see it, I'm entitled to one-third share of all future earnings on the claim, even not working it. Less your future capital investments, of course. We'll have to figure out those particulars, with receipts and such."

"One-third of my future finds!" Nate said, angry.

"I'm letting you have Henry's cabin, which is mine by California law," she said.

"Speak some sense to her, Nemacio; she listens to you," said Nate, flopping back in his chair.

"Sounds about right to me," said Nemacio.

"What the hell? This setup makes no sense," said Nate, throwing his hands up in the air.

"You don't need me anymore, Nate. You said yourself, you're strong now. Besides, you won't be alone. You have Nemacio," she said, more sarcastic than she meant.

"I can't believe you're running off now, just as the claim's paying up," said Nate.

"I'm not running off. I'll be right here in town, and I'll come visit, see how you're getting on."

"Do not travel the trail alone," said Nemacio.

"Fine! You come visit me here," she said, turning to look at Nemacio.

She knew Nate wouldn't likely make the effort to visit but hoped to heaven Nemacio might come. She looked at him clear and honest, hoping he understood she was talking to him, alone. Understood her wants floating below the surface. Understood she was asking him for it.

"What's your plan?" Nate asked.

"To sell books, and maybe my engravings, as if it's any of your business," she said.

In secret, she wondered how she'd get along alone. She'd seen no examples of how a woman might manage, except maybe Luenza, but she had her boys and her husband, Stanley, when he felt like coming around. And Nandy had her man Billy.

"You've no books," said Nate.

"I've ordered three boxes from New York. While I'm waiting for them to arrive, I've employed a man to travel to Sacramento and San Francisco to buy up all the books he can find. He left yesterday. When he returns, I'll have my store ready."

"What man?" Nemacio asked.

She didn't answer, just smirked, hoping to make him jealous.

"Who's gonna buy your prints out here?" Nate asked.

"I'd buy one," said Nemacio.

"All right, Nemacio," said Nate. "She's made a few pretty little pictures, but she can't make a living selling them."

"I suspect she can," said Nemacio.

"I've already secured a location for my shop, near the end of the main street, where the wooden buildings stop and the tents begin. In the center of activity. I purchased wood on credit from the sawyer to build my shop."

"You took out credit without asking me!"

"I don't need your permission. You forget. In California, I have the same rights married or not. I can hold property and sign contracts without a man," she said, raising her voice.

"Without your husband?" Nate asked.

"I don't need you on my contract."

"Who extended that sort of credit to a woman?"

"Mr. Stamps at the Dry Goods. I put up my portion of the claim as collateral. My third, mind you. It doesn't affect you or Nemacio. Only me. Besides, I plan to pay him back in a few months, once I get the store up and going."

"The claim as collateral! Are you crazy? What's the interest?"

"You don't need to know the particulars," she said.

Amused at his anger, she grinned, enjoying her position of power.

"What a goddam place, California! Giving a woman the right

to make a contract without her husband's knowledge!" he started, spreading his arm wide in a comic gesture. "Perhaps the whole of America will adopt these liberal laws, sending our society into ruin. What's next? Giving women the vote?"

"It's against my shares alone. And I had every right. My father gave the claim to me," she said, matter-of-fact.

"That's not how I remember it. As I recall, he left the claim to both of us, Nate and Elisabeth Parker. Husband and wife."

"Stop!" Nemacio raised his voice. "What does it matter, all this bickering, with both of your names registered on the claim? Move on. Let's talk expansion. I'm trying to save my family's ranch."

Hearing Nemacio mention his family made him feel distant and unfamiliar. But Nate smiled at hearing Nemacio say he needed more from the claim, smirking like he'd stolen Nemacio away from her.

Nemacio ordered a bottle of fancy French champagne to toast dead Álvaro, holding up the glass with a confident familiarity at using such finery.

"To Álvaro, a man who tasted the zest of life," he said.

They all sipped, and the bubbles tickled Elisabeth's throat as she wondered if the bottle had come all the way from France. Nemacio held up his glass for another toast.

"And to the fragile joy of life, which flashes so rare and fleeting," he added.

She looked at him, wondering if he was talking about their fragile joy on that rock in the middle of the Uva. But he didn't look at her. Instead, he lowered his head and started praying right there at the table, out loud, in Spanish. In California, being Papist didn't seem that different from being a Protestant, and Elisabeth couldn't even remember what her objection had been to that religion in the first place. Siding with Protestants had seemed so important back at the mill. Blaming the Catholic girls from Ireland for lowering mill wages made sense. Out west, there was no room for that sort of blame; things needed doing.

They ate a steak supper, and Elisabeth cut her meat into little pieces, savoring each bite. Nemacio took a knife out of his pocket, unfolded a blade from a bone handle, and polished it shiny with his kerchief. She listened as he and Nate discussed expanding the claim, diverting half the river, working the bed, then diverting it again and working the other half. It sounded like a herculean effort that would require many men and resources. She was glad to be done with the claim. She'd never go back now that Álvaro lay dead in the ground and Nemacio had rejected her so plain. She'd never go back to pretending to be a wife or waiting on love. She aimed to get away from them both. Make something of her own. Make Nemacio miss her.

As the afternoon wore on, the El Dorado filled with rowdy fellas ordering drinks and supper and playing monte. She wouldn't get drunk with them or wait around for Nemacio to pay her special attention. She craved quiet, with the solitude of her Emerson book.

"I'm done here," she said, standing up.

Nemacio stood with her to be polite, nodding cool and distant. Somehow she'd expected more from him, although she didn't know what. It's not like he owed her something. He wasn't obligated. They'd *both* stolen that loving from each other on the rock in the middle of the Uva, freely. Still, she was angry his loyalty fell with Nate and the claim. She'd thought the loving between them was special, like an invisible, magic string thrumming and vibrating, even at great distances. She thought he might take her upstairs, right in front of Nate. She was wrong. He didn't move. Instead, Nate escorted her upstairs, hobbling slow up each step. At the door, he asked to come in.

"I'd rather sleep," she said.

"I'll only take a moment," he said, crossing the threshold without her permission.

He looked around the room, entirely at ease, with a confidence and power new money brings a man. Propping his crutch against the wall, he stood on one leg, facing her, balanced new.

"I suspect you'd rather I didn't replace your wedding ring," he said.

Elisabeth wasn't sure if it was a question or a statement. She was about to ask when he presented her with a red velvet box. She opened it; inside lay a new pair of gray gloves.

"More practical," he said.

"They're lovely," she said, slipping them on. "Thank you."

"Won't you change your mind about coming back down to the claim? We can make a go of it again, you and me."

"I'm fixed on staying here."

"Awww, 'Lizbeth, won't you reconsider? You've been the perfect wife, taking care of me." He hesitated.

"You've not been the perfect husband."

"I'll try. If you gimme another chance."

"But . . . I'll never be a man, Nate," she said, quiet.

Nate took her fingers and brushed his lips along the gloves, kissing her hand with sweetness. He looked at her the same way Tom the dog had when he put his head in her lap, pleading. Her anger at him slipped away slight, replaced by a bubbling of understanding. An understanding of Nate's whole self, the fragility and the power pressing together like two sides of a liberty penny, head and tails, depending upon how it landed on any particular day. Whether she liked it or not, he remained the sum of his parts, just like her, with two sides, one shiny and one dull.

"Come back down to the cabin when you run out of money," he said, turning to leave. "Or when you want to see your Californio."

Ahh . . . so he knew.

"Goodnight, Nate," she said, closing the door, knowing she was done digging for scraps.

24

August 1851

My Dearest Friend Louisa May,

I write once again, begging you, please don't be sore at my contrary opinions about your father. I only meant to say I admired his efforts at experimental thinking, even as I understand his meager financial contributions cause you great discomfort. Perhaps I find myself jealous, as you enjoy a family, whole and together and in one place, even as the proximity strangles your sensibilities. Please forgive me and write to me soon, as I am in great need of your friendship, evermore now, as our little family on the Goodwin river claim has broken up. Álvaro has moved back to Spain, bestowing riches upon his family, with pride. His leaving feels as if the hardened scab of pain over losing Lucy has been ripped open, my insides oozing out messy. I miss the sound of beauty coming from his guitar, my world now filled with bleak silence in its place, deafening me in the void of his favor. I've no choice but to bind myself back up, wrap the festering loss under a bandage of courageous living. After all, it's not as if he's dead.

I value the importance of your friendship immeasurably, and am eternally grateful for the letters you have written, especially the last one with your Flower Fables, written as Flora Fairfield. You must know the ending poem from your Frost King fable lifts me up, with two lines in particular enlightening my spirit beyond measure. "Thus by Violet's magic power, All dark shadows passed away . . ." If only I possessed half the magic of Violet, or had help from those clever little fairies. Although I do appreciate your faith in me, and am bathed in the wonder of the glorious world you've created with trees and flowers and birds and joy. It reminds me to love my haven here, in all its wild unpredictability. No doubt, Flower Fables gives little Ellen Emerson a great joy knowing you wrote them specifically for her. Surely, the sweet girl is yet of an age to understand the true importance of literature in a woman's life. Dare I say, it is the life force that keeps us moving forward, blotting out our troubles with soothing words of imagination.

I think often of your troubles going out to service. It must've been simply dreadful, and paid only four dollars working yourself to the quick for the hardly honorable James Richardson! Obviously, the promise of employment as his poor sister's companion showed itself as a terrible ruse to harass your womanliness. Count yourself fortunate you had the wherewithal to escape without blackening the man's boots. I fear what might've befallen you succumbing to such humiliation. You must now reflect upon the whole horrible experience as a trove of material from which to write. Fodder for Flora, as one might say.

As for our situation, we've built a bookshop up in Coyoteville, named Split Rock Books and Prints, after my favorite spot along the American River. It will soon yield a tidy profit, as Split Rock Books is the only place to acquire literature in all of the placers. I plan to sell my engravings too, after improving my printing technique with diligent practice. It may seem as if I'm building a business at the ends of the earth, but Coyoteville is becoming the center of the universe with a tremendous amount of gold fueling a progressive society built on the merits of equality, effort, and ingenuity. The town draws in a spectacular collection of the most ambitious folks around America and the world looking to improve their fortunes. Despite the hordes of miners burrowing like coyotes into the banks of Deer Creek, it's the prettiest little place in the placers, with water sauntering through the town slow and predictable like a proper lady walking to church on a Sunday, and nothing at all like the wild tempest of the American down in the ravine. Perhaps by Boston standards it's not quite as sophisticated, but it vibrates with an energy I can't quite describe. Buzzing, but more. Ambitious and urgent. There are now 150 homes and businesses in the two-mile radius surrounding the town. The streets are situated like spokes of a wheel with mule trails leading up to miners' tents and cabins on seven surrounding hills, like in Rome, with aspiring names—Piety, Prospect, Boulder, Aristocracy, Lost, American, and Wet Hill. Lost Hill isn't meant to be negative, like being lost physically, but meant to imply being lost in pursuit of a new sort of living with delight. At the center of town is Luenza's El Dorado Hotel, and Split Rock Books and Prints lies up the road with a dozen other businesses: an assay office, a post office, two general stores, three blacksmiths, a wagon wheeler, two liveries, a barber, two bathhouses, a bakery, one shoemaker, two churches, eleven saloons and gambling houses, and four hotels. So you see, I'm not stuck out in the wilderness but am living in the center of new society full of possibility and potential.

Nate continues to manage our affairs down on the river claim, with Nemacio at his side as his partner. I've come to understand Nate holds a great affection for the man, which I find charming in its brotherly fraternity. Our triangle is not at all like that tragic tale of yours, The Rival Painters. Two in love with one. I am not at all the self-denying Madeline in your story, banishing my heart in work, "with a woman's strength, all thoughts of love were banished." *Rest assured, with Split Rock Books and Prints, I now live with purpose.*

Please post me in Coyoteville, as I've planted myself and intend to grow even stronger roots as I await your next letter with great expectation.

Your friend pursuing possibility in California,
EP

25

"That which we persist in doing becomes easier to do, not that the nature of the thing has changed but that our power to do it has increased."

She wasn't a liar, despite her letters to Louisa May. She simply couldn't bring herself to write down whole words of truth. Every time she picked up a pen, her wishes and dreams dripped down from her heart onto the paper. Her little fibs didn't hurt anyone, she told herself. They were simply imaginings that promoted a more positive position to her friend. She didn't want Louisa May to worry. Or say I told you so. Or think less of her. Besides, it's not like she'd actually lie to anyone when it really mattered. She knew right from wrong, and aimed to build herself up as a respectable businesswoman. Start new. Bury her affections for Nemacio in work.

For a fair price, the sawyer, Mr. Lockwood, lent one of his men to construct her a simple two-room cabin with plank walls fitted tight together and upright with a real window next to the front door and an old Alamo wood burner with a stove pipe vented up through a sugar pine shingle roof. She had the man build a solid oak floor that she polished proud with wax until it gleamed. She herself added on a little front porch, hammering rough boards over a covered entry. In a second room in back, she fashioned herself a single bed using rough pine and rope, topping it with new ticking she overstuffed with pine needles and the rabbit pelt blanket she'd made during that long winter past. Over the bed, she hung the Split Rock print as a reminder of how she'd earned her due down on the American. Underneath she stored her personals: night clothes, a new hairbrush and mirror, the gray gloves from Nate, and that tattered copy of "Self-Reliance" she'd been carrying around everywhere since leaving Concord.

With no banks yet established up in Coyoteville, she cut out a secret storage area underneath the floorboards below her bed, stashing away her savings in several tin boxes. Even so, the smithy made her two solid locks, one for the floor hatch and one for her front door, to keep her future secure. She wore the two keys on a rope around her neck, tucked inside her dress, against her skin.

Elisabeth loved her little cabin. It was small and simple but felt more light and airy than Henry's windowless place down on the river, crowded full with three men and a dog. She'd never before had her own place, and this little cabin was her very own. Not given to her by anyone. Not shared by anyone. Not owned by anyone but her. She carved a wooden sign and burnt the words—*Split Rock Books and Prints*—with a hot poker the way Nemacio had burnt the snake design onto Nate's crutch, and hammered the sign proudly above the door. Millie over at the Stamps Store lent her a ladder and a hammer but asked twenty-five cents for the nails.

"I hate to charge you, but they're hard to come by," said Millie.

"How about I make you something in exchange?"

Even with a comfortable savings, she didn't want to pay for the nails. She needed to keep frugal. The high prices of ordinary goods in California could break a person, and she didn't want to go belly up within her first year on her own, crawling back to Nate in defeat.

"Oh, fiddle. Why don't you make me any old sign or picture you want. Mr. Stamps doesn't have to know about the nails," whispered Millie, tucking them discreetly into Elisabeth's pocket.

Elisabeth didn't make Millie any ordinary sign but rather inked up another print of Split Rock instead, telling her about the special place where she'd sat many days listening to the river, drawing strength. Millie gushed over the picture, hanging it in her bedroom above the store.

Millie was a marvel, helping customers with patience alongside her husband while keeping an eye out for three-year-old Joe Junior pulling on her skirt behind the counter. Whenever Joe Junior got into something, Millie managed him without missing a beat, redirecting his attention away from the delicate or sharp objects causing offense. One time Elisabeth saw little Joe hiding high up on a top shelf in the store, blending in with the boxes. He winked down at Elisabeth, mischievous, putting a finger to his lips. When he teetered, she yelled, and little Joe Jr. jumped down into Millie's arms. Mr. Stamps gave him a swat on the bottom and scolded Millie.

"Keep an eye on him, woman," said Mr. Stamps.

Elisabeth wondered why it fell on Millie to watch the little one when both husband and wife worked equal side by side in the store. It seemed four eyes were better than two, but Mr. Stamps couldn't be bothered minding his own son while working, leaving all the responsibility to Millie. She felt grateful, at least, for not having Millie's burden.

Elisabeth got her book shipment with the help of James Porter. When he brought back several crates from Sacramento and San Francisco, she set up the books on shelves she'd fashioned from planks of wood balanced on the crates. Mr. Porter skittered around her in circles like a squirrel, watching her work.

"You need help?"

"Nope," she said, positioning each stack of books two inches apart.

"Anything I can do, say it. I'm your man," Mr. James Porter said, flinging about his hands.

She figured Mr. Porter meant something other than books, but she ignored his intentions, quite sure she could handle the advances of man like him. Wiry and quick-witted, Mr. Porter was more amusing than attractive, hiring himself out as an all-around-everything fixer in just about every enterprise in Coyoteville, from trading and banking to couriering and surveying claims, and any other matter, as long as it wasn't digging in the dirt. He wore a full brown beard with a thick, bushy mustache that clear covered his lips. She wondered how he ate clean. But under all that face hair, Mr. Porter had kind, eager eyes, and all the townsfolk relied on him as he was known as honest and earnest with concern for helping out his community. He even helped Luenza slaughter a pig when Stanley took off on another digging spree, not charging anything but a single pork supper and a few dram of whiskey.

Elisabeth finished setting up the shelves and paid Mr. Porter his ten-dollar fee plus the cost of the books. She thanked him over and over, making him feel far more necessary to her than he really was.

"You're a gem! Truly, I don't know how I could've managed without your help," she said.

Peppering him with questions about the happenings in San Francisco, she figured being in the know would help her business succeed. She listened in for clues as he rambled on about his travels in the valley.

"Sacramento flooded again," he said, standing too close.

"Terrible," she said, taking a step back to lean against the open doorframe.

Elisabeth made it clear to Mr. Porter and everyone else in town that her husband, Mr. Nathaniel Parker, worked their claim down on the North Fork of the American. She kept things cool yet sweet between all the fellas she met, including Mr. Porter. She intended to grow a respectable reputation, giving nobody reason to talk. Even so, she had an instinct that to succeed she'd have to crawl along the sharp edge of flirty modesty. She was learning how to gain respect with her intelligence and capability, yet flash bits of feminine weakness, however feigned, during moments when she needed a spot of help.

She ushered Mr. Porter out the door, saying she had to get working. He promised to come back to check on her the next day.

"Give it a week, Mr. Porter," she said, holding the door open wide. "So you'll be impressed with my progress when you come back."

She was toying around, yanking him along. No one could compete with the likes of Nemacio.

To Elisabeth's relief, her monthly bleeding arrived. She'd a been wrecked getting pregnant, seeing as how Nemacio had gone back down to the river without even saying goodbye. She was still fuming that he'd chosen Nate and the claim over her. But now she stewed in a mix of melancholy at being without him. To keep from thinking about him or her fake marriage or Álvaro dying, she dug into work. Staying up long past dark each night, she read all her new books by candlelight so she could explain the stories to customers. One Saturday, she began Brontë's *Wuthering Heights*, reading it straight through without sleeping. She couldn't understand why the story centered on revenge rather than love. Catherine clearly should've married Heathcliff, since she loved him. Marrying Edgar was only a foil because she couldn't handle Heathcliff's power over her. Obviously, it wasn't his lack of money or his lack of manners. Everything after bled revenge. Disappointed, she read it again, savoring the most romantic parts. She imagined the rest, filling in her dreams by placing herself inside the pages of the book. Sometimes she touched herself, but after Nemacio loving her on the Uva, her hands seemed a poor substitute. His loving had spun her core, tilted it right yet lopsided too. She longed for his passion again, but she knew she'd not return down to the claim, scrounging. Loneliness was her price of freedom from Nate.

That fall, her book sales started off slow. To get more folks interested in spending their gold on books, she walked around Coyoteville each morning while the miners and shopkeepers readied for the day, introducing herself and showing off her books, the same way Nate visited the boarding houses back in Lowell. All cleaned up in her pretty yellow dress and warm green eyes, she greeted the men, explaining the characters first, then the story. She soon learned there were plenty of educated fellas around the American River basin, and plenty uneducated ones, too, wanting to better themselves with opportunity not available to them back east. Once she got a customer hooked on a story, she'd tell the price, between three and five dollars for a novel. Poetry sold for little less, but a large volume like Shakespeare sold for considerably more at ten or twelve dollars. She had a generous policy of buying back the books once a customer read the novel through, but at half the price. She never lent a book, like Nate had; it wasn't practical with everyone shuffling around between town and claims at the least little rumor of a new strike.

Once she got up and going comfortable, Elisabeth sent five hundred dollars to Samuel at Amherst College overland on the Wells Fargo Stage with a letter explaining she'd settled in Coyoteville. It'd be a fortune for Samuel, compared to the money she'd sent from her millwork back in Lowell. She told him to buy their mother a new winter sweater, saying a woman wants something fine no matter where they're getting on through life. She promised to send more money soon, saying they'd expanded to book selling. She left out the parts about Nate's buggery or Henry's leaving, having no heart yet for honesty. She considered writing that Henry had died, but she couldn't bring herself to lie either, using up all her lying on letters to Louisa May. Either way, she worried Samuel might tell their mother the truth about Henry, breaking her soul complete and tipping her toward trying to do away with herself again.

Relived at no longer bellyaching for food, Elisabeth now lived quite comfortable between her book sales and savings, eating supper at the El Dorado almost every afternoon, and enjoying a hot bath once a week at Dukhart's Bathhouse, with lavender soap from France she'd bought from Millie over at the Stamps Store. Still, ambition nudged at her, and she worked at engraving. She paid Mr. Porter to get her a dozen boxes of tracing and printing paper and more ink from San Francisco. She started drawing out images with charcoal on tracing paper before carving them into wood she'd sanded over and over until smooth. Practicing and experimenting with various techniques, she daubed ink over the block and centered paper atop, even. Placing a smaller block over the paper, ink, and block, she smacked a mallet across in sections. She screwed up quite a bit, inking uneven and smushing up ugly images. But she kept at it week after week, washing her block images clean, and starting over again, all the while selling books. She wasn't discouraged, telling herself that learning wood engraving was simply another trade passing through her hands, like tending apples, working a shuttle at the loom, sewing shirts, and panning for gold. With long hours of practice, she improved, thinking her wood engravings and prints of rocks and trees and squirrels worthy of selling.

To advertise her printing services, she created a simple broadsheet printed with the words *Split Rock Book and Prints*, putting it up around town. Within a week, the advert brought in such a flood of book business that she raised her prices, asking nearly quadruple what she'd paid the publishers in New York and double what she paid

Mr. Porter. She figured it entirely fair, since she held the distinction of being the only bookseller in Coyoteville, or anywhere else in the placers besides Sacramento. And that town was still flooded. Besides, everyone else charged outrageous prices for their goods and services, why shouldn't she? Still, no one wanted to buy her pretty pictures. So she suggested to the sawyer, Mr. Lockwood, that she make him an advert in exchange for his pine scraps to make her book blocks.

"I got enough business," he said.

"You'll get more with an advert."

"Show me first, then I'll decide if a trade is fair."

Elisabeth created a simple wood engraving of the Lockwood Mill with curly flourishes, a large *L* and a saw cutting through a tree. It looked simple, but it took her nearly a week and four blocks to get the image engraved just right. Then she went through a quarter stack of paper, figuring out how get the inking even. When Elisabeth presented Mr. Lockwood with a dozen copies of her first printing, he held the sheet up, rubbing his fingers over the dried ink as if he'd never seen anything like it before.

"My own business, right here in print. It's fine, Mrs. Parker. Fine. I'll give you all my scraps."

Mr. Lockwood tacked his broadsheet up around town, spreading the word about his business and Elisabeth's woodblock engraving and printing services at the same time. Before long, customers came from mining towns all over the American River Basin for her advertisements engraved on wood and printed up. Mostly she created simple pictures with just a few words, as she found lettering the most difficult. But she created both a simple block-type style and another flourishing style, each kept on tracing paper and extra blocks for new projects.

Consumed by long days of selling and engraving and books, Elisabeth sometimes went two whole days without aching for Nemacio. She pushed the dull disquiet into the distant corners of her bones, striving to secure her own slice of happiness. She enjoyed suppering with Luenza, who'd sent all the way from England for a proper nanny to mind her three boys, teaching them to read and write, and keeping them safe so she could attend to her hotel and restaurant. A rich woman by any standard, Luenza acted as the honorary mayoress of sorts, holding court at the El Dorado, offering up opinions about all the coming and goings of the growing town, and earning a reputation as a generous, heavy-hearted woman who spoke her mind, taking liberties, and never asking permission from anyone, least of all a man. She even kept a drove of filthy hogs out back in a big pen, being no law against holding pigs in town. Besides, Luenza knew how to set a perfect table, complete with succulent ham slices, so no one dared complain about her or the hogs.

Elisabeth learned from Luenza, watching how she spoke to customers, ordered her bar men around, and walked with a sure, heavy-footed stride. Her tone alone made men step in line.

"How do you get 'em to respect you?" Elisabeth asked.

"Run your business honest and respect yourself. Then everybody else will too," said Luenza said, pulling out her logbook.

She showed Elisabeth how to tally up her sales and expenses, and told her not to let anyone cheat her.

"And don't give the lookers a discount. You'll be sorry for it later," she added.

Luenza didn't seem worse off without Stanley, who stayed down in the diggings most days now, even though he still hadn't found any gold.

"He's just grubbing down there. I don't know why he even bothers, when he can have all this," she said, sweeping her hand around the main dining room of the El Dorado. "Don't even know what a husband is good for anymore."

Elisabeth was touched when Luenza gave her a valuable oil lamp as gift for no occasion at all, saying it'd come in handy during the long winter nights ahead. It reminded her of when Álvaro brought a lamp to their river cabin that past winter.

Luenza introduced Elisabeth to Ginny O'Rourke, a woman running a pie shop out of a tent up on Prospect Hill. Coming up toward Ginny's Place, the smell of warm baked apples flooded Elisabeth with memories of her mother and the apple orchard, and her legs nearly gave way right there in the middle of Coyoteville. She leaned on Luenza for support.

"You all right?" Luenza asked.

"Mmmm hmmm," she said, nodding.

Ginny O'Rourke sat in front of an open fire with her legs propped up on a stool, her face white as a cloud, with bright orange freckles scattered uneven. Her cheeks puckered up severe, like she'd eaten a sour lemon. She wore a shock of stringy red hair, and a navy skirt and a clean blouse, pressed crisp.

"Now we got a regular tea party," said Ginny.

She grinned, and her pucker face gave way to a mouth with a large gap from a missing front tooth. Elisabeth wondered what befell the woman to lose it.

"Gotta get supper ready. The men'll be coming in from the diggings soon. I'm just here to make introductions," said Luenza.

"I already heard about the book lady in town," said Ginny with a thick Irish tongue.

"Good things, I hope," said Elisabeth.

Ginny shrugged.

"You here for a slice?"

"I can never say no to pie," said Luenza.

Luenza handed Ginny a few coins and grabbed the pie with her bare hands, then walked back down to the El Dorado taking big bites of warm apples, yelling back over her shoulder.

"Be nice, Ginny!"

"You want some pie?" Ginny asked Elisabeth.

Even though she could afford a slice, Elisabeth wasn't about to bleed her savings out on luxuries like pie. Denying herself seemed the right thing, for now.

"No. Thank you. I can't afford to waste my money," she said.

"Pie is never a waste, is what I say. Although it looks to me like you can't afford a full dress either," said Ginny, looking her up and down.

"No need to insult me," said Elisabeth.

"Seems you're the one's insulting my pie," said Ginny.

"My dress might look silly to you, but I'll have it easier than you walking the muddy streets come this winter with it hemmed above my ankles," said Elisabeth.

"Don't twist your britches. I'm just telling it like it is," said Ginny.

"You're just telling it like you see it, without knowing, is all. I don't have the patience for you," said Elisabeth, turning to leave.

"Don't be so quick. I'm only funnin'. I don't mean nothing by it.

A few months back, I looked like you, skin and bones in an old dress."

"This is a new dress!"

"Now I've got the money for three skirts and two blouses, and filled out nice," Ginny continued, slapping her thigh. "Baking over a thousand pies a month. Can you believe it?"

No. Elisabeth could not.

"I drag my own wood off the mountain and chop it myself, never having so much as a man to take a step for me in this country. Making fruit pies and coffee, is what I do. I also got a plan for milk. I'm thinking a dollar a pint. But that bloody cow is slow getting here on account of that damn flood down in Sacramento."

"Do you read?" Elisabeth asked.

"Of course I can read."

Elisabeth ran to her store and came back with *A Modest Proposal* by Jonathan Swift.

"An Irishman!" Ginny said, sighing heavy and wiping her eyes with the back of her sleeve.

"You can keep the book if you'll give me a whole pie. And coffee."

Ginny flipped through the pages faster than Elisabeth thought her capable.

"That's a good deal, I'll have you know," said Elisabeth.

"Shh! Be quiet, I'm reading," said Ginny.

Elisabeth poured herself a cup of coffee and sat down in the chair next to Ginny. Then she helped herself to a whole pie, digging in with a fork without even cutting it, savoring the taste of home.

After a rocky start, Elisabeth struck up an unlikely friendship with the Irishwoman. Conversations between the women always grew spirited, with Ginny poking until her Irish humor got rolling with fun and Elisabeth lightened up. She realized if Ginny didn't poke fun at you, then she didn't care much for you, either.

Keeping company with Luenza and Ginny and Millie staved off her loneliness for Nemacio, and she suggested they all meet at sunup each morning for coffee and pie. She didn't go in for prattling meaningless gossip like her mother had with the neighbor ladies back in Concord; she wanted to hear about their businesses. Learn something. Millie agreed, telling Mr. Stamps Joe Junior needed an early morning constitutional to let off of his energy before the store opened. Millie dropped him off with the Wilton boys and their fancy English nanny so she could catch a breather from all the 'round the clock working and mothering. During their morning business meetings the women talked about their weekly profits and what the mule trains brought up into the foothills and what the miners were looking to buy. They shared news of strikes they'd gotten word of so they could keep up with their own supplies based on how much might be weighing down the miners' pockets that week.

"It's all the same whether it's pie or pork or nails or books," said Luenza. "We sell what those miners need and miss terrible. If we remind them of home, they'll empty their pockets."

They discussed equal rights for women set out in the California Constitution, and exactly what it meant for them.

"There's a motive for men protecting the rights of women," said Ginny.

"What's that?" asked Millie.

"I heard it said a man name Halleck called upon all the bachelors at the convention to vote for our rights. Saying they could offer no greater inducement for women of fortune to come to California. They want wives," said Ginny.

"Well, I can't see how that helps me," said Millie. "Seeing as I've already got Mr. Stamps."

"It helps you, all right," said Luenza. "For one, Mr. Stamps can't go selling the store without your signature. And if you decide to leave him, on account some bad behavior he ain't done yet, he can't take Joe Junior away from you."

"What?" Millie held her hand to her heart, shocked.

"It gives you options, Millie. If he treats you side-a-ways," said Ginny.

"I'd never leave my husband. I love him," said Millie.

"Well, you can use divorce as a threat . . . to keep him in line," said Ginny.

Elisabeth listened, thinking if there'd been equal rights in Massachusetts Henry wouldn't have been able to mortgage their family farm like he did, borrowing and borrowing until the bank took the lot of it, leaving Mother with nothing. Not without her mother's signing on to his scheme. As it was, her mother had only been allowed to conduct orchard business while Henry traveled; she'd had no power to stop him from selling the land out from under them.

During those early days in Coyoteville, Elisabeth concentrated on building up her business without taking much relaxation. One evening, Ginny came knocking on Elisabeth's cabin, saying she'd heard of an exciting bear baiting.

"With that baby bear. You killed its mama, right?"

Putting on the gloves Nate had given her, she followed Ginny to the ring. Seeing the little bear struggle against the rope tied around its neck to a post in the center of a ring, she realized her mistake in coming. Men placed bets and yelled and drank and spat in the dirt, frothing for a fight, as a group of ladies sat along the far side of the ring, posing luscious in fine red silk and low-cut bodices with breasts popping out. Luenza had told her a few ladies of the line were now working down the street at the Nugget House. They acted haughty like that gypsy woman dancing back at the claim, only raunchier. One lady put her leg up on the rail, and her skirt slid up her thigh, revealing a light blue garter; she was acting hardly a lady. Another flung her black feather scarf 'round and 'round above her head while whooping along with the men. The whole affair smelled savage and dirty and wrong, like Nate dancing with the lady-man at the Fandango.

One man shoved a huge dog twice the size of Tom into the ring with the little bear. The dog barked and nipped at little bear's behind as it refused to fight, cowering up against the post and crying like that afternoon on the trail when it'd curled up with its dead mama. Someone jumped over the fence and let the little bear loose in the ring, prodding it with an iron rod. The men hollered and laughed. Another man led a full-grown bull in the ring. Seeing himself outnumbered, the little bear tried to climb over the fence, but the men pushed him back with sticks to face both the dog and the bull. When the bull horned little bear in the rump, making him screech something horrible, a mix of images flew around in Elisabeth's head. The mama bear. Álvaro ripped up. Nate flopping around on one leg. The panther. The gypsy moaning lusty inside her tent. Nemacio sucking her tears and breasts, ripping her soul open. She fled, leaving Ginny and the bear ring behind, running away, until her lungs burned and she slowed to a walk in a fit of cold coughing. Feeling sorely alone, she stumbled and huffed as she meandered through miner tents up toward the graveyard on the hill, collecting the last fall blooms of mini lupine in the moonlight. A few grave mounds were marked with headstones, but Álvaro's grave had only a wooden cross, tipped a little to the left. She straightened it, placing the lupines atop the mound. She sat in the cool lump of dirt, running her hands along bits of virgin grass poking up through Álvaro's grave, humming "Malagueña." Remembering.

Before that moment of loving in the middle of the Uva, she'd resigned herself to being stuck in a false marriage. She'd been so naive. After tasting real love, she'd never be satisfied. Now she understood. Even with her business, her friendships, her slice of life up on that hill. It wasn't enough. What a fool she'd been.

An ant crawled up her boot, and she lifted the little creature onto her finger, studying it careful as it led with its tiny antennae, searching. A sadness slipped over her, and she placed the ant back on a blade of grass. It crawled away in the moonlight, relieved at not being crushed. She felt just like the ant, reaching out in the ever-elusive fog of being a woman, relieved at getting through another day without being crushed under waves of sore tragedies flowing on the tides of living without love.

26

"Welcome evermore to gods and men is the self-helping man. For him all doors are flung wide."

E lisabeth convinced herself he'd come back. Come see her prog-ress with Split Rock Books and Prints. As a friend, if not a lover. She waited, drifting into the white haze of winter, wondering what kept him away. She almost went manic with want and the lack of loving, reliving that afternoon on the rock over and over when they'd moved together in love and he'd made her feel whole. She tried to forget, and help herself. She tried to concentrate on her work. Tried to push away thoughts of him. Of his loving. She poked maniacal on her temple like a crazy woman, feeling like a fool. Feeling like he'd ripped something vital out of her gut.

She pulled herself together as best she could and hunkered down during the day, losing herself in selling books and engraving new blocks until she could almost forget the loving ever happened. Con-sumed, she cut block after block with lines and more lines, until she blistered up the sides of her finger from holding the bruin too tight carving adverts for customers. Her fingers blackened ugly with ink, but she didn't care. She stashed away her hard-won earnings in the locked box under the floorboards in her back bedroom like a greedy mouse. She engraved pretty pictures of trees and rocks and flowers, and printed them up in simple blues and greens. Sometimes, she sold one. But her profits were mostly from the books and adverts.

At night, sleep couldn't lie. Nemacio came to her in dreams, and she relived their loving all over. She agonized for his hands on her. He'd become her river, flowing through her blood, essential and pulsing. He'd become her religion. She prayed to him. Prayed he'd return. Prayed she could once again worship his flesh. With fervor over her new denomination, she continued to follow his false faith, blinded from reason. In her dreams, she waited.

Thankfully, her women friends kept her from feeling so alone. She relished the morning coffee ritual at Ginny's pie shop, sharing stories and business tips. She'd taken to adding a drop of whiskey to her coffee to loosen her nerves and clear the cobwebs taking up residence in her heart after a rough night of bad dreams. A morning medicinal, she told herself, convinced the cup helped hide her want. Helped steel her for another day without Nemacio. Helped her dribble her soul back into work. Luenza and Mille and Ginny didn't bat an eye at her medicinal, knowing getting started from nothing wasn't easy for anyone in California, man or woman. She never leaned on her friends too hard. Never told them of Nemacio or her tragic family, out of fear of letting loose a ridiculous display of woman tears. And she didn't want them thinking less of her. Didn't want them knowing the truth: that she might really be just a weak woman, with too little virtue.

During the winter of 1852, Coyoteville burst open with a ruckus, riddled with thieves and shady characters crazed through by hard living in the diggings. A protective organization formed, headed by Moses F. Boyt. Vigilantes combed the muddy streets looking for signs of trouble when robberies flared up. One man named Bobby Barrett, starved mad, stole $357 in dust and coins from Arlo Corbyn's tent. The vigilantes found Bobby lying naked with a lady at the Nugget, the stolen money stuffed in a bag under the bed. A miner's court found him guilty, doling out a whipping as punishment. A fellow miner laid the stripes on unmerciful while Arlo watched, poor Bobby Barrett howling high for the whole town to hear. Two days later that stupid

Bobby Barrett stole again, in the middle of the night slipping two pies off Ginny and the cow she'd finally purchased. The night patrol caught him soothing his bloody wounds in the bathhouse, with the damn cow tied up outside. This time the protective organization erected gallows, dispatching poor unfortunate Bobby in the presence of a large concourse of townsfolk.

Ginny went to the hanging, but Elisabeth didn't, hating the ugliness of it. When she passed the gallows on her weekly visit to Álvaro's grave, she thought she might get sick right there in the street. She didn't look up, walking back to her shop fast. After the hanging incident, there wasn't any more thieving going on. Even so, she took to sleeping with her Hawken, loaded.

Word floated around town about a few men having gone so insane as to hang their own selves without the help of gallows. Ginny heard old Gerald Farmer strung a rope over a pine branch himself, then climbed up the tree and jumped down to end his misery. Another man called Square Sam shot himself in the face with a twelve-gauge double barrel shotgun behind the El Dorado privy, leaving Luenza an awful bloody mess splattered all over her whitewash paint. Square Sam doing away with himself made her think of her mother. She struggled to understand the sort of pain that could bring a person to such despair. She missed Nemacio terrible; his lack of loving ripped a jagged hole through her middle. Even so, she wouldn't end her living because of it.

The townsfolk finally agreed it unseemly for the town to still be called Coyoteville, after men digging like coyotes. Wanting to create a more sophisticated impression, they renamed it Manzanita City, after the Spanish name for all the little apple-like fruit on the red bushes covering surrounding hills. Giving the town a Spanish name slapped Elisabeth as a cruel irony, as the town assayer still refused to record Nemacio's name on the Goodwin Claim for sounding too foreign.

That winter in Manzanita City came on mild, and Elisabeth found herself wholly prepared for the unpredictable fluctuations of cold and snow and sunshine and rain of a California winter. She settled into engraving when heavy snow fell, and opened up shop when snow melted clear away the very next day under the warm winter sunshine. Mr. Porter became an amusing distraction from

Nemacio. He continued to stop by her shop regular, checking in on her throughout the winter. He brought her treasures he picked up in San Francisco that he wouldn't let her pay for, like a piece of chocolate or a vial of fancy French perfume. She led him on, giggling silly and touching him lightly on the arm, hoping he'd keep coming. She liked getting any attention from a man, even though she wasn't in the least bit drawn in by him with lusty pull. He was harmless, and simply ordinary compared to Nemacio. One afternoon, Mr. Porter came in, wanting a broadsheet to advertise a mine he bought.

"You're a digger now? I thought you didn't like getting dirty," she said, wiping her inky hands on her apron.

"My partner Drew Mack does the digging. I stick to management," he said, fingering a stack of botanical prints set out on the front shelf. "I don't need nothing fancy printed up. Just a simple picture showing a hole in the ground that's big and wide and deep."

"How many you want printed up?"

"Maybe a couple dozen adverts to gain some investment interest around here, and in Sacramento and San Francisco. Maybe even in the East. The Porter Mine's gonna pay off, over a hundred pounds in gold."

"A hundred pounds! You're fooling," she said.

She put a hand on her side and stuck her hip out pretty, and he noticed, looking at her closer.

"Maybe thousands. You interested?"

"Maybe. How much have you got so far?"

"Oh, I got plenty," said Mr. Porter, winking. "You want in?"

Elisabeth knew he wasn't talking about the gold anymore, but she didn't let on, ignoring his amateur advances. She wanted to play out the situation, see what she might gain from dragging out his affections.

"I've got plenty of my own, Mr. Porter."

"Ahhh. It's not what you've got now but what you could have. It's all in the prospects," he said, holding his arms open wide as if to advertise himself.

"Where's the claim?"

"It's over near Hangtown, east of Dry Diggins. You know the area?"

"No."

"Well you will, Mrs. Parker. You will. It will be raining gold off that dry gulch any day now. Like Ophir Hill. I simply need more funds to dig deeper. If I sell stock, that'll give me what I need to go bigger with my operation."

"Perhaps I should visit the claim first," she said, pressing him.

"What's to see? It's only a hole now. But it's all in the potential. Make the advert look good. Mention the depth. The yield. The potential. Print me up some stock certificates too. Simple ones, with a border, and maybe add a letter P to match the advert. For Porter."

"I only do simple printing."

"I don't need nothing fancy. And I want to buy the blocks after."

She wasn't comfortable selling her original blocks. They held enormous value to her, and she stored them on shelves in her back bedroom, categorized and labeled for when customers wanted more broadsheets printed.

"It's all about the deep hard rock mining now," he continued. "The rivers will be washed out soon. Some say they already are. The gold is still in there, but you gotta dig down deeper to get at it."

Concerned about Nate and Nemacio, and her share of their claim, Elisabeth hoped talk of the rivers being all dried up was only a rumor.

"How much for a one percent share?"

Mr. Porter explained his calculations were complicated, based on the most conservative prediction of gold yields. He set the value based on the depth, surrounding rock, water supply, and the estimated number of months he figured it'd take to bring up the pay dirt.

"The first twenty-five shares at ten dollars each. I won't offer stock in more than a quarter of the mine's worth. That's plain bad business, if you know what I mean."

"Oh, I do. I do," she said, egging him on for more information.

"Once word gets out, I'll offer buy-ins on the next twenty-five shares. Of course, those will cost more than the first shares. As the payload comes out and the value in the mine rises, so will the share value of early investors. So you need to add a line on the certificate so I can fill in the price. The stock price fluctuates, you understand?" he asked.

"I think so," she said, acting like she didn't quite, even though she understood completely.

She realized that investing in mining shares might be the ideal way to profit off the gold frenzy without digging herself. She wanted in but didn't yet let on to Mr. Porter.

"The Porter Company Mine shares are backed by John Langley, the proprietor of the Pioneer Bank and Trust in San Francisco. Put his name on the certificate so investors will know who to contact for dividends once the gold starts comin' up."

"I normally charge twenty dollars for a woodcut, and an additional fifty cents per printing. I never sell my original blocks," she said, flapping her eyelashes, waiting for her value to sink in with Mr. Porter.

"I see," said Mr. Porter.

He took her hand in his sweaty palm and looked into her face, serious.

"I'm going big, Mrs. Parker. You want in?"

"Well, that depends," she said, using her most seductive voice. "On what you're offering."

Mr. Porter turned her hand over, kissing the back of her hand. "You know."

"I might be willing to take fees off the top in exchange for the first shares," she said, ignoring his advances.

"Brilliant suggestion," he agreed.

"Say the first five shares in exchange for both the broadsheets and stock certificates," she said.

"That's a fifty-dollar value! I'd be giving up five percent shares, right off. "

"If you'd rather not work with me, you can go elsewhere, Mr. Porter," she said, letting go of his hand.

"No, no. I want you. We have a deal," he said.

They shook hands on the arrangement and Mr. Porter pulled her in close, kissing her sloppy and squeezing her bottom awkward through her dress with no romance whatsoever. She didn't back away, instead measured his affection, finding his touch meager in comparison to Nemacio and feeling nothing more than amusement. Pulling away, she acted shocked.

"Mr. Porter, your manners! I thought we were making a business partnership."

"You know we were talking about more."

"I did not!" Elisabeth said, playing up the drama. "What sort of a woman do you think I am, for heaven's sake? I'm married! What would Mr. Parker say about all this?"

"I thought . . ."

"Not to worry. I won't tell Mr. Parker a thing. It'll be our little secret," she said, pushing him in the shoulder playful. "Now get out of here so I can get to work. The sooner I finish, the sooner you can sell your shares."

"I'll be at El Dorado," he said, walking out of her shop with a vexed expression.

Elisabeth put off all of her other engravings to work on Mr. Porter's broadsheet and mining certificates. She kept them both simple and uniform with formal, bold lettering stating: *The Porter Company Mine.* The broadsheet advert was larger and included Mr. Porter's name and the address at the El Dorado, with a likeness of a gold nugget. The certificate had a simple scalloped border running around the edges like on the broadsheet and listed the Pioneer Bank and Trust in San Francisco. She left a blank line where Mr. Porter could fill in the sum of 1 percent share at ten dollars to be claimed upon receipt at the bank. She kept her five certificates in a wooden box under her bed, knowing trading in mining shares might be her ticket to something more.

27

*"I ought to go upright and vital,
and speak the rude truth in all ways."*

———~~~———

E ngraving on her front porch in the crisp winter sunshine, Elisabeth looked up to see Nate coming up the hill, sitting atop a
mule, pulled along by a much younger man with bushy hair and a
heavy brow. She put down her graver and stashed the woodblock
under a table, not wanting him to know. She'd been trading her
printing services in exchange for shares in three mines so far, and she
wasn't up for hearing his opinion on the schemes. Her fingers looked
nicked up and blackened as usual, but she made no attempt to hide
her hands, standing up and smoothing her dress and straightening
her hair, out of habit. She knew Nate didn't find her attractive no
matter what kind of pretty she looked.

The man helped Nate off the mule, and she saw him still using
the snake crutch Nemacio had made. He didn't lean hard on it like
she remembered, instead holding it by his side like he had two legs,
standing taller and more assured. He looked handsome, and she was
surprised at feeling glad to see him. When the man's hand lingered
on Nate's shoulder, she knew straightaway. They were lovers.

"Nate," she said, standing solid, with her hands by her sides.

"Mrs. Elisabeth Parker," he said, grabbing her by the shoulders, affectionate.

Nate introduced the man as Francis, who nodded cold. Francis stayed outside holding the mule impatient while Nate came inside. She left the door propped open with a wood stopper.

"Would you look at this," said Nate, glancing around. He picked up a book, thumbing through the pages. "Quite an operation you've got going here, Mrs. Parker. Everyone down on the river is talking about it. Split Rock Books and Print run by that literary lady up in Manzanita Town."

"Quite a few folks around here like to read," she said.

"I brag you're my wife."

"I'll bet you do."

She spoke with more sarcasm than she'd meant. There was no more need to be mean, she told herself.

"I hear you take books back for half the price."

"I'm not running things like your business back in Lowell. I only sell books, not lend."

"Maybe I should join in as your partner."

"I don't need a partner," she said, serious.

"Oh, 'Lizbeth. Can't you take a joke?"

She didn't answer and he moved off the matter, sharing news of their claim, saying they'd diverted one side of the river while still working on the quartz vein near Split Rock.

"I hear the river's played out," she said.

"Not at the Goodwin Claim," he said.

"Word is that going deep pays off," she said.

"Deep? We've collected over two thousand with simple pickaxing and sluicing," he said, handing her a pouch. "I'm giving you 450. In a mix of coins and bills."

She raised an eyebrow.

"I know. I know. It's far less than what we pulled out last summer. But that's your share, after expenses. Split between you, me, and Nemacio, like we all agreed. It's fair. I pay Francis only ten dollars a day, as my employee."

"He's your *employee*?"

"As it is, I'm eating those expenses, and for two other men we brought on. Brothers from Missouri. We've quite an operation going on down there now."

Francis poked his head in the doorway.

"You finished yet?"

"Gimme a minute," said Nate.

Francis spit a glob of chewing tobacco on the front porch.

"Don't spit there!" Elisabeth yelled. "Jeezus! Don't you have any manners?"

"Missed," said Francis, shrugging his shoulders.

"Go water Bessie in the creek," said Nate.

Nate bent down and removed the stopper. The door swung shut with a slam. Elisabeth folded her arms across her chest.

"Nemacio's uncle mailed him a citizenship document, but the assayer still refused it, saying it needed certifying by proper authorities. Wouldn't identify the proper authorities. I'm up in town posting another letter to his uncle asking more advice."

"For God's sake, he was born here!"

"We'd give up twenty dollars a month in foreign tax putting his name on the title with ours. Nemacio isn't pleased, I tell you. Complains about needing more money. "

"Seems like putting his name on the claim is worth twenty a month," she said, counting the money and handing half back to Nate.

He put his hands behind his back.

"You really want to give up your money for him?"

"You *both* need it right now more than I do," she said.

She remembered last winter down on river with too little food, even with Álvaro's monte winnings, and shoved the bills and coins back at him.

"I won't take it," he said.

"Oh, don't be ridiculous! You can see I'm living comfortable up here. You got to stock up on food stores."

Nate looked at the floor, thinking for a while. Then, he grabbed the money, tucking the coins and bills back into his vest pocket.

"You seen him?" Nate asked.

"No."

"He lays off the digging for days on end. Tramps around to who knows where. I figured he was coming up here to see you."

"Haven't seen him since I left the claim."

"I can't complain. When he's around, the man's a force. He added another room onto the cabin. Built a set of bunk beds. Dug us a new outhouse further back. Works like three men. But truth be told, he's downright dour. Missing Álvaro, I suspect. Sulks something awful. Says he's grubbing in the dirt for nothing. He thinks the work is beneath him."

She held back a smile, secretly pleased at hearing Nemacio was hurting. She'd never let Nate know how much she missed Nemacio, and how she worked herself into a stupor hoping to forget.

"Do you get lonely up here?" Nate asked.

"A bit."

"Do you miss me?"

Elisabeth tucked a strand of hair behind her ear.

"Listen, Nate. I get along fine with our arrangement. I don't need you or Nemacio watching over me."

"We got some marriage, huh? Like business partners, splitting up the claim. Carrying on formal."

What did he expect? Did he still want her down in the diggings, getting grimy for him, waiting on him like a scullery maid? She stayed quiet. He shifted his one boot. The floorboard squeaked, crackling through the thick silence.

"Not what I'd imagined when we married back in Lowell."

"Not what I imagined, either," she said.

Nate's face fell soft, his eyes pleading like Tom the dog. Genuine and bewildered. Like he searched for a softer understanding between them.

"You take no blame in the matter," he said.

She hadn't been so sure but finally settled on them never finding a way back to each other as a real husband and wife.

"I shoulder the burden, entirely," he said.

Elisabeth stayed quiet, waiting on him to continue, and his lips stretched thin like he held the words back, as if letting them fly out of his mouth might poison the air and sicken them both.

"It rests all on me," he said.

"How'd you know? I mean to ask, how'd you know for sure?" she asked.

"If a man can't share loving with a splendid woman like you. Well . . . I know, 'Lizbeth. I know for sure."

"There's nothing to be done? Nothing I could've done?"

"You've been a model wife. A woman of honor. There's no fixing it. God knows I tried. Damn it all, I married you, didn't I?"

"You were a fool to marry a woman," she said.

She spoke with honesty, thinking it might prompt him to do the same. She didn't mean to be unkind and hated herself for all the times she'd acted nasty to him.

"I wanted to be normal," he said.

Elisabeth wondered what *normal* meant out here, with everything flipped topsy-turvy. She didn't live normal either. Up in town, alone. A married woman, pining away for a Californio. Running her own business. Managing her affairs without the help of a man. They'd all ventured into the edges of the unknown, forced to rejigger themselves or fail spectacular. California was no place for narrow-minded ninnies, that's for sure. Only the folks with superb confidence and magnificent daring would make it.

"You did me wrong," she said.

"I see that now. See the truth of it. I'm getting to know myself out here."

What a luxury. Being a man. Getting to know yourself. Even so, she saw his torment was altogether different from her loneliness and loss. Much harder, with more jagged edges scratching at his soul. She felt sorry for him and found gratitude in his honesty, even now.

"I've ruined you," he said.

"I am *not* ruined."

His eyes welled up, and she hoped to heaven he wasn't going to cry standing right there in her shop. Luckily, the door opened, and Nate turned around, pulling a kerchief out of his pocket to blow his nose, collect himself.

"Welcome, gentlemen," she said, relieved at the two customers.

She went to work, eager to show him she wasn't ruined. She perked up. Smiled. Asked the fellas about themselves, looking direct at them. Nodding confident. Listening careful so she might suggest the right book to pique an interest.

"Crikey, I'm needing a spot of home," said one man. "Something to read so I don't turn barmy."

She detected a bit of an English accent in his voice, buried underneath growing up in the East with immigrant parents. She'd sold her last copy of *Oliver Twist* the day before, so she picked up an illustrated copy of *A Christmas Carol*.

"Dickens," she said.

She opened the book to a vibrant illustration of Mr. Fezziwig's Ball with folks dancing happy and kissing under the mistletoe. The man peered down at the book.

"This one's special. With spectacular illustrations by John Leech. Go on," she said, handing over the book.

The man looked down at the red cloth book with gilt-edged pages, hesitating.

"I shouldn't touch it," he said, holding out his grubby hands.

"It's meant for touching," she said, thrusting the book into his hands. She knew once a man held a book, he felt a sense of ownership. The other man spoke up.

"I don't want to read about a fancy ball, Jake," he said, drawing out the word *ball*, sounding like *bawl*, like a native New Yorker.

Elisabeth didn't let Jake answer.

"Don't misunderstand, gentlemen. This story isn't all sweet cream, believe me. It's a ghost story. Creepy. Gripping. Filled with hauntings of regret. And the salvation of redemption."

Her description hooked Jake, who closed the book with a start.

"I'm sold," he said, handing over twelve dollars.

As they turned to go, she picked up *The Last of the Mohicans* and held it out for Jake's friend.

"This one's an adventure," she said.

"No, thanks. I got plenty of adventure just living out here," he said, holding up a flat hand.

"This one is set in the East. In New York," she said, thinking that might hook him. "In the Adirondacks."

She had no idea if the book was actually set in the Adirondacks, but the passages describing the nature seemed like the East, somewhere, with its thick forests of evergreens and hardwood mixed with heavy undergrowth and swamps and ponds and brown rocky escarpments. It could be set in New York. Close enough, anyway. She knew the wordy passages would be hard for the man to slog through, but he'd not admit his trouble reading to a woman. She knew men didn't admit ignorance willingly.

"It's a story with grand battles with glorious descriptions," she said. "And a woman fending off an Indian," she said.

The man took the book, scanning the pages.

"Her name is Cora," she said.

She waited beside him quiet now, giving the man the space to think about home and the woman, Cora. Nate was leaning up against the wall, watching. Tapping his snake crutch on the floorboards. Growing impatient, he interrupted the man's thinking, picking a stack of books off the shelf nearest him.

"Get on with it, why don't you. The lady's gotta help me load up a box of books in my saddlebags," said Nate, pointing out his missing leg.

His urgency helped the man decide, and he, too, handed over twelve dollars. Elisabeth pocketed the money, all twisted up and deflated by Nate's meddling. She hadn't needed his help. She knew the man was going to buy the book, and she wanted to prove how she got along fine without him and without Nemacio.

When the customers left, Nate placed the books back on the shelf, just the way Elisabeth had organized them.

"I should demand a commission," he said.

She flashed a tight grin at the joke, tamping down her irritation. Nate crutched over and handed her a scroll.

"Nemacio found this under the bed when he added onto the cabin. He thought you'd appreciate having it."

She unrolled the paper while Nate held onto one corner. It was the picture Henry had printed of the orchard back in Concord. She fingered the trees and the apples, which looked cruder than she remembered. Her woodcut prints were far better than this one. She looked up and he smiled, and for a moment, they stayed like that, each holding an end of her father's picture, an invisible marital thread still connecting them.

"Thank you," she said, pulling the paper away from him.

"Now, what do you suggest for me?" Nate asked, turning toward the bookshelves and tapping his fingers together eager.

She explained the newer books, some of which he knew and some he didn't. He asked about each one. The quality of the story. The writing. As she explained, he listened with respect.

Elisabeth handed him *The Pathfinder*, the James Cooper novel.

"It's the sequel to *The Last of the Mohicans*. A tale of greed, civilized and otherwise. With that Natty Bumppo character you liked so much. But this one features a woman on the frontier," she said.

Nate thumbed through the pages, reading silent to himself while leaning on his crutch.

"Marvelous," he said. "You know me well, 'Lizbeth. Too well."

Nate tucked the book under his arm, and Elisabeth walked him outside. The winter sun stretched bright and dazzling. Squinting, Elisabeth handed Nate another book.

"Give this to Nemacio," she said, thinking maybe a gift might entice him to come visit.

"Ahh, *Wuthering Heights*. Just the thing to stop the sulking of the privileged don. He'll appreciate a novel of revenge and rejection," said Nate, winking. "And the confines of class."

Nate whistled loud for Francis, who sauntered over to boost Nate up atop the mule. They said polite, stilted goodbyes, and she leaned up against her porch post watching Francis lead her husband down to the river claim. The mule stole a nip of tobacco from Francis's back pocket without his notice, and she laughed out loud as a puffy cloud drizzled gray in front of the sun. She ripped up the apple orchard print, tossing those last little pieces of her father into the growling wind. Her heart pounded lighter knowing she was no longer that helpless girl waiting around for a man to fix things right.

28

"Yes, but I cannot sell my liberty and
my power, to save their sensibility."

When Nemacio didn't visit to thank her for the book, Elisabeth grew sour with a bitter resentment at all the other men who came instead, messing up that sweet little hilltop town something awful. The air smelled rancid to her now, like Manzanita City was in the midst of a grand drunk losing itself sloppy. She hated the constant raucous commotion made by over ten thousand men crawling in and around the town, stumbling, searching, hacking, picking, digging, scooping, and washing, looking like hungry animals frozen from wallowing in mud, and exhausted, vexing with equal parts determination and discontent. They disgusted her, frittering away their newfound fortune, eating and drinking and gambling in the company of ladies of the line. One stupid digger even burned down his tent, barely escaping with his life, when his campfire embers jumped to the canvas. The man staggered out, coughing up smoke just as his tent lit up like a tinderbox. Fortunately, his more sober friends ran back and forth to the creek with buckets of water just in time to stop the fire from spreading to their own tents and the whole town.

When a gust blew the wrong way, a horrid stench from too many shallow outhouse pits blasted around. At night, the gunshots turned comical. If one man shot at a coyote prowling around, twenty more idiots started shooting at nothing in the dark. She never knew if the trouble came from the vigilantes or criminals.

Luckily, hoards of customers came into her shop looking for books to pass the long winter nights. A few asked about trading printing services for mining certificates, but she only worked with the six customers who banked with John Langley at the Pioneer Bank and Trust in San Francisco after learning about his honest reputation. Many of the other men looking for mining certificates seemed shady, claiming they'd held shares in their name alone. She refused to trade certificates for those shares, charging them full price instead.

Trading for mining shares might've been gambling, but she had nothing to lose speculating with her own labor. If she remained patient, the shares might pay out handsome. Those men had planted a crop of stock certificates, and everyone, including her, waited breathless for them to grow. To her astonishment, grow they did. Investors in Sacramento and San Francisco, and even from back east, wanted a piece of the deep mines, buying up shares sight unseen, based on descriptions in her broadsheets. She followed the values of her mining stock prices in the *Placer Journal* and watched that tidy stack of mining certificates stashed under her floorboards increase in value by the week. The Porter Company Mine had gone up in value from ten to fifty dollars each, which meant the value of her twenty-five shares were now at $1,250! It wasn't even a quarter of what Luenza earned in one night of feeding miners at the El Dorado, but it was all profit since Elisabeth's only capital investment was in the paper and ink supplies to print up the original certificates and broadsheets for Mr. Porter, which cost much less than a chicken dinner. The opportunity to make something out of nothing in California was astonishing. With this much value, she'd need to eventually put her certificates, along with her savings, in a proper bank down in Sacramento.

Even with all her business success, the heavy snow draped a blanket of sadness over Elisabeth when she finally got a letter from Samuel, saying he was grateful for the money she'd sent over the past year and asking forgiveness for not writing sooner. Saying he'd been suffering from a heap of sorrow, with no words to tell of it. Gwen had finally done it. She'd killed herself, yelling "Henry, Henry, Henry," running full speed at a window three stories up at the Worcester Asylum, breaking through and falling down onto the grass below. The doctors wouldn't let Samuel see her body, with her face and neck and arms torn up terrible by shards of glass. Samuel wrote he was sorry Nate had left, saying he now understood being alone was a terrible situation for a wife to endure. He said he knew something was off about the man. She'd only written to Samuel about a cheerful marriage, never telling that she'd been the one to leave Nate, but he'd seen right through her lies. Too bad Samuel hadn't shared his opinion about Nate before she'd married; it might've saved her loads of trouble and hurt. She crumpled up his letter and threw it into the firebox.

Looking out the front window, she couldn't see even a little beauty in the white storm spinning severe, switching between freezing rain and heavy snow. Outside raged wild with fury as she hunkered, dumping whiskey down her gullet in an attempt to bury her guilt at leaving her mother all alone in Worcester. The wind flew mean through the town, rattling her front window, shaking her little shop, and ripping three holes in the roof. She only had one pot to catch the water dripping down into puddles on the wooden floor. When she opened the door to fix the roof, a heap of snow blew inside, and she heard Deer Creek running through town in a rising clatter of rocks and logs and sticks. Closing the door, she kept the fire blazing and waited for the tempest to settle.

That winter the snow fell in spits and spurts, coming down hard and heavy for a few days, then clearing defiant afterward into a crisp blue bird sky, with a strong sun melting the streets into a muddy mess. Luenza's hogs ran feral now, wandering through the town, scavenging through the streets and sleeping on wooden walkways. Elisabeth told Luenza it wasn't right, letting her hogs run the town, but she just laughed it off.

"Who's gonna complain? No one who wants my bacon, that's who," said Luenza.

Those hogs had plenty of mud holes to slosh around in, with anguished men digging up the streets into muddy holes that froze overnight and thawed to a mid-afternoon muck full of hogs. The holes looked a strange sight, and Elisabeth found navigating the street in the winter difficult, twisting her ankle more than once in a pit and mudding her skirt up something terrible. One night she found three fellas digging, desperate for gold right under the corner of her porch of all places, seeming numb to the cold.

"What the hell?" she said, holding the lamp up in the dark.

"One last try at our luck, lady," said a voice in the night.

"Not here you don't," she said, tossing the contents of her piss pot in their general direction as warning.

When the man didn't stop digging she placed a boot on his shoulder and kicked him away from her porch. He stumbled backward into the mud. When he crawled up to his knees and started back to digging desperate with his hands, she went inside for her Hawken. She pointed the loaded barrel at the men, and they pleaded, saying they'd had it with looking for gold and wanted to get home to St. Louis.

"They ain't no circus out here," one of the men muttered on. "They ain't no wild elephants, either. I never did see no elephants a 'tall. I'm going back home where I can see horses and cows and chickens and real things I know for sure. I'm done looking for that damn elephant."

Elisabeth held her lantern up to their faces, seeing them haggard and thin and sick. Maybe drunk too. One man had a horrid, raspy cough and a spittle of blood on his chin. She backed up, feeling sorry for the lot. Perhaps they'd had no luck. Or perhaps they'd had luck but spent it through doing whatever foolish men do. You never could tell a man's story out here just by looking at him. She figured them dim-witted and set out a pot of hot tea and a basket of pears, saying they could sleep up on her porch out of the rain.

"But no digging, damn it! That'll ruin my foundation," she said, bolting her front door.

Inside, Elisabeth opened a jug. She'd taken to drinking whiskey regular that winter, without the help of coffee to get it down. An *evening* medicinal to help with the uncontrollable dreams and loneliness and lingering anger over Nemacio staying away. She was sore at herself for spending her savings on drink, knowing it wasn't wise, but she couldn't help it, drinking up a dram or three when nights folded gloomy around her. She liked falling into bed clouded and fixed drunk so nothing came to her but dead sleep, however muddied and hollowed out like the frozen holes in the streets. The balance of her mind wasn't off-kilter like the men who'd hanged themselves for no good reason, or her mother. She wasn't crazy, just wallowing weak in an all-consuming ache, hoping to mute her loneliness.

By sunrise those dim-witted diggers were gone, and she washed piss off the side of her store and filled in the holes by kicking in mud and tamping it down, wondering if they'd started the long journey to St. Louis yet. Wondering what makes a person happy. Even with her own business and all her savings, she hadn't yet discovered. She'd accumulated nearly six thousand dollars hidden in a yeast powder tin box under her bed, a lifetime sum for a princess back in Concord. But in California it wasn't much savings at all, and could be spent through within a year on basic supplies if she wasn't careful. She'd turned into a greedy woman, wanting more than a fleeting slice of sweetness out of life. When she started stealing little sips from a hip flask during the day while engraving blocks of wood, she smacked with a terrible self-loathing.

She was already half-drunk by noon when James Porter came into her shop one day with a bottle of red wine he'd picked up at the Solano Mission. He uncorked the bottle and poured her a cup. She smelled it and turned up her nose.

"It's not my drink," she said.

"You might grow to like it," he said, mistaking her for a temperate woman.

She took the drink, and they clinked their cups at nothing in particular.

"You ever thought of marrying?" Mr. Porter asked.

Sipping the wine, she sized him up as being like a brother, even though he looked pleasant, tall and well kept, without any awkward smells or manners. But he moved nothing inside her, no matter his kind attentions.

"I'm already married, you know that," she said, leaning up against her table to balance herself.

"Your man doesn't care for you proper, letting you stay up here, working all alone."

"Some thing, you tossing around judgment at me."

"You ever thought about getting yourself another man?" he asked.

"Oh, dear God, I don't need another one," she said, her lips let loose with drunken honesty.

"Do you fancy being a hermit woman, is that it?"

"A hermit? No," she said, holding out her cup for more wine.

The wine tasted sweeter than whiskey, and slower to slip into her blood, but warm and lovely. She liked it.

"A fine woman like you shouldn't go to waste," said Mr. Porter.

"How does a woman get a divorce?"

He smiled hopeful, telling her how to file a claim with the Accolade down in Hangtown.

"You could say he's neglectful. Impotent."

She peered at him, feeling the wine take over her mind.

"You need someone to love you," said Mr. Porter.

"That's not what Emerson thinks," she said.

"Who's Emerson?"

"Ne te quaesiveris extra." She said the words mushy, flinging her tin cup around, sloshing wine onto the oak floor.

"You talking Latin?"

"Do not seek for things outside of yourself," she said.

"Sounds like the makings of a lonely life."

She hiccupped, and Mr. Porter shifted his feet uncomfortable, clearing his throat.

"Listen, Elisabeth," he said, stepping close. "You and me, we'd be good together."

He turned pitiful now, and Elisabeth felt sorry for his fruitless efforts. Still, he proved too easy to toy with, not at all challenging her intellect or passions. She gulped down the last of the wine, teasing.

"Oh?"

"Darling. I've hoped for this," he said, grabbing her close.

She felt him harden through his pants as he kissed her wet, pulling up her skirt, fumbling in between her legs before she knew what was happening. Her reflexes were slow on account of the wine, and from the whiskey she'd been sipping on all morning, and she let him rub her privates through her drawers for a while, curious to see how it felt. Nothing. Only irritation he acted so clumsy. She pushed him away, and he stepped back, dejected. The wine stuffed up Elisabeth's nose, making her impatient and tired. She wanted Mr. Porter out of her store. She tried to explain, calm, knowing she owed him nothing. Even so, she didn't want to hurt his pride.

"You see, here's the way of it, Mr. Porter. I'm not so fine a woman. Certainly not worthy of a man like you. Trust me. Take your bottle of wine and move on. Go find yourself a woman who *needs* a man."

Elisabeth handed Mr. Porter back the empty tin cup, and he took it with his head hanging low. Without another word, he corked the wine bottle, walked out the door, and never came around again.

29

March 1852

Dearest Louisa May,

What a joyous day indeed, receiving your latest letter! Your words greet me at a high time celebrating your hard-won rewards, as well as my own, earned through temperance and self-discipline. I congratulate you on the publication of "The Rival Painters" in the Saturday Evening Gazette. *Your success is overdue and much deserved. As you say, five dollars is a meager sum for your literary labors, but more will surely follow now that you've opened the door with a smash. I admire your resolution to build a solid foundation for your family in ways your father cannot or will not. Your efforts must feel a great burden weighing down your shoulders given what little he contributes to the household. I've no doubt you will manage with grace.*

But dear LM, it pains my heart to hear you continue railing on about your father, given that his lectures on the Conversations on Man, which you say both sexes attend, and not just the transcendentalist. Surely his lectures will spread enlightenment on the nature of conventions and expectations throughout New England, after more than a spell, perhaps. Small minds creak open slow. I do not deny your frustration with the particular principles which force him to shirk his familial duty, I simply encourage paternal gratitude. Try to find an understanding in the steady compass of commitment guiding him, even as he contributes paltry toward your financial necessities.

All families suffer from shortcomings, even mine. Of course, I am continually blessed with our prosperous claim, which allows me the fulfilling work at the Split Rock Books and Print Shop. With hard work, we've earned beyond expectation, allowing for us to send for my mother, who is recovering well from her exhaustion at the Worcester Sanitarium. I suspect she will soon make the long journey west where she will enjoy the healthy California sunshine alongside us. Consumed with classes at Amherst, Samuel is a great beneficiary of our labors. I do not understand why he holds no interest in leaving his studies in banking to join the new economy of California. Perhaps he will change his mind in time.

Oh, how I wish you might someday know my friends Luenza and Ginny and Millie! And Nandy too. They are women working with a pure exuberance far beyond their present circumstances should rightly allow, and without fear. In knowing them, I have discovered how an independent occupation gives a woman strength of no equal measure. In accordance, I've come around to the idea that we must all live our own truths, no matter how uncomfortable those truths strike our loved ones. I extend that ideal to my husband, who is living his truth for the first time, even if that truth lacks the cherished conventions of most marriages back in Massachusetts. In knowing as much, I understand that man, too, is at his very nature as equally vulnerable as we women. In searching for acceptance and compassion, I take lessons from his remarkable emancipation. California has taught me that we all deserve to fulfill our dreams, women as much as men. In my observation, men already know the value of pursuing happiness, when *the ideal has yet to take hold in the minds of women. We must find our worth anew by escaping the noose of traditional living, which confines most women. This act in and of itself will bring us happiness, where there was none before. So you see, LM, I'm finished with my old thinking, and now address my desire as each opportunity presents, however dangerous, while attempting to convince myself the notion isn't selfish, just as you and all women on this earth should do likewise.*

I await word of how you receive my new frame of thinking, along with more stories written by you as both Flora and out of the shadows as the brilliant Louisa May Alcott.

Your bookselling and engraving friend in California,
EP

30

"The mind, once stretched by a new idea, never returns to its original dimensions."

S pring arrived early, bursting forth a spray of orange poppies all over the foothills, and the women sat outside Ginny's place again, enjoying Sunday coffee and conversation. Their voices and laughter traveled like a sweet song on the cool morning breeze through the quiet town not yet recovered from a Saturday night of equal measures revelry and despair.

"Let's toast to another article added to our list of equal rights," says Luenza, reading from the *Mountain Democrat*. "Article 2633, Sec. 2. Divorces may now be granted from bed and board, or from the bonds of matrimony."

"May many a woman now be released from the yoke of an unhappy coupling," said Elisabeth, holding up her cup as a toast. "As no longer the property of our husbands. Free to start over, fresh."

She took a long drink of her morning medicinal.

"As long as we prove fault," said Luenza.

Luenza read off the list of faults like a legal expert.

"Impotence. Underage consent. Extreme cruelty. Desertion or neglect. Fraud. Habitual intemperance. Conviction of a felony. Adultery. I got Stanley on a few of those for sure," said Luenza.

Elisabeth found it difficult to find fault in Nate, even after all that had gone on between them. She'd come to understand he had no control over his peculiar predilections with men. She'd never tell the truth about his buggery. She didn't want to shame him, and besides, the truth would brand him limp, setting him off an outcast and putting his life in danger. In fairness, she couldn't accuse him of impotence either, since they'd consummated their marriage on their wedding night and a few a times after, however unsatisfactory. She hadn't been underage at nineteen when they married, and extreme cruelty certainly didn't apply, either. Nate wasn't cruel, save for marrying her as a foil in the first place. A judge wouldn't likely deem Nate neglectful of providing the common securities of life, given his amputation after the snakebite. He didn't lack temperance. Didn't treat her with force. He wasn't a felon. And he hadn't deserted her, either. Technically, she had left him. Adultery seemed the only option. She just wanted out of the marriage. She wanted her freedom.

"How does a woman prove adultery?" she asked.

"Your man step out on you?" asked Ginny, the one unmarried woman among them.

"Maybe I stepped out on him," she said, adding more than another drop of whiskey from her hip flask into her morning medicinal.

Millie raised an eyebrow.

"Oh, stop, Millie! I don't need your high-minded judgment right now. I'll thank you to keep your opinions to yourself."

"I didn't say a thing," Millie protested.

Elisabeth figured Nate would have to file for the divorce himself, accusing her of adultery with Nemacio. It seemed a small stain on her reputation, and far less severe than how Nate would fare under the humiliation of buggery allegations. The price she'd pay for getting out of her sham marriage. It was also a lever. If Nate refused to file for a divorce, she would threaten to tell the judge about his buggery.

"With all you talking of divorce, I don't even want to tell about Bucky," said Ginny.

"Who's Bucky?" Luenza asked.

Ginny told them about a handsome man called Lucky Bucky from Georgia who'd been pestering her to join him for dinner.

"I might give him a chance. Seems a decent fella. And clean. It's not like I've got anything to lose," said Ginny.

"Don't be so sure, Ginny. A man can take your happiness if you're not careful. Trust me, I know," said Elisabeth.

"What do you know, Señora Parker?"

She knew the sound of his voice like her own but didn't turn around, just kept looking straight ahead like she hadn't heard him and continued sipping her morning medicinal. Nemacio stepped in front of her, shading her from the morning sun. She didn't look up, instead stared into her coffee cup like the grounds floating on top might predict her future.

"I'm asking, Elisabeth. What man took your happiness?"

"Who are you?" Luenza asked, standing up.

Nemacio didn't answer, just kept fixed on Elisabeth. When she finally looked up, her stomach flipped. It'd been nearly six months since she'd last seen him. His curls were longer, but his face was still clean-shaven. His eyelashes curled up thick and long, and his dark eyes pierced through her, looking for something.

"What man?" Nemacio asked again.

"That's none of your business," she said, flippant.

"Who's this, Elisabeth?" Ginny asked.

He bowed with that ridiculous charm.

"I'm Nemacio Gabilan. Mrs. Parker's . . ."

"Business partner. He's my business partner," she said.

"Well, I'll be damned," said Luenza, looking Nemacio up and down like she was sizing up a hock of ham.

"You've got a partner in your bookshop?" Millie asked.

"No," she said.

"You got something on the side," said Ginny.

"No. Not in my shop. The claim."

"Isn't Mr. Parker your partner?" Ginny asked.

Elisabeth was about to explain when Nemacio threw the book on her lap, angry.

"I am not your Heathcliff," he said.

"You misunderstood," she said, slow.

"I don't think so."

Elisabeth stayed quiet, not wanting to quarrel with him in front of her friends.

"I've come for Álvaro's guitar," he said.

"It's at my shop," she said, while Ginny and Luenza and Millie looked on, dumbfounded.

"I want it," he said.

Elisabeth took her time, sipping the rest of her morning medicinal slow. Sipping and sipping for courage. Making him wait. He loomed over, patient. Finally she got up, handing Ginny the empty cup.

"You need our help?" Ginny asked.

"Nope," she said.

"We'll come with," said Millie, standing up.

"No need. I'll catch up later," she said.

"Let her go, Millie," said Luenza.

Elisabeth walked down the hill toward Spilt Rock Books and Print taking tiny steps, slow and deliberate. Her face burned up at knowing he was walking right behind. When they rounded the corner out of sight, Nemacio grabbed Elisabeth's hand.

"Elisabeth," Nemacio said.

"Don't! You've no right. After all this time. Coming up here now. And for that damn guitar, smashed up as it is!"

"Please forgive me," he said, but didn't drop her hand.

His gentleness made her even more angry.

"Don't you please me! I've not been sitting around waiting on you."

It was a lie. She'd been waiting. She'd hoped once he'd read the book, he'd come back to her. When they reached her store, she didn't invite him inside, but he came in anyway. He shut the door, locking them inside, together. Holding herself away, she watched as he blew on his hands and rubbed them together. He slipped off his coat and hat, hanging both on the hook next to the door, like he was at home. Throwing two logs in the firebox, he stoked and blew until flames lit the cabin warm. He looked around at her books and carving tools and paper and ink and prints, and peered into her little back room, seeing Álvaro's broken guitar propped up in the corner. He picked it up and came back to the front room, cradling it.

"Lo seinto, mi amor," he said.

"No!" she said, holding up her hand.

She wasn't going to fall for his Spanish words reeling her in this time. But he put the guitar down and started to sing. She nearly crumpled.

"Since the night we met, seeking in wandering. A way to forget. But it's no matter by what path I may depart. I can't escape from my Malagueña," he sang, soft.

Not wanting to lose herself again, she folded her arms over her chest, but his singing started melting her cold heart, softening her into a mushy puddle. When he finished, they looked at each other in the stillness of the cabin as the fire crackled.

"I don't want you here," she lied, hoping he'd believe her.

"Mi amor," he said, taking a step toward her.

Still a little drunk from her morning medicinal, she pushed him in the chest, but he didn't move.

"Get out," she said, weak.

He placed his hands on his heart like he was in pain. When she pushed at his shoulder again, he caught her by the wrist. She struggled, and he grabbed the other wrist, drawing her in tight up against him.

"I can't stay away from you," he said, whispering heavy into her ear. "I tried. I tried staying away. But you've got hold of me."

"Let go!"

She didn't struggle to get out from under his strength. He grabbed a fistful of her hair, strung out long and messy, pulling her head back. He brushed his lips along the side of her neck, first cold, then warming. She exhaled, shaking under his touch.

"You want me," he said.

He was so damn arrogant.

"No. I don't," she lied.

He pressed his mouth urgent onto hers then, kissing and sucking too hard at first, then slow and lush, pulling and luring until she went weak on her feet. He groped and fumbled desperate, tearing at her blouse and tugging down her skirt. When she leaned heavy into him, he pulled her down to the floor, his curls brushing her bare breasts.

"Say you want me," he said.

"I don't want you . . ." she hesitated.

He stood up. He pulled the curtain shut over the little window for privacy, and then grabbed a chair, slamming it down in front of her. He sat, waiting quiet with his brow furrowed, looking down on her.

Lying on the bare floor with her clothes peeled half off, she wasn't cold. Perhaps that's all it took for her to thaw, a man to sing. Talk about his soul. Tell her what she wanted for her own self. Tear at her clothes. Tell her to beg for him. How pathetic she'd become.

"Say it," he said.

"I . . . I," she started, her voice shaking. "I don't want you . . . leaving me again."

In front of the firelight, he kept his eyes on her while he slipped off his boots and unbuttoned each button on his shirt so slow that she could hardly stand it. When he slipped off his shirt and stepped out of his pants, she held her breath.

"I need you to say it," he said, standing tall over her, naked.

"I want . . . you," she said, breathing in big gulps.

He was on top of her then, and she gasped as he filled her world, spinning it full of promises. Consumed by want, they moved together frantic, losing themselves in each other on the floor in front of the fire, loving full, absorbing and consuming. Not out of obligation or duty or guilt or loyalty or custom or law, but with a loving they'd read about in books. The naked, wrenching, blinding love that drowns you in the deep, drains you of all reason. A powerful, truthful loving that holds the earth together at its core. Forgetting. Creating. Making a new kind of love, in and more and deeper with a rhythm both tender and urgent, unearthing a bedrock of desire buried deep. He knew how to pleasure her like she was the only women in the world, and she gave all of herself over to him arching and shuddering and trembling, as he savored her passionate.

31

"Thou art to me a delicious torment."

They stayed together in her little back room of the Split Rock Books and Prints Shop loving on each other for three days while the spring rain pattered on the roof above. They stopped just to eat and sleep. Nemacio made her thistle tea with honey and fed her pine nuts and cooked her up a slab of beef seasoned with chili peppers he had in his knapsack. As he flipped the meat in the frying pan, she watched the muscles move along in his bare back, terrified the bliss would end. She could hardly breathe for the fear of it, thinking him far better medicine than whiskey.

When they lay together in bed, she knew every inch of him. His silky curls. His smooth, delicious chest. His flat middle and arms rippled by hours of digging and hauling rock. And that little divot just below his hip bone leading down. She reached out, tracing a finger slow along the middle of his chest to his waist and below.

"Solo tengo un amor," he said.

He combed her hair with a delicate shimmering comb made from an abalone shell.

"It's a creature so strong it only needs one single shell. It grabs hold of a rock like this when it gets afraid," he said, cupping his large hand around her breast.

Goose bumps rose up along her skin, and she tingled all over.

"For you," he said, tucking the comb into her hair. "To hold your hair out of your eyes while you work."

"I'm going to divorce him," she said.

"Divorce?"

"He doesn't want me."

"Don't be so sure of that. A man doesn't give up his family so easy."

"My father did."

She flooded open, talking about her family shame. About Henry's Indian girl and her mother killing herself. About how she wracked with guilt thinking it was her fault. How she should've stayed back in Massachusetts to help set her mother's mind right again. She cried in his arms and he rocked her, reassuring.

"You did right by God," he said.

She scrunched up her nose, not understanding.

"God's got nothing to do with it," she said, wiping her tears.

"I don't believe in divorce," he said.

She peeled herself out of his arms.

"What's that mean?"

He looked sheepish, as if he had something terrible to say.

"You made a promise to him."

"That was before I knew Nate liked loving on men."

"There are no exceptions with God," he said, sitting up in bed.

"I don't give a damn what God thinks."

"You can't mean that," he said, serious.

"I do. I refuse to waste the rest of my life waiting on God to fix things. Besides, I'd say you don't care much what He thinks either, seeing as you're here coveting another man's wife."

"I didn't intend to covet what's not mine. I'm in love with you," he said, tracing his finger lightly along the inside of her wrist. "But Nate .. . he's your family. That's the part I can't reconcile. I'm wrestling with it."

"Don't worry," she said, nonchalant. "Nate doesn't care about me, and I don't need him. I look after myself, and Luenza and Ginny and Millie are more family to me than Nate ever was."

She didn't wait for him to respond but explained how she'd been trading her printing in exchange for mining shares in six claims over the past months.

"Those shares secure my future, so I don't need any man," she said, as if she really believed it.

"You need me," he said, confident, like he knew for sure.

"Want and need are two entirely different things," she said.

"Is that right?"

He pushed her backward on the bed playful, and she giggled.

"You don't *need* this?" he asked, dragging his lips gentle along her collarbone.

"Nope," she said, feigning disinterest.

"What about this?" he asked, licking her nipples, gentle.

She squeezed her eyes shut, shaking her head no.

"You *need* this," he said, kissing her tummy and down lower, putting his mouth on her sex.

She sat up, shocked. She gathered her legs up and closed her knees, embarrassed.

"Relájate," he said, tugging at her legs and pushing her back on the soft rabbit-fur quilt.

He began again, first kissing the inside of her knees, then licking the inside of her thighs with the tip of his tongue, working his way up and up. She gasped, panting nervous. He spread her knees apart, and her legs shook from her hips down to the tips of her toes, and she squirmed, feeling exposed. Laid bare. He held her legs wide open with his elbows and tasted her inside, moving his mouth down on her, sucking slow and slower until she gave in, relaxing, trusting, slipping into blind rapture. He listened to her body, nibbling harder and teasing his fingers up inside faster, until her moans echoed off the plank walls in a new voice saying, over again and again, *I need you.*

32

"Do not seek for things outside of yourself."

Nemacio came to her most Saturday nights that spring, sneaking up to her cabin in the dark so they could while away Sundays in each other's arms, shaking the universe. Come Monday morning, he always made a pot of thistle tea and kissed her passionate, telling her to drink up before slipping back down to the claim before sunup. He said he loved her. Said she was his very own soul. And she believed him, returning to engraving with a heart so full of love that she poured out her whiskey jug and even passed on her morning medicinal with the ladies, taking her coffee black. He filled her with such contentment and hope that a calm sleep came so natural now that she almost didn't wake up when smoke filled around Split Rock Books and Prints.

She sat up, coughing in a fit, not quite understanding. Running outside for air, she saw a terrible chaos let loose. An angry wind whipped through the town, sweeping up stray embers from fire rings and striking them down upon cabins, and tents and trees, lighting them ablaze, brightening up the dark night. That pretty little town was no match against the firestorm flying as a mighty force atop the flimsy wooden shanties, sending folks running through the cold night clutching their belongings and screaming, as the fire cracked and roared like a demon unleashed.

She raced inside for her books and began piling them outside until she realized the futility. Fire was sweeping down the hillside fast, consuming whatever lay in its path. She had no time for the books. Throwing on her dress and boots, she grabbed for the keys around her neck. Sweat dripped from her forehead as she fumbled open the floorboard locks under her bed. She grabbed her tin of money and mining share certificates just as flames broke through the wall, licking the room wild. Gagging with the smoke, she ran for the door and tripped, dropping her tins, scattering the coins and paper bills and certificates across the floor. Frantic, she crawled on all fours, her eyes stinging as she grabbed whatever she could reach, stuffing her savings, her livelihood, her independence, her freedom into skirt pockets before the fire broke through the roof, pressing down on her like the devil's wrath taking its vengeance. As her small sack of gunpowder leaning against the wall popped, she snatched her box of engraving tools and fled out the door with her pockets full of who knows how much, while her entire shop went up in flames behind.

She ran down the hill with the rest of the townsfolk, away from the firestorm destroying everything in its path, pushed along by the mad wind, and the smell of burning hogs filling the fiery night. She ran and ran until she reached the bottom of Deer Creek Gulch, where the whole town huddled together in the cold night as Manzanita City lit up like Hades. She found Luenza and stumbled over, hugging the boys. She drew a sigh of relief at seeing Ginny, and they all cried, watching the fire destroy so much in so little time. All of their hopes and dreams and new beginnings and hard work, gone in a spark. When Millie and Joe Stamps arrived safe in the crowd with Joe Junior, Elisabeth headed down into the river ravine, picking her way down the trail with the help of the moonlight. Down the hill. Toward the Goodwin Claim. Toward Nemacio.

At dawn she reached the cabin, flinging open the door to see Nate and Francis curled up side by side against the winter's cold in Henry's old bedstead.

"There's been a fire!" she said, gasping with burning lungs.

Nate scrambled for his nightshirt, red-faced. Francis didn't move, just rolled onto his side looking sleepy and irritated at the intrusion. Nate swatted Francis's foot.

"Get up," said Nate. "Put something on!"

Francis dropped his leg over the bed, lazy, and sat up bare naked, staring defiant at Elisabeth. She looked around the cabin, frantic.

"Tell me of the fire," said Nate, holding her shoulders gentle.

"Where is he?" Elisabeth asked, still in shock.

"Gone," said Nate.

"Because of the divorce?" she asked.

"What divorce?"

"Did he leave because I want to divorce?"

Nate rubbed his eyes, perhaps not fully understanding.

"Just said he was going home. Something about his ranch and his sister. I tried to talk him into staying, but he was out of his mind. Wouldn't listen to reason. Forced me to pay out his entire share. Said he wasn't coming back."

"When?" she asked, weak and unbelieving.

"Two weeks ago."

She stumbled backward, grabbing at the wall, and he helped her into the rocking chair.

"Settle down, now. You've been through something awful, running all the way down here in the dark," he said, wiping the soot off her face with his kerchief.

"He left?"

"He said to give you this," he said, handing her an envelope.

She took the letter, and a knot fitted itself in her neck, choking her tight. Her hands shook as she read the words, and her feet pushed off the ground nervous over and over, rocking and pitching and nearly plunging her backward. Sideways. Off-kilter, and down. She bit and chewed her nails as her head pounded in panic and fury. Pounded at her foolishness. She was so stupid to believe he loved her. So stupid to believe she could have more. She pounded and reeled, gripped in a stupor of uncertainty.

"He told me to say . . . he's sorry," said Nate.

PART 3

"We were new creatures . . . and truly not until this time were we fairly conscious that we were born at all."

—JOHN MUIR

33

A way to forget

When Elisabeth threw herself down the hill she wasn't trying to kill herself like her mother, or the men gone mad in the diggins. She only wanted to rid herself of the baby. With most of her livelihood swallowed up in the fire, she had few prospects. And tumbling down the hill hadn't been her first consideration.

At first she didn't understand, begging Nate to tell where Nemacio had gone, shaking him and shaking him until he slapped her face, and she fell down on the floor realizing the rake had used her, swooped her up in a heap of charm. Used her up for his own pleasure. Devoured her. Stolen her dignity, then lit off like a thief with her soul. What a damn fool she was for believing! Believing he'd wanted her forever. Believing he loved her.

After the fire in Manzanita, she hadn't fully understood her compromised condition. She only knew all her money was gone—nearly six thousand dollars burnt up in the fire. In the mad scramble, she'd only managed to grab a measly two hundred dollars and four out of her six mining certificates. She'd grabbed her engraving toolbox, but with all her books and woodblocks lost to the ashes, she hadn't enough heart or money to stay in Manzanita City and rebuild. Most folks scattered, looking for a new town, a new opportunity. Ginny O'Rourke left for Sacramento, determined to set up a new pie shop. Mr. Lockwood the sawyer moved to Auburn. Millie and Joe Stamps moved over to Grass Valley, hoping to come back soon. Luenza refused to follow her man Stanley on word of a new strike near the South Fork of the American, staying behind in the heap of rubble of Manzanita City with her three sons to rebuild the El Dorado.

There was no way she'd go back to living down on the Goodwin Claim with Nate and Francis loving all over each other, flaunting what she didn't have and wanted so. Cashing out what was left of her mining shares at the Langley Bank in San Francisco was her only prospect of keeping on as an independent woman.

Nate agreed to a divorce on the grounds of her adultery. The Manzanita County Court flung liberal and loose with granting divorce, and the Accolade didn't at all pass judgment on her, believing that building a better society out west required freeing up the few women available. But the liberal sensibilities of California ended at Nate's peculiar sort of adultery, and Nate was relieved at her willingness to take the fault. He gave her three hundred more dollars, saying he appreciated her discretion and promising to forward on future profits in the Goodwin Claim once she settled in San Francisco.

Elisabeth set out of the river basin, walking away from the Goodwin Claim, alone. She stopped in Culoma along the way to find Nandy living a free woman. Gold diggers had run Mr. Sappington out of town the previous summer, angry at the slave-owning pig of a Southerner for using people as property to work an advantage in the diggings. The new golden rule of California was clear: everyone works for himself.

Nandy had grabbed her freedom and flourished, taking over the Sappington cabin and renaming it the Gootch Bakery. A smart woman, Nandy had worked religiously like a daughter of Zion building the Holy Land of California, mixing flour and pounding out famous bread with butter, saving nearly three-quarters the price needed to buy her son from the slaver in Missouri in under a year. She guarded her famed sourdough starter in a pouch around her neck, as the gold earning her son's freedom. Billy assisted in the bakery, cutting the wood, stoking the fires, and turning the stoves to please his woman, while digging on the side when he got a chance.

Nandy welcomed Elisabeth back to Culoma like family, telling her to pitch a tent behind the Gootch cabin. Elisabeth helped out mixing and pounding dough while she got her bearings. Nandy felt a great comfort, like the shadow of a giant redwood on a blistering hot day. But she wasn't above setting out her opinions plain when Elisabeth threw up in the grass after getting a whiff off the sourdough starter.

"What's gone is gone. And done is done. Nothin' you can do about water slipped through your fingers," she said.

Elisabeth cursed, furious that Nemacio's damn thistle tea didn't work, sick that all she had left of him was growing inside her, and his damn letter. Nandy looked at her sideways like she was a madwoman, failing to see her condition as a terrible predicament.

"Aww, git over yourself, woman. A baby doesn't need a man anyhow," said Nandy.

"I don't want to have a baby alone. How can I get my business going again with a baby?"

Nandy didn't soften her view, pointing out being a white woman having a free baby alone wasn't such a terrible lot.

"It's not like anyone gonna be taking that baby away from you, like my little Andrew. It's time you quit being so selfish and get on with living. Stay on here. Help grow my bakery," said Nandy.

Elisabeth was fixed on her own predicament, thinking only of herself and not on Nandy's long-suffering grief at being separated from her only child. She should've been more grateful to Nandy but saw only a bleak future flipping dough down in the river basin with no man and a baby pulling on her apron strings. She'd never be content scraping and scratching and digging out a living again. A greater drive ate at her, gouging an ambitious pit of restlessness into her soul. She wanted to sell books again and engrave wood and ink up prints. She wanted her freedom.

Sinking low and wretched, she let a man kiss her behind Brook's Blacksmithy for nearly five whole minutes in exchange for sips off his hip flask. She stuffed down her shame while the man slobbered and sucked on her lips sloppy in between her sipping, until she'd drunk up nearly all the man's whiskey, desperate to forget Nemacio. His loving. His leaving. And the fate of a baby she didn't want crying at her neck, holding her down, strangling. As she stumbled back to her tent late, Nandy wasn't light on the judgment.

"Drinking that stuff'll eat up all your money. Make you lazy. Kill all that ambition you got."

Fixed with guilt, she left the next day, saying John Langley at the Pioneer Bank and Trust owed her money. Nandy sent her off with three loaves of bread and a smothering of hugs.

"Next time you come visit I'm hoping Andrew will be here. You'll meet him."

Hearing Nandy going on about her son was like a hammer of guilt hitting Elisabeth. Feeling heartless, she fled to Sacramento and hopped a steamer down the delta to San Francisco, along with every sort of poor soul, emaciated and broken by defeat, returning to homes back East they'd left on a gamble. Hugging the steamer rail, she breathed in the hot delta air, clinging to the hope of cashing out her mining shares. Fixed on the notion of building up her business again. Ignoring her condition yet knowing she had nowhere to go. Nearly three months had passed since those delicious days held up in her cabin loving with Nemacio, her monthly bleedings replaced by a twitchy flutter growing strong and promising to eviscerate her life without permission.

She settled in at the Sully Boarding House in San Francisco, which had transformed considerably from when she and Nate had landed upon its shore over two years ago. Whole hilltops now flattened, the sand pushed clear off and down into the bay, engulfing the port to make more streets. Most of the tents and flimsy wooden structures were gone, replaced by impressive buildings of brick and stone that would've looked at home on any street in Boston or New York or Philadelphia. She had a hunch San Francisco might become a city of great importance someday. The perfect place to start again.

She found the Pioneer Bank in an imposing three-story stone building with three steps up to the entrance. Walking up the steps, she wondered why the builders didn't make two or four; an odd number just seemed like bad luck. Inside, pink velvet wallpaper covered the walls, with oak squares carved ornate with laurel and ivy crawling up toward a tall ceiling. It looked far too garish for a bank but nevertheless lent an air of gravitas befitting an institution aiming to bring stability and security to the untamed city. She waited in the lobby as bankers worked in silence behind a dozen desks blanketing a vast marble floor, until a man came out of a set of tall double doors saying Mr. Langley had gone to Sacramento for the month. Said nobody was buying any mining shares.

"Everyone is waiting to see how the hard rock mining techniques will play out," he said, brushing her off. "Come back in a few months."

She begged, but the man said she'd need to talk to the bank president directly. She walked down the steps, dejected, wondering how she'd pay for the next month's rent. Mr. Sully charged a fortune for the single room and board, bleeding her savings out. Without the mining shares she couldn't care for herself, much less a baby, and she saw no clear way of managing the difficult work of building up a new business with a baby riding on her hip. She considered the possibility of giving it up to the Orphanage Asylum Society in the outskirts of Happy Valley, but seeing those cribs stuffed full of wailing babies and sick children orphaned in the past winter's cholera epidemic, she decided against it. There was no hope for a child growing up healthy in that dreadful place.

She wandered the streets of San Francisco considering her choices, drinking whiskey during the day, guzzling greedy from a cheap little tin flask she'd bought off a corn farmer at the boarding house with nearly the last of her savings. Nandy was right, of course. Drinking was futile, a bottomless pit, useless at best. She drank anyway, looking in the saloons and hotels and liveries, asking after a Californio named Nemacio Gabilan. If he knew about the baby, he might return to her. Make things right. But searching for him made her feel desperate again, like a foolish girl waiting on her father.

One afternoon, she stumbled into a cathouse on Morton Street. To be fair, she didn't know it was such. With the same name as Luenza's establishment in Manzanita City—The El Dorado—she got all wistful and weepy at missing her friends and the close sense of family she'd had up on that hill above the river canyon. She opened the doors expecting a good meal and warm cheer, and instead found a surprise of a dozen ladies lapping around lazy with next to nothing on, their breasts pushed over the top of their bodices raunchy. Lounging loose and too loud, the women draped themselves around men, kissing their necks and ears and hairy lips, making for sin. It wasn't at all enticing like the Spanish couple loving each other in the tent back at the river claim, but soiled and messy. As she turned to go, a lady wearing hot red lip paint suggested she join in the business.

"Eyes like those, you'd lure 'em in. Make up to three hundred a night," she said.

She watched the woman's lips working up and down haughty, smelling like wild roses, and considered it. Living lying on your back for money couldn't be all that hard. And three hundred a night was an awful lot. A fortune, each day. In that line of work, she'd make enough to keep the baby and hire an Irishwoman to help like Luenza had in Manzanita City. She kidded herself. She could never stand the mix of smelly men getting up on her like that, no matter how much money she'd earn. Lying with a strange man would never give her the love like Nemacio, and she'd probably just get in the same baby way again. Instead, she paid two bits to the madam for a mixture of cohosh tea, drinking a dozen cups of the nasty stuff, but that didn't rid the baby out of her, either. She just threw up the brew all night in a piss pot on the second floor of the Sully House.

With no other prospects, she chose to end it, roaming the streets with Nemacio's letter burning a hole in her skirt pocket, searching for a suitable hill to throw herself down. She cursed that damn Emerson and his "Self-Reliance." He was wrong. His words didn't apply to women. Emerson had written *that damn book* for men. Women couldn't follow his advice by relying on a future of their own making, because women couldn't choose their own fate; it came pre-determined and thrust upon them by a long history of manners and tradition and expectations and their own weaker selves and the weight of small-minded men bearing down on them. Emerson's words had been laughing at her the whole time and gave her no glimmer of hope to sort out her dreadful predicament.

She couldn't see a clear way out. She thought her broken heart was blind, as her father's words came slamming into her head. *There comes a turn far more complicated, requiring more of man than he's capable.* Maybe he was right, after all. This was her turn. It was far more complicated and required more than she was capable.

She settled on Telegraph Hill, planning to tumble down just long and hard enough to propel that damn thing out, but not too hard to put herself beyond mending. Once making up her mind, she spent the whole day circling around the bottom looking up, getting up courage. Telegraph Hill reached 350 feet high, with a north side much too rocky. The south side, facing away from the bay, offered a long steep slope of sand all the way down, steep enough to shake the baby out but soft enough not to kill her in the tumbling.

Just before dusk, she crisscrossed back and forth, up through the dirt and sand among the wild clumps of yerba buena smelling minty sweet. When her boots filled with sand, she didn't dump them out, simply let the sand creep down, scratching and tearing at her stockings, as she sipped from the cheap tin flask, growing braver and braver. Breathing heavy, Elisabeth labored up the steep hill, steeling herself against changing her mind.

Halfway up, she noticed a murder of ravens circling high overhead. They landed en mass right in front of her and started cawing and hopping around crazy over a nest of snowy plover eggs. As the murder fought among themselves, a falcon swooped down and stole the six eggs, gulping them down without one raven noticing. Elisabeth shooed the black birds out of her path, and they took flight with a clamor of irritation. As she neared the top, she found the summit not at all menacing and quite appropriate for the task at hand. The view toward the south spread out stunning, with the sandy hill leading all he way down to open rolling grasslands with goats and cows and a few adobe houses, and magnificent oak trees stretching regal in the dusking light. The bay filled around behind her and to the left, with the ocean opening up endless and encouraging.

As the sun dipped behind a blanket of fog on the horizon, the sky lit orange and yellow like a heavenly void glowing beyond the sea itself. A blanket of fluffy fog crept in toward Elisabeth, blowing in on the Pacific wind, shivering her cold and calculating. She'd left her straw hat back at the Sully Boarding House, along with her gloves; she didn't want to ruin them in the tumbling.

With her lips chapped by thirst, she lined up with an old adobe rancho at the bottom of the hill, planting her feet firm, knowing she was a savage woman gone wrong. Downing the final drops of whiskey, she coughed and spit, promising this was her last drink. Hereafter, she'd do better, turn toward temperance and fortitude and hard work requiring a sober mind. No longer feeling cold, she flung the flask into the sand, relishing the fog cloaking in misty whiteness around her face, kissing her cheeks wet. She hoped the fog might cover up her deed.

By her feet, the sand swarmed with hundreds of tiny ants. A single ant escaped the group and climbed up her boot. She wasn't afraid anymore. She captured it in her cupped hand, and it tickled her palm. She spoke into her hands as if the ant could understand.

"Be thankful you'll never have to rely on just yourself. You'll always have your little ant family marching alongside you. Looking after you. Helping you out. Lightening your load. I'm all alone, you see. I have no choice. I don't have a family caring for me," she said, with tears dripping off her chin.

Elisabeth placed the ant down with its family, then fell on her knees to pray, calling out to God for forgiveness, her sloppy voice carrying along on the wind.

"I'll stop the whiskey. I'll be a good woman. I promise. Please God, let me start over again."

She stood up, pulling Nemacio's letter out of her skirt pocket, thinking it'd help her. Help rise up her anger. The letter didn't begin "My Dearest Elisabeth." Or offer up an apology or explanation. He just wrote down the lyrics to that damn song he'd sung to her, "Malagueña," written in English. The letter left her wondering all the more why he'd left. What she'd done to deserve it.

Malagueña

Fly away! said my carefree heart
To the place where daydreams start.
Fly away! said my heart to me
To the shore of the moonlit sea.
'Tis the gypsy code to be fancy-free;
When I see a road,
Oh, that's the road for me!
My Malagueña, your eyes shamed the purple sky.
You were as fair as I dreamed you would be;

I loved and left you for I never could deny
The gypsy strain in me.
Lightly as a song, going where I please;
Journeying along with every vagrant breeze.
Up a hill, down a stream
I follow in a dream.

Long have I traveled, my love
Since the night we met,
Seeking in wandering
A way to forget.
But it's no matter by what path I may depart
I can't escape from my Malagueña.

Reading the set of words again slapped her with shame at loving the man in the first place. She resolved to not think on him again. Resolved to begin anew. Be a better woman, without a speck of him lingering inside her belly or her heart. Filled with boldness and hope, she whispered, *Fly away, to the place where your daydreams start.* Then she buckled her knees and tumbled down.

34

To the place where daydreams start

*U*p a hill, down a stream; I follow in a dream.
Tumbling, twisted, bent crumpled, she flung herself down the hill, falling, pitching, stinging sideways and up ways down, crossing the main into the current of sand, savoring the river of Lethe, delivering from within, the power and the glory of forgetting, remembering, remaking herself anew. Together, alone with herself. Only.

Seeking in wandering.

And still. A little boy leaned in. Little Nemacio with lovely hair falling soft around his face, placid and recriminating. Eyes, sorrowful and seeing.

A way to forget.

Arms were cradling her, pushing her shoulder back into place. Wrapping her ribs tight.

Wracked with pain, she fainted.

To the shore of the moonlit sea.

She woke in a small room smelling of spicy chilies and garlic. A turbid candlelight cast murky shadows dancing around spooky on the bare white walls, pointing and screaming out blame and suffering and sin. She thrashed on the pillow, trying to shut out the demons dancing in her head.

"You fell," said a woman beside the bed.

The voice sounded foggy and distant, and she wasn't sure if was coming from a demon shadow.

"You're broken," said the woman, placing a heavy hand on her arm.

"I . . . I . . . ," Elisabeth started, but her lips were cracked dry and she couldn't form proper words.

"Bébelo," said the woman.

The woman wasn't gentle, forcing her lips open and pouring liquid down her throat. It tasted foul and familiar and delicious, like the mezcal she'd shared with him that night on the ridge. She relished it warming her blood, slow and thick, as she drifted, the guilt searing between her legs a dulling *thud, thud, thud*. Reminding. Remembering.

You were as fair as I dreamed you would be.

When the woman removed a bloody dressing from inside, a painful stabbing cramped her middle. She turned as the woman tended to her bloodied dress, tearing at the seams and pulling it off.

"The baby is gone," said the woman.

The woman was a witness. She knew. Nothing more grew inside. It was finished.

Your eyes shamed the purple sky.

"This needs to go inside," said the woman.

She tried to focus on the white gauzy bulb dangling in front of her face. It looked like a little floating angel, fuzzy and soft at the edges. Murky. Fading, drifting, weak. The woman opened Elisabeth's legs and pushed in the packing. Pain seared up through her gut.

"You are free now," said the woman.

Lightly as a song, going where I please.

"Forgive . . ." Elisabeth began, trying to sit up.

Dizziness consumed her, churning up the room with haunts and sins and sickness. She vomited down her chest and fell back on the bed. The woman wiped her mouth with a soft cloth, and she burned with disgrace, spiraling in shame. No one was supposed to see. To know. She'd not planned it like this. Sorrow and relief and guilt sat heavy on her rotted heart.

"It's not my forgiveness you need," said the woman.

She offered more drink, and Elisabeth gulped and gulped and burned and closed her eyes, floating away.

To the place where daydreams start.

35

*It's no matter by what
path I may depart*

After several more days of fitful sleep, Elisabeth woke with a dull ache in her middle. Lying in an iron bedstead with a white coverlet, she saw a wooden cross looming on the opposite wall, accusing, and a red lace curtain covering a single window, barely holding back the foggy light. The garlic wasn't inside her anymore, only a light dressing between her legs.

A little girl came into the room, offering a tin cup of ginger tea. She took it, sipping eager, grateful.

"Mama. Mama. La mujer está despierta," said the little girl.

A tall woman entered the room with a straight back and a strong, soft stride. She opened the curtain, letting in the dim ray of light.

"I'm sorry . . ." Elisabeth said through labored breathing.

"You've no need for apology," said the woman.

She convalesced in the adobe of Gabriella Sanchez, a Californio woman who'd fled her mean drunkard of a husband down in Monterrey with her seven children to build one of the largest ranchos in California, with over fifty head of cattle grazing at the base of Telegraph Hill. Known all around San Francisco for her hospitality, Señora Sanchez treated every vagrant and sick and deserting sailor seeking solace and refuge. Generous and astute with healing, she used Spanish cures for any ill from dysentery to homesickness, and was well loved by Californios and Americans alike.

"How long have I been here?"

"Six days," said Señora Sanchez.

Shifting in the bed, she winced as her middle hurt.

"Two broken ribs. And your shoulder. I set it right," said Señora Sanchez, speaking in perfect English.

A tall woman with broad shoulders and strong arms, Señora Sanchez spread herself around the room. She wore a high-neck dress of raw red silk, much too fancy and clean for a working dress.

"I need to go," said Elisabeth, trying to sit up.

A sharp pain stabbed her middle again, and she fell back weak against the soft goose down pillow.

"You'll not likely carry a child again," said Señora Sanchez.

Elisabeth gulped air, relieved.

Señora Sanchez didn't ask why she did it. Didn't reproach. She simply stated the situation then allowed her to stay and heal. Elisabeth remained in bed two weeks while her bones and delicate insides stitched themselves back together, the whole time marveling at Señora Sanchez's steady constitution. Even with all those children, Señora Sanchez never seemed to rile up or drain down. Aged ten to twenty-four, those Sanchez children milled about the ranch, milking cows, plucking chickens, washing laundry. In the evenings, when Señora Sanchez's lady maid rang the supper bell, they all came from every which way to sit at a long dining table, chatting and laughing while gobbling up a supper that smelled of limes and cilantro and love.

Hiding away in that little room off the kitchen, Elisabeth grew stronger as she listened to the comforting sounds of family at the Sanchez Rancho. They made her mourn over the family she'd never have, and she couldn't wait to escape their sweetness. Beautiful children crept everywhere. Too many eyes. Too many hearts. She didn't deserve their kindness and hankered for a spot of whiskey to dull her shame. But she remembered the promise she'd made to God to quit.

By the third week, she was desperate to get out from under all that stifling Sanchez generosity. She asked for her dress; she'd been wearing an unfamiliar sleeping shift.

"Too much blood," said Señora Sanchez.

Looking out the window at the rolling grassy hills, she wondered about the letter in the pocket of her dress.

"Perhaps a boy could go to the Sully House and get my . . ."

"My daughter Carmelita will give you a dress," said Señora Sanchez.

Fitted perfect and fancy, the dress seemed made for her, in bright yellow satin, buttoned up the front with twenty buttons and white lace trim high around the neck, just like the sort of dress she always wanted. She'd been used to wearing loose dresses trimmed up short with pantaloons sticking out underneath. And she hadn't worn a corset since coming over the Isthmus of Panama with Nate three years ago. Señora Sanchez fit her up tight into a whalebone corset and bodice, saying they'd help knit her ribs back into place faster. The whole fitted ensemble felt luxurious but at the same time painful and confining. Señora Sanchez brushed her long hair until it felt soft then braided it, tying four neat plaits around her head. Grateful and overwhelmed, Elisabeth promised to return the dress once she settled back at the Sully House.

"I'll pay for your troubles," she said.

"I have no troubles," said Señora Sanchez.

"For taking me in," she said.

"You can't pay for kindness when I offer it free."

Señora Sanchez took her hands, placing the folded-up letter from Nemacio in her palm. Elisabeth tucked it away in her pocket, hoping to forget. The Sanchez children gathered around as Elisabeth climbed in the wagon seat beside Jorge, Señora Sanchez's eldest son. She smiled and waved polite, eager to begin again, without burden.

Back at the boarding house, Elisabeth climbed out of the carriage gingerly, thanking Jorge. Mr. Sully insisted she pay for the two weeks she'd been gone at the Sanchez Rancho. She found ten dollars she'd forgotten in her valise and paid him half, saying she'd go to the bank to get more. Still weak from lying in bed, she ached on her left side with each breath as she walked all the way to the Pioneer Bank on Market Street to see Mr. John Langley about her mining shares.

Back from Sacramento, Mr. Langley walked out of his office with the shiny brass buckles of his shoes flashing fancy with each step. He showed her into his office, offering her a seat. He left the door open, but Elisabeth didn't relax into the plump leather and instead sat straight so Mr. Langley might take her more serious.

An Englishman, John Langley looked near fifty, stuffed into a brown suit with a paisley brocade vest and a gold watch chain dangling from his pocket. Orange freckles splattered his sallow face just like Ginny, and a long shiny scar ran down the side of his right cheek. His red hair thinned flat down the sides of his head into bushy mutton chop sideburns. A mustache of the same red covered nearly his whole top lip, moving up and down like a fuzzy caterpillar. When he spoke with a slight lisp, Elisabeth strained to grab the uneven cadence of his words.

"Elisabeth Parker. A pleasure indeed. Tell me, what's your business with me today?"

"The Pioneer Bank holds the shares in my mining certificates."

"Which ones have you got?"

From behind a large oak desk, Mr. Langley leaned over and flashed an eager smile when she placed the certificates in front of him.

"None of my customers are doing much speculating right now. They're waiting to see what those deep well mines yield this coming summer. See what all the new digging technology brings up. There's a current pause, if you will, a hold after the flurry of buying last year," he said, passing his eyes over her lot of certificates.

"I'm in need of cashing out now, Mr. Langley."

Elisabeth explained how she'd lost her whole livelihood in the Manzanita City fire, her entire worth tied in the books and paper and wood and ink, now blown away like ashes on a wicked wind.

"A sorry plight. But I tell you, no one will buy shares in those mines until one of them shows a profit," he said, shaking his head.

"I need access to funds so I can get going again," she explained.

"What's your strategy?" Mr. Langley asked, lifting his eyebrows.

"To open another book and print shop."

He leaned back in his chair, folding his hands behind his head. He took a deep breath and explained the current business conditions in a long-winded sermon, listing off at length his stakes in the more successful ventures in California. Brannan Mining Supplies. Alfred Munroe Clothing Establishment. Ghirardelli Chocolate Manufactory. Genin Hatter. Sutro Tobacconist. The Pioneer Steam Coffee and Spice Mill. Greenberg's Brass Foundry. She listened carefully, taking notes in her mind.

"San Francisco is already filled up with plenty of printers and at least three book shops. What makes you think you'll do any better?" She wrung her gloved hands in her lap, hoping Mr. Langley thought her a proper woman from a good family, educated in eastern schools. She looked the part, with that beautiful dress borrowed from Carmelita Sanchez and that precious abalone comb from Nemacio in her long brown hair.

"I'm not naive, Mr. Langley. I know what it takes to run a shop. I've the experience."

"Where's Mr. Parker?"

"I'm unmarried."

"Not married? A lovely girl like you?"

She ignored Mr. Langley's simple attempts at flirtation. This wasn't her first go-around, and Mr. Langley looked a feeble match against her determination to own herself from here on out.

"My father died," Elisabeth lied.

Henry Goodwin *could* be dead now, for all she knew, so that wasn't exactly a lie. She looked into Mr. Langley's face, waiting. Intent. Hoping on compassion.

"I suppose I can offer you a loan against your shares," he said. "In one claim only, mind you. At twenty-five percent interest."

"That's robbery!"

"I don't take advantage of anyone, especially not such a lovely lady as yourself. Twenty-five percent is the going interest rate in San Francisco. Ask around, if you please."

Borrowing against speculation felt irresponsible at best. She wasn't stupid and would never pay such outrageous interest when she had no means for paying it.

"Why don't you buy my shares yourself, Mr. Langley?"

"As the president of the Pioneer Bank and Trust, I'm waiting to see how the market turns, just like the rest. I can't jeopardize my investments, or my reputation. My clients depend upon me to keep their investments safe."

She pushed the mining certificates for the Big Rock Mine toward him, not letting on how she'd engraved the woodblock design and printed the certificate herself, with three elaborate rectangle swirls bordered fine, clear lettering stating the strike price of twenty dollars a share.

"Buying shares in Big Rock at the strike price is good business for you. And I know this mine," she said, tapping her finger on the certificate.

"What do you know?"

"I've seen it myself. Near a huge vein of granite and quartz."

It wasn't true. She'd never visited the Big Rock Mine. But Mr. Langley would never know.

"Those boys are digging deep. Yielding considerable," she said.

"I'll pay under the strike price," said Mr. Langley.

"How much less?"

"Five dollars less."

"Mr. Langley, with all due respect. Big Rock has potential to be *the* deepest mine in the Pacers, right on Big Rock Creek with plenty of water running all summer long."

"Happy to hear, since the Pioneer Bank is heavily invested in the Big Rock Mine."

"A respectable banker like you, making a girl sell her shares underwater? Really, Mr. Langley! I expected more of you, based on what I'd heard of your reputation."

She stared at Mr. Langley, serious. He sniffled, and she kept quiet, holding firm.

"How about you go out to dinner with me and I'll consider it?"

She needed money to get by on her own in San Francisco. Needed to eat and to pay Mr. Sully for next week's room. But she had no interest in getting tangled up with another man.

"Buy my shares at the strike price of twenty dollars a piece, and I'll consider it," she said.

He laughed out loud then, a joyous laugh that roared and roared throughout his cavernous bank. She'd hooked him. Mr. Langley offered a strike price of twenty dollars a piece for four of her ten shares in the Big Rock Creek Mine. At eighty dollars, she accepted, since she hadn't paid anything for the shares in the first place, only traded her labor engraving and printing the mining certificate. For now, she'd have to wait to cash out the other six of her shares in Big

Rock and those in the other three mines. Hold off on starting up a new business. As John Langley walked her to the lobby, he offered his arm. Still feeling weak, she took it, leaning on him, grateful. Up close, Elisabeth saw beads of sweat collecting around Mr. Langley's mustache, and he smelled like old cheese.

"When shall I pick you up for supper?"

"I'll consider it, Mr. Langley," she said.

"Soon, Miss Parker. I do hope," he said.

As she walked down the steps into the drifting San Francisco fog, the words *Miss Parker* sounded strange, like she was still an innocent girl. After all she'd lived and done, she was hardly innocent. But the married "Mrs." didn't fit either, since she no longer belonged to Nate. The title before a woman's name signifying who she belonged to—father or husband—seemed unsuitable for her now. She thought there ought to be a title for a woman who didn't belong to a man but could no longer claim being a girl with the chaste innocence of a Miss. Elisabeth wanted an altogether new title for herself, a surname signifying her new, independent state. A break from husband and father. She considered changing her name altogether but knew she needed to keep things clear about her one-third title deed in the Goodwin Claim. No sense in confusing the Manzanita City assayer, and getting the title all mixed with a new name. So she settled on Miss—Miss Parker. Nothing she could do about folks thinking her more innocent than she really was.

36

February 1853

Dearest Louisa May,

Please forgive me for not writing in so many months, and for so much more. I must admit, dear LM, I lost my way, if only temporarily, brought on by the poor choices presented to me and the grand heartbreak of living and loving. If I'm truthful with myself and with you, I must also blame my own greed. I grasped for more than a virtuous woman should. In the end, I fault myself and my own fanciful thinking. I'll not commit all my transgressions to paper, as the burden would surely be too much for you to bear. I do confess, however, my honesty has been lacking, as I've set down many falsehoods to you as mere wishes and hopes, presenting a not wholly accurate accounting of events that have transpired during these past years out here in California. Fearing your judgment, my transgressions extend to telling falsehoods. I understand now how a woman beset by extreme circumstances and bleak prospects tends to choose unwisely. I do not ask for absolution but only your forgiveness, as penance is a yoke I must now wear. I assure you, I am fully sound, even with my pride stripped bare, and having lost my living beyond all boundaries. If only you were here to help me find what I'm looking for. Although, your ever-present voice is always with me, telling me I cannot find what I have not lost. Forthwith, I promise to write only truths, choosing the bright light of honesty in redeeming myself before God. I shall remain mute on detailing the more shameful matters, as I do not wish to disturb your peaceful well-being, but prefer instead you know me not as a woman with a selfish nature but as a woman of substance, seeking a path of temperance and self-restraint.

In comparison, you are not as impulsive and strong-tempered as your father complains, as it is our role as women to stretch the comfortable boundaries of men, even while damaging our souls during the process. If we remain stuck in the same place, subservient to our fathers and husbands, we wilt and die, causing them in turn to complain at our grief and immobility. Rather they grumble just the same when we fly far beyond our common places. After all, men rely on us to pull them patiently along as we soar, and will surely rejoice in the new place where we've all arrived, finding it far more beautiful than the place we fled.

Despite your father's protests, I predict your life growing full, as you hold a determination that will soon be rewarded by more publications, bringing in much-needed money for your family. Simply ignore that nasty publisher, Mr. Fields. His advice on your essay "How I Went Out to Service" is utter rubbish. He knows nothing of service. How dare he advise you to stick to teaching. A man knows nothing about the plight of a woman. Trust me, women everywhere will read your words and understand. You must steel yourself against the very nature of men like Mr. Fields, and any other man for that matter, who places a heavy weight of lies and guilt around your neck. Ignore both their criticism and praise as of no consequence in your quest, as I now do here in the West. Your essay is of great importance.

Ambition is our crux, sitting at our center as a sextant, guiding us which way to turn. I know that much, and am bolstered by the knowing of it. I don't give myself over to it blindly but am paying attention with all the good judgment and reason I can muster. At first, I fretted terrible about being alone and finding a suitable way to support myself. Fortunately, many kind California women have pulled me along, teaching me how to lean in to the challenges of living independent. The fine Mrs. Ethel Rosenblatt has given me an extraordinary opportunity to learn copper engraving. I don't know why she sees such promise in me, but I accept her generosity with gratitude. I find solace in the work, and a sort of peace, too, knowing this is where I belong at the moment. In this place. At this time. Until I discover another direction, please post me at the Pacific Print Shop on Front Street.

Waiting for your forgiveness in San Francisco,
Miss Elisabeth Parker

37

When I see a road

In truth, working in copper at the Pacific Print Shop lessened the itch for drink, keeping her hands busy and her mind focused away from the sadness, guilt, and lingering want for that damn Californio. Every day before sunup Elisabeth walked the five blocks from her room at the Sully Boarding House to the shop on Front Street, then back in the dark to take her supper with the rest of the boarders. She fell in bed exhausted each night, with images of lines and curves and crosshatches drifting in dreams, pushing out memories.

Ethel and Jacob Rosenblatt welcomed Elisabeth with an intellectual companionship and solace that pulled her away from falling off the edge of reason. The Rosenblatts ran a sophisticated operation and set high standards for Elisabeth's work. At first she wasn't at all comfortable trying to prove herself, but she pushed down her nerves and rolled up her sleeves, watching and learning. Overwhelmed, she sat sheepish among the reams of paper and shelves stacked with copper plates and the large iron press and the dozens of cans of ink, and the inked-up paper drying on lines hanging overhead, wondering how she'd possibly master the new modern printing techniques. But Ethel remained patient even while demanding perfection, explaining how to melt wax on a small round copper plate and stick the pictures atop the wax. Using a stylist as Ethel instructed, Elisabeth's hands shook as she traced along the lines, pressing the image into the wax. After the first pass, Ethel removed the paper from atop the wax to reveal Elisabeth's first engraving. It was only a simple picture of a tree, but it looked magnificent outlined in wax. When Ethel told her to trace the image straight down through the wax onto the copper below, she faltered, growing flush under the scrutiny.

"Just remember, copper is much softer than the wood you worked with. Don't press too hard, or you'll punch right through the plate and ruin it. Make your first pass light," said Ethel. "Take your time, Miss Parker. Put the plate on the sand pad and turn the copper as you engrave deeper on the second pass. Peel off the wax as you go. Understand?"

Ethel didn't take a warm tone but wasn't dismissive either, instructing with a matter-of-factness that assumed an understanding.

"Yes," Elisabeth said, feigning confidence.

Her face burst open with a nervous sweat, and she wiped her forehead before it dripped onto the wax. Ethel placed a hand on her shoulder, reassuring. Breathing slow and shallow, she held herself rigid over the copper as her still-healing ribs throbbed something awful under the bony stays in her corset. Her hands shook, but she steadied her nerves and concentrated. Compared to digging in mud, engraving copper required much less force and no luck. She fell into a deep concentration, pressing into the copper slow and luxurious, losing all track of time, pulling the burin along while turning and tilting the copper plate on the sand pad, thinking of nothing but the next line, the next curve, shape, and dot. She stopped every inch, pulling the burin out of the emerging lines, cutting the curl of copper burr off with a scraper, and peeling away the unnecessary wax from the plate. The work required more patience, more delicacy than engraving wood, and proved far less forgiving.

At one point she pressed too hard and poked right through the copper clumsy, and Mr. Rosenblatt sighed impatient and grabbed the plate out of her lap. For a slight, balding man, he seemed to take up the whole room as he held the plate up close to his nose, scrutinizing every inch of the design from behind his tiny round glasses.

"Quite crude. Very rough," he said. "Don't you have any formal training?"

"Self-taught," she admitted.

"Don't use your crude engravers on our copper," he said.

Ethel stepped in.

"Have patience with her, Jacob," said Ethel, handing Elisabeth a finer bruin.

Elisabeth continued engraving, until Ethel's simple drawing of two trees appeared beneath her fingertips in the copper as if by magic. Finished, she sat back thinking it the single finest picture she'd ever engraved, hopeful the Rosenblatts might find her work sufficient to keep her on.

"Give her the scraps of copper to practice crosshatching," said Jacob.

Ethel saw potential in Elisabeth and was as generous with her compliments as Jacob was stingy with his.

"You'll save me enormous time doing the engraving so I can focus on my drawings," said Ethel.

As Ethel's apprentice, she worked the whole of spring, learning to engrave extraordinary detailed sketches in copper including one large image of a western landscape with Indians on horseback circling a buffalo, a long line of wagons on the prairie, an Indian mother carrying a baby on her back, and an impressive mountain range. When Jacob printed the plate onto paper and hung the picture on wall behind the front counter to show potential customers a sample of what they could print, she knew he finally approved of her work.

Working for a Jewish couple that didn't believe in the baby Jesus proved less complicated than working for Christians, as they didn't reproach or throw around pious judgment but revealed themselves as high-minded, enlightened intellectuals not limited by the strict constructs of the Bible. Elisabeth hadn't even realized the Rosenblatts were Jewish until the end of her first week when they left her alone in the office Friday at sundown for their apartment upstairs. She heard them praying through the ceiling and realized she never even considered the differences between folks anymore. She didn't care if the Rosenblatts were Jews any more than she cared if Nandy was black or Ginny was Irish or Nemacio Catholic. Maybe those particularities had mattered to her in the past, when she'd first arrived in California and was naive and scared. But she now understood how a variety of folks made a place more interesting. More alive. And she'd surely benefited by being around all sorts of folks these past years. Spending time in the company of those different from herself, opened her eyes wider.

Ethel and Jacob proved as fair and industrious in their business dealings as they were exacting and precise in their printing. Elisabeth gained enormous respect for Ethel's gift of drawing and wanted to please her. She listened careful at her instruction, eager to learn every part of the printing process from the drawing and engraving to the inking and pressing. She watched the Rosenblatts careful, seeing what she might learn. Ethel proved a great model of womanly industriousness. Nearly fifteen years older than Elisabeth, Ethel's forehead lifted with thin lines of expression when she spoke and scrunched up in concentration as she sketched. Small and bony, the woman worked with enormous stamina, drawing elaborate pictures from memory all day. Some days Ethel didn't rise from drawing until dark, creating picture after picture of San Francisco: the buildings, the harbor with abandoned ships, and sandy dunes. Elisabeth struggled to keep up engraving all the pictures but soon matched Ethel's pace, only pausing long enough to ask about the best tool to use or how deep to make a particular flourishing etch.

She envied the Rosenblatts' partnership. They worked side by side, with Ethel creating the images and Jacob taking orders from customers, setting type, inking plates, and pulling the printing press. Jacob elevated Ethel's contributions equal to his own, expecting his mother-in-law, Flora, to manage their three children in the large apartment above the shop so Ethel could work. As a tender and affectionate husband, Jacob often paused his own working to ask after Ethel's progress, blinking at her with both eyes closed for a moment behind his glasses in a secret code of affection from across the room. It seemed a remarkable partnership, making Elisabeth both hopeful and sad. If she'd had this sort of setup with a man, she might've been able to keep the child. She never let on a thing about her family shame or the terrible deed she'd done. Reasonable folks could only abide so much.

Ambitious, Jacob had plans to expand the Pacific Print Shop, writing summaries to accompany Ethel's drawings, passing the printed broadsheets out for free at the more respectable saloons as advertisements. By summertime, Jacob admitted he was pleased Elisabeth had joined their shop and hoped she'd help them expand.

"I'd like you to run the store during the Sabbath, to avoid any complaints that we're not open on Saturdays," said Jacob.

Eager to manage a business again, she agreed. She took over the shop every Friday when the Rosenblatts retired upstairs for dinner and prayer, settling into a comfortable weekend routine taking customers' print orders in between engraving. She closed the shop at nine and opened it on Saturday at six in the morning until six at night. Come Sunday morning, the Rosenblatts kept their shop shuttered as required by San Francisco city laws, but behind drawn curtains Ethel and Jacob toiled away in secret. They expected Elisabeth to take off Sundays for Christian church services and perhaps rest, but they didn't judge when she chose to stay and work seven days a week, even though the Rosenblatts could only pay her for six.

"I want to learn everything I can," she said, knowing work kept her from thinking about Nemacio and drinking.

As a paid apprentice, she earned five dollars a day, a low wage by San Francisco standards. Even so, she was relieved to earn her own living, free from Nate and Nemacio and anything else holding her down. After spending three dollars a day on room and board at the Sully House, she had little leftover each month to save. Not enough for starting her own business, yet. But she stashed all her savings over at Mr. Langley's Pioneer Bank, while waiting on her mining shares to cash in, hoping her meager balance might grow into a substantial savings over time. Mr. Langley offered an extraordinary savings interest rate of 75 percent. She took the interest rate gladly. Still, she didn't want to be in his debt, or any man's debt, so she inquired about his rate, just to clarify.

"What's the going interest rate elsewhere?"

"Short-term rates are running at six percent back in New York. You can get about twenty-five percent in Missouri. I offer from fifty to seventy-five percent for larger investments. You're my exception."

"That's quite a differential, Mr. Langley. What's the catch?"

"No catch, Miss Parker. My intentions are noble. Consider your special rate my personal investment in the women of California, if you will. I assure you, I'm entirely trustworthy. "

"How can you promise such grand interest?"

He leaned over the table of his bank desk, speaking in a mere whisper.

"Land. I invest my customers' money in land."

"Where?"

"Right here, in the sand below my feet. San Francisco won't always look such a dusty windblown place, but will sparkle as the jewel of the West. Most folks don't have the courage. Fine by me. More lots for the taking. I'm buying up all I can get my hands on, block by block, all the way from the ocean to the end of the bay down the peninsula. It's a good investment, Miss Parker. Mark my word. Bound to pay off. Those little plots of land stand to increase tenfold, in very little time."

"How much time, do you suspect?"

"A year or two, at the outset," said Mr. Langley.

"Since I'm giving you my savings to buy up all that land, I'd like to take out my interest payments in monthly installments. I need something to live on until my mining shares pay off," she explained.

Once they worked out the particulars of an arrangement to cover her room and board at the Sully House, he once again pressed her to join him for dinner. She begged off as usual, reminding him that she was too busy working. He was persistent and charming, saying his day would improve mightily if she'd agree, but she always turned him down, suggesting perhaps next week. It became a silly game playing between them, him asking, her declining. She found the flattery helped bury her deep loneliness for a man. But as he escorted her to the bank door, he spoke of his family, reeling her in slowly, like a fish caught on the end of a hook.

"Didn't always look like this, you know," he said, pointing to the long scar disfiguring the right side of his face. "I was a handsome widower when I came out here in 1848 looking to make a better future for my daughter, Lily Beth. I came by way of New York as a seaman, an occupation I didn't at all enjoy. Too little for my mind to work with, you understand, Miss Parker. I had an unfortunate incident with a knife-wielding American trapper drunk off his topper. He attacked me one night, disfiguring the right side of my face with this considerable gash and cutting my tongue so bad I nearly swallowed the swollen bits. But I healed, by some miracle, with the sole mission of caring for Lily B., my sweet daughter. I don't mind scars much, knowing a true woman of substance wouldn't take my face or woeful manner of speech as deterrent."

She thought he wasn't likely attractive before the attack, with his too-pale skin and smattering of orange freckles, even on his hands. It hardly mattered. She had no romantic interest in the man.

"Turns out I have a head for banking. When a few of my more speculative investments paid off, I sent back east for Lily B., and she's been here with me ever since. She's the light of my life. A precious spark of energy. You must come to my house for supper and meet her," he said.

Standing close, that stale cheese smell exuded from his skin, not just his breath. But she ignorned the smell, in awe of the way he spoke of his daughter. His love and commitment made him feel endearing and safe.

"You promised to consider my offer quite some time ago, Miss Parker," he said, feigning hurt. "I warn you, Miss Parker. I'll only take one more rejection after today, then I'll stop asking. I won't pester a woman. A man can only take so much."

"Oh, I don't believe your ego is as fragile as all that, Mr. Langley," she said, teasing as she walked down the steps.

"But it is, I tell you," he called after her in jest. "I'll ask only one more time. One more time!"

"See you next week," she called out, waving her hand high up in the air, without turning around. "For my weekly interest payment."

She chuckled to herself, hoping he'd not stop asking. Even with his cheese odor, funny lisp, and freckly face, his weekly attentions felt surprisingly welcome. He made her feel smart and womanly, again. And she liked it.

38

Lightly as a song

After six straight months of working for the Rosenblatts, Elisabeth took a day off. She'd intended to return the borrowed dress to Gabriella at the Sanchez Rancho, now that she'd finally bought a new working outfit for herself. But she dreaded going back, seeing all those sweet children running around, reminding her of what she'd done and what she'd lost. Lacking the courage, she paid a man at the Sully House that morning to return the bundled-up clothes with a note of gratitude tucked inside, and headed off to church.

She sat on a porch outside the newly built Methodist church, mustering up the courage to go inside. She hadn't sat in a church since living back in Lowell listening to the Reverend Spillwell spouting off sermons about how a good woman should comport herself. She hadn't gleaned much out of his preaching back then, and in the years since, Emerson's "Self-Reliance" proved much more useful than the Good Book. Now humbled by all that'd come before with Henry and her mother, and Nate and Nemacio, and the tumbling, Elisabeth had lost faith in Emerson too. Yet for some reason she still carried that damn letter from Nemacio in the pocket of her skirt. She couldn't say why, as she never took it out, having memorized the lyrics to "Malagueña" as his sorry excuse for leaving.

Perhaps circling back around to God now might ease her soul, give her a slice of absolution for all she'd done. Watching folks trickle into the church, dressed fine and otherwise, she willed her legs to stand up and go inside. By eleven, the Old Ship Saloon across the street had more folks, and she felt sorry the church attracted such a paltry congregation in comparison.

"No shame is too much," said a preacher standing over her, blocking out the morning sun.

"Even God has limits, surely," she said, looking up.

The preacher looked down with prideful eyes and scratched at his bald head.

"Any woman's soul can be rectified," he said.

Maybe this preacher knew the secret to forgiveness. Knew the secret of how a woman might set her soul right enough to find a good life worth living.

"Tell me the secret," she said.

"You must follow the narrow path of righteousness, with a good husband guiding you."

She paused for only a moment before realizing he was serious. She rolled her eyes.

"Tell me now, preacher," she said. "What's a woman to do if her *man* doesn't follow the narrow path of righteousness?"

"The Bible says a silent and loving woman is a gift of the Lord."

She understood then, the church simply stood as yet another instrument of control to keep a woman down.

"You're quite a relic. You have no idea, do you? Women don't work that way out here in California," she said, standing to leave.

The preacher gripped her arm and raised his voice, angry.

"Let the woman learn in silence with all subjugation! I suffer not a woman to teach, nor to usurp authority over the man, but to be in silence," he said.

"I'm not interested. I'd rather find my salvation out in nature. But I thank you just the same," she said, shaking out of his grip.

Elisabeth strode forceful across the street over to the Old Ship Saloon, sitting down out front. When the preacher shook his finger in recrimination, she smiled wide and waved back, taunting. Although she wouldn't go inside the saloon for a drink. She intended to keep her promise to God and herself, staying off the whiskey. She hadn't turned religious, just fancied herself a woman who kept her promises. Besides, the drink no longer lured or tempted. She'd lost the taste for it, knowing from experience it didn't help much and contributed to a downfall she'd rather avoid from here on out. The Old Ship Saloon simply had a nice shady spot to sit.

In truth, she didn't quite know what to do with herself for a whole day off. Sitting idle with nothing to do felt strange. Lazy. Peaceful. Thankfully, she wasn't the novelty she'd been three years ago down on the American River. No one sat at her feet flipping coins into her cup now, as lots of women came to San Francisco on ships every day, hoping on a better life than the one they'd left. The cheeky saloon was the novelty now, a tall ship trapped on all sides by sand pushed down from the surrounding hilltops to fill in the bay for more land, stuck landlocked, still trimmed full up with rigging. On the top two decks, men leaned on the rails, drinking and laughing loud, while three women hung off windlass ropes on the bow, calling to folks passing by in the street below. A fiddler squeaked out an off-pitch tune impossible to dance along with, but people danced anyway, reveling raucous atop that strange, landlocked boat saloon, enjoying themselves. Elisabeth marveled at the delight of it all, and on a Sunday no less. As the saloon doors swung open and closed, with folks coming and going, men tipped hats and women smiled at her. No one judged. The folks seemed to hold a thick tolerance for living in fallibility, with an understanding that greater delights are only reached by first stumbling messy through a thick fog of mistakes.

She pulled paper out of her valise and began a letter to Nate. She wrote that she'd taken work at the Pacific Print Shop, explaining that she didn't yet command the wages of a comfortable woman and wanted him to send quarterly profits of her shares in the Goodwin Claim to her. She also penned a letter to Samuel, sending no money this time for his schooling, explaining a fire destroyed the Split Rock Books and Prints Shop in Manzanita City. Careful with her words, she said she'd moved on to San Francisco to expand her prospects, saying Nate stayed behind on the Goodwin Claim. She promised herself not to lie, but telling Samuel the whole truth was out of the question. Best to reveal bits and glimmers in each letter, letting shades of truth fall over him slow, so as not to offend his New England sensibilities all at once.

After dropping the letters at the post office, she walked toward the hubbub of the port. Summer in San Francisco froze her through, with a foggy wind blowing in fierce through the Golden Gate like winter back east. No trees graced the sand-swept city. No New England maples or elms. And no cottonwoods or green pines of the American River. Just blank, windswept sand. Turning a corner along the boardwalk, she saw a royal-blue tent with a crowd milling out front. A showman wearing a red silk suit and top hat called out to a crowd gathering 'round, telling of a mysterious woman inside.

"She speaks to the dead. Tells the future," he bellowed.

Elisabeth didn't actually think anyone could talk to her mother or Lucy, but she was curious and joined the crowd anyhow, paying a quarter to enter the tent. Inside, soft candlelight illuminated silver paper stars hanging from the ceiling. She took a seat in the back and waited for the show to begin. When a girl no more than thirteen stepped out from behind a curtain, the crowd hushed. Perfect brown ringlets fell around her face, innocent and sweet, and she wore a garish orange velvet dress revealing a pale cleavage and a large silver cross dangling down from around her neck. The blend of innocence and allure was jarring. The girl seated herself facing the audience on a long velvet settee and spoke in a tiny whisper. Elisabeth strained to hear, wishing she'd sat closer up front.

"My name is Sara L. V. Hatch, and I will now enter into a trance."

The girl raised her eyes to the tent ceiling with a fixed expression. Unblinking and intense, yet confident with invocation. Rapt entrancement overcame the young girl's soft face. Suddenly, the girl stood and recited an eloquent prayer to the Heavenly Divine Father. A man in the front row interrupted the girl, pressing a subject clearly beyond her expertise.

"Is the soul of a man part of the Deity?"

To Elisabeth's surprise, the little girl medium set forth on the subject at length. Mesmerized, she watched from the back row, thinking it some sort of trick. When a woman on the side asked about metaphysical abstraction, the girl launched into the subject in great detail for a whole fifteen minutes with startling confidence.

"It's quite remarkable, don't you agree?"

Mr. John Langley slid over on the bench beside Elisabeth. Seeing a familiar face at such an eerie event was reassuring.

"So very peculiar," she whispered to him.

John Langley leaned over too close, smelling of his usual stale cheese, with a hint of wine.

"I hear the dead send messages to the present through her."

"Impossible!"

"Perhaps you could reach your father," he said.

A chill ran up her spine, and her faced burned hot in the crowded tent.

"I'm a believer in letting the dead lie in peace, Mr. Langley," she said.

She kept watching the girl as John Langley scooted up close. She felt his chest heaving up and down as the crowd fell silent. When the girl opened her eyes, Elisabeth jumped and Mr. Langley grabbed her gloved hand as a pretense of comfort against the weird conjuring before them.

"It's all right. She's just a girl," said Mr. Langley.

In the dark recesses of the conjurer's tent, he cradled her hand in his lap with affection. After a time, she nearly forgot about Mr. Langley altogether, lost in watching the little girl communing with the beyond for an old man who'd dropped to his knees on stage pleading for the girl to relay a message to his dead wife. The spectacle stunned her into thinking the girl a near miracle. When Mr. Langley slid her hand over the middle of his lap, she didn't pull away. She wasn't yet uncomfortable, just assumed he'd taken too much drink. When his pants bulged up, she grew amused at his bold move, and couldn't help the thin smile spreading across her lips. She was pleased as still being able to move a man to pleasure, and wondered if maybe this sort of power might get him to give up some information about her mining shares. Mr. Langley didn't turn toward her, just kept his eyes locked toward the stage, and she had a mind to start rubbing him through his pants right then and there in the tent, in front of all those people, just to see if she might turn the tables. Get him to moaning under her control.

But the little girl abruptly stopped talking, stood up, and walked off the stage, and Elisabeth lost interest in Mr. Langley. When the crowd clapped raucous with enthusiasm, she pulled her hand away from his lap, and he stood, holding out his arm to escort her out of the tent like he hadn't just been lewd with her hand. Fed up with the man's silly overtures, she declined his arm and left the conjurer's tent, alone. She hustled off to the Pacific Print Shop. Being a Sunday, the curtains were drawn, so she knocked.

"It's Elisabeth," she whispered.

Jacob opened the door, ushering her inside.

"We must print an article about her," she said.

Pacing the shop with excitement, she told Jacob and Ethel about the little conjurer. Trying to convince them. Jacob wasn't so sure.

"We can't compete with the *Daily Alta*. Robert Semple has a powerful steam press over there, with a dozen workers to help get his paper out," said Jacob.

"But, they aren't open today, with the Sunday closing laws. We are! We can get to work on an issue now. And they've no artist like Ethel to recreate a likeness of the girl."

"We can't risk being fined for not abiding the Sunday closing laws," said Jacob.

"Plenty of saloons are open today, flaunting the law," she argued.

"They're not run by Jews," he said.

"If the police come, we'll say we began work Monday morning, early. No one can prove otherwise," she said.

Jacob twirled one end of his mustache with his fingers, looking at Ethel.

"She's right, Jacob. This is our opportunity," said Ethel.

They began immediately. Elisabeth described the medium show in great detail while Jacob asked questions and took notes. She described Miss Sara L. V. Hatch to Ethel, who sketched her likeness. A young girl. Petite. Diminutive but suggestive. Too mature for her age. Her nose is too short. Broader shoulders. Longer ringlets.

Ethel captured an approximate picture of the girl and quickly etched the drawing into a copper plate for printing while Elisabeth read over Jacob's article about the event, suggesting changes to make the article more enticing.

"Perhaps we should include the details of how the girl looked up at the ceiling when she was in a trance. Her voice got deeper when she went on about metaphysical abstraction," she said.

Jacob took her suggestions, setting the type on his press. Ethel suggested a different format.

"Let's go bigger. Like a magazine. We can fold the paper in half and include one of my drawings of the west on the other side. It will distinguish us," she said.

"We need a title," said Elisabeth.

"How about *California Illustrated*?" said Ethel, who'd already begun sketching a unique design for the new title.

"Brilliant!" said Jacob.

By midnight they began the assembly, with Ethel inking the plates, Jacob pulling the press, and Elisabeth hanging the wet sheets. As the paper dried, they took a resting on stools, grinning at each other. Flora, Ethel's mother, came down from the apartment above with warm chicken soup.

At first light, Jacob hired men to sell the first edition of *California Illustrated* at the Port, Front Street, Market, and Montgomery too. That morning, five hundred copies sold out in thirty minutes, at fifty cents apiece. No one asked if it was printed on Sunday.

That day, Jacob rewarded her with a weekly raise of five dollars, for a total salary of forty dollars a week. It was much less than she'd earned sewing a day down in the diggings, and a measly amount compared to the gold she'd dug out of the river, but she didn't care. Engraving and writing challenged her mind, made her feel as if she added something valuable to society. She wanted to spend all her time roaming around San Francisco searching for interesting stories to report about, but after the tumbling, she still questioned her own judgment. Besides, she'd never written anything other than letters. She hesitated, thinking it seemed too easy for a woman to simply lean in, grab a piece of any conceivable scheme in California, no matter how bizarre or impossible. It required a woman with a healthy dose of confidence and courage to take the opportunity, to be sure. She had nothing to lose by asking.

"You'll need a reporter," she said to Jacob.

"I suppose I do," he said, looking up from his lettering case over at Ethel. "Do you know of anyone?"

He was forcing her to ask. Step up. Grab the opportunity. He wasn't just going to hand it over.

"I can do both, engraving and writing."

"Makes sense to me," he said. "Ethel?"

Ethel nodded, and Elisabeth clapped her hands together fast.

"Yes. Yes. I'll do it," she said.

So, Elisabeth Parker became the first reporter for *California Illustrated*. For the second issue, she collected information about the harbor happenings, asking the city manager, port organizers, sailors, and even the saloon owners about the harbor getting smaller with infill. Everyone offered up an opinion, and she brought her notes to Jacob, who helped her write up the article. In the months that followed, she wrote the articles by herself, with Jacob only giving them a once-over for grammar accuracy. All her years of reading novels had made her a solid writer. Jacob helped her with the grammar particulars, but she knew how to hook in readers with a good lead. Fill in stories with just the most important and interesting facts. She wrote about a group of women who opened a new school for children, the bifurcated skirt, the Ladies Temperance Society, traveling minstrels, bicycles, and Maguire's Opera House.

Consumed with working as a reporter, she rarely ever thought about Nemacio anymore. She no longer fretted over why he'd left, closing the lid tight on that jar of sadness. She only occasionally remembered his body moving over hers. Loving her with a devastating passion and tenderness. His fiery touches and soul-sucking kisses. She sometimes imagined him living on his family rancho somewhere and wondered if he was happy without her.

She decided to overlook Mr. Langley's indiscretion in the darkness of the conjurer's tent, knowing she needed him as her banker. Besides, he never mentioned the incident and made a special point of always treating her as a respectable lady. She continued stopping by the Pioneer Bank every other week, depositing her earnings, collecting interest payments, and asking about her mining shares. Mr. Langley still advised her to hold off in selling, saying it was better to wait until solid information about the mine yields drove share prices higher. Trusting his advice, she saw no reason to do otherwise. He didn't stop flirting with her, expressing admiration, saying he read every article she wrote. But as promised, he never asked her to join him for dinner again. She missed their little game of him asking and her saying no. It had been a comfortable ritual that flattered her sensibilities.

After a year, living at the Sully House dulled, tarnished by the unsavory newcomers crowding in, looking to get rich quick. Her single room cramped dark and too spare, making her want for a single window and her own bath. Tom Sully grew weary of the crowds, too, taking to seasoning the bland food with too much salt and changing the bed linens only when someone complained of the stanky stains. He lost his temper at two young sisters from North Carolina, accusing them of prostituting, saying he'd seen them out dining alone the previous Saturday at a questionable saloon, trolling for men. She understood Mr. Sully's concern about keeping his boarding house respectable but felt uncomfortable with his accusations, as she hadn't seen those women take in any men. Not even once. Besides, a woman's got a right to enjoy a meal without a man, prostitute or not. But Mr. Sully kicked the girls out with no notice anyhow, and they cried and hollered rude obscenities when he threw their trunks in the street. She followed the girls down the steps, slipping them each five dollars to find another place to sleep.

When the Rosenblatts' new steam printer arrived from Germany, print production in *California Illustrated* increased, and so did the profits. Soon, the Rosenblatt family moved over to Hawthorne Street, into a proper two-story Victorian, built from milled redwood trees with curved windows sticking out beyond the house frame, and garish gables and rounded turrets at the top. Panels of showy fish scale shingles on the front screamed out in bright colors of yellow, brown, and red. Much too showy for Elisabeth's liking. Within a week of moving into their new home, the Rosenblatts insisted she move out of the Sully house into the apartment above their shop, rent-free.

"I don't deserve it," she said, hugging Ethel with a squeeze. "But yes!"

Elisabeth moved into the apartment above the Pacific Print Shop straightaway, into her very own bedroom with a tiny window overlooking busy Front Street, and a desk and chair and a bathroom all to herself, and real running water and a working toilet. Now she rolled right out of bed to work, saving an extra twenty dollars a week not paying rent, and getting her that much closer to opening her own shop. Wanting something more than working at the Pacific Print Shop was greedy, she knew. She couldn't help her ambition. Grateful to the Rosenblatts, she still wanted something of her own. After all, she'd endured. Lost. Given up. She deserved it. If she couldn't have a lasting love, she'd have her own successful business. It wasn't impossible. She'd done it before.

39

Mi Malagueña

"Lemme take your picture in trade," said Julie MacRob.

"I can't barter. It's not my shop," said Elisabeth.

"No matter, I'll pay for the advert," said Julie, passing bills across the counter. "I want it to say: 'Daguerreotypes taken by a lady. Those wishing to have a good likeness are informed they can have a picture taken in a very superior manner by a real live lady. On Post Street, opposite the St. Francis Hotel, at a very moderate charge. Give her a call, gents.'"

"I got it all down," said Elisabeth.

"Also, write down I birth babies too."

Elisabeth raised an eyebrow, thinking it strange a picture lady birthed babies, too, but she wrote down the wording for the advertisement in *California Illustrated* just as Julie wanted.

"It's my own shop. I own it outright," said Julie. "I like keeping my options open, just in case one or another venture doesn't pan out. Plus keeping familiar with the society ladies with children makes my picture business more respectable. Sends more customers my way."

Elisabeth didn't appreciate the woman bragging on about having her own business, and found her lack of formality presumptuous.

The woman thrust out her hand into Elisabeth's, pumping it up and down aggressive.

"Julie MacRob," she said, introducing herself.

Julie looked too sturdy, with a square jaw jutting out and an unsightly underbite causing her words to come out clumsy and too loud. Tall with wide shoulders, Julie wore two simple loops of blond hair tied up without flourish. But her unfortunate jaw and heavy brow made her look near like a man. In fact, if it wasn't for her elegant brown silk dress and fine felt hat with peacock feathers, she could've been mistaken for a man. But her undeterred confidence was irresistible.

"Whaddya say I take your picture, anyway? No charge. I'm working up a collection of art pictures, and you gotta good face. I'd like to capture those green eyes."

Remembering the womanly fellowship she enjoyed in Manzanita City, Elisabeth agreed. After closing up the shop that evening she met Julie at MacRob Photos on Clay Street. Seeing the inside made her wistful. Even small and dark, the room felt special with pale blue wallpaper, and shelves filled full and neat with stacks of copper plates and silvering chemicals, and spray of baby yellow roses in a crystal vase atop a tiny round table. She wondered where Julie found such gorgeous flowers growing in the gray, dusty city.

"My customers sit here," said Julie.

Julie pulled back a royal-blue velvet curtain, revealing two ornately carved and overstuffed chairs.

"Marvelous," she said, running her hand along the arm of one chair.

"I got the chairs off a Dutch sailing captain. Go ahead. Sit," said Julie.

Elisabeth plopped down in the chair and turned to face the large box on a tripod. Nervous, she fiddled with the folds of her silk dress. She'd never had a picture of herself made before.

"Hat or no?"

"No." Julie shook her head.

Elisabeth took off her hat and smoothed her hair as Julie slid a silvered copper plate into the camera box.

"Now act natural. No strange expressions. Ready? Freeze!"

In that intimate moment, Elisabeth sat still and unsmiling, hiding behind her green eyes, raw and wide and unblinking, as Julie looked through the box for nearly two minutes. It felt an eternity. When Julie finally pulled the plate out of the box, Elisabeth gasped, astonished at her likeness looking back. The picture looked like a mirror, but more. Tilting the plate at an angle, she saw her face appear in shadowy darkness. Tilting the plate the opposite way reflected a lighter image in opposite parts, as if the picture captured her whole true self, all that came before, with all the now and unfolding future pressed together. Mesmerized, she kept tilting the picture plate back and forth, looking for an unknown grace hidden inside her soul.

After the picturing, the two women struck up a grand friendship, taking Sunday suppers together every week at the Gold Dust Restaurant on the waterfront, eating crab, cracking and digging in the claws for meat, chatting about any old thing. Julie always ordered a brandy, and Elisabeth took only coffee with a teaspoon of sugar. When Julie asked if she was too prissy for a drink, she didn't tell the full reason.

"I've had my fill," she said.

"I'd like to hear that story," said Julie.

"Not interesting, I assure you," she said.

"Well, my story *is* interesting. Quite an adventure . . . swimming through that sea of grassland on a wagon train for so many months. I was nearly done in when the Sierra Nevadas came up tall like land ahoy . . . I'll tell you about it someday, if you're lucky!"

Elisabeth filled with both admiration and jealousy over Julie, even as the woman worked at winning her over with a bubbly and infectious disposition bursting forth as wholly agreeable, like a much-needed fresh breeze streaming into a musty, stifling room. Julie walked with a bouncy carefree stride as if nothing bothered her. No worry. No loneliness. No lost love. Much too audacious and bold, and not at all shied by her unlovely looks, Julie struck up conversations with just about everyone in the restaurant, promoting her picturing shop. Elisabeth knew a woman in the West looking for freedom required a certain level of force, and Julie reminded her of her friends Luenza and Ginny and Millie back in Manzanita City, and Nandy in Culoma Town and Gabriella Sanchez at the bottom of Telegraph Hill. It seemed all the women of California shared the same silver thread of determination and fortitude, spun up from the soul out of nothing. A silver thread required for surviving, thriving, in California.

One Sunday, Elisabeth begged off from their weekly supper, asking John Langley if he'd invite her to the opera. Julie teased at Elisabeth asking him, saying all the women in the city were after that Langley fellow, as he was on the lookout for a wife.

"Quite a catch, I hear. If you like that sort," said Julie.

"What sort is that?"

"Rich," said Julie.

"Not interested! I don't need a man bossing me. I'd rather get rich myself. Besides, I asked him to take me to the new Jenny Lind Opera House, so I can write about it for *California Illustrated*," she explained.

Of course John Langley agreed, picking her up at the Pacific Print Shop on Sunday afternoon in his very own brougham carriage, sleek and brightly polished, pulled by two gray horses harnessed up in silver. Blue paisley silk lined the inside. When the driver opened the carriage door, Elisabeth slid in beside Mr. Langley.

"You look a peach tonight, Miss Parker," he said, kissing her hand.

She blushed, pulling at the cuffs of her white lace gloves, nervous. He was just being kind. She knew her outfit wasn't quite up to par for the outing. The gray-and-white dress was good quality silk but had no ruffles, only a modest collar up to her neck. She couldn't be bothered with the latest fashions. She wore no tall hat with feathers and embellishments like the fancier ladies she'd seen around town. Instead, she simply parted her brown hair down the middle, fastening it in a bun with the abalone comb Nemacio had given her.

As they bounced along through the bumpy streets of San Francisco, Mr. Langley bragged on about his daughter Lily B. Elisabeth listened but hoped outside the formal confines of his bank he might reveal more about her mining investments.

"I'm so pleased you'll finally meet her tonight. She's coming with her new husband. They live down on the family ranch now, only coming up once a month. I miss her something terrible. She has exquisite taste, you know. She decorated my whole place up on Nob Hill. Six bedrooms, a ballroom, three parlors. Filled with beautiful art and furniture of the most cultivated sort. Turkish rugs. French armories. Lacquer vases from China. Fine bone dinnerware from

England. Venetian glass goblets. She even got me a Casilear painting of a mountain range to hang above my marble fireplace. Very classy. I give her all the credit."

Not a modest man, Mr. Langley had acquired a boastful reputation by talking up his various speculations and investments, gaining favor with many politicians and businessmen and their wives and daughters. He opened up his Nob Hill mansion for lavish parties every other Friday to all the who's who in San Francisco to enjoy good whiskey and listen to a Bach harpsichord sonata or a one-act Shakespeare play. Word floated around town he was in the market for a wife, now that his daughter had married and moved down the peninsula. Many single ladies vied for his favor, flitting about him like moths to a flame taken in by his new money. Not Elisabeth. Unable to overlook his less-than-handsome countenance in exchange for a comfortable life, she never accepted an invitation to one of his soirees. She simply found the man a charming father to his daughter.

"I admire your dedication to your daughter," she said.

"I adore Lily B., and I can't stand being all alone in my empty house without her. She thinks I need a wife. One who can appreciate all I have to offer," he said, spreading his arms wide and leaning back in the leather carriage seat.

Perhaps Elisabeth should've married a man like John Langley instead of Nathaniel Parker, as he surely enjoyed the intimate company of women over men.

"No need to sell yourself, Mr. Langley. I'm not in the market," she said, abrupt.

"A woman like you, with a quick mind and independent spirit. You're not an ornament," he said, earnest.

"I take that as a compliment," she said, feeling at the same time understood, but not entirely pretty either.

"We both know you're the sort of woman who prefers a compliment about the quality of her mind rather than the color of her eyes. Although, I daresay I do admire those just as much."

"I'm not looking for a position, Mr. Langley. I'm already employed."

He chuckled, sweet and infectious, and pointed at her.

"Clever, clever, woman. You must join me at Lily B.'s ranch . . . see the beautiful country down the peninsula."

"I'm heading up to the placers soon," she said.

"You're leaving me?"

"Researching an article about the deep well mines for *California Illustrated*."

"Can't those Rosenblatts send someone else?"

"I'm the reporter," she said.

"Come to the ranch instead."

"Perhaps when I return. In September."

"September is too far off!"

"Two months," she said.

John stroked her hand, and she realized she hadn't been touched for over a year by anyone. She enjoyed the attention.

"Why don't you take your gloves off?"

"I've working hands, John. Not as fine as most of the ladies you entertain, I suspect."

She stated a fact, no longer ashamed at her rough, nicked-up, calloused, ink-stained hands.

"It's not safe for women up there in the placers alone," he said.

"Greatly exaggerated, I assure you. I'm quite familiar with the gold country. I lived there before and found the living quite safe."

He closed his eyes and sighed heavy and exasperated.

"I suspect there's no talking you out of it," he said.

"Writing about the success of deep well mining might boost the stock prices in *both* our holdings," she said.

"Hmmm . . . like your thinking, Miss Parker," he said, tapping his temple as the carriage clattered through the streets of San Francisco toward the opera house.

"I hear word of a new contraption. A stamp mill. Crushes ore in a fraction of time it takes pickaxe operations. And quicksilver. Apparently it separates the gold from the rock. How about you give me a list of your mining investments, their general location, and such? I'll report back," she explained.

"How about I send one of my men instead."

"Nope."

He leaned over, kissing her hand in the rocking carriage, and his mouth lingered warm through her gloves, pulling her into well-charted waters. She looked into his face, examining all those freckles, thinking if she took the time she might be able to count each one and guess how many'd been cut clean off, replaced by that long scar, glistening clear and smooth.

"I know the gold country. Besides, you've got plenty of ladies to entertain you while I'm away," she said, teasing.

"I do like the ladies," he said, chuckling to himself.

"I miss the fresh air. The river."

"Ahh . . . you're looking for adventure."

Mr. Langley listened with interest as she spoke wistful of her time living down on the American and up in Manzanita City until the carriage arrived at the Jenny Lind Opera House. The three-story building rivaled the most noted theaters in Boston or New York, outfitted exquisitely inside with a grand spectacle of light pink walls, tastefully gilded with a turquoise drapery covering the stage and richly carved wooden seats with plush, tasseled cushions. Nearly a thousand folks crowded in, putting on a brilliant display of beauty and fashion. As friends and acquaintances vied for Mr. Langley's attention, he introduced Elisabeth around, fawning all over her, saying she reported stories for *California Illustrated*. When they sat in a box closest to the stage, Mr. McGuire, the owner of the opera house, came by to pay his respects.

"Do you know of *California Illustrated*? The most important newspaper in all of California? This woman here, Miss Elisabeth Parker, is the star reporter," Mr. Langley said.

Elisabeth asked Mr. McGuire a few questions about the building and the night's performance, jotting down his comments in her notebook. As the orchestra warmed up their violins and flutes, Lily B. finally arrived, bounding into the box, looking like just a girl. She had John's same light features of yellow skin, flaming with freckles, and curly red hair. Overjoyed, Mr. Langley embraced his daughter, kissing her cheek over and over as if he hadn't seen her just last month. Overcome with envy, Elisabeth turned away, thinking of everything she didn't have. A loving father. A place to call home. A man of her own.

"This is my Lily Beth. The sunshine of my life," said John.

Lily B. grabbed her by the shoulders, hugging her much too tight and talking much too fast and animated in a high-pitched, wild playacting.

"My father's writer friend, Elisabeth Parker. We've heard all about you!"

Lily B. wasn't exactly beautiful, with brown eyes too small and flecked in yellow, and a too-tiny chin, and a long pointy nose, but her giddiness made her magnetic, and her shock of red hair looked spectacular, even with her orange dress clashing in terrible taste. She pulled out of Lily B.'s grip, interjecting a mature formality to calm the girl down a bit.

"How do you do," said Elisabeth.

When the lamplighters snuffed the lights to a dim and the curtain opened, she turned to sit down.

"Wait! You must meet my husband!" Lily B. squealed.

Elisabeth turned around and nearly fell over at seeing him come in through the box curtain. Nemacio. Her Californio. Her lover. Her love. He drew in his breath at seeing her, too, and took a step back. But he collected himself quick, removing his hat and bowing, as if they hadn't once loved each other.

"Good evening," he said.

He looked the same as when she last saw him leaving her cabin in Manzanita City, full of promises. His smooth skin. His eyes, black and enticing. How absurd, seeing him here of all places. If she'd only asked John about Lily B.'s husband. Asked after her surname. If only she'd thought to ask. Thought to remember. She'd have never come.

Sitting through the performance with him just behind her felt like pure torture. Elisabeth didn't find the opera *La Cambiale di Matrimonio* even a little funny. The audience laughed and howled at the comic farce, while she remained flat, looking straight ahead at the performers. She tried not to come apart, knowing he was right behind her with his silly wife. She couldn't understand the words of Rossini's composition but got the meaning, to be sure. An ironic plot in the face of her own tragic life. The rich Tobias Mill marrying his daughter Fanny off to an even richer foreigner. Of course, Fanny is in love with another man, the modest Eduardo. Chaos issues. Secrets. Promises. Misunderstandings. Duels and tricks. In the end, Fanny gets to marry Eduardo. What cruel irony!

Just beneath the songs sung in Italian, she strained to hear Nemacio's breathing behind her like she had back in the dark cabin on the American River. But she couldn't hear a thing, just a terrible ringing in her ears. Loud and painful. When the performance ended and the lamplighters lit the lamps, the audience stood, but she remained seated, frozen in fear at facing him. She focused on the red carpet beneath her feet, as she felt him stand up behind her, next to silly Lily B., giggling gleeful. Her face grew hot, burning with vengeance. Rage. She imagined turning around and stabbing Lily B. with a sharp engraving bruin.

"You don't look well," said Mr. Langley, leaning down to touch her shoulder.

"Yes. I need to go home, straight away," she said, standing.

She hurried out of the opera box brushing past Nemacio, not looking at him. Brushing his shoulders. Slight. Touching. Remembering. Forgetting. She fled out of the opera box as John Langley struggled to catch up. She slipped away quick, disappearing into the crowd and out into the street, where she picked up the folds of her skirt and ran all the way home through the dark.

40

Since the night we met

Back in her bedroom above the Pacific Print Shop, she flung her-self onto the bed, burying her face in the embroidered linen pillowcase, shaking. *Trying to forget.* Trying to find a way to hate that man, *journeying along with every vagrant breeze!* Loving her and leaving her to forget her eyes that *shamed the purple sky,* with that damn Lily B., young and beautiful and hungry for a fancy Californio like him. What a fool she'd been to carry around his Malagueña letter in her pocket all year. And even now. She pulled it out from her skirt pocket, the paper thinned and frayed from rubbing it to death. She ripped it up, ashamed he still flowed through her blood after all this time, after using her like a dirty rag, then tossing her aside for a young American girl with a load of money behind that stupid squeal. Seething atop her quilt, she lay in a rage. Angry at herself. She'd come so far during the past year. She thought she'd moved on from all that hurt and shame. Replaced it with hard work and a load of learning. Moved on from all she'd done wrong. All the wrong choices. Wrong turns. The wrong loving that pricked with so much pain. What a fool she'd been! He'd been living in her bones the whole time. No amount of work or temperance could leach him out. Nothing could drain away that sort of love.

She wanted a drink of whiskey or mezcal. Something hard enough to dull the sharp stick of jealousy stabbing into her heart. Something to prop her up, give her strength. Digging around in her lock box, she grabbed a fistful of coins. She leaped down the steps and grabbed the front door knob, just as someone knocked. She backed up quiet, not wanting to deal with Mr. Langley. Not wanting to explain or make excuses.

"Elisabeth, open the door. Por favor."

It was Nemacio. He knocked again, and she sank to the floor, frozen.

"Please. My love. Please. I know you are there . . ."

He rapped on the door again and again as she sat quiet in a heap. She wasn't strong enough to open the door. To see his face up close. Not strong enough for his excuses. His lies. Just smelling him, she'd probably fall right back down his well of lying loving, getting trapped deep in that dark passion all over again with no way out. She stayed silent, pleased at hearing the growing desperation in his voice.

"You were married. I couldn't take you from him."

She wanted to open the door, to scream that she wasn't some damn horse to be traded. She was a woman who owned herself. He got quiet, and she wondered if he felt her through the door, listening. Holding herself back from unlocking her heart. Holding herself back from letting him in, again.

"I didn't know," he said, calmer now. "About the divorce. I didn't know you could divorce."

He knew. He just didn't approve. He'd told her so.

"I came back to the diggins. To explain about Lily, but you were gone," he said.

It went quiet, and she thought he might've left. Gone home to his red-haired American girl. She scooted up close to the door, leaning her cheek on the cold wood, and pressed her ear flat. Listening. She heard his breathing then, heavy and trembling. She felt him sad and weak right through the door, and she smiled, knowing he wasn't worth a drop of whiskey. Wasn't worth ruining all she'd built up. Wasn't worth losing her dignity.

"I had to marry. To save the ranch," he said.

She'd a never done that. She'd a never traded her love for a little money and a sweet slice of land. Not for a spot of heaven itself. She'd a never given him up. Standing, she turned away from the door. Walking up the stairs, she heard him calling out. Pleading.

"Please, Elisabeth. I only love you. Solo te quiero a ti. Solo ti. Solo ti."

As his voice faded away behind in hollow pleas, she vowed to never again settle for less than a grand love. Honest and true. And meant only for her.

41

Up a hill, down a stream

"Shhhh . . . I hear something," said Julie, putting her head down the hole.

Elisabeth listened, peering inside the hole burrowed into the side of the hill. Black as pitch and cold, the shaft stunk of rotten eggs wafting up, slapping her in the face. She turned away, coughing.

"Shhhh," said Julie.

"I don't hear a thing," she said.

Elisabeth and Julie were at the Porter Mine on a dry ravine, investigating all the deep well mines.

After seeing Nemacio at the opera, Elisabeth had convinced the Rosenblatts a feature in *California Illustrated* about the new mining techniques would sell in the thousands, and even back East too. She took off for the placers the very next day, fleeing Nemacio and his excuses and her own delicate heart. Eager for an adventure, Julie agreed to come along. They'd been out traveling for only two weeks and had already found one mine she owned shares in, the Clearwater, which turned out to be a modest operation making decent gains, and four mines from John Langley's list.

The Porter Mine was partway obscured by dried grass, so they'd nearly missed the hole altogether. Elisabeth cleared bits of sticks away from the head beam to reveal an entrance about four feet in diameter, braced up off-kilter with rickety wooden beams and a sign claiming it The Porter Mine.

"It smells like deep pay dirt. Might be over twenty feet, maybe more," she said.

"Shhh!" Julie said.

She heard it, then. A feeble tapping, like a tummy gurgling faintly with hunger. Then nothing. Then the feeble gurgling tap again.

Julie pulled her head out of the hole, with a face turned white and beading up with nervous sweat.

"It's the tommy-knockers," said Julie.

"The tommy-knockers?"

"My grandfather told all about those godforsaken imps," said Julie.

"Stop!"

"Those tommy-knockers are like leprechauns and brownies. Little green men living in the mines, knocking around, making strange noises," Julie explained.

"I don't believe in magic," said Elisabeth.

"Believe it! Those tommy-knockers are real, making mischief. Depending on their mood. That knocking means two things: either the tommy-knockers say this hole leads to richness or it's a death pit about to collapse," Julie insisted.

"Just those two choices?"

"Yep," said Julie.

"Go in for the booty or get the hell away?" she asked, mocking.

"You go ahead and laugh, but my granddaddy told me about those tommy-knockers living in the coal mines back in Cornwall. One time, he heard them knocking and ran out of the mine just as the fore section caved in. After that my granddaddy left a slice of cherry pie every Friday for those tommy-knockers, thanking them. Asking for protection. Call it superstitious, but come Monday, that pie was always gone."

"Lemme guess. Eaten by the tommy-knockers," Elisabeth said, funning.

Returning to the American River basin with Julie had improved her spirits after seeing Nemacio again. Julie proved a great traveling companion, always goofing around and making light with a warm, funny manner. She hadn't told Julie about Nemacio at the opera, preferring instead to forget altogether.

"Yes! And after, no more mine accidents," said Julie.

As the tapping turned to clomping, they listened at the mouth of the mine. When the clomping got louder and louder, they backed up.

"That you, ladies?" a voice called out, muffled and small.

A short man crawled out of the hole, scruffy with a long red beard and a hat filled with cobwebs and bits of dust that sparkled in the sun. He stood short but was still a man, not a tommy-knocker. Both women sighed in relief.

"I heard you was coming," he said.

The man introduced himself as Drew Mack, manager of the Porter Creek Mine, explaining that word had gotten around two ladies were crawling all over the hills, writing and picturing the deep pits. His boss told him to show the ladies the spoils. Explain the particulars and such.

"Who's your boss?" Elisabeth asked.

"Mr. James Porter," he said.

"James Porter! He's an old friend," she said.

"You got a picture box? I'll stand right to the side so you can see the hole," said Mr. Mack, posing tall. "The world will want to hear about the production we've got going on here."

"Where is Mr. Porter?" she asked.

"Maybe up in Auburn Town this week. I never do know the particular whereabouts of Mr. Porter at any one given moment. He's a busy man."

"I'll bet," she said. "Tell me, Mr. Mack, how do you separate the ore with no water running down the ravine?"

"Not in the summer, that's for sure. We operate in winter, full up, and in spring, too, when the rains fill the gully down there. We break up rock, more than two dozen of us, till we get out the gold."

She had her notebook out now and started scribbling with a charcoal nub along the paper, even though the mine looked abandoned with no past evidence of the production Drew Mack described.

"How exactly?"

"Ma'am?"

"How exactly do you break up the rock? You still smashing with pickaxes?"

Julie set up her tripod with a camera box as Drew Mack shifted on his feet in the hot sun.

"Make sure you write down there are no Maidu in these parts," he said, pointing to her notebook. "Last spring they all got rounded up for those Indian Farms. There's a bounty on their scalp, with the new laws. Those savages stay clear now, is all I know. You getting this all down?"

Hearing about the Indian Farms made her think of Henry and his girl. She still held soreness for them both but wasn't so cruel to want the girl to get rounded up. Penning up any person like an animal struck her as cruelty beyond redemption.

"How much have you pulled out so far?"

"See this here? I pulled this up just today."

Drew Mack handed over a nugget, brassy like a crystalline sunflower. Turning over the golden ore, Elisabeth found it hard and flat with crackled striations radiating out from the center. As she ran her thumb along the center, gold bits flaked off, sticking to her sweaty skin.

"What's the total yield?" she asked.

"Quite a bit," he said.

"How much is quite a bit?" she pushed.

"Looky here, ladies. My hat sparkles with the stuff." Mr. Mack thrust his hat in her face. "Make sure you write that down. 'His hat sparkled in gold dust.'"

"Quite impressive," she said, handing the nugget back to Drew Mack and nodding for Julie to take a picture.

"Hold your hat in one hand and the nugget in the other," said Julie. "Now keep still."

Elisabeth wondered if Mr. Mack was really that stupid, or if he just thought women knucklehead fools. Gold isn't brittle, but soft. It can't rub off in your hands and doesn't smell like rotten eggs. His golden nugget was simply iron and sulfur fused together into the heartbreaking joke of fool's gold. She didn't let on she knew the truth, just nodded in approval, grateful she'd refused marrying that lying Mr. James Porter when he'd asked.

"Give me a figure, Mr. Mack," she said.

"A figure?"

"A figure on how much gold you've pulled up so far."

"Uh . . . seventy pounds. Say seventy pounds."

She didn't ask for proof, just wrote the number down in her notebook and elbowed Julie to move on.

Following a map from the Hangtown assayer, the women traveled around on horseback, zigzagging along the new roads cut through the Sierra foothills, twisting and turning down rugged pine-covered canyons and snaking up the other side, looking for all the hard-rock mines on Elisabeth's list. The mountains teemed with activity now, with pack trains of mules carrying mail into mining camps, and Wells Fargo money stages, passenger coaches, supply wagons, and miners on foot swarming like locusts from one location to the next. Folks proved friendly as ever, eager to make small talk with the women, share in the latest word of a new strike. The road builders took tolls on the roads, and Elisabeth was happy to pay, thinking routes cut into those steep ravines a marvel of man's ingenuity and far safer than those skinny footpaths she'd once traveled with bears lurking under bushes.

Elisabeth still wasn't relaxed up on her horse. Coming overland with the wagon train turned Julie into quite a horsewoman, and she insisted they ride straddling the horses with both legs, like men.

"I've always been convinced those damn sidesaddles are some diabolical invention of a tyrannical man, made to drag women lopsided through the world. I like to see where I'm going," said Julie.

Elisabeth wasn't at all happy with her squat, dappled gray gelding, looking old and doddery with a scraggy mane and graying whiskers. But Julie insisted she needed something steady on its feet since she'd had no riding experience. Elisabeth slumped awkward atop the pony, nervous at managing such a creature, even with its small size. Although she was happy wearing her comfortable skirt, cut short, with no corset digging into her ribs.

Julie demonstrated the particulars of horse riding, sitting easy on her mare, Old Sally, showing how to steer and stop, and how to weight the saddlebags even so as not to cause the horse distress. Julie said to act casual but confident too. Let the horse know who's boss. Give him a kind talking to. Treat him just like any old man, telling him he's smart and strong.

Elisabeth hated calling her horse Burrito, thinking the name silly. Even though Julie advised it wasn't a good idea to confuse the horse, she took to calling it Tom, in honor of her dead dog.

"I refuse to call out to a Burrito the whole way," she said, grumbling.

Leaving the Porter Mine, Elisabeth still wasn't relaxed, off-balance and shaky up on Tom as usual, who moved slow and stubborn and refused to trot fast enough to keep up with Julie on Old Sally. Tom pained her, going sideways instead of straight and stopping sudden to munch on grass. She kicked Tom hard in the sides with her boots and slapped his withers unkind, pulling on his reins strong.

"I keep telling you, he don't go by Tom," said Julie, shaking her head. "His name's Burrito."

"He'll go by what I say. Git up, Tom!"

Her legs grew sore from kicking Tom over and over to git up, and from gripping tight when he got a mind to haul off at a rough unwieldy run. She yelled angry and impatient at Tom's difficult temperament.

"Quit beating on him. Talk nice. Let him nibble at the grass, a bit. They work for love."

She tried coaxing him to walk right, talking smooth talk to him. But the damn thing didn't respond, instead sulked along, laying his ears low like he knew she lied. When Tom turned and bit her knee, she felt so mad and beaten down she thought she'd cry. Over a damn stubborn horse! After that, she resigned to ignore his willful manner, letting him go on at his poky, annoying pace. She stopped smacking on him, since it didn't work anyhow, and he slowly started minding her gentle rein commands, if reluctant and with a little hesitation.

By that afternoon, the two settled into a sort of resigned agreement, and she grew grateful at least that she wasn't breaking her back walking and pushing a cart like she'd been three years before with Nate. She found the familiar nature of the American River canyon a grand comfort. Along the trail, the water's cadence over the rocks gave her chills, like a long forgotten song streaming through her once again. Her mood soared at the rich blue sky; she hadn't realized how much the wet fog of San Francisco had dampened her free spirit. Bright orange poppies and red Indian paintbrush speckled along the hillsides, burning her eyes open, as all the pines greeted her with outstretched branches like old friends.

Julie turned out an agreeable traveling companion, energetic and eager to explore the area bringing so much fuss to the whole of America. Sometimes she rattled on too much for Elisabeth, who rather preferred savoring the simple sounds of the soothing breeze whooshing through the boughs. But she didn't tell Julie to shut it, just listened to her friend chattering on about the beauty of California. Considering each day an adventure, Julie blanketed the air with cheerful optimism, offering up intelligent companionship, all while pointing out clever observations like how pine trees only collect moss on the north side, and how funny she found marmots always choosing a spectacular view atop high rock ledges to do their business, and how the American flows back up on itself in sections, eddying up into a calm whirlpool. Julie's chatty manner grew on thick, and Elisabeth came to enjoy her lively observations on all sorts of subjects. Writing. Books. Picture taking and engraving. The particulars of managing financial matters, and the prospects of a woman working on her own. With Julie along, the journey turned surprisingly lighthearted and joyful.

Two women traveling alone up through the foothills into the river basin was still a novelty to the miners they passed. The men usually stopped pickaxing near the riverbanks to doff their hats and stare dumfounded like they were looking at a mirage. Not one group let the women pass without offering them a place to stop and rest in the shade. Water their horses. Or join them for a cup of coffee. The women were polite but never accepted.

"No time, boys, gotta get on," Elisabeth said, begging off.

She told Julie there was no reason to be nervous.

"They're harmless. Just ordinary men out looking for courting company. And we're a rare sight. Precious things they haven't seen in some time digging out here among only men. Don't you mind 'em, Julie."

Looking down at the men from atop her horse as she passed, Julie mumbled to herself.

"No man ever thought I was precious, that's for sure."

Being near the American River again relaxed Elisabeth, and she soon gave up calling her horse Tom. She might as well call the damn thing by his real name, no matter how stupid Burrito sounded. She'd been foolish anyhow, trying to rename a horse after a dog she'd once loved. Those days had long passed, swept away along a river of remembrance. The gelding responded right away at hearing his name, perking his ears up sweet. She stroked the side of his neck, leaning down and whispering in his ear.

"Good boy. You're a good Burrito. That's right, good Burrito," she said.

She felt silly saying nice nothings to the horse named Burrito, but he liked the gentle coaxing, and a springy stride replaced his lazy lumbering. When Burrito started galloping along smooth, she hugged his neck, wondering how life might've turned out different if she'd only learned to control a man that easy.

She led the way up along the river basin, eager to see her girlfriends in Manzanita, and Nandy in Culoma. But as they came up the North Fork, she turned Burrito onto the Brushy Creek trail and switchbacked up to the ridge to avoid the Goodwin Claim. She wasn't quite ready to see Nate.

That afternoon they made camp high above the canyon, unsaddling the horses and giving them a lump of oats. Elisabeth performed her usual camp routine, clearing rocks and sticks and pine cones, and stamping the dirt flat with her boots. She refused Julie's help, saying she knew how to set a camp right. In truth, she needed the ritual. It gave her a sense of control. Unsatisfied with some tiny pebble poking up from underneath the canvas roll, she ripped the tent down, starting all over again with her whole exacting flattening procedure, reworking the bedrolls, as Julie kept quiet at her fussing and set up her camera box. Frustrated, Elisabeth finally gave up on the tent altogether, setting up the bedrolls out in the open.

That warm summer twilight in the Sierras unfolded thick as Elisabeth's favorite time of day, the in-between slice of possibilities and reflections, when the setting sun and trees and the granite and the sky blended together into a rich alpenglow. She looked down the ridge to the North Fork of the American River below twisting and bending through the narrow green valley. She reached out, touching the gloaming as an ever so slight breeze tickled her fingertips, reminding her of all the living she'd done down there. All the joy and suffering and loving and learning, and her heart reset itself, beating right again. She'd come out of it stronger, if alone, and wasn't waiting on any man to make her whole anymore. She inhaled all that woodsy fragrance deep into her lungs, content to soak up the fresh living. Nandy had been right after all when she'd told Elisabeth that first day they met: *The world is different out here. It presses into you . . . a gift you didn't know you needed. Once you take it, you ain't never gonna be the same.*

Elisabeth was no longer that same woman, and felt lucky for it. And knew she was lucky, too, for knowing Nandy, and for traveling around in the company of such a solid woman as Julie.

"Come on over. I don't want to miss this light," said Julie.

"What do you aim to picture?"

"Myself. I want you to take it," said Julie.

Julie showed her how to frame up the view and hold the shutter open, then walked to the edge of the ravine.

"I don't know a better moment, Lizzy. I'm gonna do it right here," she said.

Julie slipped out of her dress and dropped her pantaloons to the ground. Standing bare naked, her skin glowed creamy against the setting sun smearing red across the Sierra ridges and beyond.

"Dropping your drawers?"

"Not like you haven't seen lady bits before," said Julie.

It wasn't true. She'd never seen a woman naked before. The only person she'd ever seen naked, out in the open, was Nemacio down on the Uva.

Julie laid herself out bare and long on a smooth granite slab cropping out over the steep ravine. She reclined as if on a plush divan, not a hard rock. The light danced behind her, casting a deep shadowy crevasse between her legs, and she pulled her braid free, flinging her long hair across one breast. The other breast poked up taut. Julie posed, looking over her shoulder off into the distance.

"Put me at the bottom of the frame. With that purple sky above. Like I'm floating up in heaven," she said.

"How's it feel bare naked out in the open like that?"

"Free," said Julie.

Elisabeth looked through the viewfinder, seeing Julie not at all obscene but bold and at the same time vulnerable.

"Hold still now," said Elisabeth.

Julie remained still as a Greek statue for two whole minutes, as the cricket song grew louder in the dusking. She looked deeply beautiful to Elisabeth, and full of extraordinary power.

"Finished," said Elisabeth.

Julie slipped back into her clothes and grabbed the plate as the image appeared as a gauzy goddess under her thumb. She tilted the image back and forth, looking. Regarding herself lying out there naked in the wild like some California Lady Godiva.

As dark came on full, the women made a fire together and shared a pot of stew without talking, struck silent by the intimacy they'd shared. After, they lay beside each other in the open night, and Julie reached over for Elisabeth's hand, threading her finger through hers. In the firelight, Elisabeth saw tears streaming down Julie's cheeks. She didn't pry, just held her hand tight, glad to give a spot of comfort to her friend.

"I think my daddy knew," said Julie.

Elisabeth kept looking up at the stars, knowing, yet waiting for Julie to tell it.

"A man and babies, I just can't go for having a man laying up on me," said Julie. "My sisters, they enjoyed all that baking and washing and sewing, but I liked working in my father's picture shop, silvering up the copper plates and mounting the pictures under glass. All my sisters grew tall and beautiful, attracting fine suitors. All of 'em married, even little Mary, at eight years younger than me. I'd a been happy staying a spinster like that, working in my father's shop. But a man named Thomas Ward showed up looking for work. My daddy didn't need an apprentice, of course. He had me. But Mr. Ward came around asking after me on three separate occasions, hoping to win my father's favor. I knew he wasn't interested in me. He just wanted my job. It worked. My daddy hired him. Gave him my position. When Mr. Ward asked to marry me, my daddy insisted I accept. I didn't want that man or any other climbing all over me. I know what that gets you: six girls and a load of work wiping bottoms and washing drawers. I saw my momma under that weight, just wishing her daughters would marry and get out from under her roof. Not the life for me."

Elisabeth understood the sentiment but wondered how Julie might fare if the right man showed her the right sort of loving.

Someone who broke her open, melting her soft and weak like butter set out too long in the sun.

"I acted spiteful, telling my daddy he didn't need me anymore, now that he had Thomas," Julie said, her voice wobbling. "I said I wanted payment for working free all those years. In the end he agreed, giving me a camera and buying me passage on a wagon train going overland, sending me off with good wishes. I'm thankful for it every day," she said.

"He just let you go?"

"Yup. He knew I'd never be happy in New York, with no prospects of my own. He understood I wanted something else, and I wasn't about to miss an opportunity to picture the gold rush," said Julie.

Elisabeth waited, knowing Julie wasn't finished telling it. She waited through the long awkward pause, until Julie finally said it.

"Truth be told, I'd take any woman over a man," said Julie.

Hearing Julie tell it, she thought of Nate. How he must've felt. His struggles and the choices he'd been forced to make. Nate hadn't half the courage of Julie, who hadn't given up herself in a lie of tradition, ruining another person's life in the process. Instead, she chose swimming against the strong tide of what's expected in a woman, to live honest and true, come what may of the consequences. She held a great admiration for Julie.

"I understand," said Elisabeth.

Letting go of Julie's hand, Elisabeth leaned up on her elbow, looking at her friend in the firelight. She took a deep breath and told her story. About Henry and the Indian girl, and Nate, and Nemacio. She left out the part about the tumbling, confident no good woman could look past that terrible sin. And they talked long into the night, sharing stories without judgment.

"What was it like, having that fella Nemacio move around inside you?"

"Like I'd cracked open and filled up with a juice of honey and whiskey. A sweet drunk. Leaving me barely able to breathe for the pleasure of it."

"Honey and whiskey?"

"I couldn't get my fill," she said.

"And now?"

"Probably still," she said.

"Do you get sad, being without him?"

"I got myself. And my women friends," she said, meaning it.

She pulled the worn copy of Emerson's "Self-Reliance" from her saddlebag and handed it to Julie.

"I want you to have this," she said. "I'm finished with it."

Elisabeth lay down on her blanket roll as Julie thumbed through the pages of the book by the firelight.

"I love you, Lizzy," said Julie, matter-of-fact, without looking up from the book.

Elisabeth stared up at the stars flickering bright in the sky overhead, understanding and gaining trust in her own bearings.

"I love you too, Jules," she said.

42

The gypsy strain

Aiming to find some wild intensity, Elisabeth went looking for a man. They were in Auburn Town. She left Julie asleep in the tent and went looking. She wanted someone entirely opposite of Nemacio. Someone weak and shallow and empty. And younger than Nate.

She'd been freed. Freed from waiting on Nemacio. Freed from wondering if he'd ever come back. He wasn't coming back. He'd gone and married someone else, so she went looking for some loving of her own. She found a man in the Auburn Town Store. He was younger, with an open face and blond hair, tousled sweet and careless. He was buying coffee beans and had large beautiful hands and he smelled like wild anise. She touched his arm light when the grocer turned around toward the shelves. He followed her away from the store out into the darkness. He followed her past the bathing house and the livery. He followed her deep into the forest where the bulbous moon cast shadowy excitement all around. He said he was a Dane, from Denmark. She couldn't have picked that place out on a map, nor did she care. She didn't want to know his name.

California peeled away her old New England self, shedding that meek skin of chastity, revealing a brighter hue of flesh underneath. Revealing her new self. Thrilling yet unnerving at the same time.

She untied her straw hat, letting it drop to the ground, while the Dane stared with blue eyes, light and watery like the river. She leaned up against a pine and unbuttoned her blouse, freeing her neck, her breasts. Cloaked in tenebrous light, she was anonymous. Enigmatic. Strong.

When the Dane fumbled her hair loose and sucked on her neck, she grew beautiful. When he kissed her shoulders, collarbone, nipples, she came alive, clawing at him savage, pulling his pants down, groping. Pawing. Opening her legs lusty with desire, taking what she wanted. Taking hold of his backside and pulling him up inside. Wrapping her legs around him, she let loose hungry moans as the Dane moved in and out delicious with passion. She writhed up against the tree trunk, taking the loving she wanted. Finding her true self, free and powerful, and it was enough.

43

Going where I please

The Manzanita City town center looked nearly unrecognizable to Elisabeth. From the ashes of that horrible fire, gleaming new shops of all sorts had risen up. She didn't see any bookstores, but a water stand in the plaza held a dozen buckets full of water just in case of another fire. The El Dorado Hotel sat in the same spot as before, near the center of town, now rebuilt larger with a clever two-story outhouse attached in the back so guests wouldn't have to make their way downstairs to take care of business on cold nights. Elisabeth walked inside to see Luenza at the bar, tallying up her books. At seeing Elisabeth, she ran out from behind the bar throwing her arms up in the air, hooting and jumping up and down.

"God, I've missed you, woman!" said Luenza, folding her into a huge hug.

Luenza had packed on more than a little weight in the year Elisabeth had been gone, with a blue silk dress pulling taut over rolls of tummy fat. Luenza seemed jollier than ever, not minding her middle one bit, patting it lovingly as if the extra bit were proof she'd done well for herself. Luenza sent her barman 'round to get Millie at the

Stamps Store. Elisabeth gave them each a little square of Ghirardelli chocolate from San Francisco as a gift, and made introductions to Julie. They suppered in the dining room of the new El Dorado Hotel, which looked finer than the original, now with a piano man playing the main saloon room all day, a separate cardroom in the back, and a few tables in the front with lace table coverings for ladies who wanted tea in the afternoon. Elisabeth listened as Luenza and Millie told of Ginny not sticking around to rebuild after the fire.

"She set herself on a man who'd weaseled himself some land off a Californio in Stockton. Last I heard she sits around a hacienda all day with maids making her pies," said Luenza.

"She'll get bored," said Millie.

"Come back to us, Elisabeth," said Luenza. "Manzanita City doesn't have a bookstore since you left."

"That's not true, Luenza! I have a whole shelf of books for sale over at our Stamps Store," said Millie.

"Millie does whatever she wants now after living in Auburn Town for a few months after the fire," said Luenza, nodding in the direction of Millie. "I don't know what happened down there, but now her man treats her like a princess. I suspect he's afraid she'll hightail it with a better man."

"Never!" Millie said. "Joseph is the best partner."

"That's 'cause of all that business in bed," said Luenza. "I swear, I heard you yelling out all sorts of yummy from your open window last week."

"Stop it!" Millie said, turning red and slapping at Luenza's thick shoulder.

Elisabeth held deep affection for Millie and Luenza but had no interested in returning to Manzanita.

"I'm working in San Francisco for *California Illustrated* now. That's what brought me out here. Reporting on the deep mine technology. The stamp mill. Hydraulic monitor. Riffle sluicing with quicksilver," said Elisabeth.

"I make quite a bit on the side picturing men looking to send their likeness back home to family," said Julie.

"We don't have a picture shop yet. Why don't you stay?" Luenza asked.

"I'm sticking with her," said Julie, pointing to Elisabeth.

"I get it," said Luenza.

"You gotta man?" Julie asked.

"Used to. More trouble than he was worth, sitting on his behind all day, spending all my hard-earned money. He up and left for good after the fire, saying I was too much trouble. Well, good riddance to him. I got plenty of other men interested. Good men, mind you. But I'm finding life easier not choosing," said Luenza.

"That's 'cause she prefers loving them all," said Millie.

"Your man came looking for you," Luenza said, turning to Elisabeth.

"I don't have a man," said Elisabeth.

"You know who I'm talking about. That Californio."

"He's not my man."

"You don't want to know?"

Of course she wanted to know. She stayed silent, holding her breath.

"He came a few months after the fire, when we were still hammering nails. I had a makeshift bar out in the open, and he walked up angry, asking where you'd gone. I said I didn't know, which was true 'cause you hadn't written me yet," said Luenza, chiding. "He looked skinnier than I remembered. Carried a terrible worried look. I asked what he wanted with you. He said it was none of my damn business. He had the gall to swipe his arm along my bar, breaking four glasses. I told him to pay up, and he flung coins at me. More than the glasses worth, but still."

She didn't want to know. Didn't want to open the wound. Spill her sick soul out on the ground to rot. Besides, Nemacio was married now. It didn't matter.

"I'm not interested," she lied. "I'm too busy for a man now."

"Too busy for loving?" Luenza asked, not believing.

"We found the Red Hill Mine," Elisabeth said, moving away from the uncomfortable topic. "It looked like just a hole dug into the side of a hill, until we saw men hauling out barrelfuls of quartz chunks. They have this stamp mill contraption powered by a flume coming down off the Bear River smashing up the rocks. Noisy as all get out. They smooth the stamped pulp over wool blankets, getting more than half the gold, then push the rest into a cylinder with quicksilver to separate any leftover gold bits. Quite a sophisticated operation," she said.

She went on and on with more exuberance than she'd meant, getting excited at the telling of it. Although she didn't let on that she owned nearly a five percent share in the Red Hill Mine. Didn't brag how she'd grabbed the opportunity to trade engraving certificates for shares in five more mines when she had the chance. She had no need to show up Luenza or Millie.

Leaving Luenza and Millie in the morning, they traveled down the Codfish Falls trail, which she remembered as less steep than Brushy Creek. When they reached the bottom of the canyon, Elisabeth stopped, sitting atop Burrito, soaking up the familiar beauty of the American rushing past. Powerful and pure. But she didn't turn upriver to the Goodwin Claim, figuring that part of her life was gone now, having flowed out of her like a stream dried up. She saw no sense circling around to her past, and didn't want to see Nate living in domestic bliss with Francis. Didn't want to hear him tell how Nemacio came looking for her after the fire. And she didn't want his money, either. Besides, he probably needed her share of the claim more than she did. Instead, she turned Burrito downriver toward Culoma to see Nandy.

It'd been over a year since she'd left Nandy's bakery with a slice of Nemacio growing inside her. Many times she'd considered writing Nandy but never did. On account of guilt. And shame. Seeing Elisabeth walk up to her bakery, Nandy looked up and wiped her hands on her apron without a fuss.

"I knew you was comin'. My jay fussed up something awful this morning," said Nandy.

Elisabeth and Julie pitched their tent behind the Gootch cabin, preferring Nandy and Billy Gootch over the comforts of a hotel with strangers. They stayed on three days, letting the horses fill up on the last of the late summer grass covering the hill behind Nandy's bakery. Elisabeth was surprised to hear Nandy had sold enough bread to finally buy her son Andrew's freedom, and his wife's freedom too.

"They're coming overland. Due any week now."

"You did it, Nandy. Just like you said you would. You're a marvel," she said, meaning it with all her heart.

"I own the land you're standing on too. Gootch land. Bought the plot last month. For Andrew," said Nandy, beaming. "Me and Billy, we's gonna add on the cabin, make room for my boy and his woman. Might take a year, but I'm saving up for the wood now."

"Now you're just braggin'," said Elisabeth, giving Nandy a playful shove.

"I ain't funnin'. I did. I earned this Holy Land, flowing with milk and honey and freedom. Given to me by God. I'm never leaving."

She knew God didn't give Nandy that land. She'd earned it. Fair and square. With her own blood and sweat and anguish and hope for her son. Setting a fine example. From then on, Elisabeth started seeing California though Nandy's grateful eyes.

Elisabeth helped out with the chores, mixing and flipping dough, and washing out pans and cleaning rags. She actually enjoyed the rush of activity in Culoma Town this time around, with no heavy worry about finding Henry or making Nate happy or carrying Nemacio's baby. They suppered all together over at Captain Shannon's place, meeting new townsfolk who'd recently settled in. She and Julie even danced with a few nice fellas who asked, and she enjoyed herself without the help of any drink.

Nandy didn't ask about the baby right away, but she'd never let something like that lie. On the second day, Elisabeth was chopping wood when Nandy cornered her.

"Where is it?"

Elisabeth leaned on the axe and wiped her brow, knowing she'd never admit the tumbling to Nandy or anyone else. She'd locked that something awful deep inside the marrow of her bones, and no amount of picking and digging would ever pry it lose.

"I lost it," she said.

"What you mean, lost it?"

"Came out before its due," she said.

"Before its due?"

Elisabeth kept quiet, squirming on her feet, like a fly caught in honey.

"That's all you got to say?"

"We all got something," said Julie, walking up from washing at Dukehart's bathhouse.

"That right? What d'ya have?" Nandy asked Julie.

Julie flipped her drippy wet hair around in circles to dry.

"I've got something, too, that's for sure. I just don't want to tell it," said Julie.

"I don't pry," said Elisabeth, not letting on she knew.

"I don't pry neither," said Nandy, who let both matters drop.

They headed out on the trail the next morning, with Elisabeth promising to visit Nandy the following summer to meet Andrew. She gave Nandy a generous hug, thanking her for all she'd done to help get her though the rough patches.

Traveling out of the American River basin, the women carried all the supplies they'd need for the mining edition of *California Illustrated*. Mining reports, summaries, yields, locations, contacts, and plenty of photographs. Elisabeth carried sweet memories of visiting with her friends, and enough passion with that Dane to last a while. Coming down through the wide golden foothills toward the sun hanging low and shining hard and hot, she left behind thoughts of Nate and his lover and her father who'd up and left and Nemacio who'd married another woman and the child she'd killed and all she would never have, toward her very own guilty broken-up heart, patched but still beating strong. She walked westward toward who she was and who she was yet to become, and she didn't look back.

44

October 1853

Dearest Louisa,

Your recent letter struck me with compelling advice, if perhaps seen by many in the east as less than genteel, and even a little dangerous. I agree a woman might fare better, as you say, "remaining a free spinster to paddle her own canoe." However, I still choose to consider the prospects of a passionate love, which has been known, on rare occasion, to bring extraordinary pleasure to a woman. If not lasting, then fleeting. I hope regardless, not yet counting myself among the desperate lot without prospects. There is appeal in the expected comforts of home and hearth promised by a husband, but comfort without independence or love isn't really all that comfortable. Besides, I know many women in California who earn those very same luxuries promised by a man without the help from the stronger sex. These women have taught me we should no longer settle for the low bar of comfort alone, but strive higher for a partnership of equal measure and effort that includes the fair bargain of a grand love.

Of course, you'll never entirely paddle alone if you remain unmarried, as you'll always have your family crowded around. I find myself in a wholly different situation. At times I am discomforted in thinking how I might be bolstered through with a family of my own. How I wish you and Anna and Elisabeth and Abigail were my very own sisters, and admit my jealously now knowing you lean on each other through a life without knowing any less. You must understand, carrying around the burden of your family is just as heavy as the weight I do not carry. Our weights are made of different shapes and sizes, but each constitutes a commensurate burden nonetheless.

In circling around to my beginnings out west on the American River, I embraced the fabric of a wound, which I'd nearly fooled myself into thinking mended. My journey to the diggings proved a clearing out of sorts, allowing my mind the realization of my mistakes in keeping the company of those who'd held no true regard for my circumstance, and showed little consideration for providing me comfort in exchange for my sacrifice. My sadness doesn't stem from need but from lack of consideration, which festers as an infection of unworthiness atop my heart. I remain paddling alone, but not as the spinster with which we are both familiar. I dare to imagine a different sort of situation for myself in California, the discovery of which reveals itself as pure joy. In the meantime, I entertain the possibility of the unknown and the unknowing, which both thrill and terrify me. On opposite coasts, we must promise to find worth in ourselves, and to never stop hoping for an expected surprise.

I congratulate your efforts in finding a womanly life full of meaning and success. It is not by happenstance but your own perseverance that the Boston Theater accepted your play. I think of you in the throes of production and await news of the opening. If not too much to ask, and if time permits, a copy would find itself a welcome home in my hands, even if a poor substitute for you joining me in

California. I eagerly await word of your next book and send you love and strength in prospering with joy on your own.

Your friend, paddling alone down a river of uncertainty, out west,
EP

45

Said my heart to me

Elisabeth rode out through the wide-open valley of Central California with John Langley toward the Gabilan family rancho. Toward Nemacio and his silly wife, Lily B. Elisabeth was no longer afraid. She was strong enough to face him now.

"I warn you in advance, John. You've no chance with me," she said, sitting tall atop Burrito.

He insisted she call him John now, while she didn't invite him to call her anything but Miss Parker.

"There's always a chance," said John, winking.

"You can go on flattering all day, but you know I'm not the marrying sort," she said.

She'd accepted John's invitation to the Gabilan Rancho as research for a feature article the Rosenblatts suggested she write about the California Land Act. A legitimate assignment for *California Illustrated*, not a journey of vengeance, she told herself. After all, her last feature about the new gold mining techniques created quite a stir, earning spectacular returns for the Rosenblatts, selling out eight hundred copies in just under an hour. They reprinted it eight times, shipping it east to New York, Boston, Baltimore, Philadelphia, and St. Louis. New investors and speculators flooded to John Langley's Pioneer Bank looking to invest in the mines, further driving up the value of all California gold mining stocks across the board. The mines mentioned in Elisabeth's article gained the highest value, increasing four-fold in the first month alone, including the Porter Mine where the unscrupulous Drew Mack lied about the gold. She'd written about Drew Mack's "hat sparkling in gold," as her ethical considerations didn't quite extend to burying her interests under the foolish man's inconsistencies. His lying wasn't her problem. Besides, she nursed an unapologetic blind ambition to boost the value of her own mining interests. She intended to secure her financial future, independent from any man.

She'd cashed out her Porter Mine shares when they hit a price of $6,000, up $5,500 in value from before the *California Illustrated* feature issue on mining. The truth about the Porter Mine yielding fool's gold would come out soon enough, but she felt confident she'd never be blamed since she hadn't lied, exactly. She'd simply quoted Drew Mack's words. It wasn't her lie. Anyhow, she'd only made the one promise to God, not to nip on the drink anymore. She'd never made a promise not to stretch the truth, so she saw no harm in boosting her interests like every other man in this town did.

John Langley paid her an additional bonus for boosting his own banking interests, suggesting she invest in land for her own security. She agreed, buying three plots in San Francisco straight away. She held off selling her other three remaining mining investments until the shares gained enough value, enough to buy six more plots. She dreamed of owning a whole city block. In the meantime, she'd set herself up comfortable, with a tidy savings in the bank she could rely on, and she'd come by it independent and honest, more or less.

Elisabeth posted a hundred dollars to Nandy in Culoma with a note saying she hoped to help buy the wood for Andrew's new room. Then she sent a letter to Samuel on the Wells Fargo Stage with a secured package of a hundred dollars and the mining edition of *California Illustrated* as a wedding present. Upon graduating from Amherst, he'd gotten engaged to a local woman he'd met at the Methodist church in Amherst and secured a position as a clerk at a dry grocer in Boston. Elisabeth finally wrote how she'd divorced Nate, hoping her honesty wouldn't cast a pall on Samuel's new marriage. She'd been revealing drips and dribbles of truth over many letters through the past four years, a thimble at a time, making it easy for him to swallow, but she still found it difficult to explain all the particulars of how the California society allowed more liberal prospects for a woman out on her own. You had to live it firsthand to understand.

When the Rosenblatts first asked her to write an article about the California land disputes between the Americans and the Californios, she hesitated, saying Jacob might research that topic better.

"That's ridiculous," said Jacob. "You're the one to write that story. You know the land. The people. Far better than me."

She finally agreed, researching in earnest. First she learned all she could about the history of the Spanish in California, how they'd enslaved the Indians to build the missions with the sorry excuse of spreading Christianity. And about the Mexican War of Independence, and the Mexican-American War. Then she interviewed Senator William Gwin about the California Land Act. Senator Gwin said the Californios were irresponsible, with unethical bookkeeping methods. When he started complaining that all the old Californio families held the best sections of land, she interrupted.

"Do you suggest they give up land they've had for generations? To Americans for free?"

"No. No. For a fee, we'd gladly help the Californio families settle their deeds."

She finally understood. The Americans weren't trying to settle questionable land deeds from historical records but aiming to take away land they'd promised the Californios could keep. Unless the Californios paid off the Americans. Land was second only to gold in California, with everyone scrambling to grab a piece. No wonder Nemacio had been so desperate to find more gold; he had little choice.

Getting the Californio perspective was crucial for her article in *California Illustrated*, so she headed out to the Sanchez Ranch on the other side of Telegraph Hill to hear Gabriella's take. But Gabriella and her children were gone, having sold the Sanchez Ranch to the Murphy family from Iowa. Neighbors said she'd resettled down the peninsula on another rancho she also owned, Rancho La Purísima Concepción.

So with reluctance she took John up on his offer to visit the Gabilan Ranch. He was right, of course. Seeing the Gabilan Ranch firsthand just made sense. It would add a credible angle to her article. It was research. A necessary sacrifice in the interest of good reporting, she told herself. Besides, she was over Nemacio. Traveling back through the American River basin had cleansed her soul of him. She could handle seeing him again.

She'd refused John's offer to ride in one of the four wagons driven by his men loaded full with trunks of supplies for Lily B.: fabric, seeds, nails, boards, books, paper, a mahogany writing desk from Holland, three John Brown Sharps rifles, and several iron reapers. Atop Burrito, she wore a lacy white blouse and a pretty red calico skirt, which she hiked up to her knees. John didn't say a word about her pantaloons dangling out from underneath, just lifted an eyebrow and laughed hearty as they made their way through the flat valley passing dozens of willow bark Indian dwellings and herds of elk and more bunnies than she could shoot if she'd brought her Hawken.

They watered their horses at the courtyard fountain of Mission San Juan Bautista, a long white rectangular adobe building capped with red tiles and a tiered campanario with three bells. Pressing on south of the mission, they passed Indians working fields of corn, stacking ears onto wagon beds. The flat valley gave way to undulating foothills of bright yellow grass dotted with clumps of dark green oaks and craggy mountains rising up.

"Our ranch stretches out from here as far as you can see, in all directions. Up there in the nook of those mountains is the Gabilan Hacienda," said John, pointing. "My Lily Beth and her man have a heap of trouble on our ranch running off squatters and cattle rustlers stealing heads by the thousands. At fifty thousand acres, it's quite a load to defend. I've an army of men to help protect our interests down there. I tell you, that Land Act is pure theft, with Americans thinking it's their right to take the land outright, gobbling up whole sections piece by piece."

John proved an excellent traveling companion, funny and light-hearted even after hours in the saddle. He told long-winded stories about all manner of subjects that didn't at all bore her. His pompous banking clients. His fabulous art collection. Interesting books he'd read. And his extravagant social life. Overly solicitous, he asked about her work and travels in the mining region. In between, he attempted to sell her on the idea of becoming his wife. She couldn't quite tell if his congenial sales pitch was part of his joking manner, or if he really meant it. Either way, she had great fun playing along, and his attentions distracted her from a creeping fear at seeing Nemacio again.

"We'd make quite a team," he said.

"So you've said."

"Think about it. Seriously! Out adventuring together like this, then taking comfort in my home in the city. It'd be a good life," he said.

"I already have a good life."

"A gooder life then."

"*Gooder* isn't a word."

"Well, it should be."

"See how difficult I am, Mr. Langley? Already correcting your grammar."

"You improve me."

"Do you flatter all women this way?"

"Contrary to what you've heard, the only other woman in my life is Lily B."

"Surely you can find a more suitable woman than me. More pliable, perhaps?"

"I find the pliable ones boring," he said.

They traveled into the Gabilans, past cattle and sheep grazing, free. Two red-tailed hawks soared overhead in the bright sunlight, following them up the slope. A group of twenty or so American squatters were setting up a tent camp in the distance.

"They think they can homestead any old place," said John, sending out two men to rout them. "We've got to educate them about trespassing. Otherwise, they'll be picking off our herd of cattle by morning."

By midday they arrived at a grand white hacienda, over twice the size of Mission San Juan Bautista, at two stories tall with huge clumps of bright red geraniums dangling down from the balcony above. Elisabeth climbed off Burrito and shook out her skirt, taking in a deep breath of courage. The stable boy took their horses and unloaded the wagons. She looked around, marveling at the sprawling ranch and the vegetable garden and rows and rows of fruit trees with white cabbage butterflies flitting among the lemon blossoms. Beyond, she saw vines hanging heavy with grapes and a young boy pushing a drove of fat pigs through dozens of chickens running around. It looked a bounty of magnificence.

"The gardens are valuable, of course. But the profit's in the cows. Meat and hides," said John, leading her up to the long arched veranda.

A short stout woman came out of a finely carved oak door wearing a white silk dress and a red shawl with fringes. She embraced John, warm, and he introduced her as Doña Maria of the Gabilans, flattering the woman in a Spanish flourish that made the older woman blush. Lily Beth bounced out from behind Doña Maria, glowing precious with her yellow skin flaming with freckles, and curly red hair that she didn't even bother to pin up but instead wore down, long and wild.

"The sunshine of my life," said John, kissing Lily B.

"Mi amor is out there somewhere, helping the vaqueros," said Lily B., flinging her hair over her shoulder.

She found herself wanting to like the girl, to please John. Thinking Lily B. might like flattery, she admired her dress.

"What extraordinary lace detail on your sleeves," said Elisabeth.

Unfortunately, she couldn't find any more flattery. As she looked down at Lily B's intricate orange lace bodice clashing with that awful red hair, a dreadful jealousy tore her scabbed wounds open. Lily B.'s waist bulged large, with life growing inside.

46

I could never deny

By afternoon time, John knocked on the door of her room at the end of the long hallway on the second floor of the hacienda.

"Can I get you anything, darling?" John asked through the locked door.

"No."

"Are you unwell?"

"Tired from traveling. Need a bit of rest, is all."

"I have something for you," he said. "I'll leave it here."

After he'd gone, she opened the door to a tray with a pitcher of lemonade and a wooden box. She pulled the tray inside and closed the door. Inside the box was a leather-bound journal tooled with her first name in large block letters on the front. On the inside page John had inscribed: *To a lovely beginning. Yours, John.* The rest of the book was filled with blank pages for her words. Her writing. Her story.

John's kindness diluted her bitter mood, a little. He was an honorable man, to be sure, and considerate. A man who knew how to regard a woman, proper. He valued her work, her independence.

Her future. Unlike Nemacio. And it's not like she wanted a baby, anyhow. She was relieved at never having to worry about giving up work for mothering. Being with that Dane confirmed it. She'd never get with a baby again after that tumbling, just like Señora Sanchez said. She pushed down the guilt, resolving to forget all about what she'd done, buried under her pile of prospects. Purposeful work and financial success.

When the sun set and the crickets sang, lulled by the warm dusking of the California night, and the music wafted up from the fiesta in the courtyard below, she finally dug up the courage. Washing her face in the basin, she examined herself in the mirror by candlelight. Her face struck her as too brown from the past summer spent traveling under the California sun, but her youthful glow had not yet grown dim. She brushed her brown hair out smooth, then pinned up one side with the abalone hair comb Nemacio had given her in Manzanita City, letting the rest fall down reckless just the way Lily B. wore her hair. She slipped on her green-and-white striped silk dress and walked downstairs, leaving her gloves on the dressing table, knowing she could face him.

The October air hung gentle, smelling heady of wild roses and jasmine. The courtyard lit soft from a dozen torches, and the harvest moon rose full and bright. Nearly a hundred people attended the harvest fiesta. The whole Gabilan family. Friends, neighbors, and farmhands. Even el padre from the Mission San Juan Bautista. Guitarists strummed out a Spanish waltz, familiar, but without the soul of Álvaro's playing years ago down on the river. John Langley crossed the courtyard toward her.

"Simply breathtaking," he said, his hands in prayer under his chin.

"I'm touched by the notebook. Such a thoughtful gift. Thank you," she said.

"I'll care for you in a manner you deserve," he said, frank.

Comfortable in this crowd of family and friends, John seemed far more attractive to her than his actual appearance in garish striped pants, his broad belly stuffed into a blue velvet vest a size too small. He escorted her around the courtyard like a precious gem, bragging on about her writing for *California Illustrated* and her travels to the hard rock mines. Standing tall and stiff beside him, she remained patient, squishing down her fear and ache, looking past everyone she met. Looking for Nemacio.

"The Californios sure know how to live," he said, pulling her onto the dance floor. "Don't you agree?"

John danced her around with heavy feet, and fat hands dripping sweat in hers. But as he placed a hand on the small of her back, he felt surprisingly safe, like family, and he didn't at all smell like cheese. She tried to find the romance in dancing, but the moment didn't feel at all like when she first danced with Nemacio on the ridge outside the Fandango, no matter how much she willed the passion to come on.

"I've got just the person for you to interview for your article," he said, guiding her to a group of men standing near a low wall.

When they walked up, all the men turned. John introduced Don Pío Pico, the wealthiest cattleman in California. As John explained how Don Pico had been the last the governor of Alta California, she saw Nemacio sitting on the edge of the wall in the center of the group. He looked magnificent, with a royal-blue suit jacket covered in extraordinary swirling white embroidery and a crisp shirt knotted with a scarf just below his Adam's apple. She couldn't look away from him when John introduced the four younger Gabilan brothers, all seemingly cut from the same Californio cloth, slick with charm and deceit. She asked Governor Don Pico how Californio families could keep their ranches with all the force of the American government after their land. But Nemacio interrupted.

"Good evening, Mrs. Parker," he said, lifting his hat.

"It's Miss. I'm unmarried," she said, snapping sarcastic.

"Perdón, señorita," he said, smoothing down his hair.

Nemacio turned away from her then and started speaking in Spanish with his younger brothers, who listened to him in deference. She tried not to be taken in by his smooth lush words like before, and instead focused on any bits of Spanish she might understand. But her ears rang with his honey-toned voice, and her legs wobbled as her mind jumped to the memory of them swimming together in the Uva. His body moving over her, inside. She ignored her misbehaving memories and blurted out a question directly to Nemacio.

"How'd you settle your ranch deed dispute with the Americans?"

All four Gabilan brothers turned toward her. The brother standing next to Nemacio spoke first.

"That's private family business," he said, glaring.

"I'm wondering, of course, for the feature I'm writing for *California Illustrated*," she said.

Nemacio held up a hand to his brothers.

"It turned complicated in the end, Miss Parker," he said.

"Oh, but I'd love to hear all the details," she said.

"Perhaps another time," he said, turning away from her to call for tequila.

When a woman came into the courtyard with a tray of glasses, Elisabeth thought she looked a bit like the Indian women she'd seen digging in the American back at Chana's claim. She was short with a round face and timid eyes cast down when she served the men. Elisabeth wondered if Nemacio employed the woman, or enslaved her, like the Spanish padre who enslaved the Indians with promises of salvation in the afterlife as long as they broke their backs building the California missions in this life first.

Nemacio and his brothers drank the tequila, ignoring her. Angry, she gripped her hands by her side, trying to calm her heavy breathing like she didn't care. John seemed to sense her discomfort and escorted her away to long tables with white tablecloths and ornate wrought iron candelabras. The music stopped, and Nemacio's voice boomed through the courtyard.

"Familia y amigos! Comamos todos."

Nemacio took his place at the head of the table with Lily B. on his right. Elisabeth sat between John and Doña Maria, wondering how she'd get through a whole meal sitting so near to Nemacio. Everyone spoke Spanish. Elisabeth couldn't understand much, and seemed like the only person feeling uncomfortable. Lily B. and John seemed to understand everyone's conversation. Lily B. even spoke Spanish with Nemacio!

Elisabeth tried to enjoy the lavish feast, with bowls of figs and cheese and olives and spicy salsa, and plates of sliced steak and beans and tortillas and roasted artichoke hearts drizzled in olive oil. But she mostly picked at the food on her plate, imagining Nemacio's voice belonging to someone else. She turned to John.

Tilted her head. Smiled with all her teeth. Laughed and flirted like she hadn't a care. She drank the red wine. First a sip. Then a little more. It wasn't whiskey, she told herself, so she wasn't breaking her promise. She losened up, trying to be the lighthearted woman she wanted to be.

For dessert she ate strawberries with cream and drank a third glass of wine, trying not to look over at Nemacio with Lily B. beside him, radiant and glowing like the moon itself. She tried to hold herself in. She tried not to explode like a madwoman. When Lily B. touched Nemacio's arm, Elisabeth felt sick, like she'd eaten too much sweet cream. She ignored her insides and struck up a polite conversation with Lily B. like a sophisticated lady might.

"Tell me, Lily B. How did you meet your husband?" she asked.

"Daddy introduced us. Brought him up to our city house for tea. Love at first sight," she giggled.

"And for you, Don Gabilan, was it love at first sight?"

She prodded polite and nasty, intending to poke and pick like a crow tearing off bits of his flesh until he bled out why he'd left her for this silly girl.

"Love is a powerful thing, Miss Parker." Nemacio said slow. "Leading our hearts without permission. Don't you agree?"

She wanted to scream, "Yes, damn you. Yes! Love is a beast that leads women into a raging fire of torment."

But before she could respond sensibly, Lily B. held up her wineglass in toast.

"To Daddy's writer friend, Miss Elisabeth Parker. You are always welcome here," said Lily B.

Elisabeth downed the wine as Lily B. clapped her hands together in a buoyant enthusiasm that might've spread infectious over most people. But Elisabeth hated her.

"We live a simple outdoor life here, with a generous spirit," said Lily B., leaning back in a chair, her belly swelling full. "The rancho is absolute heaven, and I adore the fiestas!"

What began as charming chatter about the ranch turned into incessant prattle, vapid and grating, about inane topics of dress fabrics, table coverings, flower arrangements, and meal preparation for the harvest festivities. Elisabeth wasn't at all interested in the domesticity that interested Lily B. Maybe that's why Nemacio married her. For her homemaking skills.

Doña Maria seemed tired of her daughter-in-law's ramblings too, and deftly moved the conversation away from decorative particulars toward the business of the ranch. A formal air swirled around the doña, and Lily B. afforded her mother-in-law respect, listening gracious as she talked with great pride about the importance of her family, her five sons and daughters-in-law and her extended relations of sisters and nieces and nephews. Even with silvering hair, Doña Maria still looked youthful, flashing a girlish smile and speaking English directly to Elisabeth with only a slight accent. She was a formidable woman, and Elisabeth could see how Nemacio might've found it difficult going against her wishes.

"As a close family, we work together to keep the ranch prosperous. With a thousand head of cattle, we employ the Mutsun and Mexican vaqueros, providing stability and prosperity to the region. We sell fruits and vegetables Fridays in the plaza at San Juan Bautista and give cows to the mission on Feast Day, the birth of Jesus Christ our Lord," said Doña Maria, crossing herself. "We share our harvest with everyone in the Gabilans. I suggest you write about that. The Californio spirit of generosity and love. And the deep importance of family, coming first. Above all else."

Elisabeth shifted in the iron chair, uncomfortable the woman might be warning her.

"What a striking hair comb," said Doña Maria, reaching out to touch the abalone comb in Elisabeth's hair.

"It was a gift," she said.

"Abalone?"

"So I was told," she said.

Doña Maria leaned in, whispering.

"I used to have one exactly like it. I gave it to my eldest son a few years ago, for a woman he'd met in the diggings."

The old woman knew!

"Then I must return it to you. It means nothing to me," Elisabeth lied.

With no more room in her heart for shame, she pulled the comb out of her hair and placed it on the table. Doña Maria covered it quick with her bony hand before Lily B. noticed.

"Gracias," said Doña Maria.

Elisabeth glanced up to see Nemacio looking at her with those familiar eyes, smooth like polished pebbles, luring her in, churning her up in a roiling river. Disappointed at herself for still feeling his strong pull, she promised herself not to look in his direction again for the whole night.

The fiesta continued in the courtyard past midnight, carried along by more toasts and music and drink and dance. She drank far too many glasses of wine and danced into the night with all the men who asked, steering clear of him. Refusing defeat, she pretended to enjoy herself. Dancing with John, she let him hold her close and threw her head back laughing like a light-hearted woman having a joyous time. Across the courtyard, Nemacio leaned up against the wall with his brothers. Watching. He didn't dance with Lily B., who sat under the rose arbor with her sisters-in-law surrounding her like a flower in full bloom, full of Nemacio.

"I must dance with my daughter tonight. Her man is always caught up in rancho business," said John. "Do you mind?"

Even through her jealousy, Elisabeth admired John's concern for Lily B.

"Not at all. I'm ready to retire anyhow," she said, defeated.

"Shall I escort you upstairs?"

"Not tonight, John. Go dance with your daughter," she said. "I'll see you in the morning."

He kissed her bare hand goodnight. She said polite regards to Lily B. and Doña Maria, and escaped inside the hacienda. She felt her way down the dark hallway, relieved to finish the fiesta and all that joy that wasn't hers. When she heard footsteps behind, she stopped but didn't turn around.

"You still wear the hair comb I gave you," he said, from the shadows.

"Not anymore I don't," she said, steadying herself on the wall.

"You can't marry John. You'd be my mother-in-law. I won't allow it!"

"You can't stop me."

She laughed a wild sort of laugh that echoed off the adobe walls. A maddening laugh, conjuring up spite. He leapt at her, covering her mouth with his hand.

"Shhhh! Let me explain," he said, pushing her up against the wall.

He put his hands flat on either side of her on the wall, encircling. Trapping.

"I couldn't take you from Nate," he said.

"It was my choice. Not his," she said, not meaning to sound like she cared anymore.

"I was desperate," he said, his breath hot in her face.

"Desperate to stick a baby in some other girl," she said, drunk with sarcasm.

"I didn't know about the divorce," he said.

"You knew," she said, focusing on a hardened path of hate.

Sweat dripped down her back underneath her silk dress and she squirmed to get out from under him, but he stepped in closer.

"I came back to you. To explain, but you were gone. My sister Isabella was supposed to marry John, but she ran off with a Mutsun. My mother was shamed. Insisted I help. She fixed it so John would set the matter right. Get our deed in order. Pay the government to put the ranch in my name."

"In exchange for his daughter!"

"You don't understand. It wasn't supposed to be like this. John was supposed to marry Isabella," he said.

"But you offered yourself instead. I understand completely."

"We'd nearly lost our ranch. That damn claim on the river didn't pay out enough."

"After you left, I lost everything in a fire, but I didn't go marrying for money," she said, pushing his chest.

He didn't move but kept her trapped up against the cool adobe wall. He was quiet for a long while, breathing heavy. She heard the crickets' familiar refrain outside, and kept still. Knowing she could wait him out.

"Without our land, I would've been nothing," he said, finally. "A poor Californio is nothing."

"The land wasn't yours in the first place. You took it from the Indians. Did you make them slaves too?"

"The Spanish took the land from the Indians. We pay the Mutsun."

"Then you took the land from the Spanish and the Indians. Either way, you're a thief."

"I'm no thief. The Americans steal from us."

"You forget the Mexicans. You stole from them too," she said, working up her nerve.

"No! We have honor."

"Honor, indeed. Well, you've no worry now. You've got Lily B. and soon . . . a baby!"

"No more talking," he said.

He hung his head down to kiss her, and she slapped his face. He grabbed her wrists, holding her arms above her head like a prisoner against a wall. His words came out soft and shaky.

"You are the river flowing in me," he said, gripping her wrists harder.

"You're hurting me," she said weak.

She looked away, willing herself not to cry. Hoping she was stronger than this.

"You are my very own soul," he said, burying his face in her hair, breathing her in.

When he pressed up against her hard and familiar, his thighs trembled and she savored his pain. He loosened his grip on her wrists, and tasted her lips, urgent. She felt lightheaded, flooding full of him. When he freed her hands she tasted him. Only for a moment. Tasting his weakness and want and memory and love, like water after a long thirst. Only for a moment, then she remembered how he'd opened her up like an ordinary rock with crystal hiding inside, then smashed her in the mud and left her in pieces. She took hold of her senses, wiggling out from underneath his grip. She dashed up the stairs toward the room at the end of the hall, hearing only her boot heels hitting hard on the Spanish tiles, as he called out after her.

"Te amo solo a ti," he said, not quiet at all.

47

To the shore of the moonlit sea

The next morning shined luminous and entirely too bright for
Elisabeth, with her head still pounding wicked with wine from
the night before. She breakfasted outside with John and Lily Beth and
Doña Maria and a dozen other folks from the Gabilan family under
the shade of a pergola dripping with fuchsia bougainvillea. Thankfully, Nemacio wasn't among them, already out on ranch business.
They ate fried eggs, warm bread with honey, and ripe raspberries
from the garden. She cleaned her plate, listening to the water cascade
down the fountain in the center of the courtyard, knitting together
her frayed insides from Nemacio nearly tearing her to shreds again.
A hummingbird fluttered back and forth joyful through the spray,
then darted around the bougainvillea overhead, sucking nectar from
the fuchsia flowers with its tiny needle beak. Elisabeth's heart beat
stronger at seeing the power and speed of those tiny wings.

Lily Beth suggested they spend the day together canning jam.
Elisabeth would have rather hung by her knuckles from the nearest
oak than spend the day in the kitchen with women peeling and slicing and standing over steaming pots of boiling sugar.

"I'm terrible in the kitchen," she said.

Thankfully, John rescued her, saying he was taking her on a tour around the ranch.

"For her reportage," he said. "The folks of America need to know the value of Californios. What they contribute to America."

Grateful, she followed him into the walled gardens blooming bright with fragrant sweat peas, hollyhocks, nasturtiums, and yellow lilies. Solicitous, John held her hand and pointed out the peas, beans, beets, lentils, onions, carrots, red peppers, potatoes, corn, squash, cucumbers, and melons, going on as if she didn't know the plants. Beyond the vegetable garden grew fig, olive, lemon, and orange trees among lavender and roses. It seemed as if anything and everything could grow tall and strong and abundant out here in this heavenly slice of fertile earth. She'd never seen such a bounty in all her life.

"Beyond the garden are bee hives. Lily B. loves the honey," he said.

She finally understood why Lily B. had agreed to move all the way out here, away from the city. Away from her father. The place was paradise.

"These are Lily B.'s favorite," he said, snapping off a clump of tiny white flowers. "Narcissus."

The flowers smelled strong and sweet, reminding her of all she'd missed and all she'd wanted. Taking another deep whiff, she sneezed.

"Oh my," she said, sounding ridiculously flirty.

She didn't mean to lead him on, but she liked the way he made her feel important and wanted.

"Bless you," he said, placing a reassuring hand on her back.

John handed her a crisp linen handkerchief embroidered with an *L* for Langley. She wiped her nose as John pulled a pear off a tree and cut it with his pocketknife, handing her slices. She bit into the ripe, sweet pear, the juice dripping down her lips. When she swallowed the fruit, John leaned over and kissed her. She held her breath, regarding the kiss. By now she'd had some experience to compare, with Nate and Nemacio and that Dane up against a tree. He scratched her face with his stiff mustache and mashed his puffy cheeks up against her face, covering her nose, moving his lips full around her mouth in a manner not altogether unpleasant but not thrilling either. She didn't smell even a whiff of cheese on him, and hoped the kiss might grow passionate. Perhaps his whole self might prove better than this one particular piece. But she grew bored as he kept working his mouth atop hers for what seemed entirely too long. She stepped back, giving them both a break. She cast her eyes downward and demure, like an inexperienced woman might.

"I've been wanting to do that for a long time," he said, leading her to the barn.

They mounted their horses and set off into the lower slopes of the Gabilans on horseback. As they passed a herd of nearly fifty elk grazing lazy, she noticed no pines grew in Gabilans, only cracking chaparral and grand oaks among craggy rocks, brown and rugged. Overhead, silver-gray clouds gathered and separated against the stark blue sky, creating a soft light illuminating the sharp edges of the oak leaves and the rich redness of madrone branches against the yellow grass. She distracted herself from thinking of Nemacio by imagining what her life would be like as Mrs. Langley. With a kind, generous companion like John, she could surely continue the independent work she'd found as necessary as air. She'd live comfortably and want for nothing. And having Lily B., he might not mind her being barren.

They rode up and over on the south side of the mountains toward a creek flowing down to a tannery, where he toured her around, explaining each step of the tanning process. She wrote down all the details in her new notebook. The horse-driven wheel crushing a half cord of oak bark. The seven large oval vats of oak pulp and water. The cow hides soaking soft and supple.

"The tannery is the life blood of the ranch. We make more than two hundred steer hides and three hundred deer hides a year. We also have a leather working shop near the barn, where we make saddles and boots. Our workers are true artisans. They made your notebook," he said, slipping into "we" and "our" as if he owned the ranch and not Nemacio.

She didn't want to know the details of the arrangement he'd made with Nemacio. Swapping a daughter for a ranch struck her as unseemly, no matter how beautiful the ranch. Leaving the tannery, they climbed up and over the ridge, their horses stepping sure-footed down the thin path. Up on the top of the hill, the hacienda gleamed white in the far distance below as a thunderhead clapped and blue-streaked clouds streamed in front of the sun. When drops of rain dotted down delicate, she looked up, letting the sprinkles wet her face.

"Let's find cover," he said.

They galloped their horses down toward an oak grove and dismounted, huddling under a tree, laughing in the rain. She fooled herself into thinking she'd tossed off that weight of lost love still crushing her chest.

"I do enjoy you," he said, smiling broad, the scar on his cheek glistening waxy and wet.

In the distance, a rider galloped up the slope toward them. As the rider came closer, she saw it was Nemacio, wearing a wide-brimmed sombrero and brightly colored striped serape, looking like an ordinary vaquero. As he reached the oak grove the rain came down harder, and water poured off his brim. Thunder clapped, and a lone streak of lightning lit across the valley below.

"John," he said, serious. "A group of rustlers were making off with fifty head at the east border."

"Mexicans?" John asked.

"Americans. Pablo shot two. He and Jorge are holding one more down by the river. We don't want more trouble."

"Damn it," said John, mounting his horse. "Take Miss Parker to the hacienda, out of this storm. Get a rope, and meet me down by the river."

As John rode off toward the river and the rustlers, Nemacio got off his horse, dropping the reins careless in the grass. He and Elisabeth stood alone and together, numb under the oak. The rain slowed, hitting the leaves with a *drip, drip.* An eagle, tall and proud, landed on a wide branch overhead, making no noise at all, just turning its head from side to side, looking fierce with bright yellow eyes.

"I can't stand seeing you with him," he said, stepping closer.

She stepped back and he stopped. He took off his hat and ran a hand through those unruly curls, now cut short, tamed into submission.

"Mi amor. Lo siento," he said, his voice shaking with guilt.

"Don't," she said, holding a hand out, flat.

Burrito stamped his hoof in the soggy dirt as a coyote crossed the grass twenty yards from them, bouncing into a hole and pulling out a rabbit. As the coyote ran off along a gully with the catch in its jaws, out of sight, Nemacio started making promises.

"Come away with me," he said.

She backed up, untying the yellow ribbon from her hat, slow.

"You'd leave your family for me?" she asked, slipping off her hat and dropping it in the dirt.

"I'm desperate for you," he said, his voice low and quiet.

He didn't look like the proud, powerful Don Gabilan anymore. He looked ashen, with foggy, distant eyes sunken into his head like he'd been hollowed out on the inside by a worm. Even in his misery, she still wanted him. She wanted him wrapping his pain around her, throbbing with grief. She wanted his lips, full and wet all over her. She wanted them to suffer and wallow together. She untied her bodice, slow and teasing. When her breasts fell out bare, he drew in a breath.

He lunged then, pulling her down to the ground, kissing her neck and nipples with wretched despair. He smelled delicious like the dry grass and the river and bliss and hope and her own self. She touched his hardness through his pants as he trembled in agony. She wanted him moving in her like before, breaking her open, making her whole. She pulled up her dress and slipped down her pantaloons, opening her thighs. He fumbled his pants down and thrust himself inside, harder and more. He pushed her deep into the wet dirt as she wrapped her legs around him. Weak with want, she melted into him, losing herself in his desire. His love. His lies. His promises and power over her.

Filling with rage, she flung him off her. In a leap, she straddled atop him, pounding on his chest with her fists as her long hair fell loose, tumbling down around his face, messy. He dug his fingertips into her hips as she flailed and thrashed and cried. In a fury, she pressed herself down, taking him inside forceful and he grabbed hold of her bare bottom, coaxing. She slid up and down on him with a crazed passion, deeper and darker and furious, capturing more and enough, loving away the anger and sorrow and loneliness, and he moaned with hunger, calling out her name as they moved together in reckless rapture, kissing and sucking and eating and drinking and living whole lives in that precious moment, loving like they'd never been apart, plunging down together into an eternity of heartbreaking fire, erasing themselves into each other, until bursting open, shaking and shuddering as one.

Raindrops dripped off the leaves, and a cooling wind sang calm through the branches overhead as they lay holding each other, hidden in the tall grass. Still inside her, he spoke.

"My soul is yours," he said.

"I had a part of you growing in me once," she whispered in a queer unfamiliar voice, much too calm. "When you left, I killed it."

She admitted it. She admitted it to herself and to him. She admitted her choice, understanding the consequences for the first time. She faced her sin and guilt with a strange peace and resignation, looking up toward the eagle, wondering if Nandy sent him.

"Lo siento, mi amor," he said. "It's all my fault. Let's leave from here. Let me take you away. I'll say I still hold interest in the claim on the American."

"You'd lie for me?"

"We'll be together, forever. Right after the baby comes," he said.

His eyes pooled honest, saying everything. And she knew. She understood he could never leave his family, no matter how much he wanted to. He'd always be here, in his heart, no matter how far away they traveled together. She'd never ask him to leave his child, the way Henry had left her. She wanted him but wanted herself more. She wanted to be brave and strong and true, for herself.

The eagle called out with a single soft high-pitched note, talking to her. Giving her courage. She stood up. Straightened her skirt. Laced up her bodice.

"No," he said, crawling on his knees toward her.

Kneeling before her, he wrapped his arms around her legs and buried his face in the silk folds of her wet skirt.

"I can't live without you," he said.

At that moment, she knew he wasn't enough. Under the witness of the eagle, she cut herself away from Nemacio. From his beautiful body and his beautiful soul. She cut away her love and hate and shame. She forgave herself and forgave him, knowing he would stay.

He belonged here in the Gabilans. She cut herself away, leaving him behind kneeling in the dirt, his fate sealed to his land and his family. As she led Burrito toward the hacienda, the rain stopped and the sun pushed through the dark clouds into thin streaks of California light glimmering down upon her.

48

Summer 1854

Dearest Louisa,

News of your publication of Flower Fables greets me with such admiration. Your success is a long time coming, a pure recognition never more so deserving in a writer. Receiving the gift of your first published book is my greatest treasure. I read it over and over again, finding you in the pages, filled with pride in knowing this will be the first of many books the world will read from my dear friend Louisa May Alcott. In time, all of your financial worries will settle behind you, at last and for good. While you protest the thirty-five dollars from your publisher George Briggs as paltry, you must know money doesn't make a woman. It's the texture of her mind and the strength of her heart that matters in the end.

I must concede, my investments have at once removed my past distress of caring for myself alone. My mining shares paid out handsomely, so I purchased a whole city block in San Francisco, and then some. I have set down roots in California, aiming to never again fret over my future. In my bones I feel you burgeoning the same, with *proper compensation for your valuable contributions. As women, we must demand more. No longer should we apologize for our living, however halting and hard and harrowing that living strikes some. Bumbling along the way, I can say without a doubt, I will never again set my sights low like a proper lady most often does, even understanding how I've paid a high price for striving beyond the life of an ordinary woman and bear a cost which still stings even now. I've come to understand my journey in all its full truth, walking forward with the ashes of my life scattered behind as a reminder of the burnt ugliness from which I grew, and with a pride of which I am no longer capable of feeling ashamed.*

I am a self-reliant woman now, with a full heart. In turn, I let Nemacio go, and John too, knowing neither man could make me whole again. I haven't given up all prospects of passion, the possibility of which I might know again somewhere along my adventures, as I believe myself still capable of a great unreasoning love. After years of serious examination, I see truth in Emerson, after all, when he wrote, "All our progress is an unfolding . . . we must trust ourselves to the end, even though we might not render any reason."

I'm now out on the trail again, traveling with Julie in the first scouting party with James Lamon to the stronghold of the Yosemite Indians in the Sierras. We're intent on reporting its splendor for California Illustrated. *I'm committing my observations to paper, while Julie pictures it all in her camera box. Yosemite shines as my reflection, which I accept without reservation, as I capture the spectacular scene before me. Please understand my attempts to write about the grandeur of this place fall woefully short, as no mere mortal has words adequate for a proper description. Humbly, I try.*

Coming out of the woods to a rocky point, the most magnificent sight hits me. A place to end all places and the beginnings of a wondrous unknown, like the Elysium Fields at the western edge of the known earth. From a bluff, I stand in awe of massive granite walls surrounding a grand valley far below filled full of verdant pines and grassy meadows. A valley too large for the largest of giants, with an immense waterfall roaring down one sheer rock face, falling beautiful and violent, transforming, floating off the rocks as a rainbow of misty light and into a wild river below. Soaring in the distance stands a towering rock dome, cut clean in half by God Himself, yet still whole and complete in the halving, like my very own soul. The sun lights up the gray half dome in golden glory like a luminous altar beckoning me at the end of a majestic cathedral. The Yosemite call it Tissaack, which means "The Face of a Young Woman Stained with Tears," for the dark stripes dripping down.

Out here I stand in the precipice of my own perpetual prospects, expanding beyond my own limits, halving in whole. Overwhelmed with awe, I drink in the wild, in all of its beauty and terror, understanding in this moment. California is my Promised Land, giving me the power and the glory to find my own happiness and freedom. I've finally seen the elephant, and it's given me more than enough.

Always and forever, I remain your self-reliant *friend in California,*
Elisabeth Parker

~Acknowledgments

W hile *Prospects of a Woman* is a work of fiction, actual California women inspired me: Francis Gearhart, Anne Brigman, Juana Briones, Nancy Gootch, Luenza Stanley Wilson, Mary Hallock Foote, Emily Pitts Stevens, Ina Coolbrith, and Amelia Dannenberg, among others. In striving to reframe a more authentic account of women in the West, I borrowed from their lives, and I remain in awe of their valuable contributions to early California.

I'm grateful for the many friends, family, and early readers who supported me during my long journey toward the publication of *Prospects of a Woman.* A special thanks to Brooke Warner at She Writes Press and the whole SWP team for their valuable mission of promoting literature written by women, and for believing in *Prospects of a Woman.* I also owe heaps more gratitude. . . . To the Vermont College of Fine Arts community, for sheltering me in literary warmings during snowy residencies and after, and especially to Doug, for pushing me off the edge of the trail into a deep river without throwing me a life vest. To Scott James and the whole Castro Writer's Cooperative, for providing me a haven within the most supportive group of unpretentious talent in one Coop. To Paco and Kate, for requiring more at the end. To Lee, for picking me up and dusting me off. To Andrea Hurst for her critical eye. To my posse of strong California women, including Liz, Carey, Lucy, Suzy, Kim M., Kat, Kim G., Nina, Michelle, Alicia, and Hillary for showering me with continuous inspiration, support, and encouragement. To the extended VoorClan, now and generations before, for offering me countless examples of how Californians love with passionate vulnerability, respect, and equality. To Oma Heide, a powerful California matriarch, for showing me how to love unconditionally. To my mother, for teaching me how to pick the right path. To Kevin, for his brotherly loyalty. To Karen, for walking alongside as my life's witness, cheering me on with understanding and humor. To my boys, for giving me sunshine I didn't know was possible before. And most importantly, to Conrad—the single best decision I ever made—for his enduring optimism and unwavering belief in me. Finally, I acknowledge California herself, whose air and water and mountains and valleys continue to gift me with immeasurable joy and hope.

The following books helped me understand California women's true place in history: *Apron Full of Gold*, Mary Jane C. Megquier; *With Great Hope*, JoAnn Chartier and Chris Enss; *The Shirley Letters*, Louisa Amelia Knapp Smith Clappe; *Roaring Camp*, Susan Lee Johnson; *Nuggets of Nevada County*, Juanita Kennedy Browne; *California*, Kevin Starr; *They Saw the Elephant*, JoAnn Levy; *The California Indians*, R.F. Heizer and M. A. Whipple; *African American Women of the Old West*, Tricia Martineau Wagner; *Testimonios*, Rose Marie Beebe and Robert M. Senkewicz; *Behold the Day: The Color Block Prints of Frances Gearhart*, Victoria Dailey, Nancy E. Green, and Susan Futterman; *The Decline of the Californios*, Leonard Pitt; *It Happened in Northern California*, Erin H. Turner; *Gold Dust and Gunsmoke*, Jon Boessenecker; *Westward the Women*, Vicki Piekarski; *Rooted in Barbarous Soil*, Kevin Starr and Richard J. Orsi; *The Age of Gold*, H. W. Brands; *Sex, Gender, and Culture in California*, Albert L. Hurtado; *High-Spirited Women of the West*, Anne Seagraves; *Women's Voices from the Motherlode*, Susan G. Butruille; *Covered Wagon Women*, Kenneth L. Holmes; *Land of Golden Dreams*, Peter J. Blodgett; *Ina Coolbrith*, Josephine DeWitt Rhodendamel and Raymund Francis Wood; *Mining for Freedom*, Silvia Roberts; *Women and the Conquest of California*, Virginia Bouvier; *Anne Brigman: A Visionary in Modern Photography*, Ann M. Wolfe, Susan Ehrens, Alexander Nemerov, Kathleen Pyne, and Heather Waldroup; *Mary Hallock Foote: Author-Illustrator of the American West*, Darlis

A. Miller; and *Juana Briones of 19th-Century California*, Jeanne Farr McDonnell; *Self Reliance*, Ralph Waldo Emerson; *American Bloomsbury: Louisa May Alcott, Ralph Waldo Emerson, Margaret Fuller, Nathaniel Hawthorne, and Henry David Thoreau: Their Lives, Their Loves, Their Work*, Susan Cheever; and *Louisa May Alcott: A Biography*, Madeleine B. Stern.

ABOUT THE AUTHOR

Born and raised on the American River in Sacramento, Wendy Voorsanger has long held an intense interest in the historical women of California. She started her career in the Silicon Valley, writing about technology trends and innovations for newspapers, magazines, and Fortune 100 companies. She currently manages SheIsCalifornia.net, a blog dedicated to chronicling the accomplishments of California women through history. She earned a BA in journalism from California Polytechnic State University in San Luis Obispo and an MFA from the Vermont College of Fine Arts, and has attended Hedgebrook, the Squaw Valley Writers Workshop, and Lit Camp. She is a member of the Castro Writers' Cooperative, the Lit Camp Advisory Board, and the San Mateo Public Library Literary Society. She has also worked as a lifeguard, ski instructor, and radio disc jockey. Wendy lives in Northern California with her husband and two boys. Learn more at www.wendyvoorsanger.net.

Author photo © Phonethip Sritiraj, Indulge Photography

Selected titles from She Writes Press

She Writes Press is an independent publishing company founded to serve women writers everywhere. Visit us at www.shewritespress.com.

Eliza Waite by Ashley Sweeney. $16.95, 978-1-63152-058-7. When Eliza Waite chooses to leave a stagnant life in rural Washington State and join the masses traveling north to Alaska in 1898 during the tumultuous Klondike Gold Rush, she encounters challenges and successes in both business and love.

The Vintner's Daughter by Kristen Harnisch. $16.95, 978-163152-929-0. Set against the sweeping canvas of French and California vineyard life in the late 1890s, this is the compelling tale of one woman's struggle to reclaim her family's Loire Valley vineyard—and her life.

Lum by Libby Ware. $16.95, 978-1-63152-003-7. In Depression-era Appalachia, an intersex woman without a home of her own plays the role of maiden aunt to her relatives—until an unexpected series of events gives her the opportunity to change her fate.

Even in Darkness by Barbara Stark-Nemon. $16.95, 978-1-63152-956-6. From privileged young German-Jewish woman to concentration camp refugee, Kläre Kohler navigates the horrors of war and—through unlikely sources—finds the strength, hope, and love she needs to survive.

Tasa's Song by Linda Kass. $16.95, 978-1-63152-064-8. From a peaceful village in eastern Poland to a partitioned post-war Vienna, from a promising childhood to a year living underground, *Tasa's Song* celebrates the bonds of love, the power of memory, the solace of music, and the enduring strength of the human spirit.

In a Silent Way by Mary Jo Hetzel. $16.95, 978-1-63152-135-5. When Jeanna Kendall—a young white teacher at a progressive urban school—becomes involved with a community activist group, she finds herself grappling with issues of racism, sexism, and oppression of various shades in both her professional and personal life.